DRAGON LIGHT

Also by Shaun Clarke and available from Pocket Books:

The Exit Club

DRAGON LIGHT

A Novel of the SAS

Shaun Clarke

POCKET
BOOKS

First published in Great Britain by Pocket Books, 1997
An imprint of Simon & Schuster Ltd
A Viacom Company

The right of Shaun Clarke to be identified as author of this work has
been asserted in accordance with sections 77 and 78 of the Copyright,
Designs and Patents Act 1988

Simon & Schuster Ltd
West Garden Place
Kendal Street
London W2 2AQ

Simon & Schuster Australia
Sydney

A CIP catalogue record for this book is available from the
British Library

ISBN 0-671-85479-8

Typeset in Century Old Style 10/12pt by
Palimpsest Book Production Limited, Polmont, Stirlingshire
Printed and bound in Great Britain by
Caledonian International Book Manufacturing, Glasgow

For John and Barbara Bash

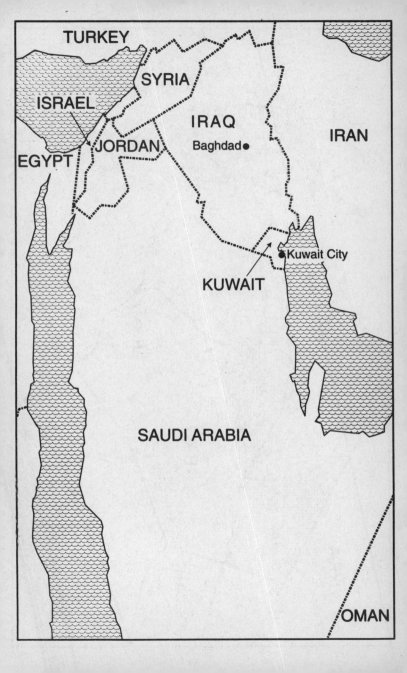

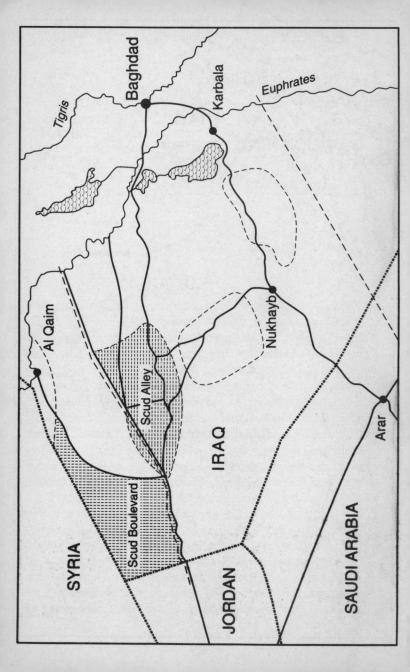

CHAPTER ONE

The forty SAS men were inserted by two RAF CH-47 Chinooks shortly after midnight on a landing zone about half a mile from the road that ran from Basra to Baghdad, though little more than forty miles from the latter. Disembarking even before the Chinooks' engines had gone into neutral, spilling out of the side into dense clouds of sand whipped up by the rotors, the troopers were wearing the normal beige beret, but without its winged-dagger badge and now camouflaged under a *shemagh*, or veil, that was wrapped loosely around the face to protect the eyes and mouth from blowing sand. They were also wearing standard-issue woollen pullovers, woven in colours that would blend in with the desert floor and match the colouring of their high-topped, lace-up desert boots.

When the rotors of the Chinooks had slowed down, letting the swirling sand settle, the men were exposed to a fabulous display of fireworks illuminating the distant horizon: immense webs of red and purple anti-aircraft fire, silvery, mushroom-shaped explosions, showers of crimson sparks and streams of phosphorous fireflies – a surreal, almost heavenly, sight that actually represented the relentless, hellish bombing of distant Baghdad by wave after wave of British, American and Saudi jets, flying in at just under the speed of sound at heights of fifty to a hundred and fifty feet, as well as Tomahawk Cruise missiles fired from ships in the Gulf, to cause appalling devastation and death.

Heavily armed, wrapped in ammunition belts, and further burdened under packed, camouflaged bergen rucksacks, the troopers looked awkward and bulky, almost Neanderthal, but they moved with surprising speed when ordered by a silent hand signal from their 28-year-old commander, Major Norman Phillips, to commence their designated tasks.

As their eyes adjusted to the moonlit darkness on the plain, they saw the towers of the two Iraqi microwave links, soaring high above the flat desert, about a quarter-mile apart, but less than twenty yards from the Basra–Baghdad road. Spreading out and keeping their weapons at the ready, they hiked across the dusty, windblown plain until they reached a point equidistant between the towers. Once there, as instructed with hand signals by Staff Sergeant Clive Morrissey, they fanned out to form a circle of LUPs, or laying-up positions, from which they could keep their eyes on the road and defend the diggers and demolition team if anyone came along and discovered them.

When the troopers were in their protective ring of LUPs, covering the darkness on all sides with their semi-automatic SLRs, Heckler & Koch MP5 sub-machine guns, thirty-round M16s with night-vision aids, and belt-fed L7A2 7.6mm general-purpose machine guns (GPMGs), Sergeant Harry Spooner, the demolition specialist, checked the alignment between the two communications towers, gauged where the fibre-optic cable was running between them, buried deep in the ground, then waved his hand from left to right, indicating an invisible line between the two towers. Speaking in a whisper, he ordered his dozen troopers to dig a series of four holes about twelve feet apart, each six foot long and as deep as they needed to go to expose the fibre-optic cables. He also told them that if they heard any transport coming along the nearby road, which was the enemy's main supply route (MSR), they were to drop into the holes and not move until given clearance.

Nodding their understanding, the men selected as diggers laid down their weapons, removed spades and shovels from their bergens and proceeded to dig the holes as required. Meanwhile, Sergeant Spooner ordered two of his eight sappers, both of whom had various explosives, charges and timers dangling from their webbing, to fix enough explosives to the base of each microwave link tower to ensure that both toppled over when the explosives were initiated. The towers were to be brought down with the aid of remote-control electronic timers at exactly the same time as the underground fibre-optic cables were blown up.

When the two sappers had headed off in opposite directions, towards the tower selected for each, Spooner supervised the digging of the holes, which took almost forty-five minutes. During that time, two vehicles came along the road, about thirty minutes apart, heading away from Baghdad, their headlights cutting a swathe through the darkness but not picking out the men who were lying in LUPs, guns at the ready, a mere twenty metres away. The first vehicle was a chauffeur-driven Rolls-Royce with white-robed Arabs in the rear, probably fleeing from the air attacks on Baghdad; the second was a soft-topped army truck, filled with Iraqi soldiers. Both passed by and disappeared into the night, their drivers and passengers not knowing how close to death they had come in what they must have assumed was a friendly area.

About twenty minutes after the army truck had passed by, one of the SAS diggers uncovered a fibre-optic cable. After inspecting it and confirming that it was indeed a part of the cable, Spooner ordered the sweating trooper to keep digging until the whole length of cable was clear. The trooper did so. When, about twenty-five minutes later, the length of cable running across the bottom of the hole was completely exposed, he jumped out to let Spooner jump in.

As Spooner went to work, laying the explosive charges that would blow the cable apart, the other diggers also completed the uncovering of their cables and clambered gratefully out of the holes, wiping mud off their hands. Spooner's remaining five sappers then jumped into the holes to fix explosive charges to the cables.

Even as Iraqi MiGs and Mirage F-1s flew overhead, heading away from the heavily bombed, burning airfields of Baghdad, Sergeant Spooner and his men coolly continued what they were doing. With Major Phillips looking on, Spooner sheared through a cable and slipped a piece into his bergen, to be shipped back to England for examination. He then packed C3/C4 plastic explosive around and between the exposed cables, fixed it in place, and attached a non-electrical firing system with a time fuse connected to a blasting cap in a thin aluminium tube. This he embedded carefully in the explosive charge. To the blasting cap he attached a detonating cord, or 'det cord', of reinforced primacord – a small high-explosive core protected by half a dozen layers of material. This was then taped together with two primers and a detonator fixed to a timing device. Finally, having completed his task, Spooner glanced up inquiringly at Phillips.

'We need twenty minutes to get back to the choppers,' Phillips told him. 'Can you manage that?'

Spooner opened and closed his right hand six times, indicating that he needed thirty minutes. Nodding to confirm, Phillips turned to his second-in-command, Staff Sergeant Morrissey, and told him to signal the men to break up their LUPs and head back to the choppers. Morrissey used hand signals to convey Phillips's instructions. At first there was nothing out there but dark emptiness, but then the men started appearing, rising up from the flat earth, silhouetted either by stars or the spectacular firework display over Baghdad.

After strapping their bergens to their shoulders and picking up their weapons, they lumbered like misshapen beasts back towards the Chinooks, which still had their rotors turning, though silently, their engines in neutral.

As the men retreated from the area, being swallowed up in darkness, Spooner and his sappers emerged one by one from their separate holes, wiping the mud off their hands. Packing up their equipment, the remaining two demolitions specialists returned from the separate communications towers and reported that they had placed the required explosives and remote-control timing devices on both of them. Satisfied, Spooner nodded, then led them all across the windswept plain, hurrying after the others.

Phillips and Morrissey came up the rear, Morrissey keeping his eye on the road. Seeing nothing, he turned away, walking faster to catch up with his men. When they reached the Chinooks, slightly obscured by the dust clouds swirling under the lazily spinning rotors, they gathered together to look back at the stretch of earth between the two communications towers. When Morrissey saw Phillips and Spooner checking their watches, he did the same.

The whole operation had taken ninety minutes and now they waited for the job to be completed.

The ground shook beneath their feet, then they saw a dark eruption far ahead, equidistant between the two silhouetted communications towers, where the holes had been dug in the ground. As the shaking ground started rumbling, the erupting earth became a dark crescent, then a black, expanding hillock, and then the rumbling became a thunderous explosion that created a gigantic mushroom cloud of smoke, dust, sand and showering gravel, billowing up from a bed of white, yellow and blue flames overlaid with crimson sparks. The mushroom cloud rose higher, expanded in all directions, and was blotting out the stars even as its tendrils coiled languorously, beautifully, back down to rain its deadly debris on the desert floor.

First one tower, then the other, collapsed and disappeared in the billowing smoke.

The roaring tapered off into a rumbling and faded back into silence.

'Let's go!' Phillips bawled.

Turning their backs on the spectacular explosion, the SAS men hurriedly filed into the two Chinooks. The first chopper lifted off the desert plain with no problem, but the second coughed noisily at the start of its ascent, the rapid spinning of its twin rotors slowed down, and then it sank back to the ground, landing so hard that its wheels buckled under it. Tilting to one side, it came to a shuddering, shrieking halt in a billowing cloud of sand.

'All out!' Major Phillips bawled.

The men spilled out of the Chinook as its erratic coughing tapered into silence and its rotors stopped spinning. The cloud of sand whipped up by the rotors settled back down, turning into drifting tendrils that painted the moonlit darkness like strips of tattered brown cloth, as the men ran away from the helicopter, fearing that it was about to explode.

Even as the SAS troopers were fanning out, automatically forming themselves into a protective circle, six Iraqi troop trucks emerged from the near blackness further along the MSR, rattling noisily as they bumped over potholes and stones, heading for the great mushroom of smoke that still boiled high above the two felled communications towers.

Realising that the trucks could only have come from an Iraqi army camp, obviously nearby but unseen in the darkness, Phillips used a hand signal to tell his men to fire at will. This they did, opening up with everything they had as the Iraqi trucks careened off the road in opposite directions, screeched around in wide arcs, rocking and tilting wildly, churning up more clouds of sand, and then turned back to form into a protective laager, with each truck practically touching another, front to rear in a circle.

A fusillade of bullets punctured the tyres of the trucks closest to the SAS troopers, making them explode and subside to a noisy hissing of air as the Iraqi troops jumped down to the sand, took up safe positions behind their vehicles, then returned the SAS fire with a fusillade of their own, firing wildly and blindly in the darkness.

Exposed in the open ground in front of the damaged Chinook, which luckily had neither caught fire nor exploded, two of the SAS troopers were killed instantly, a few more were wounded, and the remainder were forced to fall belly down and fire from that position, with soil and sand spitting up all around them as more enemy bullets stitched the ground. Others made their way backwards to the Chinook, firing on the move, to join the SAS troopers still inside. Some of them made it. Three more were caught in a convulsion of spitting sand, jerked spasmodically in the moonlight, screaming, then dropped their weapons and fell into the pitch darkness of the desert floor.

The Chinook that had lifted off returned briefly to the scene of the fire fight, but devoid of weapons it soon ascended again, out of range of the Iraqi machine guns and any anti-aircraft missiles that the enemy might possess.

Knowing that the pilot of the Chinook would report the plight of the SAS squadron to HQ at Al Jubail, Major Phillips, now kneeling with the company signaller, Corporal Ben Townsend, behind the crushed wheel of the helicopter, had no choice but to let the fire fight continue and pray that his men could hold off the Iraqis until some form of rescue was at hand. Nevertheless, he was filled with grief to see that most of his men were still pinned down in dead ground, firing valiantly from the prone position but far too exposed for their own good, even though partially hidden by the moon-striped darkness. Indeed, even as he looked on, some of them suddenly writhed violently in convulsions of spitting sand and swirling dust, peppered by bullets from a combination of semi-automatic weapons

– probably AK-47 Kalashnikovs – and machine guns. Even worse, the first of the shells from enemy mortars had begun to explode in their midst, blowing some of them into the air, showering others in falling sand and debris.

'Christ!' Phillips exclaimed. 'It's a bloody slaughter!'

However, some of the troopers on the ground, realising what was happening, began firing 40mm grenades from the M203 grenade-launchers fixed to their M16 rifles. Aimed with exceptional accuracy, with the aid of night sights, the grenades exploded behind the Iraqi troop trucks, inside the laager, with sand, soil and smoke boiling up, roaring, and wounded Iraqis screaming in pain. Then, as the SAS troopers kept firing more grenades, a couple of bold SAS men jumped out of the Chinook, one holding a 94mm light anti-tank weapon – a LAW 80 – the other a portable FIM-92A Stinger anti-aircraft missile system. Taking advantage of the exploding grenades from the M203s, the two troopers ran forward at the crouch, weaving left and right to avoid the hail of enemy bullets, which now were ricocheting off the Chinook's fuselage, until they reached its undamaged front wheel. Kneeling behind the wheel, protected only slightly, both men loaded their heavy weapons, then each selected a separate target – the trucks nearest to them in the enemy laager, outlined clearly by the starry sky – took aim and fired almost simultaneously.

Even as the man with the LAW 80 was being rocked by the backblast and obscured in a cloud of smoke from his own weapon, the 94mm warhead was streaking on a separate stream of white smoke into the first truck, smashing through the glass of the driver's compartment to explode with a mighty roar in the clearing behind it. In less than a second, the high-explosive anti-tank (HEAT) rocket of the FIM-92A Stinger was ploughing into the rear of the second truck to explode even more noisily, blowing the truck to pieces and killing the men kneeling directly behind it.

Now, with only the mangled, smouldering skeleton of the

truck remaining, the SAS GPMG team, set up behind the damaged rear wheels of the Chinook, poured a fusillade of automatic fire into the gap in the laager, decimating the Iraqis exposed there.

Shocked, the other Iraqis responded by aiming most of their mortar shells and machine-gun fire at the Chinook, blowing holes in its sides, filling the air with flying debris, and causing hundreds of bullets to ricochet off it.

Fearful that this combined fire power would eventually find and penetrate the Chinook's fuel tanks and cause it to blow up, Major Phillips used his walkie-talkie to tell the two men hiding behind the front wheel to make a rough estimate of the enemy mortar positions from the smoke rising from them and then pour as much fire power as they possessed into them. In less than a minute, a deadly combination of 94mm warheads and HEAT rockets was creating a virtual cauldron of fire and smoke inside the laager, with another truck bursting into flames, the whole laager becoming covered in a pall of black smoke, which blotted out the stars, and Iraqi soldiers screaming as they were scorched by the flames or cut to ribbons by red-hot, flying debris.

The Iraqi mortars, however, were still blowing holes in the Chinook and a shell struck its fuselage just above the front wheel, blowing out a few panels and showering debris on the two men below. Hit by a massive, red-hot, composite-metal panel, the trooper with the LAW 80 was smashed into the ground, dying instantly. The trooper with the Stinger managed to run away just before the debris reached him, but he was struck almost instantly by a hail of enemy machine-gun fire that punched him backwards, made him shake like an epileptic in a fit, then flung him violently into the sand.

Seeing that the LAW 80 and Stinger were out of action, the Iraqis again concentrated most of their fire power, including their heavy weapons, such as the machine guns and mortars, on the unfortunate SAS men still trapped out in the open, just in front of the smouldering Chinook. Luckily, as more of them were dying under a pall of boiling sand and smoke, a US Apache AH-64 helicopter – one of those widely known as the 'Dragonflies of Death' – came roaring out of the night sky. Descending low enough for its rotors to whip the sand up into a minor tornado, it poured an awesome combination of laser-guided Hellfire missiles, 70mm rockets and 30mm Chain Gun Cannon into the general area of the Iraqi laager, turning it into a nightmare of roaring, spewing sand that obliterated the stars, searing yellow-white flames that cut jagged holes in the darkness, and boiling smoke that billowed back on the breeze to choke even the SAS troopers still on the ground.

Unable to withstand the ferocity of this attack, the Iraqis jumped back into their remaining trucks and broke the laager up by racing off in different directions, leaving the spiralling sand to settle down over their dead. As the Iraqi trucks were retreating, the Apache also flew off, heading back to Al Jubail, then another Chinook materialised to descend in a whirlpool of swirling sand and dust, landing between the damaged helicopter and the former Iraqi positions.

Without waiting for instructions, since they knew what the Chinook was here for, the men on the ground jumped up and ran at the crouch towards it, weaving spectrally through the murk.

Just as the first of them were hurrying up the chopper's rear ramp, two of the Iraqi troop trucks, their officers obviously emboldened by the abrupt departure of the Apache and aware of the fact that the Chinooks carried no armaments, roared back out of the dark desert plain with their canvas tops removed and the troopers in the back firing as they approached. A couple of the SAS troopers were hit and rolled off the ramp, but most of them made it inside the Chinook before the Iraqi trucks swept around in a wide circle and returned for a second attack on the move.

Unable to cross that stretch of dead ground between the

damaged Chinook and the one waiting to lift them out, four of the SAS men – Phillips, Morrissey, Townsend and Spooner – ran the short distance between the damaged Chinook's front and rear wheels and then up the rear ramp into the loading bay. They had just managed to locate themselves in this temporary refuge when the ramp of the second Chinook was raised and the chopper, being fired upon by the machine guns in the Iraqi trucks, ascended again, rising vertically until it was out of range of the enemy's fire power, then flying horizontally back towards Al Jubail.

The refuge of the remaining four SAS men was indeed temporary. Frustrated that the second Chinook had taken most of the SAS men away, enraged because of the death and destruction wreaked not only by the SAS troopers but also by the US Apache, some of the Iraqi soldiers jumped out of their trunk and hurried up the ramp of the grounded Chinook. Knowing that they could not escape, the SAS men had already raised their hands in the air and were waiting calmly for the Iraqis to find them. When found, they were spontaneously, brutally battered by the Iraqis' rifle butts, then virtually dragged by their hair out of the chopper, down the ramp, across the cold sand, then half pulled, half pushed up into the troop trucks. The trucks disappeared into the night, heading back to Baghdad.

That was the start of it.

CHAPTER TWO

The briefing took place in the sweltering late-afternoon heat in a large tent in the transit camp of Al Jubail, an immense, modern port on Saudi Arabia's east coast, approximately six hundred kilometres from Riyadh, more than eight hundred from Kuwait City, now being used as a receiving port for the Allied equipment and supplies being brought in on over a hundred ships, mostly from European ports, but also from Cyprus, Liberia and Panama. While some of the British servicemen in transit, mainly those of the Queen's Royal Irish Hussars and the 7th Armoured Brigade, were being housed in huts and sheds originally intended for the industrial workers of the port, most were in this enormous, constantly growing 'Tent City' located in the port area and already complete with camp beds, showers, chemical toilets and food from a field kitchen run by the Americans.

From where he was seated at the end of the first row of folding wooden chairs in the big tent, Sergeant Michael 'Mike' Kilroy, of C Squadron, 22 SAS, could look out over the rows of lean-to tents divided by paths that led in one direction to the port, in the other to the airstrip, other accommodations and guarded compounds for the armoured transport and tanks. Hundreds of thousands of troops, British, American and French, were filling up the spaces between the tents, eating cold rations, drinking tea, writing letters, taking open showers, and making use of the chemical latrines known as 'thunder boxes'. Their constant movement and the ever-present wind created drifting clouds of sand and dust that made them look ghostlike in the shimmering light.

Surveying that vast camp, waiting for the arrival of the CO and green-slime Head Shed who would conduct the briefing between them, Kilroy thought of the march of events that had followed Saddam Hussein's brutal invasion of Kuwait. When the news first broke, Kilroy had been sceptical that Saddam would remain in Kuwait City, assuming it to be a bluff designed to get him his way in other matters. Since then, however, Saddam had stuck to his guns. Because of his intransigence, the UN had imposed economic sanctions and a trade ban on Iraq; President Bush had 'drawn a line in the sand' and sent thousands of troops to Saudi Arabia; twelve Arab states and the British and French had done the same; over 100,000 refugees had crossed the border into Jordan; Saddam had used British hostages as 'human shields', paraded others on television, then declared Kuwait as Iraq's nineteenth province and released the hostages as a political gesture; and the UN Security Council had voted for the use of force against Iraq if it did not withdraw from Kuwait by 15 January. By 22 December, shortly after the UN General Assembly had condemned Iraq for human-rights violations in Kuwait, Saddam had vowed that he would never give up Kuwait and threatened to use atomic and chemical weapons if attacked.

At 00.01 hours Zulu, at one minute past three, local time, or one minute past midnight, Greenwich Time, on Thursday, 17 January, two days after the deadline given for Saddam's withdrawal from Kuwait, eight US Apaches of the 101st

Airborne Division, equipped with laser spot trackers and range-finders, attacked Iraqi radars with Hellfire missiles, rockets and 30mm cannon shells, destroying two command centres to create a safe corridor for allied aircraft.

Simultaneously, Tomahawk Cruise missiles from the Coalition carriers in the Gulf rained down on Baghdad while British tornadoes skimmed at low level across the desert, also heading north for Baghdad. These were followed almost instantly by another wave of 'jammer' aircraft intent on suppressing enemy defences, top-cover fighters, more Tornado bombers, reconnaissance planes, AWACS early-warning, intelligence-gathering and target-identification aircraft, and the deadly, delta-winged F-117A Stealth fighter-bombers.

Soon the night sky above Baghdad was illuminated by the greatest firework display in history and covered in an enormous umbrella of boiling black smoke.

In the first twenty-four hours of this unusually complex, computer-controlled war, over a thousand sorties were flown and over a hundred missiles launched against 158 targets, including communications centres and Scud launching sites. As many as twelve combat aircraft at a time were refuelled in flight from tankers stacked six deep in the air.

During the day, the first Allied casualty was the loss of a single Tornado. However, during the night of the 17th, Saddam's military commanders unleashed a volley of eight Scud missiles at Israel from Iraqi airfields and secret bases in the west of the country. Two landed in Haifa and four in Tel Aviv. They were followed immediately by more Scud attacks on Riyadh, where the War Room and main communications of the Coalition effort were located.

Even as the citizens of Haifa, Tel Aviv and Riyadh were donning NBC suits or placing gas masks over their heads, Patriot anti-missile missiles were taking off with a deafening cacophony, followed rapidly by similar noises overhead as the incoming Scuds were hit and exploded, filling the sky with great flashes of silvery light, mushrooms of black smoke, spectacular webs of crimson tracers and downward-curving streams of dazzling white, yellow and blood-red flame.

By the second day of the war, RAF aircrews were attempting to trap Iraqi aircraft hidden in hardened aircraft shelters, or HASes, by bombing the access tracks and taxiways leading from the shelters to the runways. At the same time, US giant B-52s were carrying out round-the-clock, high-level attritional bombing raids designed to demoralise, exhaust and daze the Iraqi troops by denying them sleep – when not actually killing them.

By Day Three it had become clear that the major threat to the Coalition was the Scuds, particularly those on mobile launchers. This was when the SAS were called in.

In fact, as Kilroy had since learnt, certain members of 22 SAS had been working undercover in Iraq since a few days before the invasion, having flown incognito on British Airways Flight 149 from London to Delhi, with a fuelling stop in Kuwait. Finding themselves in the middle of Saddam's invasion, they had melted away, dispersing in two different directions, some to send back information from behind Iraqi lines, others to do the same from Kuwait itself, hiding in a succession of 'safe' houses and operating under the very noses of the Iraqis.

Kilroy's squadron had arrived officially on 1 January 1991, almost four months to the day after Saddam Hussein's bloody takeover of Kuwait City. Flown out on an RAF C-130 Hercules transport from RAF Brize Norton, Oxfordshire, along with members of the Special Boat Squadron (SBS), they had been set down in a holding area in Riyadh, the joint capital, with Mecca, of Saudi Arabia, located in the middle of the country and surrounded by desert. Their journey did not end there, however. Without even a rest break, they were made to unload and transfer to waiting RAF HC-1 Chinook medium-lift transport helicopters their recently acquired, state-of-the-art desert warfare weaponry. When the transfer was completed,

Kilroy and the other SAS men, after being allowed time for a hurried snack of cold rations and hot tea in the shade of the Hercules, boarded the Chinooks and were flown on to Al Jubail.

In the sprawling, sunbaked Tent City, where over half a million Coalition troops and the greatest air force in history were gathered together, they were accommodated close to the Royal Corps of Transport's Force Maintenance Area, or FMA. There the constant noise, combined with the heat, made for aggravated days and sleepless nights. After five days of relative inactivity, waiting for the arrival of the rest of their equipment being brought in by ship, the lack of sleep was certainly no help. To make matters worse, they were ordered to take NAP tablets, which were supposed to reduce the damaging effects of gas in the event of a chemical attack but actually gave everyone diarrhoea. Even before fully recovering from this embarrassing condition, they were made to spend a large part of each day on the Jerboa Range of the training ground at Al Fadhili, inland from Jubail, where they shot at targets and markers while being bellowed at by the aggressive camels of passing Bedouin and assailed relentlessly by buzzing flies and whining, biting mosquitoes.

In short, it had been five days of hell on earth and Kilroy had not been alone in feeling enormous relief when told that something was 'coming up' and they had to attend a briefing. Now that they were all gathered together in the sweltering heat of this big tent and Lieutenant-Colonel Lawrence Blair, their present CO, was entering with an unknown Intelligence Corps officer – instantly recognised as such because his beret was green instead of beige – Kilroy and the others straightened up in their chairs, displaying an interest that was absolutely genuine, since they were assuming that this briefing was for a forthcoming operation and they would soon be moved on. They were not disappointed.

'Good afternoon, men,' Lieutenant-Colonel Blair said when

he had taken up his position on the raised floor at one end of the tent, in front of a blackboard showing the theatre of operations. Wearing his full uniform, including his beige beret and badge, Blair looked infinitely more glamorous than the short, rather podgy green-slime officer who had taken a chair slightly to one side and was resting a manila folder on his lap. 'As you've doubtless already guessed, this briefing is for a specific operation.' He paused to let the general murmur of excited comments and splatter of soft applause die down. Nodding in the direction of the seated green-slime Head Shed, or senior officer, he continued, 'Before Lieutenant-Colonel Kingsley of the Intelligence Corps briefs you on the operation itself, I thought I should fill you in on the background details of the general situation here in Kuwait. This, I know, will bore you all to tears, but you'll just have to suffer.'

The CO grinned as the men hissed and booed derisively in a time-honoured tradition at the mere mention of background details, but eventually, when they settled down, he picked up where he'd left off.

'An SAS forward operating base has been established in the Gulf since August, with D and G squadrons carrying out intensive exercises, including the testing of men and equipment, in the desolate area known as the Empty Quarter. At first, our primary function was to rescue the hostages being used as a human shield by Saddam; but with the release of the hostages in the second week of December, that function became redundant. Instead, we were tasked with tracking the mobile Scud missile launchers that were causing havoc to the Coalition war effort – and calling in attack aircraft to bomb the hell out of them. This is what we're doing now, but the task isn't easy. For a start, the mobile Scud launchers are driven all over the desert and fired from many different locations. Tracking them's been made even more difficult by Saddam's use of dummy rockets that look realistic from the air and contain fuel that explodes when hit by a bomb.

This encourages our pilots to report more strikes than they've actually made. The Iraqis also used dummy mobile launchers with real crews and they, too, look genuine from the air.'

'Are you telling me, boss?' asked Roy Collinson, a darkly intense trooper from Liverpool, formerly of the Cheshire Regiment, 'that the crews of the dummy mobile launchers have to drive around the desert, deliberately trying to be spotted, in order to misdirect the fire from our aircraft?'

'Affirmative.'

'Sure, they must be bleedin' mad!' Trooper Patrick 'Paddy' Magee said. Formerly a corporal with the Irish Guards, he was short and barrel-chested, with a battered, good-humoured face and thinning auburn hair. Though a veteran of the Falklands War and the Princes Gate Siege, widely respected by his superiors, he remained an SAS trooper because of his volatile temper and lack of personal discipline. 'Drivin' round in bloody circles just to be picked off by our aircraft and become another statistic on our kill counts. Not for me, boss!'

'Anyway,' the CO continued, waving those talking into silence, 'since it's become increasingly clear that because of those dummy sites and launchers, the number of Scuds taken out by the aircrews is considerably less than at first anticipated – and as the real ones can't be seen from the air – we're now concentrating on eyeball recces and personal contact, with particular emphasis on the Scuds within range of Israel, roaming the desert round two Iraqi airfields known as H2 and H3.'

'What's Israel got to do with it?' Corporal 'Geordie' Welsh asked, brushing his dusty fair hair from sky-blue eyes and studying the CO intently. A member of the Mobility Group, formerly a corporal in the Staffordshire Regiment, he hadn't fought in a major war before and was keen to get going.

'So far, the Israelis are refusing to be drawn into the war,' the CO replied. 'Should they be drawn in, our Coalition allies are liable to turn against us. We therefore have to stop the Scud attacks on Israel before their patience wears out.'

'So how are you going about it?' Kilroy asked.

'Some teams,' the CO told him, 'stake out static, covert road-watch patrols to report the movement of Scud traffic. Other teams vector F-15 strike aircraft onto the Scuds to destroy them. A third group has reverted to the kind of campaign David Stirling ran during World War Two – deep penetration, hit-and-run raids behind enemy lines, destroying their aircraft on the ground, attacking their lines of communication, ambushing their patrols, and causing general disruption and mayhem.'

'In armed Land Rovers?' Geordie asked.

'Correct. The Pink Panthers. In and out in clouds of dust with all guns firing. A hell of a buzz.'

'Right up my alley,' Geordie said.

'But also Lurp teams,' the CO continued. 'Eight men to each team. Inserted by chopper at an LZ about a hundred and forty to a hundred and eighty miles behind the enemy border, without any transport other than desert boots and a strong will.' By 'Lurp' teams, he was referring to LRRP, or long-range reconnaissance patrols. 'Parallel with this, however, we have fighting columns of up to a dozen well-armed Land Rovers carrying one-and-a-half tons of war material each, manned by a half-squadron of thirty men or more. We have four such columns. Their job's to penetrate one of two major areas in the west, near the border with Jordan, from where the Scuds are launched. This so-called "Scud box" is a well-defended area of desert – approximately two hundred and forty square miles, including the motorway linking Baghdad with Amman. Around twelve to fourteen mobile launchers are thought to be in or near the area.'

'So that's what we're going to be doing?' Kilroy asked, growing impatient, as he did all too easily, and wanting to get to the heart of the matter.

'No,' the CO replied levelly. 'What you're being tasked with is infinitely more dangerous. For the details, I'm going to hand you over to Lieutenant-Colonel Peter Kingsley of the Intelligence Corps. Peter . . . ?'

The CO stepped aside to let the green-slime Head Shed stand up and take his place on the platform. Holding the manila folder in one hand and tugging distractedly at his green beret with the other, Kingsley nodded at them.

'Five days ago,' he said without preamble, 'D Squadron, 22 SAS, was tasked with cutting Iraq's links with the outside world. Those links were in the shape of a complex web of communication towers known as microwave links, set up in the desert, dangerously close to the enemy MSR that runs between Basra and Baghdad. According to our intelligence, it was the communications system coming out of Baghdad that controlled Saddam's trigger finger by carrying his orders to the Iraqi troops responsible for Scud operations. The microwave links also ran Saddam's diplomatic traffic to Amman, Geneva, Paris and at the UN, thus increasing his political credibility. It was the task of the SAS to destroy that credibility as well as the actual Scuds by blowing up the microwave links – and they succeeded in doing so. Unfortunately, when trying to make their escape, one of their Chinooks malfunctioned and the men from that chopper had to be rescued. Though most were lifted out in the end, four were captured by the Iraqis and taken back to Saddam's HQ, located deep under the streets of Baghdad. We want those men back.'

A heavy silence hung over the men for a moment as they contemplated what Kingsley had just said. Eventually, in order to break the silence, Captain Mark Williams, seated beside Kilroy, asked, 'So how do you know where the prisoners are?'

'We know *roughly* where they're being held,' Kingsley replied, 'because Saddam has made no secret of it. Obviously confident that his underground bunker complex in Baghdad is impregnable, he's sent messages to the various leaders of the Coalition forces, stating that he's personally holding the four men prisoner – the use of the word "personally" is our way of knowing that he means his own HQ – and that if we don't cease our attacks on his Scuds, he's going to make an example of them. As we know for a fact that Saddam has ordered all SAS prisoners to be routinely tortured for information, then executed, we've no doubts whatsoever that in this particular instance, where the SAS prisoners were not killed, he intends, if they don't break under torture, either to execute them publicly as a propaganda exercise or, even worse, use them as human shields. We can't let that happen.'

Captain Williams, though looking like a blond-haired, blue-eyed adolescent, had fought with Kilroy in the Falklands and been involved in some hair-raising R and I (reconnaissance and intelligence) exercises; he was therefore an officer who knew his business and was not shy of asking the relevant questions. 'So you want us to enter Baghdad,' he said, not trying to hide his scepticism, 'break into Saddam's underground HQ, somehow avoid his crack troops in the bunkers, find those prisoners and then make our escape. Am I hearing right, boss?'

'You are,' Kingsley said.

'And what if we see Saddam himself?'

Kingsley smiled at that one. 'You're as likely to see Saddam as you are to fly to Alpha Centauri.'

'But what if we *do*?' Williams insisted.

This time Kingsley audibly sighed. 'If you happen to see him when you're going in there, disguised as one of his men, you'll ignore him and keep going until you find the prisoners. That's your first priority. It's not to draw attention to yourself with an assassination attempt. Should you happen to see him when you're trying to break out, then by all means take a shot at him, though don't stop for a fire fight. Your mission is to get those people out. That's your priority.'

There was another lengthy silence while the men took this in. Eventually, however, Mike Kilroy, the most experienced man in the squadron, said, 'That's some tall order, boss. In fact, it's so tall I'm not even sure it's possible. Just what do we have here?'

Sighing, glad to get the question out in the open, Kingsley responded: 'We know that Saddam's HQ is a vast set of military complexes located right under the streets of downtown Baghdad. It consists of cavernous nuclear bunkers and enough command shelters and barracks to house thousands of Saddam's imperial guards. Our intelligence believes that the tunnels between the various complexes run for miles. Each complex is capable of holding twelve hundred people and has command posts, sick bays, sleeping accommodations, decontamination units, armouries, kitchens and stores for dried food and water. Theoretically, there's enough space for nearly fifty thousand people and the bunkers are covered by enormously thick, reinforced detonator slabs capable of withstanding the blast of five-hundred-pound bombs.'

'So we can't bomb it to hell before entering,' Kilroy said.

'No, I'm afraid not.'

'We have to go in cold.'

'Precisely.'

'Is that possible?' Mark Williams asked bluntly. 'I mean, how do we do that? You're talking about an enormous complex located under the enemy's capital city – a city packed with Iraqis and being bombed to hell by our own forces. You're also talking about a complex that's bound to be heavily guarded, almost certainly has electronically controlled gates, and is doubtless under high-tech surveillance. And to top it all you're talking about a complex that runs for miles in every direction, every mile packed with Saddam's crack troops. So getting in there would appear to be extremely doubtful; getting out, with or without the prisoners, could prove to be impossible.'

Lieutenant-Colonel Kingsley, as the green-slime Head Shed,

knew exactly what the odds were against these men in this particular, exceptionally dangerous, near-impossible task. He stared steadily at Williams with his wintry grey, unblinking eyes, then offered the slightest of smiles.

'We have a plan,' he said.

CHAPTER THREE

Alice was choking on sand and dust, trying to spit it out of her throat, as they dragged her by the hair across the ground, over sharp stones and gravel. Their feet were all around her, men's feet, wearing boots, and she heard their excited voices above her, calling out words she didn't understand. Pains darted through her body. Her head seemed to be on fire. Someone was dragging her by the hair, like a sack of potatoes, across the hot, dusty, sharp-stoned ground.

God, the stones hurt as well! Fear seared through her like a hot knife. She tried to remember what had happened, going down, but her thoughts were still scattering.

She had crashed, but survived. Crawled out of the cockpit. She remembered the flames around her, the smoke, and wondered if she was burnt, if her face had been scorched. Please, God, no – not that! Please stop this pain and fear. She coughed and choked up more sand and dust as her body was dragged across the ground, the sharp stones tearing her clothes and lacerating her skin.

The men were obviously excited, shouting in Arabic above her, as she remembered clambering out of the cockpit and falling to the ground. She had crashed and survived but they had captured her. Now she knew who they were.

'Stop it! *Stop it!*' she screamed.

Some laughed and one kicked her, putting his boot in her ribs, and she gasped as the pain exploded through her and knocked the wind out of her. The hand grasping her hair let go, easing the burning in her head. Then she was grasped under the armpits and heaved up over the tailboard of a troop truck, falling onto her back. Someone grabbed her by the hair again, hauled her deeper into the truck, then the other soldiers clambered up inside and seated themselves on the benches on both sides, their boots hemming her in. The man who had hauled her in let go of her hair and the pain eased again.

The truck roared into life, shuddered and moved off. She tried to sit up and was pressed back down by the boot planted deliberately between her breasts. Gasping for breath, trying to control her racing heart, she opened her eyes, but was grabbed by the shoulders and flipped over, onto her belly, one cheek pressed to the floor of the truck, her eyes mere inches away from another pair of black desert boots.

Her hands were tugged behind her back, one wrist folded on the other, causing more dreadful pains to dart between her shoulder blades. Then her wrists were bound together with rope, so tight that it hurt. She tried not to cry out, tried not to give in to panic, when another hand grabbed her by the hair to jerk her head off the floor. Before she could see anything, before she could breathe properly, a blindfold was brutally slapped over her eyes and knotted tightly at the back of her head.

A man screamed in Arabic at her, at the back of her head, then he squeezed her neck as if to choke her, though he didn't actually do so. Instead, he pushed her face back to the floor of the truck, forcing her head to turn to the side, unable to see because of the blindfold, which made the panic return.

'Please don't,' she whispered, still disorientated, thrown into an even deeper well of fear by being blindfolded.

She recalled those other blindfolds, those evenings without pity, the singular humiliations she had suffered at the hands of those supposed to have been her friends. Those nightmares rushed back in, bringing the past to the present, briefly making her believe that she was back in the Academy, on the table in the white room, trussed up like a chicken, blindfolded, kicked and spat upon, one of them standing between her outspread legs, another holding her head down.

'Are you ready for it, you cock-teaser? Do you want it right now? We're all gonna take our turn, whore, so why not tell us you want it? OK, bitch, here's the first one . . .'

Someone bellowed in her ear – words she could not understand – brutally jerking her back to the present and this even worse nightmare. They were speaking Arabic, of course. Some of them were giggling. It was a high-pitched, nervous kind of giggling of the kind she had often recalled with dread.

Please, don't let them, she thought. She knew they were looking at her. Lie still, she thought. Don't make a sound. Don't give them any encouragement . . .

But she jerked when something touched her, pressing teasingly on her rump, something cold and hard – a gun barrel – moving down between her inner thighs. Some of them laughed at that, others traded excited remarks, and for once she was glad she didn't know the language and could lie there in ignorance, though lying there wasn't easy.

Her heart was still racing. She was sweating and felt feverish. The gun barrel probed down between her thighs, causing laughter, then mercifully it moved lower, to her ankles, then withdrew altogether. She tried not to move, but shuddered helplessly, and they laughed all the more.

Lie still, she thought again. Don't make a sound. Don't give them any encouragement . . . But the fear almost choked her, knotted her stomach, making nausea well up . . .

Don't be sick. Don't show weakness.

The truck was bouncing over rough terrain, growling and shrieking in protest, its floor hammering up against her right cheek, her breasts and belly, her sweat-soaked thighs. She heard the wind beating, slapping against the canvas top, and the dust was spitting up from the wooden boards to make her choke and cough helplessly.

Blindfolded and trussed up, she felt oddly disembodied, cast adrift from her own senses, and kept flitting in her thoughts between the past and the present, confused between what was happening now and what had happened before. That brought the fear back, reminding her of what was possible. If before, with trusted friends, it had been bad, now, with these men who must despise her, it could be much worse.

Please, God, don't let them . . .

Someone screamed something at her, then kicked her and laughed harshly. She gasped and felt the shuddering of her body as the others laughed as well. The truck shook beneath her body, its roaring magnified in her right ear, but when she tried to turn her head to the other side a booted foot pressed upon it, trapping it, immobilising it, and someone bawled at her.

She froze immediately, not wanting to make him angry, and just lay there, feeling suffocated, filled with fear, choking in the rising dust. With the pains darting between her shoulder blades, she thought she might actually die there.

Luckily, the men seated around her, unseen, seemed gradually to forget her presence and fell into general, murmured conversation in Arabic, none of which she could understand.

The rest of the journey seemed endless, though this wasn't really so, and the fear of where they were taking her, of what they might do to her, nearly stripped her of her senses. She fought to defeat her panic, collect her thoughts, stay in control, but she could not stop the racing of her heart or kill the fear coursing through her. Time seemed to stretch out for ever.

Nevertheless, the truck soon stopped bumping over rough terrain and instead moved along what felt like a normal, tarmacked road. She heard the sound of other traffic, engines coughing, horns hooting. Then the truck started turning left and right, obviously making its way through a maze of side streets. Eventually it braked to a halt. There was an exchange in Arabic outside. A metal gate squeaked as it was opened, or raised, and then the truck lurched forward again.

When the temperature in the back of the truck dropped dramatically, she knew that the vehicle had moved indoors, out of the baking heat. It braked to a halt again and the engine was turned off. There was more shouting in Arabic from the rear, then the tailboard was thrown down. Some of the soldiers jumped out, their weapons jangling noisily, then two pairs of hands grabbed her under the armpits and jerked her to her feet. Barely able to walk, feeling stiff and badly bruised, she was dragged along the floor of the truck and manhandled over the fallen tailboard, then virtually dropped to the ground. Hitting it hard, she instantly collapsed and rolled onto her side.

Someone kicked her. She was grabbed again and jerked upright. Two pairs of hands held her by the shoulders and hauled her forward, her feet dragging on what felt like concrete, up steps, which hurt her toes. Then she was half dragged, half pushed up stairs, one flight, then another, and made to stop briefly at the top.

Gasping, trying to breathe, shuddering with fear and disorientation, she was just about to collapse when someone bawled in her face, the back of her head was slapped, and she was virtually dragged forward again. There was another spate of shouting, the voices reverberating, then she was stopped again. She heard what sounded like the turning of a large key in a lock, the squeaking of rusty hinges as a door was pulled open, its steel bottom dragging across a cement floor. The thongs on her wrists were loosened and she was thrown roughly forward.

Confused again, recalling the other blindfolds, the other empty rooms, she felt herself flying forward. Instinctively spreading her untied hands to break her fall, she dropped head first though what seemed like endless space and rapidly rising cold. She landed on hands and knees, on something hard and icy, hurting her knees, spraining a wrist, but fell onto her stomach and rolled over as the door slammed shut behind her.

Now sobbing helplessly, retching with fear, she sat up and ripped the blindfold from her eyes and was instantly dazzled.

It wasn't very bright at all – the sun did not shine here – but her eyes had to adjust to the dim light and for a while it seemed radiant.

This was a dreadful illusion.

CHAPTER FOUR

From Tent City in Riyadh the men chosen for the rescue operation, codenamed Operation Dragon Light, were flown in RAF Hercules transports to a forward operating base at a secret Saudi airport in the desert, one day's drive from the border of western Iraq. Though not quite hell on earth, this particular FOB was certainly no paradise, being another sprawling city of tents divided by roads of sand and dust, crammed with Challenger tanks, armoured cars, Land Rovers, Longline LSVs (light strike vehicles), Bedford RL four-ton trucks, a wide variety of jeeps, British Army trail motorbikes, and other SOVs (special-operations vehicles), many of which were being used as the 'walls' or 'supports' for the tents and their camouflaged netting. The few prefabricated buildings on the immense site were used mainly for administration, including the special forces HQ, and a sickbay; otherwise, tents were used for even such basics as the NAAFI canteen, quartermaster's stores and armoury. The showers and 'thunder boxes' were makeshift jobs, with flapping canvas to keep the sun off the men as they attended to their ablutions practically in the open. On all sides of this rough-and-ready camp there was nothing but desert, stretching fifteen hundred kilometres from the Red Sea to Kuwait and the Gulf, southwards to the Arabian Sea beyond Oman: three million square kilometres of white sand and dunes, with the heat waves shimmering up to a dazzling azure sky.

'Fucking beautiful,' Geordie said, as he and the other men gathered together on the tarmac of the airstrip, in the shadow of the Hercules, watching their kit being unloaded.

'Fucking dangerous,' Kilroy replied. 'That desert's no friend to man or beast, so treat it with care, my friend.'

'It's still beautiful,' Geordie insisted.

'Beautiful and deadly,' Kilroy replied. 'Just like a woman. You can't trust either, believe me.'

Kilroy, a Londoner, born and bred in Camden Town, was a legend in his own time, a regimental hero who had fought his first campaigns with the SAS in Northern Ireland in 1978, led one of the assault teams in the daring Princes Gate Siege in 1980, fought all over South Georgia and the Falklands during the war against Argentina in 1982, took part in the killing of eight IRA terrorists in Loughgall, Northern Ireland, in 1987 and was rumoured to have been involved in the controversial shooting of three IRA terrorists in Gibraltar the following year – a rumour consistently denied by him. Nevertheless, whether or not he had taken part, he was undoubtedly one of the most experienced NCOs in the regiment and a man who had been marked by those experiences. Rarely smiling, speaking only when spoken to, with wintry grey eyes and a two-inch scar running down his sunken right cheek – an old shrapnel wound from the Falklands War – he could seem slightly sinister, even oddly threatening, to those not used to him. Though greatly respected by the other men in the regiment, he kept himself to himself and had few close friends. Geordie knew that he was married, but that's all he knew about Kilroy's private life. Kilroy was a world unto himself and not too approachable.

'Anyway,' Geordie said as his mates, Roy Collinson and

Paddy Magee came up to join him, both squinting against the brilliant sunlight, 'I guess this is home for a few weeks.'

'One week exactly,' Kilroy replied. 'Seven days from start to finish and then we're off. That's what the CO said.'

'Sure that's long enough in this pisshole,' Paddy said. 'I'd rather go on the mission – even if suicidal – than have all this bloody retraining.'

'Me too,' Roy said, removing his beige beret from his head and running his fingers through dishevelled jet-black hair as his dark, intense gaze took in the sights all around him. Six foot tall and as thin as a reed, he towered over the short, stocky Paddy, his best friend in the squadron. 'Christ, it's hot as hell here!'

'That's where you'll end up eventually,' Paddy told him, 'so you might as well get used to it.'

'I'm heaven-bound,' Roy replied.

Though they were grinning at each other, Paddy's mention of the 'suicidal' mission had reminded them of just how dangerous the mission was going to be and made them more keen to get started. This they did when their gear was unloaded onto the tarmac and they had to sort out their individual kit. As they were doing this, they were approached by a barrel-chested SAS sergeant major who, even before he had introduced himself, bawled at them to move their lazy arses.

'Sergeant Major Basham,' he said eventually, his shock of red hair windblown and flopping over brilliant green eyes. 'Behind my back, I'm called "Bash-'em-Up, Basham", but don't call me that to my face unless you're looking for trouble.' Some of the men grinned at that, but Basham's glare froze the smiles on their faces. 'I'm going to be your DT for the duration of your stay here and you can take it as read that I'll work you hard. Now pick your kit up and get into the trucks and let's get to work. It starts this very second. No break for you crap hats.'

Realising that they had a hard man on their hands, the men

did as they were told. When their kit had been unloaded, they were herded into Bedford four-tonners and driven to what looked like a dust-covered, open motor pool near the perimeter of the FOB, containing a great number of brightly painted 'Pink Panther' Series III Land Rovers, Land Rover One-Ten Desert Patrol Vehicles, Longline LSVs and British Army trail motorbikes, all heavily armed.

'That's a sight for sore eyes,' Geordie said, being in his element here. 'My day's just been made.'

Indicating the vehicles with a vigorous wave of his hand, Sergeant Major Basham said, 'These are all yours. This is where you'll basha down. From this day forth, you'll live just as you'll have to in the desert, which means sleeping on the ground in lean-tos attached to whatever vehicle you're allocated.' This caused a few moans from the men, but Basham ignored them. 'Throughout your training, you'll have to put those lean-tos up every evening and dismantle them every morning, then pack them into your respective vehicles and take them with you into the desert when you go out there for field exercises. No trenches, no tents. You sleep out in the open, beside your vehicle, here and in the desert, so don't look forward to wet dreams. Now—'

'Excuse me, boss,' Geordie said, raising his hand in the air and grinning mischievously beneath his mop of fair hair. 'But as a member of the Mobility Group, I assume I'll be assigned a motorbike. I can hardly fix a lean-to to that, so do I get a pup tent?'

Basham grinned wickedly. 'Nice try, Corporal, but the answer is no. What you do is construct your own lean-to basha *beside* your vehicle. Got that?'

'Yes, boss.'

'Good.' Basham returned his attention to the rest of the men, many of whom were grinning broadly. 'Three men to each vehicle. You'll find your name on a piece of paper stuck somewhere on the vehicle you've been allocated. Once you've found your vehicle, you'll put up your bashas, then you've got an hour off to have a lunch of the rations you're carrying. Fresh rations will be collected from the quartermaster's stores every morning and will have to last you the rest of the day.'

'Scuse me, Sergeant Major,' Roy asked, his dark gaze concerned. 'Are you saying we're not allowed to use the NAAFI canteen?'

'No, you're not. For reasons of security, you're being segregated from the rest of the men in this FOB until you return from the mission.'

'What about the odd beer?' Paddy asked, looking even more concerned.

'We don't drink out of respect for local customs, so no beer for you.' Basham smiled sadistically, waited for the moans and groans to fade away, then continued, 'At precisely fourteen hundred hours, you'll report to that big tent for a briefing on what's going to happen over the next seven days.' He pointed to the biggest tent in the clearing in the middle of the sea of lean-tos. 'That's it. Get moving.'

The Bedford four-tonners had been turning around and heading back to the motor pool even as Basham was speaking. Leaping onto the dashboard of the last one as it rumbled past, he was carried away with it, through boiling clouds of sand. When he had gone, the men wandered through the many parked vehicles until they found their individual names on the pieces of paper stuck to them – three men to each four-wheeled vehicle; one man to each motorbike. Once they had found their vehicles, they inspected them with considerable enthusiasm, these being very special machines indeed.

The so-called 'Pink Panther' Land Rovers, or 'Dinkies', were more or less as described – painted in a desert camouflage scheme of sunset pink, earth brown and sandy yellow, which made them look a bit like cartoon or funfair cars. They were, however, highly sophisticated vehicles, with 3.5-litre V-8 petrol engines, five-speed gearboxes, alternating four or five-wheel drive, with cabins stripped down to the hull and windscreens removed. They were also bristling with machine guns, including front-mounted 7.62mm GPMGs, rear-mounted 0.5-inch Browning heavy machine guns and two M203 grenade-launchers, with additional mountings for LAW 80 94mm anti-tank missiles and a Stinger-POST (Passive Optical Seeker Technology) surface-to-air missile (SAM) system. Short-burst radio and SATCOM antennae were fixed to the sides, jutting up in the air, high above the multidirectional barrels of the guns. A SATNAV global positioning system (GPS) receiver was mounted on the vehicle (though it could also be carried by hand) and a sun compass, also used for navigation, was mounted horizontally on the front. Smoke dischargers were fitted front and rear, detachable searchlights were positioned on each side, camouflage netting was rolled across the bonnet, and there were extra storage racks for food, water, fuel, spare parts, more weapons, ammunition, and the tools required for the construction of observation posts – or OPs.

The Longline LSVs, or light strike vehicles, based on the dune buggies widely used on American beaches, were virtually no more than tubular steel frames in roll cages – no roof, body panels or windscreen – with two seats in the middle, a fat, low-pressure tyre on each corner, and a powerful engine. Nevertheless, though they looked even more like vehicles from a funfair and their payload capacity was limited, they carried LAW 80 anti-tank rockets and man-portable MILAN guided-missile firing posts, which made them ideal for hit-and-run raids on enemy targets.

The British trail motorbikes, one to accompany each Land Rover, were normal Honda machines, used as 'outriders', mainly for forward observation purposes in terrain impassable to the other vehicles, to be driven by members of the 22 SAS Mobility Group, usually with an M16 slung across the back and a Browning 9mm High Power handgun holstered at the hip.

All in all, they were mobile arsenals of highly advanced capability.

'A little beauty,' Roy said, running his hand over the body of his Pink Panther as if stroking a woman.

'He's getting a hard-on just looking at it,' Geordie responded, dumping his bergen on the ground beside his motorbike. 'God help us when he turns on the ignition – he'll probably shoot his whole wad.'

'Better believe it,' Roy said, unabashed.

When they had inspected their vehicles and found them satisfactory, they proceeded to raise temporary bashas. Those with four-wheeled vehicles hammered sticks into the ground about three feet away from the vehicle, stretched string between the two uprights, slung their ponchos over the string, with the long end hanging down to the ground, and tied the other ends to protruberances on the vehicle. Those with motorbikes used two long and two short sticks to get the same effect, which was that of a small, triangular tent. They then unrolled their sleeping bags and laid them out under the sloping roof of the shelter, using some of their kit as a pillow.

'Doing this every evening,' Roy said, 'is going to drive me crazy. Especially since we're going to have to dismantle it every bloody morning. Why can't they just give us tents?'

'Because they want you to get used to doing what you're going to have to do out in the desert,' Kilroy explained. 'So shut up and do it.'

'It's as good as done, Sarge.'

Once the tents were raised, they removed the portable hexamine stoves and rations from their packed bergens, lit the stoves and then heated the first meal they'd had since leaving Riyadh: sausage with baked beans or curry with rice in small frying pans, spooned up from mess tins as quickly as possible to stop sand or dust from getting on it, then washed down with hot tea. When they had finished, they had to wash their utensils with cold water from their water bottles, place everything back in the bergens and heave the bergens into their individual shelters. Then they hiked back to the big briefing tent where they were informed by Captain Williams that training would commence immediately, following a visit to the armoury, with weapons practice on the firing range.

'All right, men, quieten down,' Williams said when the anticipated moans and groans filled the tent. 'I know that you all feel you've had enough firing-range practice to last you a lifetime, but unfortunately this can't be avoided. The last major war waged by the regiment was in the Falklands, eight years ago, and the weather, terrain and weapons were all very different. Some of you have never been in a desert environment, so the retraining will place emphasis not only on firing the weapons, but on maintaining them in this particularly hazardous environment. Tomorrow you'll have less familiar, therefore potentially more interesting, training in high-tech surveillance and laser designation, but for now you'll have to settle for the firing range. So on your feet, please, and take yourselves off to the armoury. Sergeant Major Basham's waiting for you there and he isn't a patient man.'

Leaving the briefing tent, they made their way to the armoury where they found 'Bash-'em-Up' Basham waiting impatiently for them, his green gaze piercing and his cheeks flushed with heat as he made them enter the big tent in pairs to collect their weapons. While the personal weapons included the semi-automatic SLR, the thirty-round M16 with night-vision aids and M203 40mm grenade-launcher, the Heckler & Koch MP5 thirty-round sub-machine gun and the standard-issue Browning FN 9mm High Power handgun, they also picked up some belt-fed L7A2 7.62mm GPMGs and the LAW 80s and relatively new Stinger-POST missile systems that would eventually be fitted to the attachments on the Pink Panther Land Rovers. Also dispensed to each man were L2A2 hand grenades, Haley & Weller incendiary and fragmentation grenades, and enough ammunition to last them at least through the afternoon.

It was a hellish afternoon: four hours in the boiling heat of an open stretch of dusty ground with figure-eight targets at the end of it and the air about them filled with swarms of whining mosquitoes and fat, buzzing flies. Seemingly impervious to the flies, Sergeant Major Basham put them through their paces with the various weapons, including the LAW 80 and Stinger-POST, both of which caused deafening, spectacular explosions of sand and dust that were swept back over the men who had fired them, practically choking them. The same thing happened when they were made to throw their hand grenades at the nearby sand dunes: the exploding sand and dust were swept back over them on the constant, hot wind. These arduous endeavours were made no easier by the knowledge that the sand was crawling with venomous scorpions and other insects, though Basham ignored this fact as well.

Indeed, when the two hours of target practice had finished, he did not reprieve the sweating, filthy men but instead made them dismantle every kind of weapon being used, clean and oil them, reassemble them and cover the movable parts in stretched contraceptives to keep the sand and dust out until they had to be used again. This was far more difficult than it would have been indoors because the sand and dust, being whipped up by the constant breeze, got into the weapons as quickly as they were cleaned; nor was it made any easier by the swarms of flies and mosquitoes that attacked the men relentlessly as they tried to work. By the end of that first afternoon, they were filthy, sweaty, exhausted and extremely frustrated.

'How the fuck you're supposed to clean weapons out there is beyond me,' Roy complained. 'The sand gets back into the bastards quicker than you can actually wipe 'em clean. A right fucking waste of time, if you ask me.'

'You weren't asked,' Paddy replied.

'You always say that when I make a statement,' Roy complained. 'You say the same thing each time.'

'That's because you keep saying "if you ask me" and it's driving me mad.'

'Fuck you and your mother.'

'Sticks and stones, you Liverpudlian git.'

'A good city ruined by too many Paddies.'

'Sure it's the Paddies who make that bloody city.'

'Who gives a shit?' Roy said. 'All I know is that I'm fucking exhausted from all that garbage today.'

'Aren't we all?' Paddy said.

They were, however, given little rest. Upon returning to their open-air bashas, they were allowed another hour to attend to their ablutions, change into fresh clothing and heat up a hasty meal with the aid of their portable hexamine stoves. The instant this blissful hour was over, they were marched by the redoubtable Basham to the briefing tent for the first of their seven lessons in basic Arabic words which could be used if they were lost in the desert or captured. They were also given helpful titbits of information about local customs and warned, in particular, that, although the desert appeared to be empty of everything but sand and gravel, that appearance was deceptive, as even the most barren stretch probably belonged to someone and would be highly valued as grazing for the camels still maintained there by the Saudis, particularly those of high rank. As the Bedouin often passed the Coalition camps on their camels, it was important that the men respect Muslim customs by not flaunting their Western habits except in the privacy of their bashas.

'So why can't we drink beer in the privacy of our bashas?' Geordie asked the lecturer from the Hereford and Army School of Languages.

'The Bedouin can sniff it a mile off,' the young SAS captain replied disingenuously. 'So that ban remains, I fear.'

'Fucking A-rabs,' Roy said. 'We come here to defend 'em and still have to do what *they* say. A right fucking cheek, if you ask me.'

'No one asked you,' Paddy reminded him.

Finally, when the first language-and-local-customs lesson had ended just before last light, the men were allowed to return to their open-air bashas to sleep. However, as they learnt to their cost during the first night by their vehicles, decent sleep was not easy to come by, being interrupted constantly by the noise of the RAF Chinooks taking off and landing on the nearby airstrip, churning up great clouds of sand that swept over the SAS quarter to make them choke and cough. Also churning up clouds of sand and creating a lot of noise were the Challenger tanks being put through their paces on the sands surrounding the camp. To make matters worse, at least regarding the noise, the sky directly overhead was filled constantly with Tornado F-3 air-defence planes going to or returning from practice flights out in the desert, which the men soon came to know as the GAFA, or the 'Great Arabian Fuck All'.

Sleep was also made uncomfortable because of the surprising cold of the nocturnal desert. At night it was freezing, and the nights were extremely long – about eleven hours of darkness – so the men stretched out beside their armoured vehicles could do little to pass the time other than listen to the restricted programmes of the Forces' Broadcasting Station or study the brilliant stars over the flat, featureless, seemingly endless black desert.

The rest of the week was taken up with extensive training in a variety of other skills required for modern warfare in the desert. First was the maintenance of their vehicles, which could suffer severe mechanical problems due to sand ingestion. Even when using special filters, most engines, including the normally more powerful helicopter engines, were reduced to about a tenth of their normal usage and the power packs of the Challenger tanks were failing so often that 7th Armoured Brigade's desert training had to be curtailed. Supply vehicles that were perfectly fine in Europe and had performed superbly in the Falklands sank into the sands of Iraq. Container trucks were so useless that the SAS had been forced to borrow M453 tracked vehicles from the Yanks and use them in conjunction with wheeled vehicles for staged resup journeys. Water for men and vehicles had to come from the desalination plant at Al Jubail, but if the SAS missed the REME supply columns, or if they were out on patrol, they had to drink fossilised water from the prehistoric aquifers beneath the desert floor. If even more desperate, they had to filter and sterilise water, recycle water already used for cooking, shaving and washing, or, as a last resort, purify their own urine. All of this they were taught to do in the blazing heat of the desert.

'Great, ain't it?' Roy complained. 'First they say you can't have beer, then they teach you how to drink your own piss. What kind of war *is* this?'

'A war in a furnace,' Kilroy told him, 'so learning to purify your own piss might come in handy. You won't complain if you get lost out there and run out of water.'

'Who's complaining?' Roy asked rhetorically. 'I'm just airing my thoughts.'

'Your thoughts aren't worth airing,' Paddy told him, 'so keep 'em in the closet.'

'Very funny,' Roy said.

They were also taught desert navigation, which, because of the lack of topographical features, was particularly difficult. Navigation by night was conducted pretty much as it was elsewhere in the world – by reading the stars – but navigation by day presented more problems and a wider variety of systems, including the use of maps, prismatic compasses, the SATNAV global positioning system (GPS) receiver, both when mounted on the vehicle and when carried by hand, and the sun compass mounted horizontally on the front. More primitive but surprisingly effective methods of navigation for emergencies, technology being highly unpredictable and not always reliable, included the 'distance-marched method' (pacing) and the use of razor blades or needles as makeshift compasses.

'One minute we're finding our bearings by listening in to satellites circling the earth,' Roy said, referring to the GPS as he studied the Magellan NAV 1000M receiver in his hand, 'the next we're doing the same by stropping razors against the palms of our hands, magnetising them, then dangling them from wee bits of string. Navigation in the desert with the SAS is a weird and wonderful business.'

'From the cave to the stars,' Paddy replied. 'We make the leap in seconds every day. We're men of initiative, mate.'

Once they had mastered navigation, they were taken out into the desert, both by day and by night, to learn how to drive and hike over the physically demanding landscape – the undulating gravel plain known as *dibdibba*, broad wadis, dried-out flash-flood depressions, small hills, sand dunes and ridges – without succumbing to dehydration, sunstroke or sunburn, with particular emphasis on water discipline and personal hygiene. Doing this, they soon learnt that intense thirst was an indication that dehydration was already setting in, that it was important to drink *before* feeling thirsty, and that fourteen litres of water a day was not an unusual amount for a trooper to drink. Personal hygiene covered the proper cleaning of eating and cooking equipment, correct disposal of garbage and human waste, and protection of utensils from flies to prevent intestinal diseases. Last but not least, they were taught how to look out for, and prevent being bitten or infected by, poisonous spiders and scorpions as well as the lice, mites and flies that carried diseases such as scrub typhus and dysentery.

'Sure, why should we worry about Saddam Hussein's crack

troops when we're in more danger from the creepy-crawlies?' Paddy asked of his mates. 'If we can survive all the diseases mentioned by Bash-'em-Up Basham, we can survive anything Saddam Hussein throws at us. It'll all be small beer after this, boyos, and we'll feel like John Wayne.'

'Before or after the Big C?' Geordie asked him.

'After,' Roy said. 'Wasted away with dysentery and diarrhoea and God knows what else.'

'You lot have already got acute diarrhoea,' Mike Kilroy said, staring at them with his chilly grey eyes, his scarred face unsmiling, 'and it's all purely verbal. I've never heard so much bullshit in my life.'

'So sorry, Sarge,' Geordie said.

'He has a rubber mouth,' Paddy explained.

'A punctured balloon letting out hot air,' big Roy added helpfully.

'Just shut up, the lot of you,' Kilroy said, not remotely amused, 'and let's get back to work.'

'Yes, boss,' Geordie said.

Finally, during the last of their seven days, just as they were feeling that they could learn no more, they were given a crash course in the most recent high-tech surveillance methods, using the equipment they would be taking on the mission. These included Thorn EMI multi-role thermal imagers, Davin Optical Spylux image intensifiers, STG (Surveillance Technology Group) audio surveillance probes, transmitters and optical receivers; and laser designators, which could be used by hand or be mounted on the vehicle to illuminate a chosen target – ground-based air defence systems, nuclear, biological and chemical research facilities, and military production centres – with a laser beam detectable by airborne laser-guided bombs, such as the GBU-10 Paveway II.

Those final lessons were given on the evening of the seventh day. At 22.00 hours, just as the men thought they were going to be able to raise their bashas and put their heads down, four of them – Sergeant Kilroy, Corporal Geordie Walsh, and Troopers Paddy Magee and Roy Collinson – were called for a special briefing, to be conducted by Captain Williams, their squadron commander.

From this they gauged instantly that they had been selected as part of the special team for Operation Dragon Light.

'We're the crème de la crème,' Kilroy said without the trace of a smile. 'Who else could they pick?'

CHAPTER FIVE

The cell was narrow, gloomy and cold from lack of sunlight, with a stone-flagged floor, hatched steel door, and no windows, its only light beaming in weakly through the open top half of the hatch. It contained only a badly stained foam mattress with two folded, tattered blankets placed at one end of it. At the far end of the cell, a wooden stable door led into a tiny washroom, consisting of no more than an uncleaned lavatory bowl, over which flies swarmed, and a cold tap hanging just above the ground from loose, rusty piping. There was no soap or towel. Large cockroaches crawled all over the floor and around the foam mattress in the cell itself.

The stone walls were covered with scribbling in Arabic, which Alice couldn't read, and various drawings that made her shiver when she studied them: men hanging from gallows or being shot behind the head as they knelt in last-minute prayer. Clearly, Iraqis had been imprisoned here before her and had guessed what their eventual fate would be. The walls revealed the history of the cell and gave Alice nightmares.

Of course, the walls were only part of it. She had been here three days, all alone, left to her thoughts, weakened by the lack of decent food and proper sleep, her only human contact the brown eyes that peered at her though the top half of the hatch, the barked words she could not understand, the food poked through the slot. The food came once a day, at any time in the morning, and was always the same dreadful mess: a vomit-coloured soup with a piece of dried bread, both covered by a swarm of fat black flies. At first she'd refused to eat it, but hunger works miracles and soon, after retching a few times, she managed to swallow it. When the voice barked and a hand came through the slot, she handed the empty plate back: that was her sole human contact.

She was still in her flying suit and boots, but covered in filth, only able to clean her face by splashing it with cold water and drying it with her oil-smeared sleeve. The cell was hot during the day and the suit made her sweat profusely, but she didn't dare take it off because of those peering eyes.

At nights, when the cell was freezing cold, she wore the suit under the blankets, grateful to have it on, including the boots, even though it reminded her of being shot down, the flames in the cabin, crashing, scrambling out of the burning chopper, leaving the dead crew behind, including Dave – oh, God, her beloved Dave! – then falling to the ground and losing consciousness, recovering only when they dragged her across the ground by a hunk of her hair.

When not recalling the crash and suffering anguish, in particular, over Dave's death, haunted by the sight of him, scorched and bloody in the wreckage, she sought refuge in recollections of her parents, her older brother and younger sister, her friends from high school and university, the white-painted farmhouse in Iowa, her own bedroom with its childhood bric-a-brac, the love and friendship she had known before entering the US Air Force Academy in Colorado.

Invariably, however, this latter recollection led her back to the other blindfolds, the other humiliations in cold, locked rooms, surrounded by sneering, threatening men.

All her nights were an ordeal.

Going to the toilet was a further ordeal, squatting over that squalid bowl, and the paper she used, passed through the slot by the guard, could only be thrown in the bowl, thus remaining exposed, covered in dried shit and buzzing flies. The cockroaches were everywhere.

She vomited a lot. The second day she had diarrhoea. By the third day, when she felt weak and nauseous, she was even more frightened. She hadn't been able to sleep at nights, being tormented by anguished thoughts of Captain Dave Bamberg, by thoughts of what might happen to her at the hands of the Iraqis, and by the scurrying sounds of the many giant cockroaches, which she often imagined were rats. Also, in the darkness, she often thought that she was still blindfolded and grew confused between recollections of her journey here in the troop truck and recollections of the other blindfolded sessions in other rooms in the past.

She had tried to forget all that, or at least put it behind her, but the instant they had blindfolded her in the truck it had all rushed back to haunt her.

It was for your own good, she had been told. You must accept that if you're shot down, if you're captured, you'll have much worse to endure. Don't complain. Don't show weakness.

The sanctimonious bastards.

She wanted to hate them now, but she was too frightened of the others: the ones who would eventually come for her as they had come for the others, the ones outside her cell. She had heard the others in the adjoining cells, Iraqi men and women, marched away by the armed guards, often babbling hysterical protestations as they moved past her cell. Some were dragged back a few hours later, groaning with pain and nearly unconscious. Others never returned.

When Alice saw the drawings on her walls, she didn't have to imagine what happened to those who did not return.

She knew they would come for her, take her into another room, and she wondered what would happen in that room and the thought terrified her. She could not forget the feel of that rifle barrel prodding her buttocks, poking between her legs, aware that the soldier who had done that had wanted to do more; knowing full well that the men in the interrogation room, when they finally came for her, might do even worse. Thinking about that, she shivered.

She was shivering when the door was finally opened and they came in to march her out.

Weak and disorientated, covered in filth, humiliated, she looked up and saw brown faces, black berets on their heads, olive-green uniforms, brown eyes looking her up and down, teeth white as they grinned and made jokes. Then one of them barked fiercely and threw something at her. Catching it, she saw that it was a particularly filthy *dish-disha*, the plain, one-piece Arab shirt that reaches from the throat to the feet. The guard barked at her again and jabbed his finger at the washroom. Grateful for this modicum of protection from staring eyes, she went into the washroom, shucked off her flying suit, and put the *dish-disha* on over her head, letting it fall over her brassiere and panties.

Even with the long gown on, she felt naked when she returned to the cell and saw the eyes of the guards move up and down her. The leader barked again and pointed into the wash-room. Realising that he wanted the flying suit, she went back for it and handed it to him. He shook his head, indicating that she should hold it, then barked another command and pointed at her feet. Sitting on the floor, she removed her laced-up desert boots. Before she could stand up again, another order was barked at her and she realised that he wanted her to remove her socks as well. She did so, feeling even more naked, and finally stood up, hugging the flying suit, boots and socks to her breasts, her bare feet cold on the stone-flagged floor, the *dish-disha* falling down from her neck to just above her ankles.

'*Yalla!*' the guard bawled, indicating with his free hand that she should follow him.

Aching all over from lack of exercise, weak from hunger, trembling helplessly with fear but trying not to show it, she followed the armed guards along the corridor, which had a row of cells on one side and a solid concrete wall on the other, with no windows to let the light in. At the end of the corridor she was led down what she took to be the two flights of stairs that she had previously come up blindfolded, then marched across a spartan hallway, containing only wooden benches, to a closed wooden door.

The guard in charge of the group, the one who had barked instructions at her, knocked on the door with his fist and called out to those inside. A male voice responded, also in Arabic, and the guard opened the door and motioned to Alice to enter. Trembling even more, now clutching the folded flying suit, boots and socks to her bosom for comfort, she entered and was followed in by the armed guards.

She stopped automatically when the door slammed shut behind her, but one of the guards pushed her roughly forward with the palm of his hand, then grabbed her shoulder and forced her down onto a wooden chair, facing a large desk covered in papers. An Iraqi with grey-black hair, hostile brown eyes and a bushy moustache like Saddam Hussein's, wearing a plain grey suit with an open-necked shirt, was seated behind the desk. Two other men, both in Iraqi army uniforms with black berets, both with similar black moustaches, were standing one on each side of the seated man, neither looking friendly.

Seeing them, Alice could not help thinking of the men who had surrounded in her in the other rooms in the Academy in Colorado, of those singular nights of terror and humiliation. The recollections, as they always did, brought back the fear and made her tremble in full sight of the enemy.

Don't let them get to you, she thought, as she had thought

in those grim rooms in the Academy. Don't let the bastards see weakness.

Without saying a word, the man behind the desk motioned with his right hand, indicating that she should place her flying suit, boots and socks on his desk. When she had done so and was sitting back in the chair, he cupped both hands over his breasts, shook them a little, as if making an obscene joke, then used a hand gesture that unmistakeably meant she should remove her brassiere.

Shocked, but too frightened to refuse, she tugged the *dish-disha* up to her knees, then slid her hands up inside it and, with a great deal of difficulty, seeing those eyes watching her and feeling utterly humiliated, she managed to unclip the brassiere, tug it off her breasts, then pull it down and out from under the bottom of the long cotton garment. When she had placed it on the desk and was sitting back again, the man grasped his own crotch with his right hand, held it there for a moment, this time smiling slightly, then removed it in a way that suggested he was removing his underpants.

Even more shocked, now burning with shame, Alice did as she was told. Having removed the panties, again with a great deal of difficulty, seeing the two officers smirking, she placed them on the desk beside the rest of the clothing, then sat back, feeling naked and defenceless, aware that, even though she was still covered in the long *dish-disha*, her nipples were outlined under the thin cotton and the men were staring brazenly at them.

Folding her arms over her bosom and trying to avoid those staring eyes, she glanced sideways and saw, against that wall, a long wooden table that looked like a butcher's block and was stained with dried blood. Over the table, on hooks in the wall, were what looked like whips made of bamboo and leather. Shocked again, she lowered her gaze, saw more stains on the floor around the wooden table – more dried blood – and so returned her gaze to the front.

One of the officers stepped around the desk and leant down to gently but firmly make her unfold her arms and place both hands on her thighs. He then stepped back to his position behind the desk and smiled slightly at her. Once more she felt naked.

The interrogation began routinely with the man behind the desk, not smiling, his gaze still suspicious, introducing himself in English as Mohammed Samir and explaining that he was an intelligence officer. He then asked for her name, rank and serial number, which she readily gave him.

'You are an American.'

'Yes.'

'From?'

'Des Moines, Iowa.'

'A member of the US Air Force.'

'Yes.'

'And your unit?'

Alice took a deep breath. 'As a prisoner-of-war, I'm not obliged to answer any more questions. Under the Geneva Convention—'

'You were found by the wreck of a crashed UH-60 Black Hawk helicopter,' Mohammed interjected impatiently, 'wearing a flying suit with the insignia of the US 101st Airborne Division. There were three dead crew members found with you.'

'That's true,' Alice said, welling up with grief and horror at the thought of those three dead men – and of Dave Bamberg in particular, who had, after the nightmares of the academy, helped her regain her self-respect.

'What was your function in the aircraft?' Mohammed asked.

'Co-pilot,' she replied, almost weeping at the thought of Dave, her pilot, lover and friend. Just thinking about him filled her with pain, but it also helped her to bear this.

'And the others?'

'A pilot, a navigator and a gunner.'

'What was the purpose of your mission?'

'I'm sorry, but I can't answer that question.'

Mohammed closed his eyes, as if pained, then opened them again to stare impatiently at her. 'I repeat: what was the purpose of your mission?'

'As a prisoner-of-war, I'm not—'

The army officer who had smiled at her walked around the desk and slapped her face so hard that she was bowled off the chair and sent flying to the floor. He then kicked her in the ribs, hauled her back into the chair, slapped her twice more and leant down to bring his face close to hers, his eyes bulging with hatred.

'American whore!' he bawled. 'You will answer the questions or suffer the consequences. Do you understand, whore?'

He slapped her again, once, twice, a third time, now holding her by the shoulder to make sure that she didn't fall out of the chair again.

Alice had blood on her lips when the real interrogation began – and this was just the beginning.

CHAPTER SIX

In fact, they *had* picked someone else. The men knew it the minute they entered the briefing tent and saw Captain Williams, wearing desert clothing, with the beige beret on his head, standing beside a man who looked twice his age, was built like a bear, and was wearing the uniform of the US Delta Force. Both men were standing in front of a blackboard covered with a map of the war zones of Iraq. The American had his arms folded on his chest and looked as solid as a rock, his bright blue gaze taking in the SAS men with unblinking fearlessness. Beside him, looking rather uneasy, Williams seemed even more like a schoolboy.

'What the fuck's this?' Geordie whispered to Kilroy.

'I hate to say it, but I think that's our sixth man.'

'A fucking Yank?'

'Looks like it,' Kilroy said.

Once the men had settled into their seats, Williams coughed into his fist, still looking uneasy, then said, 'Good evening, men. Sorry to bring you out at this late hour, but I take it you've already guessed from this late call-out that you've been chosen as the special rescue team for Operation Dragon Light.'

The four men seated in front of him nodded, though most of them were looking with curiosity and a certain degree of suspicion at the US Army master sergeant wearing the beret of the US Delta Forces.

'The operation commences at last light tomorrow,' Williams continued. 'I'm commanding the rescue team. For reasons which will be explained shortly, our sixth man will be Master Sergeant Bill Kowalksi of the First Special Forces Group. He'll talk to you in a minute about that, once I've filled you in on the general details.'

As Williams picked up a pointer and turned to face the blackboard, the four SAS men stared at Master Sergeant Bill Kowalski, who stared back with admirable boldness, his thick arms still folded across his broad chest. The US Delta Force was the American equivalent of the SAS and the latter were always quick to swop derogatory jokes about the former. Kowalski would be aware of this – his own men would have done the same with regard to the SAS – and doubtless he realised that his presence here would cause suspicion, if not outright resentment. If this was so, he was certainly not being intimidated by it, as they all saw by his blue-eyed, unblinking gaze and proudly rigid stance.

'As was explained at the intelligence briefing,' Captain Williams said, 'the target is Saddam's underground HQ in Baghdad.' He tapped the word BAGHDAD with the pointer. 'However, as the bombing of that city precludes a parachute insertion, the rescue team will be inserted to territory presently patrolled by the Coalition forces and then make their way overland to the RV, accompanied by an entire squadron broken up into separate raiding parties. By this I mean that the whole group will fight its way to the outskirts of Baghdad, causing as much disruption as possible en route. Once near Baghdad, the rescue team will attempt to enter the city on their own and then make their way into Saddam's HQ. After that, they'll be on their own.'

He paused to let his words sink in, understanding the gravity of what he had just said and wanting it to be fully impressed upon those listening. Eventually, he turned sideways again to tap the map with his pointer, this time indicating the desert area between SCUD BOULEVARD and SCUD ALLEY. 'This,' he continued, 'is the area you have to make your way across. It's presently divided between the British and US territories in the most distant of the three main supply routes running north-east from Baghdad to Amman. The Americans operate mostly to the north of it, in the area they call Scud Boulevard, or the northern Scud Box, while we stick to Scud Alley, south of the main road. The squadron will be inserted in Scud Alley, near the area protected by our Road Watch South, and make their way from there through enemy territory, engaging the enemy en route until we reach Baghdad. This may entail entering Scud Boulevard on occasions, in which case we have to avoid an own goal with the US Delta Force.'

He meant the situation most dreaded by all servicemen, including air force pilots: engaging by accident in a fire fight with friendly forces. This often happened in darkness between friendly patrols not aware of each other's whereabouts or when air pilots, mistaking friendly patrols for the enemy, bombed or strafed them.

'Who's in charge of the two Scud Alleys?' Kilroy asked, glancing from Williams to Kowalski.

'We each have autonomy over our own territory,' Williams told him. 'The US Delta Force in Scud Boulevard, the SAS in Scud Alley – but we trade information and, sometimes, troops. At the moment, for instance, with the cooperation of the American Special Operations Central Command, we're working hand in glove with Five Special Forces Group, the Amphibious Sea Air Land, or SEAL, units, the US Air Force Special force, and the Psychological Operations and Civil Aid or, to be brief – and I'm sure you know the lingo – Psyops and Civaid.'

'How are they being patrolled?' Kilroy asked, always keen on getting his facts straight.

'Mostly with Lurp patrols and raiding parties. But since it's perfectly clear that the outcome of any war with Saddam Hussein will be determined by air power, the patrols are concentrating on the use of lasers for target designation with the Tornado and other bombers. Front-line reconnaissance, however, is still under the control of the Fifth Special Forces Group and US Marine Corps recon specialists.'

'God bless the Americans,' Geordie said sardonically.

'I'll ignore that remark,' Master Sergeant Kowalski retorted, 'until it's my turn to speak.'

The SAS men grinned, admiring the Yank's chutzpah, then Kilroy, ever mindful of business, asked, 'What's the terrain like?'

'Our territory, Scud Alley, is the Jordanian lava plateau, a relatively high, hilly area with deep wadis that are often flash-flooded after storms. Loose rock instead of sand, though dense sandstorms are blown in from other areas. Lots of rain instead of burning sun. Freezing cold at nights. In fact, it's more like the Falklands than some place like Oman, so you shouldn't find it *too* strange. Unfortunately, a lot of that land is less flat and open than most parts of the desert, which means a lot of hard hiking.'

Glancing outside the big tent, Kilroy saw the moon over the flat horizon, casting its pale light on the darkened white plain. As he watched, a Chinook helicopter passed across it, looking like an ink-black cutout suspended on invisible threads. It crossed the face of the moon and then passed on, disappearing in darkness. Turning his gaze back to Captain Williams, Kilroy asked, 'Do we move by day or night?'

'Mostly by night. It's not an Empty Quarter. Bedouin come and go constantly and there's also a surprising amount of civilian traffic, much of it generated by fear of Western vengeance on Baghdad. Last but not least, because it's a critically important military zone, it's filled with Iraqi military personnel of all kinds, including Scud crews and the militia.'

'How do we insert, boss?' Paddy Magee asked.

'You'll be lifted in by RAF Chinooks, with the Land Rovers, LSVs and motorbikes in underslung loads. The rescue team will travel in their own two Land Rovers, each accompanied by an outboard rider on a British Army Honda. Once you reach the outskirts of Baghdad, you'll detach yourselves from the main group, camouflage the vehicles, and hike the rest of the way to the main supply route leading into Baghdad. An OP will be raised overlooking the MSR and once you see a method of hitching a ride into Baghdad, as previously discussed, you will do so. Upon leaving Baghdad, you'll make your way back to the hidden Land Rovers and use them to return to the RV, where you'll rejoin the rest of the squadron.'

The method previously discussed, Kilroy remembered, was for the rescue team to lie low on the outskirts of Baghdad, ambush a passing Iraqi troop truck, neutralise the troops without damaging the truck, then dress themselves in the clothing of the Iraqi soldiers, including their *shemaghs*, and, after dying their faces, wrists and hands to roughly the colouring of the Arabs, drive on into Baghdad in the truck and move through the city. The hope was that they would be mistaken for just another bunch of Iraqi soldiers and somehow, still dressed as Arabs, get into Saddam's HQ. It was a high-risk operation of the kind not practised by the SAS since the notorious Keeni-Meeni raids in Aden in 1964, when the men had also dressed up as Arabs to move amongst them in the city streets. Unlikely as it must have seemed at the time, it worked so well that the Keeni-Meeni teams operated successfully in the disguise of Arabs for years. If it had worked then, it might work again, but Kilroy had his doubts.

'Why only six men, boss?' Roy Collinson asked, his dark eyes glinting restlessly under his jet-black hair. 'The SAS normally operate in four-man teams. Why the change this time?'

Williams paused, as if deciding whether to give an honest answer or not, then said, 'Because you're going in there dressed as Arabs, we thought the less of you there were, the less likely you are of being noticed. Also . . .' He hesitated again before letting it out. 'Well, to be frank, the odds against you getting out are fairly high, so six men is as many as we want to lose if you come to a bad end. If that happens, the Iraqis will have a propaganda victory that we have to minimise. Six is the least we can send in; it's also the highest figure we're willing to risk. I trust that answers your question.'

'It sure does,' Roy replied.

'It's nice to know that the Head Sheds are filled with optimism,' Paddy added. 'Sure, it makes m' heart sing, that does.'

'What's a Head Shed?' Kowalski asked Williams.

'A senior officer,' Williams explained.

'Oh,' Kowalski said, grinning slightly. 'I heard you guys had a lingo all your own. I guess I heard right.'

'You did indeed,' Captain Williams said. Turning back to the men, he continued, 'So that, for good or ill, is the reason the number is six, operating in two three-man teams, one to each Pink Panther when required. One man driving, the second on the front-mounted GPMG, and the third on the rear-mounted point-five-inch Browning heavy machine gun.'

'That sounds a better reason to me,' Geordie said. 'At least it's more positive. What about my motorbike?'

'You're off it and in the Pink Panther. Sorry about that, Corporal.'

'Shit,' Geordie said softly.

'I'll let that comment pass,' Captain Williams said, 'though it's hardly constructive. Are there any more questions before I hand you over to Master Sergeant Kowalski?'

'Yes,' Kilroy said quietly, evenly, staring directly at the big American. 'As this is an SAS mission, specifically raised to rescue SAS men, why are we taking along a representative of the US Delta Force?'

It was a blunt question, designed not only to clear the air, but to put the American on the defensive. Unabashed, the Yank took a couple of steps forward, until he was standing just in front of Captain Williams, then he unfolded his thick arms and placed his big hands on his beefy hips.

'Master Sergeant Bill Kowalski,' he said, loud and clear. 'Known to certain of my men as Wild Bill because I'm not inclined to take any shit from anyone.' He stared directly at Kilroy, then continued, 'First off, I'm not a *representative* of the US Delta Force; I'm a *member* of it – and I've been in it a long time. I'm as experienced as any man in this tent, so bear that fact in mind.'

He waited for a moment, keeping his gaze fixed directly on Kilroy. When Kilroy nodded in acknowledgement, not smiling but showing respect, Wild Bill nodded back, then turned his attention to the other three men.

'I won't beat around the bush,' he said. 'I know damned well that you guys are going to resent having me along, but we have a pretty good reason for it. Before I tell you what it is, could I just clear the air by pointing out that while I'm happy to let the SAS bullshit about the US Delta Force, bullshit it always was and will remain. In case any of you are harbouring doubts about my capabilities with regard to this mission, let it be known that the American SEAL special forces have been doing in Scud Boulevard everything your SAS friends are doing in Scud Alley. That includes searching for Scud missile launchers, kidnapping Iraqi officers, stealing SAM missiles, cutting communications, and using hand-held laser designators to illuminate enemy targets for our bombers and fighter planes. In fact, while you guys were still powdering your asses back in Hereford, I was driving an LSV through the night streets of occupied Kuwait to hit the Iraqis where they were least expecting it. A lot of us lost our lives doing that, but we damned well did it. So while I'm not claiming any superiority over you guys, I *am* insisting that you give credit where it's due and treat me as equal. OK?'

There was silence for a moment while the SAS men took in this forthright outburst, glancing in surprise at one another. Eventually, turning back to the front, they nodded one by one at the rocklike Yank.

'No problem,' Kilroy said in his soft, even way. 'So why are you joining us?'

Pleased, Wild Bill let his breath out and said, 'A couple of days ago, not long after your intelligence briefing, one of our female helicopter pilots, Lieutenant Alice Davis of the 101st Airborne Division, was shot down in her UH-60 Black Hawk and captured by the Iraqis. We happen to know from sources inside Baghdad that she was taken to a detention and interrogation centre there. Now, it's one thing for that bastard Saddam to put a couple of male pilots on TV, as he did with your RAF guys, but it'd be a whole different ball game if he put on a woman, particularly if she looked as beaten up as your Flight Lieutenant John Peters. We just can't let that happen, so I'm going in with you guys to personally take her out of there while you look after your own.'

'We're going to rescue a *woman*?' Roy asked, his face a picture of disbelief.

'Correction,' Wild Bill said. '*I'm* going to rescue a woman. And I'm gonna bring her back here safe and sound, no matter what you guys do.'

'But we work as a team,' Geordie said. 'We try to keep them together.'

'That's the idea,' Wild Bill said. 'And to do it, we have to change our plans slightly, which may or may not amuse you.'

No one was amused. On the other hand, they all looked interested, so Wild Bill continued.

'The detention centre is located near Karrada – ironically,

an upmarket shopping street frequented mostly by English speaking expatriates. Our Baghdad source is an Iraqi who was held in that detention centre for months of interrogation. He says that the captured British pilots were initially held there, before being moved on elsewhere. He also says that your SAS buddies and our Lieutenant Alice Davis are being held there and were still there when he, our informant, was finally released. Our informant is well connected – he has a friend in the complex – and he says that as far as he can gather, that's where they're still – on the second floor, where our female pilot is also being held.'

'Were they being tortured?' Roy asked.

'No. They were housed in filthy cells and interrogated repeatedly, often with verbal abuse and other psychological tricks, but they weren't actually tortured. Eating shit and not allowed to sleep too much, but not really physically abused. On the other hand, if Saddam loses his patience, there's no knowing what he'll do and we're not about to wait for that to happen. Not with a female prisoner, buddy.'

'What's the building like?' Kilroy asked.

'A three-storey concrete blockhouse with a courtyard and a guarded gate out front. The guards usually stay in the prefabricated hut just inside the gate. The downstairs floor of the main building is taken up with interrogation and administration rooms. The top two floors contain nothing but prison cells with hatch doors.'

'So we enter Baghdad,' Kilroy said, 'and find our way to Karrada and somehow enter the building.'

'No. The building's well known as a detention centre and suitably feared by the locals. For that very reason, the Iraqis, if they except an attack at all, will be expecting it to come from their own dissidents and therefore from the front. What we plan to do, then, as distinct from your original plan, is split this team into two. The original part of the plan stays put in the sense that we go in disguised as Iraqi soldiers. But the new plan requires us to hijack two Iraqi Army vehicles instead of one, with three of us to each of the vehicles. Our informant has given us the layout of Saddam's underground complex. It's fucking enormous, believe me. So here's what we do.'

Wild Bill turned to the blackboard and pulled down a large sheet that covered the original map of the battle zones. The new sheet was a line drawing of Saddam Hussein's elaborate underground HQ, with its tunnelled roads, nuclear bunkers, command shelters, barracks, stores, parking bays and many other areas. All of these were shown in three dimensions: vertically, horizontally and viewed aerially. As shown by the aerial plan, the complex began at the south-western outskirts of the city and stretched as far as downtown, terminating under the Presidential Palace and the Ministry of Defence. Certainly it was a labyrinthine complex of enormous proportions.

'Holy fuck!' Roy said softly.

Wild Bill wagged his finger as Captain Williams, just behind him, quietly smiled. 'We don't have to get through it all,' Wild Bill said. Taking the pointer from Williams, he touched a line on the drawing that showed the southern extremity of the complex, just outside the city. 'This is the entrance,' he said, 'leading straight out to the main supply route running all the way to Kuwait, via Kirkuk and Basra. It takes the form of your standard Iraqi hardened aircraft shelter with blast-proof steel doors – which is just what it looks like from outside. A main road runs from inside those doors all the way down through the centre of the complex to the very far end.' Wild Bill tapped the parallel lines that showed the main road on the map. 'All the command shelters and bunkers are in side tunnels leading off that main road, which terminates just under the Presidential Palace. Elevators run up through the various walkways – three in all – to just under street level. One of those elevators, this one' – he tapped an elevator with his pointer – 'ascends to the detention centre where the prisoners are being held. So three of us, dressed as Iraqi soldiers and in one of their army trucks, will drive down that road, then take the elevator up to the detention centre.'

Placing the pointer on the low table under the blackboard, he grinned at Williams and turned back to the other men.

'HAS doors,' Kilroy said in his flat manner, referring to hardened aircraft shelters, 'aren't the kind you can walk through.'

'Damned right,' Wild Bill replied. 'So we don't even try. Which gets us back to the hijacking of a couple of Iraqi Army vehicles, preferably troop trucks.'

'At least a dozen troops in each truck,' Kilroy said. 'Not that easy to neutralise without doing damage to the trucks.'

Wild Bill nodded, appreciating the observation. 'According to our intelligence,' he said, 'Iraqi troop trucks go in and out of that HAS all day, to enable the Imperial Guard and other Iraqi soldiers to go out on practice manoeuvres and also engage in R and I patrols. Those patrols often sleep out at nights, scattered all over the area. What we do, then, is launch assaults on the troops of two separate patrols as they're sleeping by their trucks. After putting them to sleep permanently, we tint our skin dark, then put on their uniforms and *shemaghs* to cover most of our faces. Just before first light, the three men in the first truck prepare to enter the complex via the HAS doors. The three men in the second truck illuminate the doors with laser designators to enable US Stealth F-117 fighter-bombers to come in and attack them with laser-guided bombs. That air raid, even if not damaging the HAS, will encourage the Iraqis to open the doors and let their patrol vehicles back inside. The three men in the first captured truck will enter the complex with those other vehicles and continue down the main road as part of the Iraqi convoy until they reach the elevator leading up to the detention centre. In the excitement generated by the continuing air raid, they can park the truck in the parking bay by the elevator, get out as quickly as possible, and make their way up to the rear of the detention centre, where they'll force their way in and recapture the four SAS men and one female prisoner. Meanwhile, the three men in the second Iraqi truck, having guided the Stealth fighter-bombers in, will drive into Baghdad, which will also be under a massive Coalition air attack, and make their way to the front of the detention centre. When the rescue team inside, hopefully having poleaxed the Iraqi guards, bring the prisoners out, they'll all pile into the second truck and be driven back out of Baghdad, taking advantage of the ongoing air attack on the city. Once outside the city, assuming that they haven't become victims of an own goal – which is a chance we'll have to take – they'll drive on to their two parked, camouflaged Pink Panthers, transfer the rescued troopers and female pilot to them, then hare across the desert, back to the RV. It's as simple as that.'

'It sounds as simple as Dante's Inferno,' Kilroy said.

'Are you in or out, Sergeant?' Wild Bill asked.

'We're all in,' Kilroy said.

CHAPTER SEVEN

Alice spent most of her time in the cell doing physical exercises and fighting the urge to cry. She knew that crying would help her, releasing a flood of despair and fear, but she also sensed that it would weaken her resolve and give them the advantage. She never cried during the interrogations, determined not to show weakness, and although at times she came close to crying in the cell, she resisted because she knew that they were watching her every hour of every day.

The guards even watched her when she was in the sordid washroom, squatting over the toilet bowl, surrounded by buzzing flies, and although they couldn't actually see her there, the knowledge that they knew what she was doing humiliated her even more. They watched her through the opened hatch, the brown eyes of the changing guards, as she slept, exercised or crawled into the washroom, now ignoring the cockroaches, and although the guards never said a word to her, she could never forget them. Sometimes she screamed at them, hammering the door with her fists, and when she did the eyes usually moved away to give her peace for another hour.

She had been here for five days, but it seemed like five

years and she wondered if she would ever get out, let alone
stay alive. Her thoughts were in disarray, always scattering
here and there, settling on her childhood, which had certainly
been happy, drifting painfully around thoughts of her dead
lover, Dave Bamberg, often wishing that she had died with
him, or circling back reluctantly, relentlessly, to the horror of
her present predicament and how it might end.

Exercising, she touched her toes, did press-ups, stretched
her body, but invariably, when she did so, the brown eyes
appeared at the hatch, looking at her with curiosity and sexual
hunger. Feeling naked in the thin cotton *dish-disha*, she would
immediately stop.

'Fuck off, you pervert,' she sometimes whispered, finding
strength in defiance.

She was not, however, defiant during the interrogations,
which would have been a mistake. She hadn't learnt this at
the Academy in those rooms filled with men, with the light
blazing into her eyes and gobs of spit on her face. Those
bastards had taught her nothing but fear and made her feel
only shame. Now, here, with this set of very different men, she
was learning it all by herself and remembering the lessons.

She tried not to antagonise them, avoided showing defiance,
refused to answer most questions but did so in a quiet voice,
reiterating that as a prisoner-of-war she did not have to do so.
Duly punished with slaps and blows, she tried not to resist,
apart from covering the most sensitive parts of her body and
silently praying.

They had not sexually abused her, but that fear never left
her and virtually consumed her each time they came for her,
taking her back to the interrogation room, which they did two
or three times a day, sometimes even at night. She sat there,
feeling naked, wearing only the Arab gown, sensing the eyes
of her interrogators crawling over her like spiders, alighting
too often on her breasts, the nipples visible through the thin
cotton; on her thighs where the gown fell between her long

legs; some- times even on her bare feet, which were small, delicate and white, though now covered in dirt. Her white feet fascinated them, making them want to see more. They knew that she was naked under the gown and this knowledge excited them.

They wanted an excuse, she knew. They breathed too heavily for her liking. They made jokes that she couldn't understand and then giggled nervously. This was, she sensed, bravado. They were working themselves up to it. Sooner or later, their frustrations would explode and they would do what they wanted.

Alice knew what they wanted.

She was even more frightened because of what her fellow cadets had done to her back in the Academy. She would never forget that experience, the awful fear and humiliation, and now no one would ever convince her that they'd had a good reason. They'd had their sport with her, gloated over her, enjoyed themselves, then had thrown her back, sobbing, onto her bed and walked out making lewd jokes. She'd often heard their ribald laughter in her ears even when they weren't there. The fear had haunted her that much.

Later, when she complained, stating her case to the commanding officer, she had been told that it was for her own good, to prepare her for the future; that what might happen to her if she was captured by the Iraqis might be even worse. Of course, she hadn't believed him – his mocking grin had revealed the truth – and now, in this hellish cell in Iraq, she still didn't believe him. What he'd prophesied had come true – she had been captured and was being abused – but what they had done to her in the Academy hadn't helped her at all. In fact, it had only heightened her fear of what might now befall her.

The Iraqi interrogations went on for hours and could take place at any time. Dragged out of her cell, sometimes out of sleep, she would be marched down two flights of the stairs to the room with no windows. Once there, she was seated on a hard wooden chair, in front of Mohammed's desk. Mohammed, also seated, was always flanked by the two Iraqi Army officers and had three or four armed soldiers standing behind her to help with the beatings.

So far they hadn't tortured her, at least not overtly, but they bawled abuse at her, repeatedly slapped her face, threw her off the chair, sometimes kicking her as she lay on the floor, then picked her up and placed her back on the chair to slap her some more, often grabbing the hair of her head to jerk her face up, tugging it this way and that. She refused to tell them anything – at least, so far she had refused – but she lived in dread of what they might do to her if their patience ran out.

She could never forget that table by the wall to her right, that butcher's block with the stains on it, all around it, and the whips hanging above it. She knew just what they signified.

Indeed, her fears about what they might eventually do to her were only exacerbated by the sounds emanating from the cells on either side of her. The normal silence of the hallway outside was constantly broken by the pounding of many booted feet on the concrete floor, the bawling of Iraqi soldiers, the screeching of steel doors being dragged open, then cries of protest and screams of pain as Iraqi and Kuwaiti prisoners were set upon with boots, fists and the rubber truncheons carried by all the soldiers. Sometimes Alice could actually hear the sickening thud, thud of truncheons repeatedly hammering human flesh, the cries of pain dwindling to half-conscious whimpering, followed, when the soldiers had departed, by the most dreadful moaning.

Once or twice the screaming of the prisoners was abruptly terminated by pistol shots, after which there was only the sound of a body being dragged out of the cell and along the corridor towards those two flights of stairs. For Alice, that was the worst of all.

The Coalition bombing of Baghdad went on night and day.

Brought here blindfolded, Alice had no idea of where she was, but she recalled that the truck had driven along what had seemed like a smooth highway, then turned into a maze of noisy streets. That recollection, combined with the often-repeated sounds of air attacks and the Iraqi response, forced her to conclude that she could only be somewhere in Baghdad. As a trained Black Hawk pilot, she recognised many of the sounds: Tomahawk Cruise missiles flying in low at 500mph; the thunderous explosions of 2,000-pound precision-guided bombs; the combined roaring high overhead of giant B-52s dropping thousands of tons of explosives, EF-111S Ravens flying in to jam the Iraqi radar systems, and F-4Gs, or Wild Weasels, firing their HARM rockets to destroy the enemy's radar-guided SAM missiles. On top of that bedlam was the exploding of missiles in the sky; the relentless pounding of the Iraqi's 'Triple A' anti-aircraft artillery; and, above it all, very high up in the sky, as if in the very heavens, the muffled rumbling of the AWACS: immense aircraft covered with radar mushrooms that could scan the ground for hundreds of miles and with spectacular accuracy.

Though Alice could see none of this from her windowless cell, she had seen it before, from the distance, when, in the greatest helicopter attack ever launched, she and other women pilots, in Black Hawks, Chinooks, Hueys, Cobras and Apaches, transported paratroopers and supplies of the 101st Airborne Division deep into Iraq to tighten the noose around Baghdad. Alice had managed to insert her paratroopers, but was shot down just after turning back and caught, she could only surmise, as that Iraqi Army patrol was circling around behind the advancing American divisions. Before that, however, while inserting the paratroopers, she had witnessed the bombing of distant Baghdad and been stunned by that immense fireworks display, a dazzling *son et lumière* spectacle of phosphorescent green and purple tracer rounds, crimson balls of flak, the snaking white plumes of rockets, silvery explosions, yellow-and-white flames, and great mushrooms of boiling black smoke, obliterating the stars. It had been an awesome spectacle, beautiful and surreal, but she knew that it signified mass destruction on a terrible scale. The Iraqis, knowing she was a pilot, could only hate her for that.

And hate her they did. Not only because she was an American pilot, one of the vile breed now bombing Baghdad, but also because she was a woman, which outraged their male pride. So, they continued interrogating her, screaming at her, spitting upon her, tugging her head back by the hair, slapping her face and throwing her onto the floor to repeatedly kick her. Still, she refused to talk, repeating, through her gasps of pain, only her name, rank and serial number, silently praying that they would not torture, rape or kill her.

They were close to doing all three, she knew. She could see it in their eyes. She could hear it in the sound of their heavy breathing when she lay sprawled on the floor, the thin cotton of the flowing *dish-disha* flowing over her body, emphasising her female curves and her firm, perfect breasts. They spread their legs to stand over her, breathing heavily, spitting upon her, nudging her with their boots and sometimes trailing their rubber truncheons over her body, between her legs, down the cleft between her breasts, exciting themselves by exploring her soft flesh. She could see their hardening, the bulging in their trousers, and she knew it was coming.

It was just a matter of time.

Alone in her cell, with the flies and the cockroaches, with those brown eyes constantly reappearing at the open hatch of the steel door, Alice lived with the dread of each new visit, wondering what it would bring. The Academy, though making her suffer almost as much, had not prepared her for this.

She could hear her own heartbeat.

CHAPTER EIGHT

Just before midnight, three of the RAF's CH-47 Chinook helicopters lifted the squadron of SAS and their vehicles deep into the desert of western Iraq, in the area known as Scud Alley. Looking through a porthole just before landing, Kilroy, sitting between Wild Bill Kowalski and Paddy Magee, saw some of the US HH-53J Pave Low and HH-60G Night Hawk helicopters just below and ahead. Equipped with special electronic and night-flying systems, they were extremely efficient as pathfinders. They were, however, also transporting some of the Pink Panthers, LSVs and Honda motorbikes in underslung loads, which seemed to be flying mere feet above the desert plain. The others, which Kilroy couldn't see, were slung below the three Chinooks, including the one he was in.

Removing his gaze from the porthole and glancing around the long, narrow, dark hold of the helicopter, Kilroy saw the RAF loadmaster moving to the side door and knew from this that they were about to land. This was confirmed when the Chinook slowed down, stopped moving forward, hovered briefly, shuddering and rattling, then began its vertical descent.

'Prepare for landing!' the loadmaster bawled over the din as a red light came on above the side door.

Immediately, the men seated along the hold ran a last-minute check of their safety belts, weapons and other equipment. Some were armed with semi-automatic SLRs, others had Heckler & Koch MP5 thirty-round sub-machine guns, and yet others had the heavier M16s with M203 40mm grenade-launchers. Also, they were sharing between them the various components of a wide variety of heavy support weapons including the L7A2 GPMG, the 94mm LAW 80 anti-tank weapon, the FIM-92A Stinger SAM system, a couple of 51mm mortars and, of course, the HEAT rockets, anti-aircraft missiles and HE bombs to go with them. Each man also had his standard-issue Browning 9mm High Power handgun, his sykes Fairburn commando dagger, his water bottles, his survival kit and all the spare ammunition he could carry. Given this, as well as the packed bergens, the men looked like beasts of burden when they stood up to take hold of the overhead straps, preparing to disembark.

When the RAF loadmaster slid the door open, the slipstream howled in across the men, beating fiercely at them and giving them a hint of the freezing cold to come. The Chinook hovered for some time while its underslung loads were set down gently and released, then it moved forward again, away from the disengaged cargo, and touched down on the desert floor farther on. It bounced lightly a few times, then its roaring eased off as its still-spinning rotors went into neutral.

'Go!' the loadmaster bawled when the overhead light changed from red to green.

Forming a long line that ran the length of the hold, with Captain Williams in the lead, the men jumped out, one after the other, the first of them spreading out at the crouch, leaning against the slipstream and swirling sand, to form a wide protective circle around the chopper. Going out behind Wild Bill Kowalski, Kilroy was startled by the cold, struck by it as he hurried under the spinning rotors and beyond the swirling sand of their roaring slipstream. Tying his *shemagh* across his face to protect his nose and mouth, he noticed that the other men were doing the same. With the *shemaghs* and camouflaging over their berets, they looked like Arab militiamen.

The sky was clear of clouds, but the sweeping sand obscured the stars and the horizon was barely visible through the murk. The dropped vehicles, still in their netting, were about a hundred yards farther back and the other two Chinooks, each of which held forty-four fully equipped troops, were about to land a good distance away in the opposite direction.

They touched down simultaneously, creating a minor tornado as the rest of the men from Williams's Chinook surrounded the vehicles disengaged from the underslung loads and started removing the nets in which they had been carried. Williams and Kilroy joined them, followed closely by Wild Bill, who was gazing around him with a great deal of interest. Glancing across the desert, he and the others saw the men from the other Chinooks jumping out one by one, ghostlike in the swirling sand. Williams called Paddy over and asked for the mike to his PRC 319 radio, which he used for a chat with the officers commanding the other groups. Satisfied that they were OK, he told them to keep their eyes peeled for any sign of landmines.

He waited until the conveyance netting had been removed from the first Pink Panther and the satellite communications (SATCOM) system fixed to the vehicle, then called HQ in Riyadh, giving his grid reference and confirming that the landing had been OK. Having received permission to proceed as planned, he turned off the SATCOM system and studied the activities of his men as they removed the netting from the other vehicles, attached the separately packed equipment, and in general prepared them for use. As they were doing so, members of the Mobility Group, watched by the envious Geordie, prepared their British Army Honda trail motorbikes, kicking the engines into life and revving them noisily to ensure that they worked. With their M16 rifles slung across their shoulders, their Browning handguns holstered on the hip, their faces covered by fluttering *shemaghs*, their eyes hidden by Litton night-vision goggles, and their exposed facial skin camouflaged in blackening 'cam' cream, they were a sight to behold.

'Lucky bastards!' Geordie exclaimed softly.

'We're taking one bike in the back of each Pink Panther,' Kilroy told him, 'only to be used when we're out there on our own. One for you and one for Paddy, so go and find that mad bastard, pick yourselves two bikes, and strap them securely to the back of our vehicles.'

'Fucking terrific,' Geordie said, lowering his *shemagh* to give Kilroy a big grin. 'Whose idea was that?'

'Mine,' Wild Bill said. 'I thought they might come in handy.'

'I worship the Stars and Stripes,' Geordie replied, then raced away to find Paddy.

A sudden, staccato series of mechanical coughs and roarings reminded Williams and Kilroy of the troopers disgorged from the other two Chinooks. Looking sideways, they saw that they were starting up their Pink Panthers, LSVs and motorbikes even as the two Chinooks were lifting off in a billowing cloud of sand. That cloud swallowed the men below, but they soon burst out of it, driving their assorted, brightly coloured vehicles across the flat plain to encircle Williams's group and skid to a halt, churning up more sand and dust. Meanwhile, the Chinook behind Williams and Kilroy also took off, soon joining the others in the sky, where they hovered together for a moment, as if communicating with each other, then headed back to the border.

When the men around Williams had settled down, he

climbed up on the back of his Pink Panther and called his rescue team in around him for a final briefing.

'Apparently the Iraqis still have about a dozen mobile Scud launchers in this area. The USAF and US Navy have put heavily armed F-15Es, F-16 Fighting Falcons, A-10A Warthogs and A-6E Intruders on round-the-clock patrols over the Scud Boxes – north, where their men are, and south, where we are. However, the pilots need precise targeting information before they can launch attacks. The men we're travelling with have been inserted here as mobile teams to put eyes on the ground. For this purpose, they'll be setting up covert OPs to cover key roads, spread from here to the outskirts of Baghdad. When Scud convoys are spotted, they'll either mark the target with their laser designators or pass the grid reference on to an E-3 AWACS command aircraft, using their SATCOM systems. They'll rendezvous for resupplies at midnight five days from now in Wadi Tubal, which is marked on our maps.'

'Presumably that's our RV as well,' Wild Bill said.

'Yes. We'll travel some of the way with them, then head off on our own, using the MSR leading to Baghdad as our reference point. Once in sight of the HAS doors of that underground complex at the end of the MSR, we'll set up our own OPs and wait for the best opportunity to hijack a couple of Iraqi troop trucks. We'll have to find them more or less at the same time and then use them immediately, before their absence is noticed. When we escape, *if* we escape, we'll all meet back at Wadi Tubal and return with the main party to this RV to be lifted out. If we miss them, we'll have to make our own way back to friendly territory as best we can. Any questions?'

'We're all set to run, boss,' Kilroy said.

'Good. Let's get to it. Corporal Welsh and Trooper Collinson will share my Pink Panther. Trooper Magee will be with you and Master Sergeant Kowalski.'

'Who's PC of our team?' Kilroy asked pointedly, meaning who was going to be the patrol commander.

Realising that in formal terms the American outranked Kilroy, Captain Williams glanced uncertainly at him. Wild Bill just shrugged his shoulders and said diplomatically, 'This is an SAS mission and I'm just a gatecrasher, so I reckon Sergeant Kilroy is the logical choice.' He turned to Kilroy and offered a wicked grin. 'My pleasure, Sarge.'

'Mine, too,' Kilroy said.

After splitting up into their separate teams, they climbed into their allocated vehicles and prepared to take off. As PC of his team, Kilroy sat up front, behind the mounted GPMG. Wild Bill took the driver's seat, and Paddy, who was also in charge of the PRC 319 radio set, manned the rear-mounted 0.5-inch Browning heavy machine gun. The LAW 80 anti-tank rocket-launcher and Stinger-POST had also been mounted, one on each side of the Pink Panther, between the front and rear seats, under the short-burst radio and SATNAV antennae. In the other Pink Panther, now revving into action and moving up parallel with the first, Roy Collinson was driving, Captain Williams was acting as navigator and also manning the front-mounted GPMG, and Geordie was in the rear with the Browning. They were all set to go.

In fact, Williams didn't have to give the hand signal as the whole column was already advancing across the dark, moonlit plain, with the Pink Panthers and LSVs spread out to form a broad front and the motorcyclists racing on ahead or taking positions on both sides. Acting as outriders, the bikers would constantly disappear in three directions, the front, left and right, to reconnoitre the terrain and check for enemy troop movements, trailing billowing clouds of sand that obscured the stars. Also obscuring the stars, however, was the great umbrella of sand and dust being churned up by the column in general, now spread out over a front of at least a mile. It was, Kilroy thought, a spectacular sight and one that inspired him.

Sitting in the rear of the Pink Panther, behind the five-inch

Browning heavy machine gun, Geordie was less inspired and instead studied the great column of vehicles with a jaundiced eye.

'Excuse me, Master Sergeant,' he shouted out to Kowalski, who was concentrating on his driving, 'but why are we using those American dune buggies instead of just the Pink Panthers? I mean, those things look like rides in a funfair – and from what I hear, they only have a third of the range of our Dinkies. So what's the use of them, boss?'

Keeping his hands firmly on the steering wheel of the Pink Panther and his eyes on the vehicles spread out ahead in clouds of boiling dust, Wild Bill shouted back, 'Those dune buggies, as you call them, may be small, relatively frail and have a shorter range than your Pink Panthers, but they're also pretty damned powerful and can go where the Pink Panthers can't. They also have quiet engines and reduced radar and infrared signatures that make them pretty difficult to find or hit. *And* they carry MILAN guided missile firing posts, which makes them shit-hot for hit-and-run raids. That's why they're popular with our Special Forces – and why you sons of bitches borrowed them from us. Any *more* questions, Trooper?'

'No, boss. Got your message.'

'Fucking A,' Wild Bill said.

For the next six hours, the column made its way deeper into the desert, navigating in the darkness with the aid of the SATNAV global positioning systems and stopping once every hour for tedious vehicle maintenance checks by the light of hand-held torches: tyre pressure, carburetters, oil, water, and the removal of excess sand where it might cause the engine to seize up. More than once, when on the move, they passed Bedouin tents, the camp fires still smouldering, the camels standing on three legs, with the left front leg raised and tied by the foot to the other, to prevent them from running away while the Arabs slept, oblivious to the muffled rumbling or sudden roaring of the aircraft flying frequently overhead. The wind, which blew constantly across the plain, was shockingly cold.

Throughout the journey, the motorcycle outriders continued to disappear for forward observation. Each time they reported the movement of a mobile Scud unit or Iraqi troop trucks, some of the SAS vehicles would break away from the main column and race off in that direction, guided by the outrider, either to attack the Mobile Scud or to set up OPs overlooking the enemy supply route. As one outrider after another returned with news of the enemy, causing yet another Pink Panther or LSV, sometimes both, to break away from the main column and head for that RV, the large column of SAS vehicles was gradually whittled down and eventually numbered hardly more than a dozen, including those of Captain Williams and Sergeant Kilroy.

The remaining vehicles were still heading through the darkness, trying to cover as much distance as possible before first light, when a muffled thunderclap was heard from up front, accompanied by a jagged, silvery flashing that briefly, eerily, illuminated some of the vehicles on the dark desert plain. All the other drivers braked instantly to a halt, then the men lowered the *shemaghs* from their faces, letting them dangle under their chins, and squinted into the vast, moonlit darkness.

'Landmine,' Wild Bill said flatly.

'Had to be,' Kilroy said.

Williams had stopped his Pink Panther beside them and instantly got on the radio to check what was happening up front. Replacing the receiver, he nodded and called out, 'Minefield up front. You can all take a break. They've called HQ on the SATCOM and ordered up an AWACS command aircraft to fly over and detonate it. He should be here in about forty minutes. Meanwhile, we can rest up and have a snack – but no smoking and no hexamine stoves. Just cold rations and water.'

Relieved to get a break, the men hopped out of their vehicles, hauled off their bergens, and settled down against the wheels of the vehicles, which protected them from the freezing wind, to a snack of high-calorie rations and cold water from their water bottles. It was not the most palatable of meals, but it did the job.

'Fuckin' shit and piss,' Paddy said, commenting on his meal. 'The fuckin' A-rabs eat better.'

'I've had worse,' Wild Bill said, seated on his formidable arse between Paddy and Kilroy, facing Captain Williams, Geordie Welsh and Roy Collinson, who had parked their Pink Panther just a few feet away.

'I'll bet,' Paddy responded cockily. 'American hamburgers.'

'Nothing wrong with American hamburgers,' Wild Bill replied. 'Have you ever had one?'

'They're all over England, Master Sergeant. We've *all* choked on that filth.'

'Not the genuine item, Trooper.' Wild Bill was amused. 'If you had a real American hamburger, you'd know it. It's a whole different ball game.'

'I'd rather have soda bread,' Paddy informed him, 'with black sausage and bacon. Sure that makes a *real* meal.'

'That's a heart-attack breakfast,' Geordie said, grinning at them from the shelter of the Land Rover opposite. 'Too many of those and you're in a box with your toes in the air.'

'Ha, ha,' Paddy said.

'You're Irish, right?' Wild Bill asked.

'We call him Paddy and the Yank asks if he's Irish,' Geordie said in disbelief. 'Does he know English, or what?'

Aware that the SAS was noted for the informality of its exchanges between ranks, Wild Bill was unperturbed and merely grinned when framing his next question. 'So where in Ireland do you come from?' he asked.

'Belfast,' Paddy told him.

'You support the IRA?'

'I'm a Prod',' Paddy informed him. 'From the Donegal-Road. That's Orange Lodge territory, Sarge, and we don't like the IRA.'

'You don't want a United Ireland?'

'Sure I never thought about it. I left when I was seventeen years old an' I never went back, like.'

'But you're still Irish,' Wild Bill insisted. 'We're talking about the freedom of your country. That must mean something to you.'

'It means more to you fuckin' Yanks than it does to the Irish. What most of the Irish want is a bit of peace and quiet. They're not romantic about it like you fucking Yanks, who all imagine you've got ancestors back there and that they're all freedom fighters. When it comes to Ireland, the Yanks are a bunch of wankers with their heads in the clouds. Come back when you've had a relative kneecapped or put in his box. Then we'll talk some more, Sarge.'

'Didn't mean to offend you, kid,' Wild Bill said, more interested than perturbed and not offended by the Irish trooper's forthrightness.

'You didn't offend me at all, Sarge. Sure I'm as foreign to Ireland as you are, when all's said and done. I left it a long time ago and I don't want to go back. It's all bullshit to me.'

'Your conversation's bullshit,' Roy said, 'but we all have to endure it.'

'Bloody right,' Geordie said.

'I think you men should concentrate on eating,' Captain Williams said pointedly, 'before that AWACS command plane comes over and upsets your digestion.'

'I second that,' Kilroy said.

Glancing sideways at Sergeant Kilroy and trying to read him, Wild Bill came up with no more than a blank wall. Kilroy, he judged, was in his late thirties and had the granite face of a man who's seen more than he wants to remember. He was, as Wild Bill knew from his conversations with Williams, one of the most respected NCOs in the SAS, having kicked off his career in the mean streets of Belfast, led one of the assault teams on the now legendary Princes Gate Siege, fought all the way from South Georgia to the Falkland Islands during the war against Argentina, returned to Belfast for unspecified tasks, then reportedly took part in the shooting of three IRA terrorists, including one woman, on Gibraltar in 1988. He was, then, a hard man and he certainly looked it, with that two-inch scar running down his sunken right cheek and his occasional smiles never reaching his wintry grey eyes. According to Williams, he was also married with two kids and had no reputation for playing around outside that marriage. Now, gazing at those same wintry grey eyes, Wild Bill, himself a father with three healthy, happy kids, wondered how such a man, so remote and seemingly unfeeling, could be a loving father and loyal husband.

No doubt about it, Sergeant Kilroy was a mystery. He was also a man who demanded respect and would react in a forthright manner if he thought he wasn't getting it. Wild Bill decided to keep this fact in mind if the going got rough.

'An RAF Tornado's on its way, boss,' Roy Collinson said, having clambered back up into the Pink Panther to receive an incoming signal on the SATCOM system.

Pleased, Williams clambered up beside Roy and contacted the officer in charge of the other Pink Panthers and LSVs at the head of the column, which had moved back from the edge of the minefield to avoid an own goal by the Tornado. After speaking at some length, he turned back to the men still seated on the ground by their vehicles and said, 'When that minefield's exploded, it's going to cause an almighty din and spectacle, which might bring any Iraqis in the area running to the scene. So when the minefield's been cleared, the rest of the convoy is going to split up and head off in different directions, leaving us to our own devices. We'll then head straight for the MSR to Baghdad and try to get as far as possible before first light. OK, men, mount up.'

Packing their kit back into their bergens, the men clambered up into the Pink Panthers and waited for the Tornado to arrive. About a minute later, they heard it overhead. Using the SATCOM, Williams confirmed the grid readings to the pilot and the Tornado swooped down a few seconds later. Even in the moonlight, it was an awesome vision, a beast of many limbs and appendages, with its air-to-air refuelling probe; massive, movable 'swing' wings; high fin with ESR, or electronic surveillance measure; underslung fuel tanks and alarm anti-radar missiles; plus underwing electronic counter-measure, or ECM, pods and protruding TRB 199 twin engines. It was indeed a monster, but one possessed of alien beauty, and with its terrain-following radar and computerised cockpit, it was able to fly in as low as fifty feet above the ground to drop its JP233 bombs. Including a series of cratering devices, the bombs drifted down from the aircraft by parachute and detonated just above the ground. That detonation propelled various charges deep into the ground. When they exploded, they heaved up the surface and created many large holes beneath it. Those multiple, underground explosions caused a vast area of desert floor to rumble and shake. Then it erupted in a spectacular, cataclysmic mushroom cloud of sand, dust, gravel, smoke and swirling tendrils of gaseous flame. The noise was deafening, the impact shattering, and the mushroom expanded to form an immense canopy over the desert floor, blotting out the moon and stars.

Only when the great mushroom cloud had started to collapse, falling back in upon itself, did the men in the Land Rovers, LSVs and motorbikes drive off in many different directions, all heading even deeper into Iraq. As they did so, the remaining two Pink Panthers, one driven by Roy Collinson, the other by Wild Bill, headed in the direction of the MSR to Baghdad, still located far beyond where the black plain of the desert cut a line through the shimmering stars. The faint pink light fanning across the stars was announcing the break of day.

CHAPTER NINE

They came in the darkness, ordered her out of bed, and led her from the room, still wearing her nightdress and in bare feet, along a dimly lit corridor, down stairs and into another room, this one brightly lit, containing only a desk and some wooden chairs. They had done this so often now, it seemed like a bad dream that could only get progressively worse, which in this instance it did. They were wearing their uniforms, though without their jackets, some of them with their shirts half unbuttoned, showing their bare chests. They started bawling at her the second they slammed her down on the chair, calling her a bitch and whore, a syphilitic cunt, as they repeatedly tugged her hair and slapped her face, their eyes bright with excitement. They laughed at her when she sobbed, then screamed at her to stop. When she failed to do so, they threw her to the floor and rolled her onto her back. One of them straddled her chest, his knees pressing against her face, then started unbuttoning the top of her nightdress while another held her shoulders down. She begged them to stop. 'That's what you all say,' one said. 'That's what you say when you really want to have it and we're about to oblige.'

She sobbed and tried to break free. Someone tugged her legs apart. She felt the nightdress riding up her legs, all the way to her thighs, then a hand sliding upwards. She struggled and someone said that if she didn't stop he would piss on her face. She stopped struggling then. She felt the hand moving upwards. She heard them laughing with nervous excitement, and then—

Alice awakened, jerking upright on the mattress, gasping as she felt her heart racing and saw only the darkness. Sweating even in the cold, disorientated by the nightmare, she had to struggle to get her senses back and realise where she was. In the cell in Iraq. Not back in the Academy. She had many nightmares now, one bleeding into the other, and even when awake, in the interrogation room, she often confused the Iraqi Army officers with the air force cadets, the ones who had threatened to do to her what might yet be done here.

She took deep, even breaths, trying to slow that racing heart, hearing the cockroaches scurrying all around her, and no longer caring. She cared more about other things, about what might happen to her, and yearned to be back in Des Moines, in the comfort of her childhood bed with her parents sleeping next door. She almost wept at the thought, knowing how far away she was, wondering if she would ever see her home again or feel her parents' embrace. It was possible she might not. She might rot here for ever. She might even get a bullet in the head and an unmarked grave in the desert. Before that, though, they would almost certainly make her nightmares become all too real.

I'm gonna do it to you now, you little whore, and then pass you around. Just close your eyes and enjoy it.

The Iraqis hadn't said that yet – a fellow cadet had said it – but the Iraqis used the word 'whore' a lot and seemed to relish the sound of it. They were edging closer every day, working themselves into a lather, and she knew they were thinking more and more about it as their eyes crawled all over her. This American whore. This bitch who had bombed their people. This piece of forbidden white flesh who was naked under her cotton robe. This whore deserved to be broken. Her very silence was a mockery. She deserved to be treated as what she was and she was theirs to command. White meat to be played with. American pride to be degraded. They would do it and feel justified and have their pleasure as well. Alice knew it was coming.

She raised her legs, wrapped her arms around them and rested her chin on her knees. As her eyes grew adjusted to the early-morning darkness, she saw the hatch in the doorway, its top half still open, letting a pale light from the corridor beam in. A lot of guards had stared through there. She knew they liked to look at her. She knew they were under orders to check her constantly, but she also knew damned well that they liked to do it, that she gave them a thrill. She was starting to hate them and the hatred gave her strength. They came for her at all times, night and day, and they were coming right now.

She had cried out in her sleep and the guard must have heard her and reported on the phone that she had awakened. They often came when she'd had a nightmare, taking advantage of her nervous state, and now she heard their booted feet clattering along the corridor, their voices raised in the usual mindless shouting, deliberately awakening the other prisoners, adding to their torment.

Alice braced herself, fought to freeze her emotions, tried to become remote from herself and not let panic wreck her. Nevertheless, as the cell door was swung open, letting the light beam in, silhouetting the first soldier, she wondered if this would be the morning when they'd go over the edge. That thought made her nauseous.

The first soldier rushed in and brutally grabbed her by the hair, nearly tearing it out of her head as he jerked her to her feet. She cried out automatically, not able to stop herself, but he just dragged her across the floor, then threw her out into the corridor, into the midst of the other waiting soldiers. They all bawled abuse at her as they manhandled her along the corridor, pushing, pulling, slapping repeatedly at her head and face, one even putting his boot on her backside to kick her along. First the corridor, then the stairs, two flights down, pushed and battered, then hammered between the shoulders with a fist until she had reached the closed door. She was deafened by the shouting and could hardly think straight when the door was opened and they pushed her into the room and slammed her down in the wooden chair. She sat there, trying, to breathe, sweating profusely, her heart pounding, and looked across the desk at the calm, cold-eyed Mohammed as the door was slammed shut again. The two Iraqi officers were standing near Mohammed, one on each side of him, and both of them glared fiercely at her, as if wanting to kill her.

'What was the purpose of your flight over Iraq?' Mohammed asked without preamble.

'I'm not permitted to answer that question.'

'Whore!' one of the Iraqi officers screamed.

'I could have you shot as a spy,' Mohammed said.

'I'm a pilot and you found me by my helicopter. I'm not a spy and you know it.'

'Lying American bitch!' the other officer screamed.

'You were flying a transport helicopter,' Mohammed said with quiet persistence, 'so you must have crashed after lifting in American troops. Where did you insert those troops and what was their mission?'

'I'm not permitted to answer that question.'

'You will answer!' the first officer screamed.

'Or die!' the second one screamed. 'You understand, whore? You die!'

Alice did not respond, though a shudder passed through her. She lowered her head, looking down at her own feet, trying to pretend she was somewhere else.

'Answer, you whore!'

She was grabbed by the hair and her head was jerked back, then another hand slapped her across the face, once, twice, a third time, making her dizzy. She felt blood on her lips.

'American bitch!'

'Whore!'

Opening her eyes, she saw both officers leaning over her, practically breathing into her face, a wild light in their eyes.

'What was your mission?'

'Where did you drop your troops?'

'What information did you have about Baghdad?'

'Answer, whore, or you'll die!'

She closed her eyes and raised her hand to her lips to wipe the blood off. Someone smashed the back of her hand with a rubber truncheon, causing terrible pains to explode through her fingers and shoot up her arm. Crying out involuntarily, feeling tears spring to her eyes, she was slapped another couple of times and then thrown off the chair. She hit the stone floor with her shoulder, cracked her head and saw stars, then felt a boot kicking her in the ribs and flipping her onto her back. Gasping, feeling as if she was about to choke, she opened her eyes again. Looking up, she saw the two officers staring down, that wild, devouring light still in their brown eyes.

'Sooner or later you will tell us,' Mohammed said, his voice floating from behind and above her head and sounding utterly reasonable. 'So why not tell us now? Save yourself this discomfort and humiliation. If you don't, it will get worse.'

'My name is Alice Davis, my rank is lieutenant, my serial number is—'

'Whore!' One of the officers, leaning down, spat the word in her face, then actually spat on her. Not satisfied, he spread his legs to straddle her and sit on her stomach, pressing her shoulders back against the stone floor with his big, heavy hands. In that position, her breasts were thrusting up against the thin cotton of her gown. He glared at her, then lowered his gaze and almost stopped breathing. Instantly realising what he was doing, he glared at her again, then grabbed her head in both hands and banged it repeatedly against the stone floor. She felt dreadful pain, a dampness in her hair – she assumed it must be blood – then saw spinning stars and felt like throwing up. 'Answer, bitch! Our patience is running out! Why did you fly into Iraq? What was your mission?'

'My name is—'

He banged her head on the floor again and pressed his groin down on her stomach and she felt – she was convinced she could feel – his growing erection. She raised her legs without thinking, trying to writhe out from under him, and felt the hem of the gown falling back to uncover her thighs. One of the soldiers muttered something. Another laughed nervously. In a panic, she straightened her legs again and tried to stay still. The man on top of her slapped her face – repeatedly, brutally. He then banged her head on the floor again, so many times that she almost blacked out and heard her own distant moaning.

'Whore! Jewish bitch!'

She actually smiled at that. She was a green-eyed, blonde WASP. Obviously enraged by the smile, the man on top of her attacked again, banging her head against the floor, slapping her face repeatedly, pressing himself down on her belly, either attempting to crush the last breath out of her or slyly rubbing against her. She could hear his harsh breathing.

'Enough,' Mohammed said quietly. 'Pick her off the floor.' Alice felt a great flood of relief – until she heard his next words. 'Put her onto the table.'

She opened her eyes as the man sitting astride her raised himself off her. She caught a glimpse of his sweating face, his gleaming eyes, his sadistic smile, as he grabbed her by the hair and tugged her back up to her feet. As she stood there, swaying, seeing the walls slowly spinning, he took hold of her shoulder, viciously squeezed it, hurting her more, then flung her towards the table that looked like a blood-stained butcher's block. He slammed her face down on the table with her feet still on the floor, then tugged the hem of her gown up to her waist, leaving her exposed from the waist down. Before she could straighten up or even cry out in protest, two of the soldiers had stepped up to the table, one to hold her head down, the other to press heavily on her shoulders, both of them preventing her from moving. She heard a rattling sound above her – someone grabbing a whip – and against her will, her whole body shuddered in spasms of helpless dread.

'No!' she screamed.

Her voice reverberated eerily in her head, gradually turned into a keening, distant wailing, then was submerged in a familiar ringing sound that grew louder and louder – a telephone ringing.

Mohammed picked up the phone. There was silence as he listened. When he slammed the phone down and shouted something at his men, the two officers ran out of the room, bawling instructions back over their shoulders at their startled soldiers. The soldiers released Alice, dragged her upright, then rushed her out of the room and back to her cell, hammering her with their truncheons all the way. They threw her in and locked the door. There was a lot of shouting outside. As she struggled to her feet, almost too weak to stand, the shouting outside grew louder. She heard more shouting from the stairs, Iraqis shouting, then English voices – *English* voices – then the sounds of a lot of men struggling as they entered the corridor. She heard the dull thud of the truncheons. There were grunts and cries of pain. Other soldiers were dragging Iraqi prisoners from their cells and manhandling them back along the corridor past the struggling men. New prisoners were being brought in. They were putting up a great struggle. 'Iraqi shits!' one of them bawled and then, obviously struck by a truncheon, gasped the single word, 'Fuck!'

English voices!

A cell door was slammed shut. It was two cells down from

Alice. She heard the sounds of a struggle outside the adjoining cell, then that door was slammed shut as well. Alice squinted through the hatch as two other prisoners were dragged past, still struggling and bellowing obscenities as the Iraqis punched them with fists and struck them with the butts of their rifles. Those two men were flung protesting into cells at the other side of Alice, then the cell doors were slammed shut. They'd been wearing British uniforms, she was sure of it.

'Iraqi bastards!' one of the men bawled as the soldiers departed.

There was silence until the clattering of the boots of the departing soldiers had faded away. Then one prisoner called out to the others, 'Are you men still in one piece?'

The other three men replied in the affirmative, all speaking English.

'Oh, my God,' Alice muttered, still feeling elated to hear those voices, then she stood on tiptoe, put her mouth to the hatch, took a deep breath and called out, 'Hi, there!'

'Am I hearing right?' someone asked.

CHAPTER TEN

The rescue teams travelled unimpeded for the remaining few hours until first light, searched for a suitable resting-up place, found a low ridge with dramatic rock outcroppings, which offered protection from enemy aircraft, and decided to make camp there until the late afternoon. After parking the two Pink Panthers in the shadow of the rocks, they covered them with camouflage nets with hessian stitched in to keep out the sunlight. When this was done, each man constructed his own laying-up position by digging a shallow 'scrape' in the gravelled earth with his short-handled spade, unrolling the sleeping bag in it, then raising his waterproof poncho over it on Y-shaped sticks to form a triangular tent with its long, sloping side facing the wind. Unable to light a fire for their portable hexamine stoves, lest the smoke give away their position to passing enemy patrols, they break-fasted on cold high-calorie rations and water, then relaxed with cigarettes. When the rest period was over, they labo-riously checked and cleaned their weapons yet again, then took turns at catching up on lost sleep, three men sleep-ing while the other three kept watch in three-hour shifts.

As the sun rose higher in the sky, the heat became ferocious.

Even here, in the immense, windblown wilderness, the flies and mosquitoes tormented them relentlessly. Though the desert itself was silent, that silence was constantly disturbed by the sudden roaring of jet fighters passing overhead or the bass rumbling of the immense AWACS aircraft higher in the sky. Those on watch occasionally saw enemy troop trucks on the horizon, eerily distorted by shimmering heatwaves, and colourful Arab caravans, the camels trotting in what seemed like slow motion against the radiant blue sky, the robes of the Arabs flapping in the breeze. As the operational brief was not to engage the enemy until reaching Baghdad, the rescue team let the enemy convoys pass unmolested, merely taking notes on their size, location, direction of movement and, where they were close enough for the binoculars to reveal details, their weaponry.

'I can never get over the sight of them fucking A-rabs,' Roy whispered to Geordie when both of them were sharing the watch. 'Stealth aircraft overhead, like fucking *Star Wars*, and Arabs on camels on the ground, just like in biblical times. It's a funny old world, right?'

'Right,' Geordie confirmed, blowing a cloud of cigarette smoke. 'It's a bit hard to grasp, mate.'

In the early afternoon, when all of the men had had their three hours of sleep, Captain Williams decided to move on again, in hopes of reaching their RV near Baghdad before last light. As they were now travelling alone, without the protection of the rest of the squadron, he ordered Geordie to untie one of the British Army trail motorbikes from the Pink Panther and go ahead of them to reconnoitre the terrain for signs of enemy troops.

'Right,' Geordie said, beaming with pleasure. 'You picked the right man, boss.' Formally a member of the Mobility Group and a two-wheel specialist, he was clearly delighted as he untied the motorbike and lowered it lovingly to the ground beside the Pink Panther. After checking it carefully, he tied the *shemagh* around his face, leaving only his eyes exposed, which he covered with a pair of goggles. His M16 was slung across his back and the Browning handgun was holstered on his hip.

'Fucking Evil Knievel,' Paddy said, where he was sitting on the ground in the shade of a Pink Panther, checking the £800 worth of gold he had been given, as had the others, to help if he was caught by the enemy or found himself cut off and faced with non-friendly civilians. 'Sure doesn't he think he's the ant's pants?'

'Sticks and stones,' Geordie responded. 'You're just jealous, mate.'

'Jealous, shit,' Paddy replied. 'If I have to have something under my bum, I like to know it has four wheels.'

'You're old before your time,' Geordie said.

He kicked the start pedal and the motorbike roared into life. As he was experimentally revving it, Captain Williams approached him and said, 'No nonsense out there, Geordie. I'm only after reconnaissance. I want warning of any enemy troops ahead and that's all I want. No engagements, no fire fights, no heroics. You keep out of sight, you keep your eyes peeled, and you report back here immediately if you see anything.'

'You can depend on me, boss.'

'You travel for twenty miles towards the MSR, then turn back to let us know if the route's clear or not. If it is, we'll follow the route you took and repeat the process again. Have you got that?'

'Yes, boss.'

'Right. On your way.'

Geordie gunned the engine, practically swivelled around on the rear wheel, then shot off in the direction of the unseen MSR, deliberately showering Roy and Paddy in spewing sand. Cursing, they rolled out of the way, covering their faces with their hands. When Geordie had departed, soon shrinking in the distance and eventually disappearing, they sat up again and dusted themselves down.

'Cocky bastard,' Paddy complained.

'You shouldn't have wound him up,' Roy said. 'Have you still got all your gold, mate?'

'I have,' Paddy replied. 'I'm worth something to someone at last. It makes me feel like a rich man.'

Roy had already checked his gold and was now studying a chit written in Arabic, promising that Her Majesty's Government would pay the sum of £5,000 to anyone who returned the soldier safely to friendly territory or persons.

'You won't feel so rich if you have to use it,' he said. 'Either that or this promise of five-thousand smackers to any Arab who helps you. They'll probably help you by turning you in to the Iraqis and asking *them* for the money.'

'The Lord's will be done, mate.'

'All right, you men,' Williams said as he and Kilroy removed the camouflage netting from one of the two Pink Panthers. 'Let's get ready to move out.'

Roy and Paddy jumped up to uncover the second vehicle, then between them they dismantled the LUPs and filled in the shallow scrapes, leaving no signs of their having been here. This done, they sat down again in the shadows of the vehicles, to have a smoke and wait for Geordie's return.

Kneeling in the shade of a Pink Panther between the granite-faced Kilroy and Wild Bill, Williams unfolded a large line drawing of Saddam Hussein's underground HQ complex and spread it out on the ground in front of him to study it thoughtfully. Kilroy and Wild Bill moved closer to him as he placed the blunt end of his ballpoint pen on the indicated complex entrance, ran the pen along the main road, past a series of numbered loading bays with elevators, then repeatedly tapped number ten, which was circled with a red marker pen. It had a large arrow pointing to a square with the words 'Interrogation Centre' scrawled across it.

'That's it,' Williams said. 'The elevator in the tenth loading bay. It ascends through three floors to the interrogation centre at ground level. Loading Bay Number Ten is on the right-hand side as we drive down, located approximately one-and-a-half miles along the road. The complex has three levels with open walkways that run the whole length of the road on both sides of it. The walkways are open on the side overlooking the road, with steel safety railings running along them. The inner side of the walkways are lined with doors that lead into the various areas of the complex. The Iraqis use the walkways constantly, either to get from one end of the complex to the other or to enter the inner areas, and they have a clear view of anything passing along the road.'

'Which means that anyone on the walkway can see the trucks moving along the road below,' Wild Bill observed.

'Correct.'

'Which means they'll see us.'

'They'll see our *troop truck*,' Williams corrected him. 'With luck, that truck will enter with a lot of others, so we'll just look like part of the general convoy. Iraqi troop trucks have canvas covers, so the men on the walkways can't see who's inside.'

'What about those on the ground?' Kilroy asked.

'It's a calculated risk, but I'm assuming that if we're in the middle of the convoy, we'll just be waved through the entrance with all the others. The driver, Sergeant Kilroy, will have his face tinted and be wearing an Iraqi Army beret taken from one of the men from the hijacked truck. Most of his face will be covered with a *shemagh*. So, given that the truck will be on the move, he probably won't be seen as anyone out of the ordinary.'

'What if an Iraqi guard at the main gate speaks to him?' Wild Bill said.

'I speak a bit of Arabic,' Kilroy told him. 'I don't know much, but what I know I speak fluently.'

'Oh?' Wild Bill stared speculatively at him. 'So where did you learn it?'

'The Hereford and Army School of Languages.'

Wild Bill nodded. 'Good one. I should have known with you bastards.' Turning back to the drawing on the ground, he studied it thoughtfully, then asked, 'Are those loading bays numbered in Arabic?'

'Yes,' Williams said.

'And naturally, Kilroy here can read the numbers.'

'That's right,' Kilroy said. 'I can also count. If we can't see the numbers, we simply count the bays off one by one as we drive along. Then we turn into Number Ten.'

'I feel in safe hands already,' Wild Bill said. 'This is all hunky-dory. So we just drive down the road and turn into Loading Bay Number Ten. Just like that, right?'

'Right,' Captain Williams said.

'And what if one of the other trucks pulls in there as well?'

'We don't think that will happen. According to our inform-ant, the bays are only used for loading equipment and the troop trucks all park in a big parking lot near the end of the complex, under downtown Baghdad.'

Wild Bill was persistent. 'Then they'll sit up and take notice if we turn off from the rest of the convoy and head into that loading bay.'

'Not necessarily. They may assume that we're offloading equipment before driving on. If they don't, we should be inside that elevator and heading up to the interrogation centre while they sound the alarm. That gives us time to get into the centre, recapture our men, and make our escape through the front entrance before they get to us.'

'And recapture our female pilot.'

'That as well,' Captain Williams said. 'We know that the

elevator, when it reaches ground level, opens to the waiting room of the interrogation centre. That room has three interrogation rooms leading off it, all with guards at the doors. We dispatch the guards and clear the rooms, destroy the elevator with explosives, and leave one man down there while the others get up those two short flights of stairs to where the cells are located. There's usually only one guard in charge of the cells at any time. He has the keys to the cells. We know that as of yesterday our men were placed in those cells, where your female pilot's been held for some time.'

'So we dispatch the guard, take the keys and let 'em out.'

'Correct. And from that point on, you'll be in charge of the woman, though we'll all stick together.'

'By which time we'll almost certainly have to shoot our way out of the building, leaving through the front entrance.'

'There's only a guard gate, manned by three or four Iraqi soldiers. We emerge through an underground car park to the inner courtyard where the guard gate's located. With the elevator out of action, and hopefully blocking the entrance to the interrogation centre, we should be able to reach the courtyard before reinforcements for the guards arrive. Given that, we can dispatch the guards and get out into the street before any other Iraqi troops can get to us. I'll be waiting outside with the second truck and we'll all pile into it and get the hell out of there as quickly as possible. Any *more* questions, Master Sergeant Kowalski?'

Wild Bill grinned. 'I don't think so. I just think we'll have to move like greased lightning to get out in one piece.'

'You're with the SAS now,' Kilroy reminded him, 'and we move even faster than lightning.'

'I sure hope so,' Wild Bill said.

Kilroy was just about to reply with an acerbic comment when a trail of billowing sand in the distance, far across the flat desert plain, announced that something was coming in their direction. Instantly, all of the men rolled out of the shadow of the Pink Panthers and adopted firing positions belly down on the ground, aiming at that approaching cloud of sand. They relaxed when the speck in the distance took shape as a single man on a motorbike and eventually they recognised Geordie. He roared at them, then skidded to a halt and turned his engine off. After swinging his leg off and propping the motorbike on its steel support, he sauntered towards them, lowering the *shemagh*, raising the goggles to his forehead and grinning through the film of sand caked to his face.

'I really enjoyed that,' he said.

'So what did you see?' Captain Williams asked.

'I reached the MSR, boss, and took up a watch position for fifteen minutes. It was on a high ridge and that ridge ran in the direction of Baghdad as far as the eye could see. I saw a lot of Iraqi troop trucks coming and going in both directions, to and from Baghdad. I also saw a couple of mobile Scud launchers heading into the desert.'

'What was your location?'

'According to my map, about forty miles from the outskirts of Baghdad.'

'What about off the MSR? Anything there?'

'No. Everything was on the MSR. The desert between here and there was empty except for some Bedouin.'

'So we can follow your route.'

'I reckon, boss. Though I can't guarantee that something won't materialise in the meantime.'

'Right.' Williams and the others were all on their feet now. 'We'll move out right now,' Williams told them. 'Geordie will go out ahead again and keep us posted of any enemy movements. We follow him all the way. When we reach the MSR, we'll drive parallel to it, protected by that ridge, until we're in sight of the entrance to the complex on the outskirts of Baghdad. Geordie will stay ahead of us at all times, keeping us informed of enemy troop movements. OK, let's get going.'

Roy Collinson took the driver's seat in Williams's vehicle

and moved off as soon as Williams had clambered into the seat beside him, following Geordie, who was already racing back the way he had come, churning up a long column of billowing sand. Kilroy, Wild Bill and Paddy followed in the other Pink Panther, with Wild Bill driving, Kilroy in the seat beside him, behind the mounted GPMG, and Paddy on the five-inch Browning heavy machine gun in the rear. Geordie stayed well ahead of the two Pink Panthers – a mere speck in the dust under that column of boiling sand – but he carefully kept the same distance between himself and those behind him, to ensure that they could follow him without trouble.

Though the sun was starting to sink, the heat was still ferocious, a virtual cauldron, and the men were all wearing goggles and their *shemaghs* to protect them from the sand churned up by the wheels of the vehicles and boiling up around them. The desert plain was flat and seemingly endless, but gradually, as the twenty miles were whittled down, a series of high ridges materialised in the distance, golden brown against the azure sky, and the cloud of sand the men were following eventually subsided, indicating that Geordie had reached his watch position. About five minutes later, the two Pink Panthers braked to a halt beside Geordie's motorbike. Geordie was stretched out on his belly on the edge of the high ridge, looking down through his black-painted binoculars on the MSR far below.

Alighting from their vehicles, the men joined Geordie on the ridge to gaze down on the MSR. They were just in time to see an Iraqi Army convoy moving along the road in the direction of Basra. A mobile Scud launcher was in the middle, protected by the troop trucks.

'They're heading for the border,' Williams said, 'intent on some mayhem.'

'They'll get short shrift if they wander into Scud Boulevard,' Wild Bill said. 'My pals in the Delta Force will make sure of that.'

'They'll have to go through Scud Alley first,' Kilroy told him, 'and our SAS mates won't let them get as far as your pals.'

Wild Bill just grinned. 'Maybe so, Sarge. Either way they're in trouble.'

'Either way they're not our concern,' Williams said, 'so let's get on the move again. We'll follow this ridge as far as we can, keeping far enough back from the edge so as not to be seen by the traffic on that road below. You lead the way, Geordie, and report back if anything's up ahead.'

'You've got it, boss,' Geordie responded enthusiastically as he jumped back to his feet and swung himself onto his motorbike. 'I'm on my way.' He kicked the starter, revved the engine and then shot off in a cloud of sand. The other men clambered back into their Pink Panthers and followed him, heading along the ridge plateau, but well away from the edge. For the next hour, as the Pink Panthers bumped and rattled over stretches of the gravel plain known as *dibdibba*, broad wadis, dried-out flash-flood depressions, low hills, sand dunes and secondary ridges, Geordie kept the same distance between them, just far enough ahead for them to be able to see him as a black speck under a column of churning sand. Then, suddenly, he shot out of sight and the cloud of sand subsided.

'What the hell's he doing?' Wild Bill asked. 'He's supposed to stay in our eyeballs.'

'I think he's seen something,' Kilroy said.

This turned out to be true. After remaining out of sight for about ten minutes, during which the two Pink Panthers kept advancing in the same direction, Geordie reappeared on the summit of a stretch of high ground, heading straight towards them. Williams hand-signalled both drivers to brake to a halt and await Geordie's arrival. When he reached them, he stopped beside Williams's Pink Panther, looking excited.

'Baghdad is just over that hill,' he said. 'From up there you can see where the MSR runs parallel to the six-lane highway leading into the city. The two roads are about a mile apart. The MSR terminates at a massive HAS. Troop trucks and Mobile Scuds are entering and leaving by the HAS doors on a regular basis.'

'That *has* to be the entrance to the complex,' Williams said.

'It looks like it, boss,' Geordie said. 'An awful lot of traffic went in there – and came out as well – so it must be more than just a hardened aircraft shelter. It must be bloody enormous. So what else could it be, if it's not that underground complex? And judging by the grid references on my map, that's where the entrance should be.'

Excited, Williams checked the grid reference on Geordie's map against his own, then looked up to where the sun was sinking behind the horizon as a great crimson ball, turning the blue sky pink. 'That's it,' he said. 'If we advance to there immediately, we'll arrive before last light. We'll erect an OP before darkness falls and keep the entrance under surveillance throughout the night and the following day. When we have a good idea of what's happening down there, we'll commence the operation. Right, men, let's go.'

Following Geordie again, they moved on until they reached the end of the ridge, which curved away to the west and gave a panoramic view of the distant skyscrapers and rooftops of Baghdad and the surrounding plains. Almost directly facing them, but far below on bleached desert, the MSR curved away from the direction of the Baghdad–Basra highway and terminated at what looked like a particularly enormous hardened aircraft shelter: pyramid-shaped and flat-roofed, with sliding steel doors, half buried in heaped-up earth and sand to make them blend in with the desert.

Even as Williams was studying those HAS doors through his binoculars, they slid open to let out a convoy of Iraqi troop trucks, which headed along the MSR in the direction of Basra. When the last of the trucks had emerged, the great doors slid shut again.

Williams checked the location of that entrance against his map, then looked up and said, 'That's it, men. It can't be anything else. Let's construct our OP here and settle down for a lengthy period of observation. We'll commence the operation tomorrow when we know just what's happening. Now let's get to work.'

This time they dug a long-term OP, large, deep and rectangular, with one narrow end as the rest bay, the other, facing the MSR, for the observers and sentry, and a kit well in the middle, where they placed the weapons, spare ammunition, radio equipment, batteries, water cans and dry food. The OP was covered in canvas, which was then liberally sprinkled with sand and gravel taken from the surrounding area. The observation bay was screened with black hessian and contained a black-painted telescope on a tripod, military binoculars, a tripod-mounted Thorn EMI multi-role thermal imager which would enable them to see in the darkness, a 35mm Nikon F-801 with Minimodulux hand-held image intensifier, spare film, aerial photos previously taken by reconnaissance aircraft, codes and ciphers for burst radio transmissions, and logbooks and maps. The construction of the OP was completed just before last light, with the spoil removed and scattered over the ground a good distance away. From the plain below and from aircraft flying overhead, it would have been practically invisible.

By the time the sun had gone down, plunging the desert into moonlit darkness, the men had settled into the OP and were engaged in their various tasks.

It would be a long night.

CHAPTER ELEVEN

'Yes,' Alice called out to the English-speaking male who had, she had noticed as he was dragged past her by the guards, been wearing some kind of British Army uniform, 'you're hearing right. Alice Davis, US Air Force. Who are you guys?'

'Twenty-two SAS,' the voice called back. 'British Special Forces. I'm Major Norman Phillips.'

'Sergeant Harry Spooner,' a second voice identified himself from another cell.

'Staff Sergeant Clive Morrissey,' said a third.

'Corporal Ben Townsend,' said the fourth. 'Nice to meet you, Alice.'

Just as Alice was about to reply, there was the clattering of footsteps down the concrete floor of the corridor, a pair of angry brown eyes glared through the open hatch, and the Iraqi guard started screaming, obviously telling her that talking wasn't allowed. Startled, Alice stepped back from the door and stood there, listening, as the guard marched up and down outside, screaming similar words at the four SAS prisoners.

'Go fuck yourself,' Spooner said and the guard, though not understanding English, screamed even louder.

'Don't antagonise him, Sarge,' Major Phillips said. 'You'll only make matters worse.'

'How much worse can they get, boss?' Spooner asked.

'Much worse,' Phillips replied. 'So please try to stay cool.'

'OK, boss,' Spooner said.

The guard kept marching up and down past the five cells, screaming angrily at his prisoners, until, satisfied that they would speak no more, he returned to his chair at the far end of the corridor, near the top of the stairs.

Filled with exultation that she was no longer alone, even though she was aware that these men were also prisoners, Alice returned to her mattress and sat down, leaning her head against the wall, closing her eyes and silently shedding tears of relief. Surprised to find that her heart was racing, she leant her forehead on her knees, took deep, even breaths, eventually managed to stop crying and just sat there deep in thought. Gradually, as her senses returned, she faced up to the fact that the men in the other cells, though members of the legendary SAS – the British equivalent of the US Delta Force – were as trapped as she was and would be no help in getting her out of here. Nevertheless, their very presence here was an undeniable comfort, making her feel less alone.

This feeling was pleasantly strengthened when she recalled that though the guard normally kept the steel door at the end of the corridor open, sitting in his chair right beside it, he closed and bolted it at regular intervals throughout the day, for very brief periods, presumably when he went to the toilet. Remembering this, she became excited again and sat up straight to listen for the sound of the slamming door.

Waiting, she studied the small, gloomy cell and realised that even the large cockroaches crawling constantly all over the floor no longer bothered her. On the other hand, as so often happened, the very sight of the grim cell made her yearn for the comfort and security of her home in Iowa.

Though born in Dayton, Ohio, where her father had been a career officer at Wright-Patterson Air Force Base, she had spent her early childhood moving with her family from one location to another, each time her father was posted to another base. She had enjoyed the constant changes. Her father had taught her to enjoy it. Flying B-52 heavy bombers in Vietnam, he had been overseas a lot, but always loving and attentive when at home, so Alice had only good memories of her childhood with an equally loving mother, her older brother, Tom, and her younger sister, Melanie. The frequent moving had made them close, dependent upon one another, but it had also given Alice a feel for the service, for the peculiar insularity of the life, for the flamboyance of most of the pilots her father mixed with. From a young age, as far back as she could remember, she had wanted to be one of those men and her father, who also loved the Air Force, never discouraged her.

Eventually, when Alice had turned fourteen, her father retired from the service and moved the family back to his home town of Des Moines, Iowa, where he purchased a pretty white farmhouse just outside the city limits and began his own business, selling farming products to the local farmers, the same business his own father had been in. Nevertheless, while he thoroughly enjoyed his work, he frequently told Alice about how much he missed the Air Force and she, taking after him and having had adolescent crushes on some of his Air Force friends, continued to dream of becoming a pilot like him. So she went to college, had crushes on boys her own age, finally lost her virginity, worked hard and graduated with honours. Encouraged by her father, she enlisted shortly after graduation and was posted to the US Air Force Academy in Colorado, becoming one of the few girls in a world of men.

She paid the price for that. My God, she did! If she went

in full of dreams, excited with an expectation that had grown relentlessly throughout the years, mixed up, as it was, with her adoration for the men she had met on so many Air Force bases, she was brutally disillusioned when she entered the Academy and was faced with the full extent of male resentment at the few females cadets coming in. What happened there devastated her.

If her father had known what had been done to her, he would have been outraged. So great was his love for the Air Force, however, that she had never been able to bring herself to tell him, knowing that if she did so he would have stormed off to the Academy and kicked up a fuss and her career in the Air Force would have ended. Surprisingly, though she was shocked by how she had been treated, she still loved the idea of the service and wanted to stay in. What she could not cross then and could hardly face now was the gap between her romanticised view of the older pilots, her father's friends, and the callous brutality, disguised as duty, of the younger men she was forced to deal with in the Academy. Within weeks, her enthusiasm to work with those men had turned into fear and revulsion. Those feelings still tore at her.

Even now, when she thought about it, she felt ill. Even now, when her only bad dreams should have been about her current plight, she had nightmares when she thought about the Academy.

They had said it was for her own good, to strengthen her for the future, but she knew that they had resisted having female cadets and had applied that degradation and terror only to make her resign. She had not resigned. She had refused to give in to them. Her parents had given her pride and that helped to sustain her, but eventually her will was almost broken and she revolted against it. After submitting a formal complaint, she was called to see her commanding officer and informed that if she made her complaints public she would be forced to leave. Though this made her despise him, as she did the younger men, she refused to let them push her out and withdrew her complaint. They stopped tormenting her after that, but never apologised, and only when she graduated, becoming a pilot, did they relent and treat her as one of them. They bought her drinks, shook her hand.

'You did good,' they told her.

Still, she hated them, repelled by what they had put her though, despising their condescension, and now, when she thought about it, she was filled with a destructive combination of rage and helpless fear. This was all she had learnt from them.

The fear was hardest to deal with, consuming her in the present, reminding her that the other men, her Iraqi tormentors, might soon take to the absolute limit what had been rehearsed so brutally months ago in Colorado. Indeed, sitting there on the foul mattress, leaning against the cold stone wall with its drawings of torments and executions, already bruised from previous beatings and smeared with dried blood which she hadn't bothered to wipe off, she remembered that last interrogation and shuddered to think of what would have happened had those Iraqi soldiers not been interrupted by the arrival of the SAS prisoners.

Next time, however, she might not be so lucky. She was certain that when they held her over that butcher's block of a table, also smeared with human blood, with her legs and buttocks exposed, they would do more than whip her. Almost certainly they would do what they had dreamed about doing all along, pretending that what gave them pleasure was administered as punishment.

They'll tell themselves that it's their duty, she thought, and when they've managed to convince themselves of that, they'll be able to rape me. They're on the brink of that now.

Alice shuddered with dread, then laid her forehead on her raised knees and closed her eyes, trying to empty her mind. She did not succeed. The pain of grief was too great. She kept thinking of how, growing up in a good home, she had revered her father and romanticised his friends; of how, when she had entered the US Air Force Academy, her romanticism had been brutally shattered by her treatment at the hands of the men she had thought she would admire; of how, when she had graduated from the Academy and been posted to Langley AFB, Virginia, she had gone there already prepared to hate her fellow pilots; and, finally, of how, when she had been posted to the Gulf, she had shared her UH-60 Black Hawk with Captain Dave Bamberg and quickly fallen in love with him.

God, yes. She had loved him and he had loved her and already, mere weeks after they had met, even before they'd had the chance to sleep together, he was dead, burnt up in the crash while she'd survived to find herself here, tormented by his memory, even as she was tormented by the Iraqis and by what she had suffered before meeting him.

Please come back, she pleaded silently. Please don't leave me here. I can take anything those bastards dish out if I can just have you back. *Please, God, send him back to me.*

But Dave wouldn't be coming back.

Of course, she knew that. She had known it the instant she'd recovered consciousness in the crashed chopper, seen his rigid, bloody body, the flames reaching out to engulf him. She had known it as she did the only thing possible, crawling away through the smoke, away from him for ever, to jump out and crash to the ground and be knocked unconscious again. She had known it as she had regained consciousness a second time, being dragged by the hair across the ground by those fucking Iraqis. She had known it then and she knew it right now as the pain cut clean through her.

Oh, dear God, he was gone.

Alice had been allocated as his co-pilot as soon as she had arrived in Kuwait and, given her experience in the Academy, had been prepared to loathe him. Five years her senior, already experienced in combat, he had greeted her with a smile, warmly shaken her hand, radiated warmth from his brown eyes and said, 'Welcome to the Screaming Eagles, Alice. You're in for a pretty rough ride, but you look like the right stuff. I'm sure you'll do fine.'

And she *had* done fine. She had done it with him. He didn't treat her with contempt, nor even condescend to her, but took her aboard as an absolute equal and made her a welcomed member of the team. They had been a good team, too, under his courageous leadership, and whether attacking enemy positions or inserting troops behind the lines, they had done it together, as friends, and the experience had renewed her.

She fell in love with him – perhaps because of his kindness – and she was sure that he felt the same way, though the subject was never raised. They had been together for six weeks, from the very first air raids to the beginning of the land war, but to Alice it seemed like six months and she had never been happier. They fought the air war together, saw each other when not flying, told each other about themselves, held hands, embraced and finally kissed. Those kisses sealed their love, unconsummated though it was, and gradually they reached that stage where each sensed what the other was feeling, even though neither was willing to commit in the midst of this bloody war.

'It'd sure be nice to still be seeing you,' David had said, 'when this crap is all over. Let's make it a date.'

'Yeah, Dave, let's do that.'

Now Dave was dead.

Six weeks together. A lifetime of love crammed into six weeks. That's all they'd been given.

Resting on the sordid mattress with her forehead on her knees, stoned by nervous exhaustion and relentless, choking fear, Alice was torn between her contempt for all the men who had abused her – the cadets in Colorado and the soldiers here in Iraq – and the love and respect that she felt for Captain Dave Bamberg. Now he was rotting in a crashed

Black Hawk in the desert while the others – those back in Colorado and the ones outside her cell – were still causing her pain.

God, yes, how she loathed them!

The rage gave her strength and it was all that she had left. She was still sitting there, forehead resting on her raised knees, eyes closed, fists clenched, dwelling on love and loathing, nurturing healthy rage, when she heard the steel door slamming shut at the end of the corridor.

Instantly, she jumped to her feet, stood close to the wall at the end of the mattress and knocked on it repeatedly with her knuckles.

'Hey, you!' she called out, keeping her voice as low as possible, though loud enough for the man in the cell next door to hear her. 'Major Phillips! Can you hear me?'

There was silence for a moment, then the muffled voice of Major Phillips came from the other side of the wall.

'Yes, I can hear you. But the guard—'

'He's gone,' Alice interjected. 'That slamming door means he's gone to the john. We can talk until we hear the door opening again. It makes a lot of noise, that door.'

'Excellent,' Phillips said. 'You're US Air Force?'

'Yeah. A chopper pilot. Crashed and captured five days ago. I've been here ever since.'

'Are you all right?'

'Not bad.'

'How have they treated you?'

'It could be worse.'

'What does that mean?'

'So far they've only slapped me around but they're losing their patience. The last time . . . They were about to do worse and were only interrupted by your arrival. If you hadn't been brought in, I suspect . . .'

Alice tailed off. She couldn't bear to even mention what it was that she assumed was coming next.

'I'm sorry,' Major Phillips said, speaking softly and sounding as if he meant it. 'I trust—'

'It's OK,' Alice interjected. 'I'm OK. How about you and your men?'

'We're all right so far.'

'SAS, right?'

'Yes.'

'Like our Delta Force, right?'

'Exactly. They caught us in the field and here we are. They've been interrogating you for five days?'

'Yeah.'

'Do they have a system?'

'Yeah. They do it a lot and at all times of the night and day. Disorientation through exhaustion and being jerked out of sleep. One, the interrogator, speaks like a reasonable man; the others bawl at you a lot and do the slapping and kicking. So far, as I said, I've only been slapped and kicked, but the next time . . .' She hesitated again, then said, 'But you guys . . . they might not wait that long. I mean, I've heard that the SAS . . .'

When she stopped, wanting to bite her own tongue, Phillips said understandingly, 'Don't be embarrassed. I know what you were going to say. Saddam has a standing order that all captured SAS are to be tortured for information, then executed. We're fully aware of that fact.'

'Yeah . . . Well, I'm sorry.'

'I'm sorry, too, Alice.'

Alice leant her forehead against the wall, deeply moved by the realisation that, although she should hate men, she had been in love with Dave Bamberg, deeply respected the others who had died with him in the crash, and desperately wanted to be able to reach through the wall and touch this unseen, softly spoken, English officer. He sounded so civilised, so . . . *concerned* for her. And yet he knew, as did she, that he and his comrades were condemned men. This brought tears to her eyes.

'Is there any chance ... ?' she asked, then faltered again, unable to find the words, aware of their futility even before she managed to utter them. 'I mean ... Any chance that they might not ... ?'

'I would like to think so,' Phillips replied, sounding very calm, 'but I'm not optimistic. They'll want us to talk and they'll have no scruples in attempting to make us do so. After that, whether or not we tell them what they want to hear, they'll either use us as human shields or execute us outright. In short, the prognosis isn't good.'

They were silent for a moment, neither quite knowing what to say, then eventually Phillips said: 'However, you, being a woman ...' This time he was the one to hesitate. 'Well, perhaps they'll ...'

There was another uneasy silence, but this time Alice was the one to break it. 'They might let me live,' she said, deciding to air the subject and be done with it, 'but I won't get off lightly. They're already ... Oh, hell!'

Starting to weep again, she turned away from the wall and flung herself down on the bed. As she did so, the steel door at the end of the corridor squealed open and she heard the sound that had become so familiar and which she always dreaded: the clattering of many boots on concrete and the deliberate, frightening bawling of Iraqi soldiers hurrying down to the cells.

She knew just what that meant – only this time they hadn't come for her, but for an SAS man.

'Fuck you!' the victim bawled defiantly before they brutally laid into him with their rubber truncheons.

Alice heard the repeated, sickening blows of the truncheons against the man's body, followed by his cursing and helpless crying out. Then, temporarily silenced, he was dragged out of his cell and along the corridor to the stairs at the far end.

'Bastards!' Morrissey bawled as they dragged his friend along the corridor and down the stairs.

'Iraqi shits!' Townsend added.

'You men be quiet!' Phillips called out to them. 'That won't help Spooner.'

It didn't help them either. Within seconds of those outbursts, the Iraqi guard was back, shrieking hysterical warnings through the hatches. Less than a minute later, while the guard was still shrieking, more soldiers, all bawling, raced into the corridor, divided into separate groups, opened the cell doors of the SAS men.

Alice heard the bawling soldiers, the cursing and gasping of the victims, the repeated, sickening sounds of rubber truncheons thudding into human flesh. She closed her eyes and covered her ears with her hands, trying to blot it all out.

The awareness that their suffering was her reprieve made her feel deeply guilty.

CHAPTER TWELVE

Throughout their long night in the OP, the men of the rescue team divided their time between watching the HAS gates with the aid of their night-vision sights and eyeballing the spectacular Coalition air attacks on Baghdad. While the Iraqi radar systems were being jammed by US Navy EA-6 Prowlers and USAF EF-111S Ravens, the awesome aerial blitzkrieg against Baghdad was conducted with a combination of Tomahawk cruise missiles, all on pre-programmed flight paths, fired from ships and submarines anchored in the Gulf; 2,000-pound precision-guided 'smart' bombs fired from radar-invisible Stealth F-117 night fighter aircraft, HARM rockets fired by the Wild Weasels, or F-4Gs, and relentless carpet bombing by giant B-52 bombers, F-14, F-15, F-16 and F-18 fighter-bombers; Tornados, Harriers, Phantoms, British and French Jaguars and AV-8B jump-jets.

From their position on the high ridge overlooking the city, the SAS rescue team could clearly see the glittering web of lights, which no one had thought to turn off, the brilliantly illuminated minarets and domes of the Kadhimiya mosque, the flame, smoke and lines of purple tracery being fired by the Triple-A anti-aircraft guns on the rooftops of skyscrapers, and even the Ottoman building known as the Abbassid Palace but used by the Iraqi Defence Ministry and recently struck twice by cruise missiles. They could also see laser-guided bombs skimming low over the rooftops, often below rooftop level, before slamming with awesome precision into doorways, windows, ventilation shafts, bridges, and gas and oil refineries, to explode into balls of vivid fire and more billowing smoke.

'Just look at 'em go,' Geordie said, as he and Collinson stood at the viewing hole of the OP, watching cruise missiles flying just above the rooftops of the city, following the terrain below, then disappearing below rooftop level as they ploughed into their targets to create more spectacular explosions, followed by immense showers of boiling smoke and bright crimson sparks. 'Those fucking rockets are more precise than piloted aircraft.'

'I used to read about things like that in science-fiction books,' Roy replied, 'but I never thought I'd see it in my own lifetime. It's something to see, right?'

'It sure is,' Geordie said.

'Sure, it's beautiful,' Paddy said, crawling up to join them at the viewing hole. 'It's just like in the movies.'

'Beautiful from here,' Geordie said, 'but hell on earth down there.'

'Poor bastards,' Paddy said in genuine commiseration. 'And I wouldn't like to be those pilots, either. I wouldn't like to fly in there. Look! There goes another one.'

High above the city, above the undeniably beautiful, almost surrealistic fireworks display of modern aerial warfare, the sky was webbed with the smoke plumes of the Iraqi's radar-guided SAM missiles and, with dreadful consistency, the balls of fire formed by exploding enemy and Coalition aircraft, which rained down their hellish debris on the burning, smouldering city.

'They're mostly Iraqi casualties,' Roy said as the three of

them watched another plane turn into a ball of fire, then break apart and fall in pieces to the rooftops. 'Those Triple As can't even see our Stealth fighters. That's why they call them ghost planes.'

'Fuckin' amazing,' Paddy said.

All in all, the Coalition air raids formed an overwhelming spectacle of sight and sound that continued throughout the night while the men of the rescue team either caught up on lost sleep or went about their various tasks: taking turns on watch, eyeballing and photographing the HAS gates and surrounding desert, keeping track of enemy troop movements on the MSR and dirt tracks leading off it, making their individual entries into logbooks, and repeatedly cleaning and checking their weapons. When not sleeping, they had no time to be idle.

By the afternoon of the following day, when the aerial blitzkrieg had ceased for another twelve hours, leaving only the smouldering skyscrapers and the vast, sunscorched desert all around them, the rescue team had seen a lot of military traffic passing both ways on the MSR below the ridge, including mobile Scud launchers heading away from the underground complex into the desert. What they also saw on the MSR were mobile Scud decoys, constructed in East Germany, complete with their own crews, only there to draw the fire of Coalition aircraft and encourage the pilots to submit false 'kill' reports.

'Clever sonsofbitches,' Wild Bill Kowalski said as he knelt beside Kilroy at the viewing hole of the OP, looking down on the HAS gates through his black-painted binoculars while Kilroy took photographs with the Nikon. He had been doing this all night with the aid of the Minimodulux image intensifier, but now, in the brilliant light of the afternoon, he no longer needed that. 'Not that I'd want to be one of the poor sonsofbitches on those decoys. They must get shot all to hell.'

'*We* certainly shoot them all to hell,' Kilroy replied. 'I don't know about your lot.'

Wild Bill grinned. 'We do OK, pal.'

Given the benefit of their panoramic view, they were able to see that the Scud mobile launchers and decoys travelled only a short distance along the MSR leading away from the complex, then turned off it to use the old dirt tracks crisscrossing the desert, thus avoiding the AWACS aircraft. The mobile launchers were surprisingly large – enormous, in fact – raised up on the backs of wheeled platforms towed by trucks, and invariably they were accompanied by trucks filled with Iraqi troops.

'They'd be pretty easy to take out, even from here,' Wild Bill said. 'Just hammer the mobiles with Stingers or MILANS while raking the troops with GPMGs. Piece of cake, if you ask me.'

'I'm not asking,' Kilroy said.

'Afraid to get your fingers burned?'

'No,' Williams interjected. 'It's nothing to do with burnt fingers. It's to do with the fact that we're not here to take out either Scud launchers or decoys, but to hijack a couple of troop trucks and get into that complex.'

'So when do we do it?' Wild Bill asked. 'Have you worked out the scam?'

'Yes,' Williams replied. Putting the logbook aside, he turned around and pointed down through the viewing hole. 'We have a clear view for miles east and west, so what do you see?'

Wild Bill and Kilroy glanced in both directions and saw the tracks of troop trucks cutting fine lines in the flat plain. They also saw in the distance, also in both directions, Iraqi troop trucks forming irregular circles.

'I see Iraqi laagers,' Kilroy said.

'Watch patrols,' Wild Bill clarified.

'Right,' Williams said. 'The mobile Scuds and decoys disappear over the horizon, obviously heading across the border to Scud Alley and Scud Boulevard, but the troop trucks only go out about twenty miles from the outskirts of the city to form watch patrols.'

'No argument there,' Wild Bill responded.

'Good,' Williams said. 'Because according to my notes, those watch teams are changed every four hours, which means that the ones out there should be returning to that underground complex about two hours from now – just when the sun sets.'

'That's so convenient.'

'It certainly is. What it means is that we can leave here an hour from now, neutralise one of those watch teams, take their trucks, then join the other watch-team trucks as they return to the complex at last light. Any arguments, gentlemen?'

'Not from me,' Kilroy said.

'I'm burning my ass off sitting here,' Wild Bill added, 'so I'm all set to go.'

'I'm so pleased,' Williams said. Resting on his knees, he surveyed the land below through his black-painted military binoculars. Putting the binoculars down, he jabbed his finger towards the west. 'There's an Iraqi laager of four trucks over there to the west,' he said. 'About five miles from the bottom of this ridge. They've hidden themselves in a dried-out wadi bed, which means we can approach them on foot without being seen and then attack from the top of the wadi. My suggestion, therefore, is that we keep the Pink Panthers hidden here and proceed on down there by foot. We leave the mortars behind – they're too heavy to hump that far – but we take a GPMG, the LAW and the Stinger SAM system. We'll also need the laser designator to pinpoint those HAS gates for our aircraft when we finally call them in.'

'That's some load to hump,' Will Bill said.

'Not for us,' Kilroy told him.

'When we reach the top of the wadi,' Williams continued before Wild Bill could retort to Kilroy's jibe, 'we take up attack positions and wait until the sun is practically down.

Just before last light, the Coalition air raids against Baghdad will commence again, making for a welcome distraction and a hell of a din. That's when we open fire on that Iraqi laager and, hopefully, dispatch all those men and capture their trucks. As five miles is still a long way to hike, I suggest we start right now.'

'Agreed,' Wild Bill said.

Turning aside, Williams told Paddy, Geordie and Roy what was happening and then ordered them to start demolishing the OP. The six men shared this task by first packing their personal kit back into their bergen rucksacks, then removing everything else from the OP and transferring the various items, including the bergens, to one or other of the two camouflaged Pink Panthers. The weapons required for the planned attack were stacked up outside the OP; the OP was then dismantled and the canvas rolled up and placed in one of the vehicles. When this was done, the rectangular hole was filled in and the topsoil raked over. Finally, the two Pink Panthers were covered again with camouflaged canvas, in turn sprinkled with sand and gravel, rendering the vehicles virtually invisible from the air. The men then shared out the various components of the heavy weapons, picked up their personal weapons and prepared to move out.

'Hallelujah,' Wild Bill said to Kilroy, belting the FIM-92A Stinger SAM system across his broad shoulders and picking up his Heckler & Koch MP5 sub-machine gun. 'Let's go and rescue your buddies at last.'

'*And* your girlfriend,' Kilroy emphasised.

'I've never met her before,' Wild Bill said with a cocky grin, 'but I'm sure she's a sweetheart.'

'Sweethearts shouldn't fight wars,' Kilroy said. 'They should stay at home and in their kitchens.'

'That's a sexist remark, Sergeant Kilroy. Some of *our* sweethearts fight like wild cats and fly as if born with wings. You don't *like* girls, or what?'

'I like 'em OK when they're in their place,' Kilroy replied, adjusting the LAW 80 anti-tank weapon on his back and simultaneously checking his SLR. 'I just happen to think their place is in the home – not fighting wars.'

'Some do OK at that,' Wild Bill said.

'Not many,' Kilroy insisted. 'They're just not cut out for it. They aren't as strong as men, they're far too emotional, and they tend to be highly unpredictable. Women are born to raise kids; they're not made to be soldiers.'

Wild Bill grinned. 'If you said that in America, Sergeant Kilroy, you'd be lynched from the nearest tree.'

Kilroy didn't return the grin. 'You fucking Yanks and your political correctness,' he said. 'I couldn't live with that shit. Now I've got to go and rescue a *woman* and get her back in one piece. I don't like the thought of it.'

Wild Bill shook his head from side to side as if he couldn't believe his own ears. 'Oh, boy!' he exclaimed. 'We've got a real live wire here.' He grinned again at Kilroy. 'Well, Sarge, you can relax, 'cause *I'm* the one who's rescuing that woman and bringing her back. She's off your hands, buddy.'

'I hope so,' Kilroy said.

'Are you men all ready to move out?' Williams asked.

'Yes, boss!' came the collective reply.

Williams raised and lowered his right hand. 'Move out,' he said.

Heavily burdened with weapons and ammunition, they marched down the sloping side of the ridge as the sun started sinking beyond the western horizon, casting great shadows over the plain below and, as they noticed, over the Iraqi laager in the distance. They marched in single file with Kilroy out front on point, Williams behind him as patrol commander, Geordie bringing up the rear as Tailend Charlie, and the other three in the middle, protecting Roy Collinson, humping the PRC 319 radio system. It was not an easy hike. The heat was still fierce and the steep slope was covered with loose gravel and large stones that could trip the unwary or break ankles. Eventually, however, they reached the flat plain where the Iraqi laager, in the deep wadi, disappeared from view and the heat, in the shadows cast by the sinking sun, was greatly diminished. As they moved across the plain, taking their sense of direction from the sun on the horizon, they kept their eyes peeled for signs of enemy patrols, but luckily nothing materialised until, an hour later, they were approaching the wadi. Once there, the five men behind Kilroy lay belly down on the ground while he advanced cautiously, at the half-crouch, to the rim of the wadi. Then he, too, went down on his belly to crawl forward and look down on the enemy laager. Obviously satisfied, he raised his right hand and waved it to and fro, indicating that the rest of the men could advance and join him. When they did so, they spread out along the rim of the wadi and cautiously looked over it.

The four enemy trucks were forming a rough semicircle, a defensive laager, at the bottom of the wadi, hardly more than fifty yards away. Most of the troops were seated around the campfire in the middle, scooping couscous up from steaming bowls, while a couple lethargically kept watch from where they were perched on the bonnets of two of the trucks, their Kalashnikovs lying across their thighs.

'No men outside the laager,' Williams whispered. 'None out on point.'

'Fucking dumb,' Kilroy said.

Williams turned to Wild Bill. 'How accurate are you with that Stinger?'

'Is that a serious question, Captain?'

Williams smiled. 'Can you land a couple of rockets right in the middle of those men around the campfire?'

'Bull's eye guaranteed,' Wild Bill said and immediately started unbelting the Stinger from his back.

Williams turned to Paddy, who was carrying the HEAT

rockets for the Stinger. 'You keep him well supplied, Paddy,' he said, 'and don't stop until I give the signal.'

'Right, boss,' Paddy said and started removing the HEAT rockets from his satchel.

'I want you, Kilroy,' Williams continued, 'to take out those two trucks with the LAW – the ones those men on watch are sitting upon. And you, Corporal Welsh and Trooper Collinson, will rake the whole area with the GPMG until there isn't a soul left standing. You'll all commence firing simultaneously at my hand signal. OK, get ready.'

While Roy and Geordie between them set up the L7A2 general purpose machine gun, Paddy slithered up beside Wild Bill to pass him the HEAT rockets and Kilroy loaded his LAW 80 anti-tank weapon with a 94mm missile, then placed more missiles on the ground beside him. As they were preparing for the assault, the sun started sinking beyond the enemy laager, a great ball of crimson lava spreading along the darkening horizon, and the first of a mighty armada of Coalition aircraft – Stealth fighters, support aircraft and B-52 heavy bombers – was winging overhead to commence the nightly air raid. Williams raised his right hand and waited until the first explosions were heard and seen from the city. Then he dropped his hand.

Instantly, the silence was shattered by the combined bedlam of the rescue team's weapons. The HEAT rocket from Wild Bill's Stinger and the 94mm missile from Kilroy's LAW 80 shot on plumes of smoke towards the laager as Roy and Geordie opened up with their GPMG, Roy feeding in the belt while Geordie fired the weapon. The HEAT rocket exploded in the midst of the men around the campfire, blowing the fire apart and engulfing the men nearest to it in a ball of vivid whitish-yellow fire. The missile from Kilroy's LAW 80 then smashed through the windscreen of the truck, blew the driver's cabin apart, and hurled the Iraqi guard off the hood. Even as he sailed through the air like a rag doll, his clothes on fire, trailing smoke, the fusillade of bullets from the GPMG was turning the clearing between the trucks into a convulsion of spitting soil and sand, cutting down the Iraqis who were desperately trying to run for cover.

Paddy dropped another HEAT rocket into Wild Bill's Stinger and the American fired again as some of the Iraqis, hiding behind the untouched trucks, fired back with semi-automatic rifles. The HEAT shell exploded just short of the first one, blowing more Iraqis into the air on billowing clouds of smoke as Kilroy fired a LAW 80 missile at the truck the second guard was sitting upon. This time the missile tore into the covered rear of the truck, blowing the sides off, setting fire to the shredded canvas, and rocking the vehicle so hard that the guard was thrown from the hood with his weapon flying out of his hands. Having picked himself off the ground, the guard had just started running towards his fallen weapon when Kilroy lowered the LAW 80, picked up his SLR and fired a short, deadly burst. The running man was punched backwards, throwing his hands above his head, then staggered in a circle of spitting soil and collapsed in a cloud of dust. Kilroy instantly raised the LAW 80 again, reloaded it and fired another missile into the centre of the clearing just as a third rocket from Wild Bill's Stinger exploded there, also. The combined explosions created a mushroom of boiling sand that engulfed the Iraqis even as some of them were blown into the air.

As the boiling sand subsided to reveal many dead Iraqis littering the area around the exploded campfire, those remaining divided into two groups, one giving covering fire from behind the remaining two trucks, the others advancing at the crouch, firing on the move, and zigzagging up the lower slope of the wadi, darting from one boulder to another. Not wanting to damage the two untouched trucks, Wild Bill and Kilroy, obviously thinking alike, lowered their heavy weapons to the ground and, joined by Paddy, aimed a fusillade of fire at the advancing men while the GPMG continued to rake the clearing. Two of the advancing Iraqis were caught in that fusillade and became whirling dervishes in a pool of spitting sand and soil, then collapsed and were still. The others, now pinned down behind the rocks, continued firing uphill, as did those still hiding behind the untouched trucks.

Using hand signals, Williams indicated that he and Paddy would keep the men behind the rocks pinned down while Wild Bill and Kilroy circled around behind the laager and came up behind those hiding behind the trucks.

'Fucking A,' Wild Bill said.

Carrying only their personal weapons, he and Kilroy slithered away from the rim of the wadi until they were out of sight of the enemy. They then turned west and made their way at the crouch along the slope until they were approximately five hundred yards away. Making their way back up to the rim of the wadi, they looked along it and saw that the fire fight was still engaged, though the Iraqis on the lower slopes of the hill, realising that they could not advance any farther, were gradually making their way back to the laager, to join those sheltering behind the remaining trucks.

'When they rejoin the others,' Kilroy surmised, 'they'll probably try to get away in one of those trucks.'

'So let's stop 'em,' Wild Bill said.

Unseen by the frantically engaged Iraqis, they slithered down into the bed of the wadi, hugging the rocks, then made their way up and over the far side. Out of sight of the enemy, they made their way along the slope until they were parallel to the enemy laager, where the roaring of a machine gun had been added to the relentless firing of semi-automatic weapons. Going belly down again, Kilroy and Wild Bill slithered up to the rim of the wadi and gazed down at the men in the laager. The two trucks hit by the HEAT rockets and LAW 80 missiles were blazing and pouring black oily smoke. Their tyres were melting and sinking into the sand. One of the dead guards was lying face down on the sand, the remains of his clothing still burning. The other guard, though not on fire, was equally motionless, and more dead littered the ground around blackened shell holes. The last of the men who had retreated from the lower slope of the wadi were practically throwing themselves back into the laager while their comrades, bunched up behind the two remaining trucks, continued firing up the slope at the SAS men. A machine gun had been mounted on a tripod and was being fired by a two-man crew from its protected position behind a two-foot-high rock between the two trucks. There were eight Iraqis left and all had their backs to Wild Bill and Kilroy.

'Sitting ducks,' Wild Bill said.

'But close to the trucks,' Kilroy reminded him, 'and we can't hit the trucks. Do you think you can manage to dispatch them without doing that?'

'Can pigs shit? Can birds fly?'

'You take the four behind the left-hand truck. I'll take the others. Don't make any mistakes.'

'Worry about yourself, Kilroy.'

Wild Bill aimed his Heckler & Koch MP5 at the men behind the left-hand truck while Kilroy aimed his SLR at those behind the other truck. Both men fired simultaneously, using short, precise bursts, moving their weapons from left to right, picking off the Iraqis one after the other and as quickly as possible. Four were hit in the back and punched forward into the trucks; another two were just turning around to fire back when they were caught in the third bursts and smashed backwards into the dirt; and the remaining two had just managed to turn all the way round and fire a couple of shots before they, too, were cut down. They both jerked epileptically in a convulsion of spitting sand, then dropped their weapons and crashed to the ground.

Wild Bill and Kilroy kept firing for a short period, raking the whole group of eight prone men and stopping only when they were sure that they were dead. Even then, they waited for another few seconds, checking for any signs of movement. Seeing none, Kilroy carefully stood up to slowly raise and lower his right hand. At that signal, the SAS team behind the rim of the opposite slope stood up, holding their weapons at the ready, and advanced very carefully down the hill.

Moving with equal care and spreading well out, Kilroy and Wild Bill moved down the slope, towards the pall of smoke that was drifting from the two blazing trucks to mingle with subsiding clouds of sand. By the time they reached the laager, the sand had subsided and they could clearly see the devastation wreaked by their gunfire, with dead bodies and black shell holes littering the ground around the exploded campfire. As they entered the laager, choking slightly in the thinning smoke, Williams led the others into the opposite side of the clearing and indicated with a hand signal that the men should spread out to check if any Iraqis were still alive. Wild Bill and Kilroy did the same while Williams checked that the two remaining lorries were intact and in working order.

Moving amongst the fallen Iraqis, nudging them gently, carefully, with his booted foot, Wild Bill, hard as nails, was pleased to note that the ones he checked were all dead. Suddenly, however, the silence was broken by the short, savage burst of an SLR.

Jerking his head around, Wild Bill saw Kilroy standing with his legs spread above the body of an Iraqi who was lying face down on the ground and must have been still alive when Kilroy checked him. Kilroy's SLR was pointing at the Iraqi's back and tendrils of smoke were drifting out of the barrel. Looking up, his face absolutely unreadable, Kilroy caught Wild Bill's eye.

'No choice,' Kilroy said.

Wild Bill stared steadily at him for a moment, slightly shocked but knowing what Kilroy meant.

Wounded men could still talk.

'Right,' Wild Bill said. 'No sweat.'

CHAPTER THIRTEEN

The bombing of Baghdad was intensifying every evening and could be heard quite clearly in Alice's cell. Familiarity had taught her to distinguish between the high, keening wail of the incoming Tomahawk cruise missiles and the louder wailing of the air-raid sirens, the bass throbbing of the giant B-52 bombers, the harsh chatter of Triple A anti-aircraft guns, the exploding of rockets and aircraft in the sky, and the crashing of falling debris all around the interrogation centre. Alice knew that out there, beyond the walls of her prison, the city was burning and smouldering, with Iraqi citizens huddling up fearfully in their shelters and the anti-aircraft gunners firing their Triple As from the rooftops; and while she knew it was necessary, while she approved of it in principle, she also lived with the fear that sooner or later one of the cruise missiles or 2,000-pound bombs could destroy the interrogation centre and her with it. That knowledge and the appalling, relentless noise combined to strip her nerves bare. She had to fight to control herself.

Don't give in, she often thought to herself in the midst of an air raid. Don't let it get to you. Don't panic and don't let those bastards out there see that you're frightened. You're a woman and we're stronger than men. Hold on to that. *Cling* to it.

That resolve was not broken but it was constantly threatened by what was happening to the men in the cells on both sides of her. If anything, the Coalition air raids appeared to intensify the rage and fear of the Iraqi guards, making them take out their frustrations on the male prisoners. Alice was beginning to be tormented by the knowledge that each time she heard the guards running along the corridor, bawling excitedly as usual, she shrank into herself with dread and then helplessly dissolved into relief when they entered the cells of the SAS men, who now excited their attention more than she did.

According to whispered conversations with Major Phillips in the next cell, none of the SAS men had been overtly tortured so far during the interrogations, though all of them had been badly beaten and torture was almost certainly on the way. The beatings in the cells, however, were particularly bad and made dreadful for Alice because she could clearly hear it all and, even worse, was aware that the Iraqis' hatred for the SAS men was buying her a reprieve. She sympathised desperately with the men being beaten, but she could not help being flooded with relief when the bawling Iraqi guards ignored her cell. The guilt she felt was considerable.

Usually, when the noisy beatings were going on in the adjoining cells, with the Iraqi guards bawling insults and their victims shouting back defiantly, Alice would huddle up against the wall, sitting on her squalid mattress, then close her eyes and cover her ears with her hands, trying to blot out the noise. She also tried to distract herself from the grim reality of her situation by recalling her life at home with her family before she left to enter the Academy. Her recollections were of happy days, innocent pleasures, simple fun: barbecues in the back yard of their white-painted house, evenings spent with teenage friends in a bowling alley in Des Moines, swopping romantic secrets with her sister, teasing her brother about his girlfriends, nervously necking at the movies with her own first dates, baking bread and cookies with her mother in their flower-filled kitchen, travelling around the county with her father when he sold his farming products and told her about his early years in the Air Force, never sounding less than wistful when he did so. She had been an overprotected child, well looked after by both parents, and it was only when she had gone to the Academy that everything had changed. In her lonely cell, she tried to forget that, concentrating on earlier days, travelling in her mind back to her childhood when the days all seemed summery. She used those memories to sustain her in misery and block out her dread.

The fear was always there when the guards beat up the SAS men, their truncheons thudding into ribcages, their hands slapping brutally and noisily, their boots kicking and trampling. Those sounds sickened Alice, making her stomach constrict, but she was heartened by the defiance of the British soldiers and was compelled to admire them. Phillips, in particular, who often whispered to her through the wall, made her think of Dave, the man she had loved, who had been as courageous and decent as the man next door seemed to be when he spoke to her.

'Are you all right?' he would whisper.

'Yes,' she would reply.

'Try not to be too disheartened, Alice. Things could be much worse.'

'Do you think we'll get out, Major?'

'This war will be over quickly. If we manage to survive until it ends, then we'll probably get out.'

'Do you think we'll survive that long? That they won't kill us first?'

'I think the chances are high that they'll want to use you, rather than kill you. You're a woman and that makes a big difference in political terms.'

'You give me hope, Major.'

'I'm glad to hear that, Alice.'

'You say they'd rather use *me* than kill me. That's reassuring, Major. But what about you and your men? You've avoided that subject.'

'It's a subject best not discussed, Alice. I feel it's best to be positive. I'm very hopeful that you're going to survive and that makes me feel better. You'll be fine. You'll survive this.'

Alice knew, as did Phillips, that Saddam Hussein had ordered all captured SAS men to be tortured and killed. She also knew that Phillips, obviously an English gentleman, was avoiding the subject because he thought it might upset her. She admired him for that, for his courage and decency, and was reminded by it, as Dave Bamberg had reminded her, that not all men were bad. She badly needed that reminder and was glad to be given it.

'Thanks, Major,' she whispered through the wall. 'Thanks a hell of a lot.'

'Not at all,' Phillips said.

Often, usually at nights when the silence was broken by the groans of tortured Iraqi civilians in cells farther along the corridor or the soft whisperings of the ever-defiant SAS men on either side of her, communicating through the stone walls, Alice was reminded of other whisperings, her own tormented groaning, those younger, less admirable men who had come in the darkness, first quietly, then noisily, to torment her and fill her with fear and shame. They had almost destroyed her faith in men, made her fearful of their nature, and even now, when she thought back on that time, she was consumed with deep hatred. She still possessed that hatred, the shock of her disillusionment, and only lost it when she thought of Dave and how much she had loved him. He had treated her with respect, as her father had done, and as Major Phillips was doing here, but she still felt that such men were rare and that most were her enemy.

The SAS are the same, she thought. All men in a male world. Major Phillips, whose face I've yet to see, is probably better than most. He must be a rare bird.

Not so rare, she knew, were the guards who did the beating and, during her interrogations, stared at her with eyes grown too large. During that last interrogation, when they had thrown her over that butcher's block of a table to commence her first whipping, she had felt that it would be merely the prelude to sexual assault. They all wanted their share of her, would queue up to have her, and once started would not be inclined to stop until they had totally wrecked her. She had been reprieved at the last minute by the arrival of the SAS, but she knew that sooner or later, when the Iraqis had finished with those unfortunates, they would come back for her . . . and when they did, they would go a lot farther than they had done before.

God help me, she thought.

This particular evening, as she thought of the sun setting unseen outside and heard the distant rumblings of approaching Coalition aircraft, arriving to commence their nightly air raid on Baghdad, she was filled with all the longing of a woman who had not physically known the man she loved and desperately wanted to do so. She had known a few men that way, though not with any great satisfaction. They had been adolescents, not mature men, making awkward love to her in high school and university, at the movies, in the back of cars, none experienced enough to please her – and now she yearned to be touched by Dave Bamberg and know what it felt like. She wanted only him, those brown eyes gazing upon her, his hands, which she had held with such tenderness, awakening her body. But Dave was dead and gone. He would not be coming back. Instead, she would be brutally violated by men who despised her. She dreaded the thought, recalling those nights at the Academy, understanding that the humiliation and shame could be much worse than pain.

Please, Dave, come back to me.

Alice wept. The tears rolled down her cheeks and dripped onto her cotton gown as the air-raid sirens wailed and the Iraqis' Triple A anti-aircraft guns roared from the rooftops. Alice heard a different wailing – the high-pitched, keening cry of the incoming cruise missiles – and her tears fell as the missiles exploded not too far away. She wept for herself, for the civilians dying outside, for the SAS men in the cells beside her, who might soon be dead. She was frightened yet filled with yearning, wanting Dave, and in knowing what might soon befall her she thought that death might be preferable. She heard a rumbling from outside, B-52s flying overhead, and when their bombs began exploding all around the building, she prayed for one to come closer.

Get it over and done with, she thought. Before those bastards come for me. Let it all end tonight.

Letting the tears roll down her cheeks, not bothering to wipe them off, she raised her forehead from her knees and gazed up at the ceiling, drawn by the rumbling of the bombers and wanting to see them. They were almost overhead, and she silently prayed that one of those bombs would drop right through the ceiling.

Instead, she heard another sound, now familiar and dreaded: the pounding of booted feet in the corridor and the bawling of angry men. A cell door was dragged open. Spooner started cursing. The Iraqi soldiers bawled even more hysterically and started using their truncheons. Spooner bawled back. The truncheons hammered him into silence. Morrissey and Townsend started shouting obscenities as Spooner was dragged from his cell and back along the corridor. The steel door was left open. Spooner was dragged down the stairs. The Iraqi guard came hurrying along the corridor to scream threats through the hatches.

'Quiet, men,' Phillips said when the other two SAS soldiers shouted back at the guard. 'You won't help Spooner that way. You'll just make matters worse.'

The Iraqi guard kept screaming. The SAS men fell silent. The bombs continued as the guard marched away. Alice sat there on her mattress. She covered her ears with her hands. She remained that way for a long time, shedding tears, praying for death, hearing the explosions all around her, in the city, and willing them closer.

She was jerked out of her reverie by a short burst of gunfire that came from the top of the stairs at the end of the corridor. It was followed by more bawling outside, though this time in English.

Her cell door was dragged open.

CHAPTER FOURTEEN

Darkness was falling on the laager and the Coalition air raid on Baghdad was just beginning when the men of the rescue team, ignoring the dead Iraqis sprawled in the sand all around them, hurriedly darkened the exposed parts of their skin by applying a mixture of coffee, lamp-black, iodine and potassium permanganate. As this basic mixture could be lightened or darkened as required, they checked each other to ensure that the resultant tint had made their skin colouring similar to that of the Iraqis. With the darkening of their faces, hands and wrists completed, they turned their attention to the dead soldiers, searching among them for those whose pullovers were not too visibly torn by bullet holes, stripping them off, putting them on over their own desert shirts, then placing the black Iraqi Army berets on their own heads. Finally, they covered most of their faces with the *shemaghs*, leaving only their darkened foreheads and eyes exposed above the fluttering veils.

'Right,' Williams said when the men had completed their tasks and were cleaning and oiling their weapons yet again. 'That air raid will continue most of the night and offer plenty of distraction when the rescue truck enters the city. First, though, we have to encourage the Iraqis to call in their watch patrols and open those HAS doors to let them in. Once the doors open, I'm going to set a precise timing for the second truck's entrance into the complex, allowing ten minutes to reach the elevator.'

'That's cutting it pretty close,' Wild Bill said.

'Then don't be slow.'

Using the SATCOM system, he contacted HQ in Riyadh, gave the exact location of the HAS doors and arranged to have them bombed twice: an initial attack, commencing immediately, to encourage the Iraqis to call in their watch patrols and open the HAS doors; and another attack to commence ten minutes after his second message was received and designed to distract the Iraqis inside the complex just as Kilroy and his men were entering the interrogation centre. The same aircraft would be used for both attacks and would circle over the area until the second message was received, enabling the pilots to launch the second attack almost instantly.

Knowing that his message would be relayed from HQ in Riyadh to the US Tactical Aircraft Control, from there to an AWACS aircraft, and then on to an F-15E already in the air, Williams checked his wristwatch. Satisfied that the timing was right, he told Kilroy to pinpoint the HAS doors with the laser designator, a device which 'illuminates' the target with a laser beam, enabling it to be detected by the seekers inside laser-guided bombs.

Mounting the large, camera-like laser designator on a tripod and kneeling behind it, Kilroy aimed the device at the doors, but did not turn it on. As he waited for the SATCOM system to announce the arrival of the USAF F-15Es, the other men coordinated their wristwatches, then divided into their two separate groups, with Geordie and Roy Collinson taking the truck that would drive into Baghdad under the command of Captain Williams. Wild Bill and Paddy knelt beside Kilroy, as did Williams, and were still beside him when, about thirty minutes later – as the spectacular air raid was still engaged, with purple tracers crisscrossing in the sky and the dark sky coloured with yellow flames and black smoke – the SATCOM system announced the imminent arrival of the AWACS command F-15Es.

Instantly, Kilroy activated the laser designator and 'illuminated', or 'painted', the distant HAS doors with a laser beam. The designator also incorporated a laser rangefinder that would calculate the distance from the designator to the HAS doors by the delay between the transmission of the beam and the reception of laser radiation reflected back from them. When the F-15Es flew down towards the target, streaking across the starlit sky, the laser radiation received by the silicon detector in the seeker heads of their GBU-10 Paveway II laser-guided bombs enabled the guidance computer to steer the bombs towards the target with remarkable accuracy.

The device obviously worked. When the two F-15Es released their laser-guided Paveways just ahead of the grid location received through the SATCOM system, the bombs, honing in on the intense spot of light, were directed with pinpoint accuracy and exploded into vivid balls of fire and violently billowing clouds of sand and smoke. The two F-15Es raced up and away, then returned for another attack, swooping in low and releasing their laser-guided bombs to cause more spectacular explosions of vivid white flame and boiling clouds of sand and black smoke.

The explosions did not damage the HAS doors, but they weren't really meant to. Instead, once they had drawn the Iraqis' attention to the fact that they were being attacked, the F-15Es, again guided to their targets by Williams on the SATCOM system, flew off in opposite directions to attack the watch patrols in the surrounding area, their aim being to force them back to the underground complex, rather than actually destroy them. This worked as well. Within minutes, even as the billowing dust was settling down in front of the HAS gates, the roar of explosions was heard, first from east and west, then, shortly after, from north and south, and the darkness was erratically illuminated by the flaring light and boiling black clouds of distant explosions. Minutes later, while the explosions were continuing, the trucks of the Iraqi watch teams being 'attacked' started racing in towards the complex from all directions. As they came in sight of the complex, the immense HAS doors started opening to receive them.

'Let's go!' Williams snapped, standing upright as Kilroy began removing the laser designator from its tripod. Williams checked his wristwatch, then looked at Wild Bill and Kilroy. 'You have exactly ten minutes to get from here to Loading Bay Ten inside that complex. You have no more than another ten minutes in which to enter the interrogation centre, dispatch the guards, and get those prisoners out to the front of the building where, if things go OK with us, we'll be waiting to pick you up. Good luck to all of you.'

'Same to you, boss,' Kilroy said.

'I second that,' Wild Bill said.

As Williams clambered up into the driving seat of the Iraqi troop truck, where Geordie and Roy were already seated, both looking convincingly like Iraqi Army troops, Kilroy humped the laser designator onto the floor of the driver's cabin of the second truck and told Wild Bill and Paddy to get in. Kilroy was slamming the door closed when Williams took off in the other truck, bumping across the flat, dark plain, away from the HAS doors, heading for the six-lane highway that led into downtown Baghdad, which was still being hammered. Williams's truck was already being swallowed up by the darkness when Kilroy turned on the ignition of his truck, slipped it into gear and then headed for the MSR that terminated at the opening HAS gates.

'We're just in time,' Wild Bill said. 'The first trucks of those Iraqi watch patrols are already entering the complex.'

'The others are still pretty far out,' Kilroy replied, 'so we should be OK. With luck, we'll be in the middle of the column and get in undetected.'

Glad to have the *shemagh* protecting his nose and mouth as well as disguising his features, he glanced through the dust billowing up outside the truck and saw the trucks of the Iraqi watch teams trundling in from all directions to converge on the MSR leading straight to the HAS gates. Staring straight ahead, he saw what at first appeared to be a great rectangle of vivid white light in the distance, growing wider as the immense HAS gates continued to open. A truck entering that rectangle of light was briefly silhouetted by it, then its shape was distorted, then it moved on and disappeared inside. Gradually, as Kilroy drove closer to the gates, he caught a glimpse of what was inside: silhouetted figures moving to and fro, tall dark shapes that were probably piles of crates, black lines that he assumed were the outlines of the steel-railed walkways running back into the complex and vanishing beyond the light haze.

'Christ!' Paddy softly exclaimed. 'It really *is* enormous!'

'It sure is,' Wild Bill said. 'According to our maps, it spreads out for fucking miles under the city. We could easily get lost in there.'

'Not if we stick to the main road,' Kilroy told him, 'and stop at Loading Bay Ten. All the loading bays are located on both sides of the main road before it starts branching off in all directions under the city. If we're not spotted as we drive along that road, we won't miss the loading bay.'

'Let's hope you're right,' Wild Bill said.

Heading obliquely across the dark plain, towards the MSR, Kilroy saw the spectacular fireworks display over Baghdad. Glancing up, he saw formations of B-52 heavy bombers, blotting out the stars, protected top and bottom by a variety of British, French and US jet fighters. Lowering his gaze to the desert plain, he saw the trucks of the Iraqi watch teams coming in from all directions to converge on the

MSR, forming a column heading towards the open HAS gates.

As Kilroy drove towards that column, preparing to slip into the middle of it, Wild Bill removed the safety catch of his Heckler & Koch MP5. Paddy did the same. Then both men instinctively checked that the *shemaghs* were securely tied around their faces, exposing only their tinted foreheads and the area around their eyes.

Approaching close to the Iraqi trucks on the MSR, Kilroy was relieved to note that they were spaced well apart and partially obscured in the clouds of sand being churned up by their tyres. Most of the trucks had now come in from the desert and Kilroy noted that he was joining the last of them and would therefore be close to the end of the column, rather than in the centre. Nevertheless, approaching the column obliquely, as the other trucks were doing, he turned into the lengthy space between two of the trucks, keeping the same space between himself and the truck in front as the column rumbled on towards the heavily guarded, brightly lit entrance.

Paddy let his breath out in a tense sigh.

'Here we go,' Wild Bill whispered.

There were, Kilroy judged, three or four trucks behind him, which placed him still well within the column. As the trucks ahead entered that white haze one by one, he noted with relief that the armed guards, standing at each side of the gates where the end of the MSR met the start of the road inside, were not stopping the trucks but merely glancing up at the men inside as they drove past.

Soon there were only three trucks in front of Kilroy.

Then two.

Then one.

Kilroy kept driving, not varying his speed, carefully keeping the same space between him and the truck up front, and suddenly found himself driving between the guards, into the brightly lit interior of the complex. As Wild Bill waved a tinted hand at the guards on his side, Kilroy merely nodded at those on his own side and followed the other truck, bumping from the rough surface of the MSR onto the smoother, tarmacked surface of the road inside the complex.

Suddenly he found himself surrounded by the high, slightly curving walls of an immense tunnel that seemed to run for miles ahead and had three walkways running along it on either side, one above the other. The walkways were illuminated by overhead lights and lined with steel doors that obviously led into the underground corridors and other areas of the complex. A great number of Iraqi soldiers were visible on the walkways, either standing guard with Kalashnikov semi-automatic rifles or entering and leaving by the many doors. The walls of the complex were obviously blast proof and the ceiling, also curved, was made of heavily reinforced slab concrete. The sides of the road were, indeed, lined with various loading bays, spread about half a mile apart, and the spaces between were filled with vehicles of all kinds and packing crates stacked high, one upon the other.

The HAS doors, he saw in his rear-view mirror, were closing behind the last truck.

As Kilroy kept driving, passing one loading bay after another, he saw with a sinking heart that though some of them were empty, Iraqi soldiers were working in others, either moving or unloading packing crates.

'Shit!' Wild Bill exclaimed, having seen this also.

'Be prepared,' Kilroy said.

The loading bays were identified with large, red-painted Arabic numbers. Though able to read the numbers, Kilroy carefully counted off the loading bays as he drove past them, knowing that to make a mistake would lead to failure and death.

There were many armed Iraqi troops at the sides of the

main road, some entering or emerging from the doors at floor level, others being marched along the footpaths on either side, yet others sitting in raised watchtowers, surveying the trucks as they passed. Though the eyes of the watchtower guards often glanced towards Kilroy's truck, they appeared to take no particular notice and Kilroy realised that the combination of darkened skin, Iraqi Army berets and *shemaghs* was working so far. The trucks were moving at about twenty miles an hour, so the guards couldn't see much.

He drove past Loading Bay Five, then Loading Bay Six.

The HAS doors, he noticed in his rear-view mirror, had now closed completely. Even as he saw this, he heard the thunderous roar of Paveway laser-guided bombs exploding outside.

Instantly, a lot of the Iraqi soldiers were galvanised into action and began running, bawling loudly at one another, along the main road.

'Good,' Kilroy whispered.

The trucks ahead, he noted, were continuing to drive straight along the road, heading for the parking lot at the very far end of it, under downtown Baghdad. This, he knew, could draw attention to his own truck when he turned off into Loading Bay Ten, though the bomb attack on the HAS entrance would cause a welcome distraction.

Tensing, he drove past Loading Bay Seven, which was occupied by Iraqi soldiers stripped to the waist and breaking open large packing crates.

Driving past Loading Bay Eight, he noticed with relief that it was empty.

Driving past Loading Bay Nine, he noticed with growing relief that it, too, was empty.

'Get ready,' he said.

Driving along that final stretch to Loading Bay Ten, he

passed a column of marching Iraqi troops, another watchtower and another great mountain of packing crates. Suddenly, as he passed the last of the packing crates, Loading Bay Ten came into sight.

Kilroy slowed down, pulled out of the column and drove into Loading Bay Ten.

Three Iraqi soldiers were sitting in the loading bay, just in front of the closed elevator doors, their Kalashnikovs lying across their outspread legs, their ears cocked to the sound of the bomb attack against the now distant HAS entrance.

Kilroy braked to a screeching halt.

Instantly, before the Iraqis could even rise to their feet, Wild Bill jumped out of his side of the truck and sprayed them with a short burst from his MP5. His bullets were already peppering the Iraqis and ricocheting off the walls of the loading bay when Paddy landed on the ground beside him and also started firing, hitting the last of the three men as the first two were punched off their chairs and slammed backwards into the closed doors of the elevator. Paddy's victim was spinning off his chair and falling towards the floor as Kilroy jumped down, turned his back to the others, and aimed his SLR at the road where Iraqi troops, their attention drawn by the gunfire, were already racing towards the loading bay, weapons at the ready.

Kilroy opened fire immediately, bowling over some of the troops and sending the others scurrying for cover. He continued firing, keeping the Iraqis pinned down, as Wild Bill hauled the bloodsoaked dead soldiers away from the elevator and Paddy, with a canvas bag slung over his shoulder and his SLR in his free hand, frantically punched the button to open the doors.

The elevator doors opened, showing an empty elevator, and Paddy immediately darted inside, followed by Wild Bill.

'Let's go!' Wild Bill bawled.

But Kilroy didn't immediately follow them in. Realising that the Iraqis advancing towards him would press the elevator button to stop it from ascending, he glanced left and right, then saw what looked like a drum of oil. After firing a final, sustained burst at the advancing Iraqis, which made them dive for cover behind some packing crates, he tipped the oil drum over and rolled it towards the open doors of the elevator. Jumping over it and turning around again, he backed towards the elevator, rolling the drum towards him with one hand as he did so. When the drum was about six feet from the elevator, he jumped in between Wild Bill and Paddy.

'Close the doors!' he bawled.

Paddy punched the button inside to close the doors and make the elevator ascend to the third floor. The doors started moving in towards each other. Kilroy waited until they were mere inches apart, giving him a narrow view of the oil drum and the Iraqi soldiers advancing upon it, then he fired a short burst from his SLR, peppering the drum with bullets and causing it to explode with a thunderous roar, forming a ball of flame that expanded in all directions, engulfing the advancing Iraqis and sweeping out to the elevator just as the doors closed.

'Jesus Christ!' Wild Bill exclaimed softly as tendrils of oily smoke curled about him and he scratched his singed eyebrows.

The elevator was ascending.

'It'll take them a few minutes to put that fire out,' Kilroy said. 'They won't be able to use the elevator until they do, which buys us some time.'

'They'll come around the front,' Wild Bill said.

'We have to get out before they get there.'

The elevator ascended through the first floor, then the second, then finally stopped at the third, which Kilroy prayed was the interrogation centre.

The doors opened.

Kilroy saw a square-shaped room.

Iraqi soldiers were staring straight at him, their eyes widening in disbelief.

CHAPTER FIFTEEN

Kilroy, Wild Bill and Paddy fired simultaneously, peppering the two Iraqi soldiers, who were standing right in front of them, and making them jerk backwards and collapse while other bullets ricocheted noisily off the walls. The soldiers were still collapsing when Kilroy burst out of the elevator, his SLR at the ready, followed by Wild Bill and Paddy. A quick glance confirmed that the room was square, had closed doors in three of the walls, obviously leading to other rooms, and a short corridor that terminated at a flight of stairs – exactly as described in the SAS intelligence drawing of the interrogation centre.

A second soldier racing out of that corridor was dispatched by a short burst from Wild Bill's MP5 and he was still being punched backwards by the fusillade of bullets when Kilroy and Paddy each took separate rooms, kicking the doors open and, mindful that SAS prisoners might be present, hurled stun grenades, or 'flash-bangs', inside.

As Kilroy rushed into the room he had chosen, squinting against the sudden flaring of light caused by the flash-bang, he heard Paddy firing and the explosion of another flash-bang, where Wild Bill had tackled the third room. In a split-second glance Kilroy took in the whole room and saw a bunch of startled soldiers breaking away from a butcher's block of a table where they had been holding down a white man stripped to the waist, obviously in the process of being flogged. Kilroy fired a series of short, precise bursts at the soldiers, carefully avoiding the white man, as they tried to dive for cover, and managed to hit two of them as he saw, out of the corner of his eye, another Iraqi in civilian clothing leaning sideways in his chair behind the desk, pulling something from an open drawer.

'He's got a pistol!' the white man bawled.

Kilroy fired another short burst at the Iraqi soldier, who had dived behind the flogging table and was withdrawing a pistol from his holster. The soldier's head turned into a bloody pomegranate and he was falling backwards into the wall as Kilroy spun on the ball of his foot and fired another burst at the civilian behind the desk. The civilian was just straightening up, aiming a pistol at Kilroy, when the burst from Kilroy's SLR smashed his chest all to hell and he was thrown backwards into the wall, his shoulder and elbow shattering the glass of the window overlooking the courtyard before he slid to the floor.

Still scanning the room and seeing the white man straightening up, now recognisable as Sergeant Spooner, his back dripping blood from his flogging, Kilroy jerked his Browning 9mm High Power handgun from its holster and threw it across to him. Spooner caught it, cocked it and turned sideways, spreading his legs and holding the weapon two-handed, to fire a 'double tap' into the remaining Iraqi soldier who had dived behind the desk and was rising beside the dead civilian, aiming a Colt .45-inch handgun at Kilroy's head. The two bullets precisely entered the man's heart, making him drop his handgun and spin backwards, slamming into the wall and then sliding down it.

'Let's go!' Kilroy snapped, stepping out of the room, followed by Spooner, who was pulling his shirt back over his bloody body as they entered the main room.

By this time Wild Bill and Paddy had cleared the other two rooms and were taking up defensive positions, Paddy covering the front entrance to the building, overlooking the courtyard, and Wild Bill blocking off the corridor that led to the stairs. As Spooner buttoned up his shirt and waved cheerily, Paddy handed him the heavily packed canvas satchel that he'd been carrying all along.

'Put that elevator out of action,' Kilroy explained, 'to keep those fucking Iraqis from getting up here. I'll be back in a minute.'

As Kilroy stepped around Wild Bill and hurried along the corridor to the stairs, Spooner knelt by the open doors of the elevator and quickly opened the satchel at his feet. He removed a small pack of C4 plastic high explosive, a time fuze and a non-electric blasting cap, then quickly and expertly embedded the cap – a thin aluminium tube – in the explosive charge, attached the detonating cord, lit it and threw it into the elevator. Standing up, he pressed the button to close the elevator doors and then stepped well away from them. Twenty seconds later, the charge exploded inside the elevator, causing a muffled roaring that made the elevator visibly shake and causing smoke to seep out between the closed doors. The lights above the elevator doors blinked out and Spooner was satisfied.

'That fucker won't be going anywhere,' he said. 'They won't get up *that* way.'

With Paddy covering the front of the building and Wild Bill covering the corridor behind him, Kilroy hurried up the two flights of stairs to where the drawing of the complex had indicated that the cells were located. Briefed by intelligence that an armed guard was always placed at the top of the stairs, he held his SLR at the ready. He was nearing the top of the stairs when he heard the muffled explosion from the elevator below. Instantly, the legs of a wooden chair scraped on the floor just above him, indicating that the guard's attention had been distracted by the explosion. That guard appeared at the top of the stairs, already raising his weapon, and Kilroy fired at him on the move, taking him across the body and throwing him backwards onto the landing.

Racing up the last few steps, Kilroy confirmed with a quick glance that the man was dead, then he pressed himself against the wall by the chair and tentatively stuck his head out to glance into the corridor running alongside the cells. As he was doing so, Spooner ran up the stairs behind him, holding his Browning High Power at the ready. Kilroy saw that the corridor was empty and he was just stepping into it as Spooner knelt beside the dead man and unclipped the cell keys from his belt. Straightening up, he joined Kilroy in the corridor, shouting, 'They're in the first five cells!'

'Get them out,' Kilroy said. Turning his back to the corridor, he kept the stairs covered as Spooner opened the first cell, bawling excitedly, 'SAS! All out!'

Ben Townsend hurried out of the first cell, blinking against the unexpected light and looking more than stunned to see Harry Spooner standing in front of him.

'Jesus!' Townsend exclaimed.

'Get down those fucking stairs,' Spooner told him. 'You've got a few friends down there.'

Townsend hurried along the corridor, grinned as he brushed past the grim-faced Sergeant Kilroy and hurried down the stairs as Spooner moved on to open the second cell. Major Phillips stepped out, said, 'Nice to see you, Sarge,' then followed Townsend down the stairs, nodding and smiling at Kilroy as he passed.

Spooner moved along to the next cell. When he opened it, he saw a young woman with short-cropped blonde hair and blood-smeared lips, wearing a filthy Arab *dish-disha* and sitting upright on a torn, stained mattress, her bare feet surrounded by cockroaches.

'SAS!' Spooner bawled again. 'Out! Get down the stairs!' The girl looked at him in a daze, as if not comprehending, so Spooner stepped into the cell to grab her by the wrist and jerk her to her feet. Instantly galvanised back to her senses, her face glowing with relief, she nodded vigorously and left the cell to follow the other two men down the stairs. Spooner then left the cell and moved on to open the next one. When Clive Morrissey stepped out, Spooner asked, 'Is there anyone in the other cells?'

'Only locals,' Morrissey replied.

'Then let's get the fuck out of here,' Spooner said.

Together they hurried back along the corridor to join Kilroy at the top of the stairs.

'That's the lot?' Kilroy asked.

'All done,' Spooner said.

'OK, let's go.'

The three men hurried down the two flights of stairs and found Wild Bill still covering the corridor while the five rescued prisoners, all in bare feet, including the girl, had gathered together in the main room.

'Any Iraqis likely to come from there?' Wild Bill asked, nodding to indicate the stairs and still keeping the corridor covered.

'No,' Kilroy replied, brushing past him to enter the main room. 'There was only one guard.'

Satisfied, Wild Bill followed Kilroy into the main room, where Kilroy shouted out to Paddy, still covering the front door, 'Any sign of anyone coming?'

'No,' Paddy replied. 'I don't think they heard the gunfire.'

'But the ones down below must be coming around the front by now,' Wild Bill said, 'so they'll get to that courtyard pretty soon.' He turned to the blood-smeared, blonde girl. 'Lieutenant Alice Davis?' he asked.

'Yeah,' the girl said.

'You stick with me,' Wild Bill told her.

'So how do we get out?' Paddy asked.

'That door leads to the stairs that take you down to the basement car lot,' Alice told them. 'They brought me in that way. You make your way to the far end of the car lot and emerge to the courtyard at ground level. There are armed guards at the gate of the courtyard, but that leads out to what sounded to me like a pretty busy part of Baghdad.'

'We know where it is,' Kilroy said, 'and we have a truck waiting. OK, let's go. Me and Master Sergeant Kowalski will lead. You people behind us. Trooper Magee bringing up the rear.'

'We don't have any weapons,' said Phillips. 'What about your Nine Millys?'

'Right, boss,' Kilroy said.

As Spooner already had Kilroy's Browning High Power, Paddy handed his to Phillips and Wild Bill gave his to Morrissey.

'What about us?' Alice asked.

Kilroy shrugged. 'That's all we've got.'

'At least give me a knife,' Townsend said. 'Otherwise I'll feel naked.'

Grinning, Paddy handed Townsend his Sykes Fairburn commando dagger.

'Me, too,' Alice said.

Kilroy stared steadily at her. 'You want a knife?' he asked.

'That's right,' Alice said. 'I want a knife. You think I can't use one?'

Kilroy shrugged and handed over his commando dagger, then said, 'Let's get going.'

With Kilroy and Wild Bill in the lead, they left the main room and made their way carefully down the stairs. Reaching the bottom without problems, they emerged in a large, gloomy basement car lot, filled with civilian cars, Iraqi Army jeeps and a lot of canvas-topped troop trucks.

Kilroy glanced enquiringly back over his shoulder at Alice and she jabbed her forefinger at the far end of the car lot, where a dim light indicated the exit door. Nodding in acknowledgement, Kilroy led their advance through the car lot, indicating with hand signals that those behind him should spread out and make their way forward by darting from one car to the next. They were about halfway along, spread well across the lot, when Kilroy saw an armed guard just ahead, leaning against a jeep, facing the other way and smoking a cigarette, his Kalashnikov rifle lying carelessly on the bonnet of the vehicle.

When Kilroy stopped, the others stopped also.

Automatically, Kilroy reached down for his commando dagger, then recalled that he had given it to Alice. Frustrated, he turned back to the others and was about to pick someone to dispatch the guard when Townsend, positioned to his left, padded forward on bare feet and wended his way stealthily between the parked vehicles. Reaching the jeep that the guard was leaning against, he was faced with the problem of how to come up on his victim from the rear when the vehicle was between them. Seeing the problem instantly, Wild Bill moved first, making his way stealthily forward until he was hidden behind a troop truck that was parked parallel to the jeep. After pausing for a second, he stepped out from behind the truck and waved to the guard.

Startled at first, the guard soon collected his senses and turned quickly sideways to pick up his weapon and aim it at Wild Bill. Just as quickly, Townsend padded around the front of the jeep, came up behind the guard, then slapped his left hand over his mouth, jerking his head back, and cut his throat with one quick, expert slash. As the guard dropped his weapon and went into convulsions, his throat spurting blood, Townsend wrapped his other arm around him, hugged him tightly, then lowered his still-quivering body to the floor.

Alice winced and glanced down at her own hand knife.

Kilroy stared at her. Townsend disappeared behind the jeep with the dead man, holding him until his convulsions had ceased, but rising eventually to wave the others forward.

Again, they advanced across the car lot, spreading well out and darting silently from car to car. Just as Kilroy and Wild Bill were reaching the exit door, three Iraqi soldiers, obviously alerted in the guardhouse by a call from inside the complex, came running down the ramp leading into the car lot. Even as they were bursting out of the striations of light beaming into the gloom, Kilroy and Wild Bill fired simultaneously at them. The men went down like ninepins, but shuddering and screaming, as the rest of the bullets ricocheted noisily off the walls behind them.

'Let's go!' Kilroy bawled.

Knowing that the guardhouse had been alerted, they no longer had a reason for silence and advanced as quickly as possible up the ramp with Kilroy and Wild Bill still out front, their weapons at the ready. While still on the move, Kilroy fired another short, decisive burst from his SLR and another Iraqi came slithering down the ramp, rolling like a log, forcing Alice and the others to jump out of the way. Meanwhile, Kilroy and Wild Bill reached the top of the ramp, taking opposite sides of the broad exit, and saw the floodlit courtyard with the guardhouse at its far end and the sky beyond illuminated by flames. The main gate was still closed, but Iraqi troops were passing through the guardhouse from outside and emerging into the courtyard, where they spread out to advance towards the car lot, firing on the move.

'Hand grenades!' Wild Bill bellowed, tearing one from his belt and releasing the pin. Kilroy did the same. Both men hurled their grenades as Paddy's SLR roared into life lower down the ramp, indicating that more Iraqis had somehow got into the interrogation centre and were now in hot pursuit across the car lot. The L2A2 fragmentation grenades exploded simultaneously in the courtyard, tearing up concrete, filling the air with smoke and debris, and blowing some of the advancing Iraqis off their feet to sprawl with smouldering clothes on the ground.

As Paddy kept the Iraqis in the car lot pinned down with repeated bursts of fire from his SLR, Kilroy and Wild Bill raced across the courtyard, firing on the move at the Iraqis still there and supported by single shots from the Browning High Powers of Phillips, Morrissey and Spooner.

Covering an arc of fire to the left of Kilroy, Wild Bill stopped firing just long enough to grab Alice with his free hand, tug her close to him and race with her towards the guardhouse. As he reached it, a guard stepped out, taking aim with a short-barrelled sub-machine gun. Wild Bill released Alice and fired his MP5 before the guard could get off a shot. The guard screamed and spun away, dropping his weapon, and Alice raced forward and picked it up and advanced on the guardhouse. Wild Bill tugged her back, threw in a hand grenade, waited until it had exploded, blowing out the guardhouse windows, then nodded and led her inside. She and Wild Bill opened fire as they entered, firing blind and swinging their weapons from left to right in order to cause maximum damage to those still alive. They heard screaming, then silence, and advanced into the smoke as Kilroy came up behind them, his back turned to them, to give covering fire to those still in the courtyard, including Paddy, who, bringing up the rear, was firing his SLR at the Iraqis emerging from the car lot.

'Come on, Paddy! Let's move it!' Kilroy bawled as the others filed past him to enter the devastated, smoke-filled guardhouse.

As Paddy backed up to the inner door of the guardhouse, firing on the move, Wild Bill and Alice stepped over the dead Iraqis in the small, smoke-filled building until they reached the outer door. They were just about to step outside when more Iraqi soldiers raced along the street, having come around the main building, and spread out to encircle the guardhouse and its main gate.

'Shit!' Wild Bill exclaimed.

Suddenly, even before Wild Bill and Alice could open fire on the soldiers in front of them, an Iraqi Army truck roared down the opposite street, which was narrow and packed with Arab civilians, to plough straight through the advancing Iraqi troops, running some down and causing the others to scatter. As the truck screeched to a halt in front of the gate, an SLR roared from inside the driver's cabin, cutting down some more of the dazed Iraqi troops.

'In the truck!' Wild Bill bawled, grabbing Alice by the arm and tugging her forward. Jerking free, Alice raised her captured AK-47 assault rifle and fired semi-automatic bursts at the Iraqi troops, aiming from the hip as she ran towards the truck. Wild Bill was right behind her. Glancing up as he passed the driver's cabin, he saw Williams, in Arab dress, staring down at him. When he reached the back end of the truck, standing beside Alice, still firing her AK-47 at the Iraqi soldiers, the tailboard was thrown down by a man with tinted skin, wearing a *shemagh* and black Iraqi Army beret. Recognising Roy Collinson, Wild Bill bawled to Alice to get into the truck. She did so only after firing another short burst from her AK-47 as other members of their group, led by Kilroy, burst out of the smoking guardhouse and also ran to the back end of the truck, firing on the move, some with their SLRs, the rest with Brownings.

By now, Paddy was the only one left at the guardhouse exit, giving covering fire as the others clambered up into the truck. Kilroy remained on the ground, first firing, then hurling a hand grenade into the midst of the firing Iraqis and bawling at Paddy to run. The grenade exploded, bowling over more Iraqis, and Paddy made his short run to the truck, firing on the move, weaving left and right to avoid the bullets kicking off dust all around him. He made it and clambered up into the truck as Kilroy, still on the ground, continued firing at the remaining Iraqi troops.

Inside the truck, Wild Bill bawled at Williams to move out. At the open end of the truck, Paddy and Alice opened fire on the Iraqis, giving covering fire to Kilroy, and were still firing when the truck roared into life and lurched forward. Paddy and Alice carried on firing as Kilroy turned away from the Iraqis and clambered into the truck, just as a hail of Iraqi bullets ricocheted off the tailboard below him.

'Move it!' Wild Bill bawled. '*Go!*'

Driven expertly by Williams, Geordie still firing from the seat beside him, the truck reversed, screeched around in a semicircle and then tore back up the narrow street, causing Iraqi civilians to dive into doorways. A fusillade of bullets from the Iraqi soldiers whined about the truck, striking some of the civilians, killing some and wounding others, and ricocheted off the walls as the truck reached the top of the short street and swung right, leaning heavily to one side, tyres screeching.

Thrown all over the floor in the back, the men cursed and then sat up again to be dazzled by the brilliant lights of a broad street filled with fancy shops. Though the windows were adorned with expensive European goods, most of the shops were closed because the bombs and rockets were still raining relentlessly on the city.

'This must be Karrada,' Wild Bill said. 'The main shopping centre. It's pretty damned upmarket and normally used by English-speaking expatriates, but they're not out tonight.'

'I don't blame them,' Alice said, raising her eyes from the shops to the swarms of Coalition aircraft in the flak-filled night sky above the red glow of the flames of the many burning buildings. 'I'm just amazed that the Iraqis haven't turned out the street lights.'

'They never do,' said Phillips.

Nevertheless, the Iraqis could be seen on the rooftops

of the skyscrapers, firing their Triple A anti-aircraft guns, with smoke belching from the barrels, lines of scarlet tracers webbing the dark sky and ugly clouds of black flak exploding between the aircraft. Iraqi civilians were running along the pavements, ducking into doorways, sheltering from the debris that rained upon them when Cruise missiles and 2,000-pound bombs exploded. The shops gave way to burning buildings and smouldering ruins, with dead littering the rubble.

'Poor bastards,' Paddy said. 'This must be driving 'em mad.'

'Every goddamned night,' Wild Bill said. 'Rather them than us, buddy.'

Though the truck was careening recklessly along the street, around mounds of rubble, often passing Iraqi gun posts protected by sandbagged walls, the soldiers on the ground took no notice of it, recognising it as one of their own vehicles and seeing only the black berets and *shemaghs* of the men in the back.

'Get up the front,' Kilroy told Alice, 'before they see your blonde hair.'

'Yeah,' said Alice. 'Right.'

Seeing Kilroy as a hard man, but recognising the common sense in his observation, she reluctantly made her way to the front of the truck. There she could at least see the road ahead through a narrow window, between the heads of the SAS officer driving and the trooper beside him. The officer driving, an SAS captain, obviously knew where he was going and had turned off Karrada, made a few more turns and was now burning along the six-lane highway leading out of Baghdad. Because of the ongoing air raid there was little traffic on the highway and gradually the burning, exploding buildings of the city gave way to the flat, moonlit plains of the desert.

'God, I'm free!' Alice exclaimed impulsively, feeling joy in her heart.

'Not yet,' Kilroy responded. He was staring out of the back of the roaring truck. 'I think we've got company.'

CHAPTER SIXTEEN

Staring out of the back of the bouncing, rattling truck, they saw the spectacular firework display of the Coalition air attack over distant Baghdad and, much lower, twelve separate beams of light that splayed out across the darkness of the desert, moving up and down, shaking, turning this way and that.

'It can only be the Iraqis,' Kilroy said. 'Six troop trucks. Judging by the position of those headlights, I'd say one of them's coming straight along the highway and the others are spreading out on both sides of it, hoping to find us.'

'Right,' Wild Bill said. 'Better tell Capt'n Williams to get the fuck off this highway and then douse his lights. He can drive by the moonlight.'

'Right,' Kilroy said, then turned and glanced to the front of the truck, to where Alice was huddled up against the back of the driver's cabin. 'Can you convey that message, miss?'

'Lieutenant,' Alice corrected him.

I'll be damned if I'll take that from *him*, she thought. Hell, I even outrank him.

Sergeant Kilroy stared steadily at her for a moment, not smiling, then nodded and said with emphasis, '*Lieutenant*.'

Alice nodded back, also not smiling, then turned and knocked on the wire-mesh grille with her knuckles until the SAS trooper sitting beside the driver turned and stared at her.

'Hi,' he said. 'Corporal Geordie Welsh. You're Lieutenant Davis?'

'Yeah.'

'Nice to see a pretty face,' Geordie said, sounding as if he meant it, though he didn't bring a smile to Alice's face.

'We're being followed by half a dozen Iraqi troop trucks,' she told him.

'I'm Captain Williams,' the driver said, speaking over his shoulder. 'What's the position of the troop trucks?'

'One's coming up behind us, right here on the highway, and the others are spreading out on both sides, obviously trying to find us.'

'Then I better get off this road and turn out my lights.'

'That's what we thought, Capt'n.'

'Hold on,' Williams said.

He turned the steering wheel sharply and the truck leant to the side on screeching tyres as it cut across a couple of lanes, bounced over something solid, thumped back down and then raced across the desert, leaving the highway behind. Alice had grabbed hold of the wire-mesh grille, but she was still bounced about quite roughly, though not nearly as badly as the others in the back, a couple of whom fell off the benches and landed on hands and knees on the floor, cursing automatically. Just as Alice sat up straight again and stared through the mesh-wire, between the heads of Geordie and Williams, the headlights of the truck blinked out, leaving only stark darkness straight ahead. Alice was wondering how the hell the SAS captain could drive in that when the stars slowly reappeared, pale light shone on the sand, and she realised that her eyes were adjusting to the desert's moonlit darkness. The truck bounced and rattled on through that semi-darkness and occasionally the stars were obscured when sand was blown across the windscreen.

'Tell those men at the rear to keep their eyes on those trucks,' Williams said.

'Yes, Capt'n,' Alice replied. Shivering, she suddenly realised just how cold she was. She was still wearing only the cotton *dish-disha* and she was naked beneath it. Instantly, she felt very self-conscious, but she gradually turned away from the driver's cabin to face the men in the rear. 'The capt'n says that you men in the rear are to keep your eyes on the trucks.'

'What else do we have to look at?' Collinson asked rhetorically.

'That air raid over Baghdad,' Paddy said. 'It's like a great fuckin' light show.' He glanced at Alice and added, 'Sorry, Lieutenant.'

'What for?' Alice asked. Still trying to grasp that she had actually been rescued, that she was out of Iraqi hands, she was torn between disbelief and elation and a startling ingratitude. She was indebted to these men – they had risked their lives to get her out – but now that she was free, she wasn't about to take any shit from anyone. She had taken too much of that in the past and now the past was behind her. This time she would fight for her rights and not be abused. 'Any of you guys got something I can wear?' she asked, tugging demonstratively at the *dish-disha*. 'I'm freezing in this thing.'

'We'll all be changing back into our own outfits,' the burly US Delta Force master sergeant said, 'and we've brought desert clothing for you as well, Lieutenant. They should fit. I got your size from your records.' Grinning, he tugged the olive-green Iraqi jumper up over his shoulders and head, then handed it to her. 'Put this on in the meantime.'

Alice took it from him and put it on. 'Thanks.' She felt warmer almost instantly, but she also felt ridiculous, with the lower half of the Arab robe ballooning out from the tight jumper and her bare feet showing. 'I must look real fashionable.'

Most of the men grinned – all except that Kilroy – but they also seemed a little embarrassed to have her here with them.

'You look pretty good to me,' Wild Bill said. 'A sight for sore eyes in fact.'

'My eyes are getting sore watching those trucks,' Collinson said. 'At least three of them are coming in our direction and they're gradually catching up.'

'They can go faster than we can,' said Kilroy, 'because they've all got their lights on.'

'That's right enough,' Paddy said with an accent that was unusually harsh to Alice's ears – an Ulster accent. 'Let's just pray that Captain Williams, drivin' happily in the dark, doesn't land us at the bottom of a fuckin' wadi, six feet deep in a flash flood.'

'You get *floods* in this desert?' Alice asked.

'Better believe it, Lieutenant.'

That was Kilroy. He hadn't even looked at her as he spoke – he was staring at the lights of the Iraqi trucks in the distance – but she sensed his toughness, his air of icy remove, in the tone of his voice. He was a hard man, the kind she now feared, and she resented him for it.

'You feeling OK, Lieutenant?' the US Delta Force master sergeant asked, turning his head on that bull's neck to give her a genial grin. He was built like a bear and had a truck driver's rough, good-natured face, with red hair and very bright blue eyes that did not condescend.

'Frankly, Sarge, after what I've been through, right now I feel great.'

'You'll feel better when you get your uniform back on.'

'I sure will.'

'One of those trucks has turned away and struck out east,' Kilroy said. 'They must be spread out all over the place. There's only one left behind us now.'

'Master Sergeant Bill Kowalski,' the American introduced himself to Alice. 'They call me Wild Bill.'

'I won't ask why,' Alice said.

Together, they stared out of the back of the truck and saw two headlights beaming from the darkness a good distance away.

'Sure, he's comin' right towards us,' Paddy said.

'He'll catch up pretty soon,' Collinson added. 'I think we should take him out.'

Kilroy left his place on the bench and moved, crouched over, to the front of the truck, brushing Alice's shoulder as he passed but not looking at her.

'I think we should stop, boss,' he said, talking to Captain Williams, still driving. 'Most of the trucks have spread out and are all over the place, but one of them's hot on our tail and catching up fast.'

'I can't drive faster without headlights,' Williams replied. 'If I turn them on, the Iraqis will see us. Are you suggesting we lay up?'

'I think so, boss. If we keep driving, they'll catch up. If we neutralise them, the noise we make might attract the others – either the noise or the flashes or the explosion if we blow their truck up. So I say we lay up and let them pass and then follow them and hope that they turn off in some other direction.'

'And if they don't?'

'We attack them at first light, by which time we'll be near the Pink Panthers.'

'Right, Sarge, let's do that. There's a couple of low hills straight ahead and I'll tuck us in there.'

'That sounds good to me, boss.'

When Kilroy turned away from the mesh-wire window to make his way back to his seat, Alice asked, 'What's a Pink Panther?'

'You'll find out,' Kilroy said, then sat back on his seat, leaving Alice annoyed at his refusal to answer properly. 'We're going to lay up in a minute,' he told the others, 'and let that truck pass us.'

'Do we lay up long enough to catch some sleep?' Roy Collinson asked.

'No,' Kilroy said.

'Might've known it,' Paddy said.

A few minutes later, the truck turned sharply to the west and bounced over rougher ground, heading up a gradient, then ran slightly downhill again until it came to a halt in low ground surrounded by ridges. The engine was turned off, the driver's door squeaked open and was slammed shut again, then Williams appeared at the back, looking surprisingly young and handsome to Alice, almost a schoolboy. Indicating the ground behind him with a jabbing thumb, he said smartly, 'All out.'

Grateful for the chance to stretch their legs, everyone tumbled out of the back of the truck. The blond SAS corporal, Geordie Welsh, was standing beside Captain Williams, crooking an SLR over his right arm and grinning impishly at some of his fellow troopers.

'You just about made it through that guardhouse,' he told them. 'Aren't you glad I was there, lads?'

'We needed you like a hole in the head,' Roy replied. 'All we needed was Captain Williams driving.'

'Don't come that bullshit with me—' Geordie started retorting until cut short by Williams, who said, 'No talking, men. No smoking and no noise from your mess kits. I want you to take up firing positions at the top of that ridge and watch that truck until it passes by. Should it stop, we'll have to try dispatching its occupants with personal weapons, avoiding the use of hand grenades or anti-tank weapons, since their explosions could be seen for miles around. Right, let's get up there.'

Realising that they weren't about to get a rest, some of the men rolled their eyes at each other but made no sound as they left the low ground and clambered up the shallow rise to the top of the ridge. Alice went with them, carrying her captured AK-47 assault rifle, and lay belly down with the others on the ridge to stare across the vast desert plain, dimly lit by moonlight. Staring back the way they had come, she saw the approaching headlights of the single Iraqi troop truck and, far beyond them, the spectacular firework display of the Coalition air raid. It was much more distant now, the skyscrapers of the city hidden from view and the crimson light of explosions and webs of scarlet tracery rising eerily from the dark line of the horizon.

Out of the corner of her eye, she saw Kilroy jabbing his finger to the east. When she glanced in the direction, she saw two other sets of headlights beaming into the darkness as they moved inexorably across the desert. Glancing in the opposite direction, she saw exactly the same. Clearly, the other Iraqi troop trucks were still in pursuit and had spread well out on both sides of the MSR between Baghdad and Basra. Alice realised, when she saw those headlights, that she was not free yet.

The truck following them was now approaching, bouncing and rattling over the flat plain, its headlights beaming down on the hard-packed sand to illuminate the tracks of the captured truck being used by the SAS.

'Damn!' Williams whispered when he saw that.

'They'll be able to see where we've turned off,' Kilroy said, 'and they'll follow us all the way up here.'

'That means we can't surprise 'em,' Wild Bill said, 'so the first to strike wins. I say let's use the anti-tank weapons and blow that truck all to hell. We can't depend on only our personal weapons if they know that we're here.'

'If we use the anti-tanks weapons, the other trucks will see the explosions,' Kilroy said.

'I agree with our Delta Force friend,' Williams said. 'We've lost the element of surprise and a fire fight could go on all night. We have to do as much damage as quickly as possible with the anti-tank weapons, then hightail it out of here before the others get to us.'

'Come to think of it,' Wild Bill said, 'this could work to our advantage. If we set fire to that truck, the glow will attract all the other trucks and draw them to this single spot. By that time, we'll be a pretty long way off. From our new location, we could pinpoint the trucks with the laser designator and guide a couple of F-15Es in to bomb them. That should effectively get them off our trail and leave us free to travel on to the RV.'

'Excellent,' Williams said.

'I agree,' Kilroy added.

Without another word, he and Wild Bill hurried back to the Iraqi truck to get out their anti-tank weapons. As they were clambering up into the truck, Williams turned to the other men and said, 'Geordie, you and Trooper Collinson set up the GPMG and open fire on anything that moves down there once the truck has been struck by the anti-tank rockets. Don't wait for my hand signal. As for the rest of you men . . .' Here he turned to Alice, glanced at her captured AK-47 and smiled. 'I include you in this, Lieutenant Davis.'

'I should hope so,' Alice said.

Williams politely ignored the remark. 'You all fire your personal weapons the minute the GPMG opens up. You keep firing until nothing moves down there or until I tell you to stop. Right, lads – and ladies – get to it.'

Surprised to find that Captain Williams's reference to 'ladies' had not offended her, possibly because the comment had been made without malice, Alice slithered higher up the ridge and aimed down to where the Iraqi troop truck was approaching. As she was settling into firing position with her AK-47, beside Paddy, taking aim with his SLR, Wild Bill and Kilroy returned with their anti-tank weapons and Geordie and Roy went off to fetch the GPMG. Wild Bill and Kilroy were both set up, resting on one knee and already taking aim when Geordie and Roy returned with the GPMG and hastily set it up. They had just managed to do so when the Iraqi truck below ground to a halt, reversed slightly, then turned up the slope, following the tracks of the captured SAS vehicle.

The headlights of the Iraqi truck beamed upward and splayed out, clearly illuminating the top of the hill and the two men aiming their anti-tank weapons.

Kilroy fired first, followed instantly by Wild Bill. The 94mm missile from the LAW 80 smashed directly through the advancing truck's windscreen and exploded with a deafening roar, demolishing the driver's cabin, with shards of glass and pieces of metal blown out on clouds of smoke mere seconds before the HEAT rocket from Wild Bill's Stinger SAM system slammed through the radiator and exploded on contact with the engine, blowing it to pieces and setting fire to the petrol in the ruptured tank. As the truck shuddered to a halt and its front turned into a great ball of yellow-white flame surrounded by billowing black smoke, Collinson opened fire with the GPMG, first putting out of his misery the burning, screaming man who had fallen out of the driver's cabin, then aiming the rest of his fusillade of bullets at the rear, peppering the canvas top with holes and setting off more screams from inside.

The Iraqi soldiers not killed by this fusillade jumped out of the back of the truck, some running for cover, others boldly kneeling behind the rear wheels to fire up the hill with their assault rifles.

Instantly, Alice and the others returned the fire with their personal weapons, aiming at specific targets and then firing bursts to the left and right to take in those kneeling nearby. From where she was lying, Alice couldn't be too sure if she had hit anyone or not – the whole target area was encircled by lines of spitting sand and dust, with men screaming and collapsing within from the combined SAS fire power – but she felt an undeniable exhilaration that vaguely shocked her even as it swept through her. Though her UH-60 Black Hawk helicopter had frequently attacked the enemy with bullets and rockets, she had never personally fired upon a human being until that moment when she and the others had made their break from the guardhouse. Alice had felt exultant then, just as she did now, experiencing the pure thrill of revenge as she helped cut down the enemy.

The flames covering the driver's cabin set fire to the canvas top and illuminated the darkness around the dying Iraqis. With the truck emptied, Roy was able to turn his GPMG on the Iraqis kneeling beside it, or behind the rocks on either side, and the resultant devastation was almost total.

The few remaining Iraqis were hiding behind the burning truck, exposing their heads and shoulders only for long enough to fire off short bursts of semi-automatic fire from their assault rifles, when Kilroy and Wild Bill, no longer required to fire their anti-tank weapons, raced off at the half-crouch in opposite directions, then advanced down the hill on both sides of the burning truck. Stopping at a point parallel with the Iraqis, where they could see them clearly behind the truck, they opened fire simultaneously, Kilroy with his SLR, Wild Bill with his MP5, and managed to dispatch all of them, either wounding them or killing them outright before they could fire back.

'The others are coming!' Williams shouted down the hill. 'Stay there and we'll pick you up.'

The anti-tank weapons and GPMG were humped back into the truck and followed in by Alice and the men. Behind the steering wheel again, Williams drove without lights down the hill and stopped beside the blazing Iraqi truck, surrounded by its dead and wounded, just long enough to let Kilroy and Wild Bill clamber aboard. Glancing across the moonlit plain, Williams saw the lights of four other trucks heading towards him and gradually converging, so he gunned the engine and roared off again, heading south, still without lights, in the general direction of the RV. However, he had driven for only five minutes when he braked to a halt again, jumped to the ground, and went around to the back of the truck where Kilroy had already climbed down and was reaching up to take the laser designator off Paddy.

'The rest of you men stay in the truck,' Williams said. 'You can relax and have a drink and cold rations, but no smoking, I'm afraid, as even the glow of cigarettes could be seen from where those Iraqis are. When the F-15Es knock out those trucks, we'll move on again.'

He turned away to join Kilroy where he was kneeling on the ground behind the truck and mounting the laser designator on its tripod. As Kilroy was thus engaged, Williams contacted HQ Riyadh on the SATCOM system and called up two F-15Es to fly to the location, where he would give them more precise instructions with the aid of his hand-held Magellan GPS (Global Positioning System). The F-15Es, he knew, would already be in the vicinity, taking part in the nightly air raid against Baghdad, and would be rerouted to this location by an AWACS aircraft. In contact with HQ Riyadh, Williams was informed that the aircraft would be at the location in about ten minutes.

'Let's just hope those Iraqis don't move out before the planes get here,' he said to Kilroy. 'They'll be able to follow our tracks all the way and then we won't have a prayer.'

'They won't waste much time,' Kilroy replied, 'but I think they'll tend to their dead and wounded first, which should buy us a breathing space.'

This turned out to be true. The lights of the Iraqi trucks were still grouped together and motionless around the burning vehicle when Captain Williams learnt through his SATCOM system that the F-15Es were approaching. He conveyed this news to Kilroy who, having already aimed his laser designator at those closely grouped pairs of lights in the distance, now turned the system on and 'painted' the side of one of them with the laser beam.

Almost instantly, the two F-15Es materialised in the sky

above, sweeping gracefully across the stars, and released their GBU-10 Paveway II bombs which, guided by the laser beam, slammed with deadly accuracy into the earth between and around the Iraqi Army trucks. As the F-15Es streaked back up and away, a brief, bass rumbling sound turned into a distant roaring and the desert erupted into jagged sheets of searing white flame and boiling clouds of black smoke.

Watching from a safe distance, the SAS men and Wild Bill and Alice knew that those black clouds contained the flying debris from the exploded trucks and the dismembered limbs of men blown apart. The great white sheets of flame shrank back to reveal the dimmer, smaller flames of the burning trucks, but the F-15Es returned for a second run and again the Paveway bombs caused massive explosions, with the erupting sand and billowing smoke blotting out the stars. This had hardly settled down when the F-15Es returned for their third and final run, making the desert erupt again and leaving a dreadful pall of smoke where the trucks had once been. Finally, even before that drifting smoke had settled down, the F-15Es flew over the SAS positions and did a roll, their salute, to indicate that the job had been done and that the area was cleared.

Instantly, without a word, Kilroy packed up his laser designator, passed it to Paddy, and climbed back up into the truck. He glanced at Alice with his humourless grey gaze as he sat between Wild Bill and Paddy. Williams took his seat behind the steering wheel and the truck moved off again, heading across the desert to the RV, this time with no pursuing lights behind it.

'Nice to know we're alone at last,' Geordie said.

'Not for long,' Kilroy said. He turned his head to stare steadily at Alice. 'They won't give up easily.'

'Neither will I,' Alice said.

CHAPTER SEVENTEEN

It was still dark when they reached the RV in the high ridges overlooking distant Baghdad. Disembarking from the dust-covered Iraqi Army truck, the former prisoners stretched themselves, breathed the fresh morning air and gazed about them as if they couldn't quite believe that they were free, at least for the moment. One of them, wearing a major's epaulettes and with the features of a young aristocrat, albeit badly bruised from his beatings, approached Alice and said, smiling, 'So you're my former neighbour. I'm Major Phillips. Nice to meet you, Lieutenant.'

He put his hand out and Alice, feeling oddly touched, shook it. She then realised that her emotional feelings were possibly due to the fact that this man's presence in the cell next to hers had kept her on an even keel and that his civilised conversations had kept her morale up when it was at its lowest.

'It's swell to meet you, too, Major,' she responded as he released her hand. 'It was sure nice to hear your voice back there.'

Major Phillips smiled. 'Not the best of circumstances, I'll admit, but we did all right.'

'Let's just hope we make it back.'

'We'll make it all right, Lieutenant. It might become a little difficult here and there, but I don't doubt that we'll make it. These men ...' He indicated the men milling about her, including the former prisoners. 'They're specially trained in desert survival and all highly motivated. They won't give up easily. Are you comfortable travelling with them?'

Alice shrugged. 'I'm not sure. I feel a bit rocky. I'd certainly feel a lot better in a helicopter, but I guess I'll be OK.'

'I'm sure you will,' Major Phillips said. 'You were fine when we made the breakout, so you should survive this bit.'

'I'll sure try,' Alice said. Yet the very mention of the word 'helicopter' had reminded her of the crash and the death of Dave Bamberg, the man she had loved. Suddenly near to tears, she turned away from Phillips and surveyed the land below. Though the sun had not yet risen, the Coalition air raid over the city was tapering off and the last of the aircraft were winging overhead, flying back to Riyadh and elsewhere in Kuwait, as the men uncovered the Pink Panthers and quickly checked them to ensure that they had not been touched. In the event, they had not been.

'Those Land Rovers are Pink Panthers?' Alice asked Wild Bill as he rummaged about in the back of one of the two heavily armed vehicles, looking for the uniform he had brought along for her.

'Yeah,' he said, opening a cardboard box and pulling out USAF desert clothing of disruptive-pattern material, with an olive-green T-shirt, rubber-soled boots, soft hat with upturned brim and even underclothes. 'It's because of their near-pink colouring and the fact that they're capable of travelling in any kind of desert terrain. Pretty impressive, right?'

'Yeah,' Alice said, taking the clothes off him and holding them against her bosom. 'Right. So where can I change?'

Wild Bill grinned and shrugged. 'Pick your spot, Lieutenant.

It's still pretty dark and you've got a lot of rocks to hide behind.'

Alice glanced around her and saw Paddy Magee and Roy Collinson transferring the heavy weapons from the Iraqi truck to one or other of the two Pink Panthers. At the same time, Geordie removed a Honda trail motorbike from the back of one of the Pink Panthers, Captain Williams studied an open map with the aid of a small torchlight, and all of the former prisoners, except herself, sat against the wheels of the vehicles, eating cold high-calorie rations as if they were having a gourmet dinner.

After that shit we had in the prison, Alice thought, those cold rations probably taste like gourmet food.

She was hungry herself, but more keen to get out of the filthy, revealing *dish-disha* and back into uniform. As she was standing there, undecided, Sergeant Kilroy came towards her, obviously wanting to talk to Wild Bill, and she found herself hurrying past him, avoiding his gelid gaze, and turning behind the nearest outcropping. Once there, well away from prying eyes, she removed the *dish-disha*, felt the shock of the cold morning air on her naked body, then proceeded to put on the USAF desert clothing. As she dressed, she imagined Kilroy's eyes, filled with cold curiosity, staring at the other side of the rocks, trying to see her. The thought made her shiver, but also oddly excited her, and she found herself blushing a little as she stepped out again, dressed in uniform at last, holding the *dish-disha* in her right hand.

Kilroy was staring straight at her.

'What do I do with this?' Alice asked him, holding out the Arab robe.

Kilroy removed a small spade from his webbed belt and handed it to her with no trace of a smile.

'Bury it,' he said.

This time flushing with anger, Alice nearly spat out that he should address her as 'lieutenant', wanting to remind him that she outranked him, but her awareness that these SAS men interacted with unusual informality – the other ranks calling the officers 'boss' instead of 'sir' and the officers often addressing the other ranks by their first names – made her hold her tongue.

'Right,' she said. 'Bury it.'

As Alice walked a few yards beyond the Pink Panthers to dig a shallow hole beneath the rock outcropping and bury the *dish-disha*, Wild Bill came up beside Kilroy, followed Alice's progress with an appreciative gaze, then said, 'If she wiped all that dirt off her face, that lieutenant would be one attractive broad.'

'Then it's best she keeps the dirt on,' Kilroy replied. 'We want no aggravation.'

Will Bill stared at him, still intrigued by the impassive face. 'You think she'd cause that?' he asked.

'She might,' Kilroy replied.

'I don't think she's the kind.'

'I'm not saying she'd do it deliberately; I'm just saying that she's attractive enough to cause some dangerous distraction. Getting back is going to be difficult enough without the extra burden of a woman – and a blonde at that. She's all yours, Master Sergeant.'

Wild Bill couldn't help grinning. He thought Kilroy was off the wall. 'She handled herself OK when we broke out,' he said, 'and she certainly made her contribution with that AK-47. She'll be OK, Sarge.'

'She better be,' Kilroy said.

The last of the Coalition B-52 heavy bombers had passed on, their bass rumbling fading away to the south, when the sun started rising as a great cauldron of crimson fire that appeared to be pouring along the eastern horizon. As light ate at the darkness, sweeping across the flat plain, it revealed the blackened remains of the two Iraqi trucks destroyed by the SAS attack earlier in the morning (to most of the men, it seemed like days ago) and gradually illuminated the immense HAS doors on the edge of the city. Even as Alice hurriedly gulped her share of the cold rations and the men prepared to board the uncovered Pink Panthers, an Iraqi reconnaissance helicopter appeared above the skyscrapers, heading south, towards the ridge, and the HAS doors opened to let out more troop trucks, also heading south.

'That looks ominous,' Wild Bill murmured.

'OK, men,' Captain Williams said crisply, addressing the whole group, 'we're going to pull out and we're going to do it now. We can't use the Iraqi truck because we're going to be pursued by others and we need something faster than they are. In other words, we have to leave the truck behind and use only the Pink Panthers. With the five rescued, we're now a total of eleven, but Geordie will be on his motorbike, which means we'll be five to each Pink Panther, which I'm sure we can manage. Geordie will ride out front on point at all times and keep us informed of enemy movements ahead. I'll be in command of one Pink Panther, with Sergeant Kilroy and Master Sergeant Kowalski on the front and rear guns, Trooper Magee and Lieutenant Davis in charge of personal weapons, the Stinger SAM system and hand grenades. Major Phillips will be in command of the second jeep with Corporal Townsend and Trooper Collinson on the front and rear guns, Staff Sergeant Morrissey in charge of the LAW 80, Sergeant Spooner the explosives and the radio systems.'

He glanced back over his shoulder to where the Iraqi helicopter gunship was coming towards them and the troop trucks were still heading south, away from the closing HAS doors. Turning back to the front, he said, 'We have to make it back to Scud Boulevard or Scud Alley and the Iraqis are going to follow us all the way. The rescue of our prisoners will be a propaganda coup for us and a resounding blow to them, so they're going to want their prisoners back. For that very reason, we have to make the safe delivery of the former prisoners our prime concern, no matter the personal cost to us. Please bear this in mind throughout the journey back to our own lines.'

'You're worth something to someone at last,' Geordie said to the three former prisoners grouped beside him: Morrissey, Spooner and Townsend. 'Now isn't that nice to know?'

'I've been worth more than you from the day I was born,' Spooner retorted, 'so don't come it with me, sprout.'

'I lay down my life for my mates,' Paddy said with a wicked grin. 'What lucky bastards they are.'

'I wasn't born out of wedlock,' Townsend said, 'so don't imply otherwise.'

'A mere slip of the tongue, mate.'

'All right, men, that's enough,' Williams said, glancing over his shoulder to see the helicopter in the distance, flying out from Baghdad, casting its shadow on the troop trucks on the brightening plain below. 'I've no doubt that those trucks heading along the MSR are going out to join the other five in the search for us. As for that helicopter gunship, it's heading in this direction and it's going to see the wreckage of their other truck and know we're in the vicinity, so I think we have to move out right now. Let me repeat that our main priority is the protection of the people we've rescued. If that helicopter gunship attacks us, blow it out of the sky without stopping. OK, let's get going. On your way, Geordie.'

As the others clambered up into the Pink Panthers, Geordie kicked his trail bike into life, gunned the engine, and took off in a shower of spewing sand, bumping dangerously down the hill and then racing away across the flat plain, heading south. Even before the last of the men had clambered aboard their Pink Panthers, the vehicles were roaring into life, also, and following the trail of billowing sand left in Geordie's wake.

Alice was squeezed into the back of Williams's Pink Panther, to the side of Kilroy, who was manning the front-mounted

7.62mm GPMG, just to the side of Wild Bill Kowalski, manning the rear-mounted 0.5-inch Browning heavy machine gun. Williams was driving with Paddy Magee seated beside him, cradling his SLR over his knees, the SAM Stinger system stacked up behind him. Alice had her captured AK-47 over her knees and was squeezed tightly between crates of ammunition, spare water bottles, and boxes of British Army L2A2 and American M26 fragmentation hand grenades. As the vehicle raced across the flat, increasingly hot plain, the wind whipped the antennae of the short-burst radio and SATCOM system and sunlight was reflected off the sun compass mounted on the front. Glancing through the whipping antennae, Alice saw the other Pink Panther a good distance away, trailing slightly behind and bristling, like this vehicle, with weapons and communications antennae.

Gradually realising, with an odd sense of discomfort, just how close she was to the legs and hips of Sergeant Kilroy, she glanced up and saw his profile outlined against the azure sky, his nose slightly flattened like a boxer's nose, his full lips forming a grim line, his gelid eyes squinting against the wind and brightening sunlight. He was handsome in a rough way – the scar on his right cheek made him look like a gangster – but again she was struck by just how distant and unreadable his face was.

He probably despises women, she thought, and that includes me. He's waiting for me to crack and give him problems, but he won't have that pleasure. I'll make damned sure of that.

As if reading her mind, Kilroy suddenly glanced around and asked, 'Are you all right there, Lieutenant?'

'Sure,' Alice replied, surprised to find her cheeks burning. 'Why shouldn't I be?'

'You seem to be squeezed in by all that kit. You want me to move some?'

'I'm OK,' Alice said, surprised that he'd even thought about the matter. 'Besides, where could you move it to?'

Kilroy studied the kit piled up around her and then nodded thoughtfully. 'I guess you'll just have to suffer.'

'I'm not suffering,' Alice said.

He studied her for a moment, then nodded again and returned his watchful gaze to the azure sky. He tensed imperceptibly.

When Alice followed his gaze, she saw the Iraqi helicopter flying low across the plain, hovering temporarily over the scene of the last fire fight, then heading on across the flat plain, obviously following the trail of the clouds of sand being churned up by the two Pink Panthers. It was catching up fast.

Seeing it, Williams raised and lowered his right hand whilst simultaneously easing his foot off the accelerator, indicating that he wanted both vehicles to stop. When they did so, parking a good hundred metres apart, he explained to Kilroy, 'That helicopter's following our dust trail, so if we let it settle down, he might not see us.'

'He might see our tracks,' Kilroy replied.

'He might not. The wind's fairly strong and blowing the sand across the tracks. Also, though he's flying low, he may be too high to see anything as fine as tyre tracks. But if he does, we'll start up again and try bringing him down with the machine guns while on the move.'

'Got it,' Kilroy said. As he swung the GPMG in the direction of the advancing helicopter, Wild Bill did the same with the 0.5-inch Browning machine gun in the rear and the two gunners in the other Pink Panther, Alice noticed, were doing the same. Abruptly, however, the helicopter changed direction, heading west, and gazing in that direction, as the barrels of the machine guns carefully followed the chopper, Alice saw another trail of boiling dust cutting across the desert about a mile away from the parked vehicles.

'Geordie,' Kilroy said. 'He must have seen the chopper as well and he's trying to draw it away from us.'

'Mad bastard,' Paddy said.

'Mad bastards have their uses,' Wild Bill said. 'We owe that guy a beer.'

As the Iraqi helicopter approached the trail of sand being churned up by the motorbike, Geordie deliberately headed away from it, zigzagging expertly. Nevertheless, the chopper descended lower, coming down on top of him, and the distant roaring of its machine guns reverberated across to the men in the Pink Panthers.

Pointing east, Williams said, 'There's a line of low hills on that horizon and I think we should make for it while Geordie leads that chopper off in the opposite direction.' After raising and lowering his right hand to indicate that the other Pink Panther should follow him, he gunned the engine of his vehicle and shot off in a cloud of sand, heading for the eastern horizon. The other Pink Panther followed and soon both vehicles were racing across the flat plain, leaving trails of billowing sand in their wake.

The harsh chatter of the Iraqi helicopter's machine guns could clearly be heard above the roaring of the two Pink Panthers, but Geordie, zigzagging dangerously at high speed, was still managing to elude those pursuing him.

Abruptly, however, the helicopter changed course, turning around in a wide loop and then heading straight for the Pink Panthers.

'The pilot's seen us,' Kilroy said.

'Yes,' Williams replied, shouting over his shoulder. 'And we're a damned sight more important to him than a single motorbike outrider. Prepare to fire on the move.'

Kilroy and Wild Bill swung their mounted weapons in the direction of the advancing helicopter and opened fire as it descended upon them. The combined roar of the two machine guns was deafening and made instantly worse by the return fire of the enemy.

'Hang on!' Williams bawled and turned the steering wheel

left and right, putting the Pink Panther into a zigzagging course to avoid the parallel lines of spitting sand being kicked up by the guns of the helicopter. Alice had to brace her legs and cling to one of the wooden crates, uncomfortably aware that it was packed with hand grenades. The lines of spitting sand swept behind the zigzagging Pink Panther, though some bullets ricocheted noisily off the rear and went whining back into the sky as the chopper hovered just above, still firing its automatic weapons. By now, Kilroy and Wild Bill were firing their machine guns almost vertically, practically hanging backwards from the handgrips.

Glancing to the west, Alice saw by a trail of billowing sand that Geordie was racing back towards the Pink Panthers. Glancing at the other Pink Panther, which had been zigzagging about a hundred metres away, she saw that it was now racing directly towards her with Townsend and Collinson already firing their machine guns at the helicopter, making it ascend out of range before returning for another attack.

This time, the helicopter fired its rockets. Alice saw them as parallel trails of smoke that raced obliquely downward, hit the desert floor, and exploded just ahead of Captain Williams's Pink Panther, causing the desert to erupt in twin columns of swirling sand and boiling black smoke. Alice was blinded by the sand and felt the blast from the explosions, then the Pink Panther was racing through the smoke and back into the sunlight.

Kilroy and Wild Bill were still firing their machine guns, swinging rapidly from left to right and raising the elevation to try hitting the helicopter as it swept overhead. Bullets ricocheted off it, but did little damage, and soon it was circling around for another rocket attack.

'Fuck this for a joke!' Paddy exclaimed, then he grabbed the American Stinger SAM system, braced his two feet against some packing crates, dropped a HEAT rocket into the tube, and took aim at the descending helicopter as the Pink Panther raced away from it. Paddy fired the Stinger just after the helicopter released its own rockets and the three explosions were virtually simultaneous. Alice caught a brief glimpse of the smoke trail from the Stinger's HEAT rocket racing towards the helicopter, then she was temporarily deafened and blinded by the two explosions from the Iraqi rockets, which this time had slammed into the desert floor just beyond the Pink Panther and deluged it in a shower of raining sand and gravel and boiling smoke.

When the Pink Panther emerged from the smoke, back into the dazzling sunlight, Alice saw the helicopter ascending again, but pouring smoke and rocking wildly from side to side. The gunner in the helicopter fired a final defiant burst, with some of his bullets ricocheting off the sides of the Pink Panther, but then the pilot, obviously aware that he was in trouble, turned away and flew back towards Baghdad, still trailing oily smoke.

Paddy whooped with glee and then put the Stinger down between his legs and stuck his thumb in the air.

'Got the fucker,' he said.

'He got us as well,' Kilroy said.

Water was spurting noisily out of bullet holes in the spare-water cans, flooding the floor of the vehicle.

'Goddamn it!' Wild Bill exclaimed softly.

As the two Pink Panthers, spreading out again until they were a hundred metres apart, continued on across the flat, hot plain, heading towards the low line of hills in the east, Geordie came up between them on his motorbike, raised and lowered his right fist in a gesture of solidarity, and then raced on to check that the way was clear. Returning as the Pink Panthers were approaching the shadows cast by the rocky hills, he indicated with another hand signal that he had seen no sign of the enemy ahead. The Iraqi helicopter, still pouring smoke and wobbling dangerously, limped out of sight beyond the horizon as the Pink Panthers slowed down and finally braked to a halt in a natural clearing formed by a mile-long stretch of rocky hills.

When everyone had clambered down to the ground, the two Pink Panthers were inspected for damage. Though dented by bullets, neither vehicle had been harmed, but a great deal of water had been lost from the punctured cans.

'That leaves a pretty bad shortage,' Williams said, 'so we'll have to ration the water out more carefully in future.'

'The rest won't spread very far,' Wild Bill told him.

'I know,' Williams said. He glanced up at the dazzling sky, across the sun-baked desert, then wiped sweat from his brow and said, 'I think we should lay up here for the day and only move on again after last light, under cover of darkness. Does anyone disagree?'

When his question was greeted with silence, he gave the order to make camp.

CHAPTER EIGHTEEN

Their first job was to park the two Pink Panthers about a hundred metres apart, in the shadow of the overhanging rocks, then cover them in camouflage netting. When this was done, they constructed three short-duration, star-shaped OPs, located near the vehicles. The star-shaped OP has four legs with an open drainage well in the centre, into which access water will run in the event of a rainfall. One leg is for the sentry, the second for the observer; the third is a rest bay and the fourth is used either for a second sentry or, when required, as a personal admin bay where the patrol commander, or PC, can read maps, make entries into his logbook or complete any other tasks requiring paperwork. With its four legs, the star-shaped OP gives good all-round visibility. It is also easy to 'bug out' from.

'We're one man short of twelve,' Williams said when the three OPs were completed, 'which means that one of the OPs will have a spare leg. As Lieutenant Davis is the sole woman in the group, I suggest that we give her the extra space by putting her in the short-changed OP.'

'Thanks for the thought, Capt'n,' Alice responded, 'but

I don't want special privileges just because I'm a woman.'

Williams smiled. 'I know you don't, Lieutenant, and I appreciate your concern, but as someone has to have that extra leg room, choosing the sole woman in the group saves any arguments. It's not a special privilege, believe me, but simple common sense.'

'So who do I share it with?' Alice asked, glancing nervously, without thinking, at Sergeant Kilroy, who was squatting on the ground by the next OP, cleaning and oiling his SLR.

'Me for a start,' Wild Bill said. 'My instructions are not to let you out of my sight and I take my work seriously.'

Though Alice liked Wild Bill, she felt frustrated that she outranked him and still he had been placed in charge of her. On the other hand, she understood the logic of it and was forced to accept it under the circumstances. What she could not accept was the way she was treated by that male chauvinistic pig, Kilroy. His dumb insolence enraged and intrigued her by turns, so she certainly didn't want him in her OP, which would be far too unsettling. 'Who's the second man?' she asked.

'Me,' Williams said. 'I'm the squadron commander and my brief is to ensure the safe return of the former prisoners at all costs. You, being a woman, have been given the highest priority, so Master Sergeant Kowalski and I will stick to you like glue.'

'Because I'm a *woman*,' Alice emphasised bitterly.

Williams wasn't perturbed by the outburst. 'That's true enough, Lieutenant, but you're interpreting it incorrectly. We're not trying to treat you as someone in need of special care, which clearly, judging by your behaviour during the break-out, you are not. The question of sex is more to do with the political ramifications of a Western woman captured and possibly abused by the Iraqis. Whether or not you like it, your rescue and safe return are of vital importance to the propaganda war. It's as simple as that.'

'I still don't like it,' Alice said.

Williams shrugged. 'There the case rests,' he said. 'You share the OP with us.'

'No hard feelings, Captain.'

'None taken, Lieutenant.'

With the sun now high in the sky, the men were at last able to light their portable hexamine stoves and make themselves a decent meal in the form of a fry-up and hot tea. They partook of this outside the OPs, squatting around the stoves. Alice had been inordinately relieved to learn that she would not have the shared intimacy of a small OP with Kilroy, but now, picking at the greasy fry-up made for her by Paddy Magee, sitting between him and Wild Bill, with Kilroy almost directly opposite, she felt just as unsettled as she would have been if she'd been asked to share an OP with him.

'Is that OK, Lieutenant?' Paddy asked, nodding at what was left of Alice's plate of fried eggs and bacon.

'It tasted wonderful, Trooper,' Alice replied. 'And I was pretty damned hungry.'

'Do you eat a lot normally?' the dark-eyed, intense trooper, Roy Collinson, asked her.

'Just average,' Alice replied. 'Why?'

Collinson shrugged. 'No reason,' he said.

But Alice knew what lay behind the remark. You have a pretty good figure, he was thinking. Pity you're an officer.

'I haven't had the chance to thank you men for getting me out of there,' she said.

'Sure, there's no need for thanks,' Paddy said. 'It was our job and we did it, like.'

'I want to thank you anyway,' Alice said.

'We didn't get you out,' Kilroy said, staring steadily, disconcertingly, at her. 'We were sent to get our own men out and you just happened to be there as well. You were Master Sergeant Kowalski's responsibility and he tagged along with us for the convenience. So we didn't do anything that we wouldn't have had to do anyway. You're here almost by accident.'

The ignorant bastard, Alice thought. He can't even accept a thank-you with good grace. Where the hell does he come from?

'Thanks anyway,' Alice repeated stubbornly.

Kilroy just shrugged.

Having eaten, they were allocated their separate tasks, including the order in which they would be allowed to catch up on lost sleep in two-hour shifts, one man at a time. While the lucky man slept in the rest bay, still wearing his uniform and zipped up in a sleeping bag, the second and third men in each of the two teams paired up as sentry and observer, each to his relevant leg in the OP, and the fourth was inhabited by the PC – Captain Williams in one OP, Major Phillips in the other – who would alternate between sleep and keeping notes on what was reported to him by the sentry and observer. Before settling down to this, however, Williams was reminded by Kilroy that the puncturing of the water cans had led to the requirement for more water.

'My feeling,' Kilroy said, 'is that we should conserve what water we have for when we're on the move and take what we need from the desert while we're laying up.'

'Our own desert still,' Williams said.

'Right, boss. And Paddy Magee's an expert at that.'

'Then set him to work, Sarge.'

Nodding, Kilroy turned away from Williams and called Paddy over with a hand signal. Already fascinated by how the British SAS worked, Alice listened in as Kilroy informed Paddy of his requirements. When Kilroy had finished talking, before the Irishman could turn away, Alice said, 'I'd like to see how you do that, Trooper. Do you mind if I tag along?'

Both the men stared at her, Paddy with amused embarrassment, Kilroy with slight annoyance. Then, before the former could reply, the latter said, 'I think it's best he does this alone, Lieutenant.'

Instantly annoyed again – Kilroy easily annoyed her – Alice retorted, 'Goddamn it, Sergeant, do you think I can't look after myself when I'm only a few yards away from the camp?'

Kilroy's gelid gaze was steady. 'That's not the point, Lieutenant.'

Now Alice was really annoyed, convinced that Kilroy was trying to keep her in her place, acting like a chauvinistic bastard, letting her know that she was only a woman and couldn't be trusted. 'So what *is* the point, Sergeant?' she asked him. 'All I want to do is watch Trooper Magee make a desert still.'

'Thing is—' Paddy tried to interject.

'No, Trooper!' Alice snapped, now losing her temper. 'You stay out of this. This is between me and the Sergeant here.' She turned back to Kilroy. 'So, tell me, Sergeant. What the hell's the problem? You think I can't be trusted out there? You think I'll get lost, or step on a mine, or what? Please tell me, Sergeant.'

Kilroy stared impassively at her for a moment, breathing evenly, calmly, then he turned to Magee and said, 'Why don't *you* tell her, Paddy?'

Paddy grinned and turned to Alice. 'Thing is, Lieutenant, that to make a desert still I have to dig a hole about three feet deep, fill it with vegetation, then soak the vegetation with my own urine. So, you know . . .' He shrugged his shoulders. 'Well, I guess your presence there wouldn't be appropriate, like.'

Burning up with embarrassment under Kilroy's relentless gaze, Alice heard herself ask stupidly, as if she hadn't heard correctly, 'You use your own *urine*?'

'Sure, that's right, Lieutenant. I'll go down to that level ground at the bottom of the hill and look for the place where water's most likely to collect. When I find it, I'll dig a hole about three feet deep, fill it with local vegetation, then, to put it bluntly, I'll piss on it. When it's soaked in my urine, I'll place a metal container in the centre, cover it with plastic sheeting that has a rough under-surface, cut a hole in the sheeting, then slide a drinking tube through the hole. I'll leave one end inside the container and the other extending out to the side, like. The sheeting will be held down by stones placed around its circumference, with another couple of stones in the centre to depress the covering directly over the container. And that's it – that's your desert still.'

Aware of Kilroy's steady gaze, still burning up under it, Alice asked disbelievingly, 'And you get drinkable water from *that*?'

'Sure, that's right, Lieutenant. By collecting the condensation that forms beneath the plastic and then drips into the container, the still provides up to a litre of drinking water every twenty-four hours. Pretty good, right?'

Before Alice could reply, Kilroy said, 'OK, Paddy, get to it. We haven't got all damned day.'

Still grinning as he unclipped the short-handled spade from his webbed belt, Paddy marched down the hill towards the level ground at the bottom. Scarcely able to meet Kilroy's steady gaze, Alice nevertheless managed to turn to him and say, 'Sorry, Sergeant.'

Kilroy nodded. 'No problem.' Then he turned and walked off.

Suddenly grateful for the privacy of her star-shaped OP, wanting to get out of range of Kilroy's ambiguous, steady gaze, Alice clambered down into the sleeping bay and zipped herself up in her sleeping bag as Bill Kowalski took up his watch position in the sentry's leg, his MP5 resting on the rim of raised soil, and Captain Williams, in the administrative leg, jotted notes in his logbook.

The sun was now high in the sky, blazing fiercely over the hilltop, and though Alice closed her eyes, she felt the light burning through her eyelids and filling her head. Convinced that she wouldn't sleep, she was surprised to find herself being shaken awake by Wild Bill, who said, 'Sorry, Lieutenant, but your two hours are up. It's your turn on watch.'

Yawning, rubbing the sleep from her eyes, she crawled into the sentry bay and took up her watch position with the barrel of the MP5 that had been given to her by Wild Bill resting on the rim of the hole. The sun, she soon realised, was practically overhead, burnishing the desert plain, and already, after the two hours in the sleeping bag, she was soaked with sweat. Unable to stand the glare and also swept by clouds of fine dust, she put on a pair of tinted goggles and then covered the lower half of her face with the *shemagh*, also supplied by Wild Bill. As she was settling in to her two-hour watch period, Williams decided to send Geordie off on his Honda for eyeball reconnaissance of the area which they would have to travel through that night.

'Look out for minefields,' Captain Williams told him, 'and enemy patrols that may be looking for us. You can also check on Scud bunkers, mobile units, and the movements of any other military traffic on the desert or along the MSR. Use binoculars as often as possible and lay low when you're still out of eyeball range. Call the enemy positions in on your portable GPS receiver, just in case you get your balls blown off before you manage to get back here. No fire fights. No heroics. Have you got that, Geordie?'

'Yes, boss!' Geordie said. 'No problem at all.'

Alice had already inspected Geordie's impressive motorbike and knew that, though the desert was vast and relatively featureless, he would generally navigate with the sun compass mounted horizontally on the handlebars of the vehicle. The portable GPS receiver mentioned by Williams and carried in one of the motorbike's two pillion bags gave more precise positionings by comparing coded signals from various satellites in fixed orbits around the earth: it could, in fact, calculate its position to within fifteen metres. However, its complex electronics could fail, which is why the less accurate, though more reliable, sun compass was always carried as well. Now, as Geordie kick-started the motorbike and raced away across the desert, his tyres churning up a long, snaking trail of billowing sand, Alice was impressed once more not only by the quality of the machines being used by the SAS, but by the informality of the exchanges she had so far heard between the regiment's officers and the other ranks.

'Doing all right there, are you, Lieutenant?' Williams asked with a smile as he slipped back into the OP to return to his paperwork in the personal admin leg.

'No problem at all,' Alice replied, deliberately echoing Geordie's statement.

Captain Williams smiled at her. 'Well, I'm glad to hear that,' he said, then sank out of sight.

When the trail of billowing sand left in Geordie's wake had settled down and Geordie had disappeared on his motorbike over the horizon, Alice was left with only that vast, empty wasteland to contemplate. Bored, she glanced at the other two OPs and saw Kilroy's head and shoulders on the rim of the one nearer to her, his profile etched sharply against the blue sky, his eyes squinting into the brilliant sunlight. A swarm of fat black flies was buzzing about his head, but he appeared not to notice. Disturbed, as she always was by the sight of him, she swotted away the flies also swarming around her and concentrated on the vast, empty plain that was stretched out before her.

Time passed slowly. At first Alice assumed that she would see nothing, but gradually, as one hour slid imperceptibly into another, she realised that she had reached for her notebook quite a lot, recording her sightings of Arab caravans crossing the sunbaked plains, the robed Beduoin looking exotic on their slowly ambling camels; distant convoys of enemy troop trucks obscured in boiling clouds of sand; the helicopters and aircraft overhead, flying to and from Baghdad. Some of those troop trucks, she knew, were searching for the SAS rescue team and the thought that they might actually find it caused a tremor of dread.

Geordie returned on his motorbike just before her shift ended, whipping his goggles off to reveal circles of dust around his eyes, under wind-blown, dust-covered blond hair.

'There are Iraqi troop trucks all over the area,' he reported to Captain Williams, 'and clearly they're looking for something.'

'*Us*,' Wild Bill said laconically as he unzipped his sleeping bag and sat upright, flattening his mussed hair down with his big hands.

'Right,' Geordie replied, then turned back to Williams. 'The Iraqis are travelling out in every direction, so if we move out tonight, I can take the lead and come back to warn you if anything is up front, in which case we can lay low until they pass. It's mostly flat land we'll be crossing, but it's webbed with deep wadis and we can always hole up in one of those if we need to remain out of sight. If there are any minefields, they've been pretty well smoothed over, so we'll just have to take our chances in that particular direction.'

'*You'll* be taking *your* chances,' Wild Bill said, again speaking laconically as he stood up and stretched his tall, broad body. ''Cause you're the guy who's gonna be out ahead on your cute little motorbike.'

Geordie grinned. 'Right,' he said.

'According to my calculations,' Captain Williams said, 'we could make it back to Scud Alley in another day and two nights if we travel throughout both nights and manage to stick to a fairly straight route. But we won't necessarily be able to do that if the Iraqis are all over the place and we have to keep making detours to avoid them. In other words, our journey could take a lot longer than we think.'

'Why can't we just call in a couple of choppers to lift us out?' Wild Bill asked.

'It's too dangerous,' Williams told him. 'We can call in strike aircraft if we get into serious trouble, but the choppers are slower and would have to land, which would make them easy targets if they tried a rescue. Also, officially, this operation never took place. We don't want it to be known that our men – and Lieutenant Davis, for that matter – were ever captured in the first place; we only want a morale victory over Saddam and his generals, who now know that we've gone in and come out again, taking their prisoners with us. That shock to his system, combined with the nightly air raids on Baghdad, should seriously demoralise the officers and put egg on Saddam's handsome face.'

'In other words, we're on our own,' Wild Bill said, 'no matter how wide or high the shit flies.'

'Neatly put,' Williams said. He glanced up to note that the sun was starting to sink on the western horizon. He turned back to Wild Bill as Kilroy, relieved of his two-hour watch duty, as was Alice, came up to stand by the three-man OP and listen in on what was being said.

'You heard that, Sarge?' Williams asked Kilroy.

'Yes, boss, I heard it.'

'Any comments?'

'Yes, boss. I say that if the Iraqis are all over the place, sooner or later, whether we want it or not, we're going to make contact with them. So we might as well forget this business of moving only under cover of darkness and instead try to get back to our own lines as quickly as possible. That means moving out at last light, travelling all through the night, and not stopping even during the following day.'

'That's some heavy demand you're making,' Wild Bill said.

Alice had now come up to stand by Kilroy, but he ignored her as he turned a little to the side and swept his hand from left to right, indicating the vast expanse of the desert. 'As Geordie's just confirmed, it's mostly flatlands out there, so trying to lay up during the day is going to be difficult, if not downright impossible. The Iraqis have had choppers and reconnaissance aircraft out all day and once we emerge from the shelter of these rocks, they'll be able to see us, especially in daylight.'

'We can camouflage the Pink Panthers,' Williams said.

'You won't be able to camouflage our tracks,' Kilroy said, 'and those chopper pilots, at least, will come down so low that they'll be able to see them. So I say we'll be safer on the move, even during the day, than we'll be laying up.'

'That makes sense to me,' Wild Bill said.

'I think you're right,' Williams said. 'If the Iraqis are spread out in every direction, looking for us from the air as well as on the ground, then we're not going to avoid them by laying up out on sunlit flatlands. Given that, as well as the fact that we're going to have to make detours, possibly a lot of them, I think the imperative is to get back to our own lines as expeditiously as possible.' He glanced at the ground and nodded, as if addressing himself, then gradually raised his eyes again. 'Right,' he said. 'We move out at last light and keep on the move until we reach Scud Alley. We'll try going without sleep for at least tonight and tomorrow, but should the journey take longer than that, we'll snatch some shut-eye where and when we can; even, if necessary, when on the move, taking turns at sleeping in the Pink Panthers.' He glanced up again, squinting into the sinking sun, and saw that it would soon touch the horizon. 'We've approximately forty minutes to last light,' he said, 'so let's cook up what might be the last warm food we'll have in a long time. Then we pack up and shake out.'

'Hallelujah,' Wild Bill said.

Williams turned to Kilroy. 'Right, Sarge, tell the rest of the men what's happening and make sure that they all make themselves a decent, cooked meal. Make sure, also, that they don't use the water already in the water bottles, as we're now badly short. Instead, get Trooper Magee to bring up what water he finds in his desert still and share it around. Send someone with him, to help him dismantle the still and clear that area completely, leaving no trace behind.'

'Will do, boss,' Kilroy said.

'Speaking literally,' Wild Bill said before Kilroy could turn away, 'I have to remind you that Paddy's water will be piss.'

'The still will have sterilised it,' Kilroy explained, glancing briefly at Alice, 'and it'll taste OK when boiled for a brew-up.'

'A *what*?' Alice asked.

'A cup of char,' Geordie said.

'Hot tea,' Kilroy explained without a smile, then turned back to Captain Williams. 'Right, boss, I'll do that.'

When Kilroy returned to the second OP and had a brief chat with Paddy, the Irishman jumped out and, in the company of Roy Collinson, made his way down the hill to the flat ground below. As Alice looked on from the summit of the ridge, Paddy drained the water from the still into a large metal pot with the aid of a rubber tube, then he and Roy between them dismantled the makeshift apparatus and placed its separate components – metal container, plastic sheeting and drinking tube – into a black plastic bag. With the bag packed, they removed the urine-soaked, now dried, foliage from the hole, then used their short-handled spades to shovel the loose soil back into it. Once they had done this, they sprinkled the foliage back over the soil and smoothed the sand out around it, making it look more or less as it had done before. Paddy then picked up the pot of water, Roy picked up the plastic bag of components, and together they made their laborious way back up to the ridge.

'A nice drop of piss, is it?' Clive Morrissey asked laconically.

'Sure, it's as good as draught Guinness,' Paddy replied.

'I'll bet,' Spooner said.

Nevertheless, regardless of personal doubts, all of the men let Paddy fill up their small kettles with the water and then proceeded to boil it over the flames of their hexamine stoves, alternating this with the heating of canned food, which was eaten, steaming, directly out of the cans.

When Paddy offered Alice a cup of hot tea, she took it off him, studied it nervously for some time, then, feeling the eyes of everyone upon her, closed her eyes and gulped some of it down.

'Terrific,' she said, meaning it, when she'd had her first swallow of the hot, sweet tea and was suitably surprised. 'That's a great brew, Paddy.'

'Sure I'm a man of hidden qualities,' Paddy replied. 'Now isn't that a fact, love?'

'*Lieutenant*,' Alice corrected him.

'Sure, isn't that a fact, Lieutenant?' Paddy responded, unperturbed and grinning.

'It sure is,' Alice said.

Forty minutes later, when the sun had sunk, the air was turning cold and all traces of the three star-shaped OPs had been erased, the two heavily burdened Pink Panthers headed into the eerily silent, moonlit darkness of the vast desert plain.

CHAPTER NINETEEN

Seated behind the front-mounted 7.62mm GPMG, listening to the healthy roaring of the Pink Panther's 3.5 litre V-8 petrol engine, Kilroy felt the icy wind beating at him, blowing dust into his face, and was glad to have the Arab *shemagh* covering his nose and mouth. After the burning heat of day, the cold of night was shocking, but Kilroy knew that it would become even worse in the early hours of the morning. Already, he could see frost glinting off gravel and the low rocks thrusting up through the sand. The stars were exceptionally bright and the moon was a luminous orb, casting its mottled light in webs of pale light on the desert floor. Though relatively flat, the desert floor was filled with potholes, patches of loose gravel, slippery rocks and areas of soft sand that could trap the wheels of even the most sophisticated vehicles; so, even in the Pink Panthers, the journey through the dark, freezing morning was a bone-shuddering affair.

Geordie was somewhere far out front on his motorbike, but though Kilroy strained to see him, or the light of his single headlamp, he saw only the dark line of the horizon cutting through a swathe of stars.

Glancing to the side, he saw the other Pink Panther with Major Phillips driving, Ben Townsend and Roy Collinson on the front- and rear-mounted machine-guns, Clive Morrissey in charge of the LAW 80, Harry Spooner hemmed in by a PRC 319 radio system and canvas bags filled with explosives. Because the essence of the escape operation was now speed instead of care, the two Pink Panthers were travelling with dipped headlights which showed the ground only a short distance in front of each vehicle, leaving the rest of the surrounding area couched in darkness.

Though Williams was still driving this particular vehicle, Wild Bill Kowalski, who wished to stick close to Alice, had switched positions with Paddy Magee, who was now on the rear-mounted 0.5-inch Browning heavy machine gun. Wild Bill was now back in charge of his own American Stinger SAM system, cradling his Heckler & Koch MP5 across his heavy thighs and resting his feet on an open-topped packing crate filled with US M26 and British L2A2 phosphorous and fragmentation hand grenades.

Glancing in that direction, Kilroy saw the woman seated beside Paddy, separated from him only by the crates of supplies and ammunition strapped down between them. Both had their mouths and noses covered with fluttering *shemaghs*, protecting them from the wind-blown sand, but they were still managing to make conversation.

'Are you married, Paddy?' Alice asked.

'Ackay. Been married for eighteen years. Four kids, three girls an' a boy, all back in our wee house in Redhill, Surrey.'

'A good marriage?'

'We get on all right, apart from the fact that my missus resents my bein' away so much.'

'With the SAS?'

'Nat'rally.'

'How long have you been with the regiment?'

'Sure it's bin nearly ten years,' Paddy replied. 'I transferred from the Irish Guards.'

'Is this your first war?'

'Ack, no. Sure I fought in the Falklands eight year ago – me and Kilroy here.'

When Alice glanced at him, Kilroy returned his gaze to the desert straight ahead, though he couldn't help overhearing what was being said.

'Did you see much action there?' Alice asked.

'Enough to make m' toes curl,' Paddy replied. 'Me and Sergeant Kilroy, sure we hauled sledges up the Fortuna Glacier in South Georgia, inserted in Stromness Bay in Gemini dinghies, took part in the assault on Grytviken, inserted by helicopter, then were flown on to the Falkland Islands, where we crashed into the Atlantic in a Sea King helicopter with eighteen of our mates killed.'

'Oh, no!' Alice exclaimed.

'Ackay,' Paddy said with the air of a man who has put his bad experiences well behind him. 'Then we went on to establish OPs all over the place, took part in the diversionary raid of Goose Green, and fought our way from there to Port Stanley. We were there when Port Stanley fell.'

'You did a lot,' Alice said. Paddy just shrugged. 'And that was it until this war?' Alice asked him.

Paddy nodded. 'Aye, more or less. I mean, a couple of years before the Falklands War, me and Sergeant Kilroy here took part in the Iranian Embassy siege in London. Nineteen eighty, I think. That an' the Falklands was my lot until now.'

'That's plenty,' Alice said.

'Not enough for me,' Paddy said. 'Now Sergeant Kilroy here, he also took part in—'

'That's enough of that talking,' Kilroy interjected, knowing Paddy was going to mention that he had been in Northern Ireland and also taken part in the notorious killing of three IRA terrorists, including a woman, in Gibraltar in 1987. 'We're not supposed to talk about our work and you're blabbing away there.'

He glanced sideways and saw the angry glance of the woman as Paddy, looking flustered, said, 'Sorry, Sarge. I wouldn't normally talk about it, but Lieutenant Davis being a USAF officer an' all, I thought it would—'

'You thought wrong,' Kilroy snapped, ignoring the angry light in the woman's green eyes above the *shemagh*. 'We don't talk about our work, period, and that's all there is to it.'

'Sergeant Kilroy's right,' Captain Williams shouted over his shoulder, trying to make himself heard above the roaring of the Pink Panther and the wind's constant beating. 'We don't even discuss our work in front of Delta Force NCOs like Master Sergeant Kowalski – not without good reason – so let's drop the subject, please.'

'Right, boss,' Paddy said.

Realising that the woman was angry with him, as she often was, Kilroy met her gaze and saw the incandescence of her lovely green eyes emphasised by being framed between the fluttering *shemagh* and the wide brim of her desert hat. Though previously he hadn't given a damn what she thought of him, he was glad that Captain Williams had spoken up in support of him. In fact, it wasn't the need for secrecy that had made Kilroy reprimand Paddy – though, God knows, he wanted no one to know that he'd taken part in the Gibraltar killings – but the simple fact that he always felt uncomfortable when people spoke of what he had done as a member of the regiment. The woman, however, was certainly angry again with him; though, as he met the brightness of her narrowly framed eyes, he saw the anger receding into veiled embarrassment.

'I'm sorry,' she said, filling in a lengthy silence. 'That was my fault, Captain Williams. I shouldn't have asked Trooper Magee those questions. I should have known better.'

'No problem,' Williams replied distractedly, still concentrating on driving with dipped headlights through the sand-streaked, moonlit darkness.

Alice hadn't removed her steady gaze from Kilroy as she spoke and he realised that there was an unresolved conflict between them, largely based on her belief that he despised her. This wasn't quite true, though he had to admit to himself that he could have done without having a woman along. He really believed that women weren't as strong as men, should not take part in war, and were more naturally adept at keeping home and raising children. Of greater importance, however, was the fact that he didn't want to be reminded of his wife, Diane, now sitting in her chair at home, suffering all the torments of the damned and blaming him for it. In all truth, one of the reasons he most enjoyed being with the regiment was that it took him away from home, away from his wife and kids; twelve-year-old Tom and ten-year-old Teresa. Though he loved both kids deeply, he saw little of them and was uncomfortable with them during his visits, always aware of Diane's angry, accusing gaze and his own crushing guilt. He loved the regiment – and, most of all, he loved war – because it distracted him from all of that.

Now, however, this woman, this Lieutenant Alice Davis, who seemed to burn with her own brand of suppressed rage, was a constant reminder of what he had left behind and wished to forget. She, too, was blonde. She was green-eyed and accusing. She burned quietly with an anger whose nature he could not know and he found himself constantly wondering what it was and how he could soothe it. He wanted to do that – to soothe her rage and bring her closer – but he sensed that breaking down the wall between them would not be easy. He wanted to do it – to help himself by helping her – but he didn't yet know how to approach her. He was baffled and unsettled by her presence and that made him tread carefully.

'Looks like Geordie's coming back,' Wild Bill said, squinting into the hissing sand that blew across the racing Pink Panther. 'I see a trail of dust out there.'

'A single headlight,' Kilroy said. 'That's him all right.'

When Geordie had materialised fully out of the swirling sand and moonlit darkness, becoming recognisable, Williams used a hand signal, indicating to the other Pink Panther that he was stopping. Geordie braked to a fancy halt right in front of both vehicles, skidding dramatically sideways in a cloud of swirling sand and jumping off with the grace of an acrobat. Pushing the dust-covered goggles up onto his forehead, he sauntered over to speak with his squadron commander.

'What's happening?' Williams asked.

'The whole area between here and Scud Alley's been blocked off by Iraqi troops,' Geordie replied. 'They're all over the place, boss. Swarming like ants out there. I went the whole north–south axis of the old Road Watch North, Centre and South locations, between RT10 and H1, and found Iraqis scouring the whole area. We just can't get through that way.'

Williams nodded thoughtfully, then said, 'OK, Corporal, thanks. There's hot tea in thermos flasks in that other jeep, so go and have a cup, tell the others to take a break, and send Major Phillips over to me.'

As Geordie walked off to the other Pink Panther, Williams turned sideways in his seat and picked up a map. 'The same goes for you lot,' he said. 'Take a break, have a brew-up. You can even smoke. God knows, the glow of a few cigarettes will make little difference now.'

Grateful for the opportunity, the others set about pouring tea or lighting cigarettes as Williams spread the map out on the seat beside him. Kilroy, smoking a cigarette, and Wild Bill, sipping tea, leant over the seat as Captain Williams shone a torchlight on the military map and studied it at length. Eventually, while Williams was still deep in thought, Major Phillips arrived from the other Pink Panther, nodded at each of the men in turn, then gave Alice a warm smile.

'Enjoying the trip, Lieutenant?' he asked.

'The thrill of my life, Major.'

'At least it beats being back in that prison cell.'

'You can say that again.'

Phillips grinned, then turned to Williams, asking, 'What's up?' Williams explained the situation. 'So what's our alternative?' Phillips asked.

'We have to make a lengthy detour,' Williams said.

'I would have assumed so,' Phillips replied. 'But to where, exactly?'

Williams tapped his finger on the map where it was illuminated in the narrow beam of the torchlight. 'Going east will take us back to urbanised Iraq. Westward takes us to Jordan, which, as you know, is a noncombatant ally of Saddam Hussein.'

'Right,' Wild Bill interjected. 'And as those sonsofbitches recently handed over some crashed US pilots to Saddam, they're unlikely to help us if we make it that far.'

'Which leaves north and south,' Phillips said.

'South,' Williams said, 'takes us back to the MSR leading from Baghdad to Basra, so clearly we have to avoid that. Which leaves us with only north – or, more precisely, northwest – and the frontier with Syria.'

'Syria's a member of the anti-Iraq coalition,' Phillips said. 'So it's clearly the best bet.'

'Then that's where we'll head for,' Williams said. He folded the map up, tucked it away, then glanced around the flat, moonlit desert, seeing clouds of swirling sand erasing the stars; frost glinting on gravel and low rocks. 'Damned cold,' he said, shivering.

'It sure is,' Wild Bill agreed.

'We'll stay warmer if we keep moving,' Kilroy said. 'And the quicker we move, the quicker we'll get back, the less we'll be endangered by our shortage of rations and water. Both are running out fast.'

'Right,' Williams said. 'So we'll head for the location of the old Road Watch North, circle around north-west to Al Qaim, then head from there towards Scud Boulevard.'

'Get there,' Wild Bill said, 'and we stand a good chance of being picked up by my Delta Force buddies.'

'And failing that,' Williams said, 'we keep going until we cross the border into Syria.'

'Agreed,' Phillips said. 'And I think we should move out immediately.'

'Let's do that,' Williams said. 'Please send Corporal Welsh out ahead again with instructions to report back every thirty minutes. Should he not return within that time, we'll know that something's amiss.'

'Right,' Phillips said. He turned away and marched back to the second Pink Panther.

'I don't envy that mad biker,' Wild Bill said as he settled back into his position, cramped between the Stinger SAM system and a crate of grenades. 'He's entirely alone out there.'

'Sure it's his job,' Paddy said, slipping back into his position behind the rear-mounted 0.5-inch Browning heavy machine gun. 'He thinks it's perfectly nat'ral, like.'

'Rather him than me,' Alice said, settling down in her cramped position between crates of supplies and ammunition as Kilroy seated himself behind the front-mounted GPMG, mere inches from her.

'Let's move out,' Williams said. He raised and lowered his right hand in a languid forward motion, indicating that the other Pink Panther should move out as well. Instantly, Geordie kicked his motorbike into life and shot across to Williams's Pink Panther where he skidded into a sideways halt and grinned at them out of a cloud of swirling sand.

'You want me to go ahead again, boss?'

'Yes, Corporal. Thirty minutes at a time. Fifteen minutes out, a quick reconnoitre of the area, then another fifteen minutes to report back. In the case of an emergency, make contact through your Landmaster transceiver. OK, off you go.'

Geordie grinned cockily at Paddy. 'Must be pretty boring sitting there and getting only a sore arse.'

'Sure it's better havin' a sore arse than losin' yer balls when somethin' hot and bright explodes under yer saddle. Rather you than me, mate.'

'At least I've got balls to lose,' Geordie retorted, 'which is more than some here can say.'

'He thinks he's Evil Knieval,' Paddy explained to Wild Bill. 'That motorbike's his wee toy.' Then, turning back to the grinning Geordie, he said, 'Piss off, you lunatic.'

'I'm on my way,' Geordie said.

He gunned the engine, raised the front wheel off the ground, then roared off again, leaving his customary trail of boiling sand behind him.

The two Pink Panthers advanced in his wake, gradually spreading well apart to contain the damage in the event of a surprise attack by the enemy. Soon they were both racing across the sand at a brisk forty miles an hour, following the trail of billowing sand left by Geordie and then relying on their SATNAV GPS to guide them in the right direction.

Seated behind his front-mounted GPMG, Kilroy scanned the desert ahead, straining to see through the moonlit darkness and occasionally glancing at Alice, surprised at how much he was thinking about her and haunted by the thought of his wife back in Hereford, still and silent, her gaze bright and accusing. Tormented by the recollection, he tried to suppress it and concentrated even more on the landscape ahead, that sheet of stars broken up by the irregular blackness of low mountain ridges.

Geordie kept coming and going, roaring in and out on his motorbike, either reporting that the road was clear or recommending a change in direction to take them around the enemy forces he had seen up ahead. This made the journey longer, with the distant mountain ridges seeming to shift their position, but they managed to keep going throughout most of the night without making contact with the enemy.

Eventually, about an hour before first light, Geordie returned to tell them that the road to the abandoned SAS Road Watch North location was clear. Ordered by Captain Williams to go on ahead again, he roared away in a cloud of dust.

He had just been swallowed by the darkness when the sound of an explosion was heard from far ahead, accompanied by a jagged flaring of light that briefly wiped out the stars before receding into a pool of darkness and ominous silence.

Instantly, the two Pink Panthers braked to a halt and the men in them strained to see and hear what was happening far ahead. Eventually, after an interminable, uneasy silence, Williams glanced at Kilroy.

'Landmine,' Kilroy said.

'That could mean a whole minefield.'

'I think it does.'

'You think Geordie's bought it?' Wild Bill asked.

'Yes,' Kilroy said.

'He might still be alive,' Alice said.

'That's true enough,' Williams said. 'So let's go and find out – but let's do it slowly.'

Using a hand signal, he indicated that the second Pink Panther should drop behind and follow him at a safe distance. Then he drove forward slowly, not shifting from second gear, towards where he could just about make out a subsiding column of sand, indicating where the mine had exploded in a narrow gorge between two low mountain ranges that stretched east and west for as far as the eye could see.

The closer the Pink Panther came to the subsiding cloud of sand, the more slowly Captain Williams drove until he was down to first gear and hardly moving at all. At this point, Kilroy, without waiting for orders, jumped out of the side of the jeep and advanced ahead of it on foot, checking the ground as best he could for signs of land mines. Even as he was doing this, the sun was rising over the horizon, a bright yellow crescent that turned the blue sky along the low mountain ridges into a crimson flood. That light fell on the mountains and the flat plains below, gradually bleeding into the darkness, and Kilroy stopped walking, making the Pink Panther halt behind him, when the advancing light gradually reached Geordie.

He was lying beside his mangled motorbike, having been thrown off it by the blast. He was only about two hundred yards away, at the entrance to the gorge.

Suddenly, he let out a scream that tore hideously through the morning's silence before fading away.

Kilroy could see him writhing on the ground, trying vainly to move his mangled legs and hammering his clenched first against the ground, again and again. Then he let out another dreadful scream that tapered off into sobbing.

'Damn!' Kilroy whispered.

Slowly, carefully, he lowered himself onto his belly and squinted along the flat ground, gradually discerning through its drifting mantle of sand a series of barely perceptible mounds which could only be landmines. They had been planted closely together in the ground, almost certainly from wall to wall across the gorge and along the whole length of it. As there was no visible route around the mountain ridges, the mined gorge was the only way through to the desert beyond.

'Fuck!' Kilroy whispered. Raising himself onto his knees, he bellowed, 'Geordie! It's me! Kilroy! Can you hear me?'

For a while there was only the sound of Geordie's anguished sobbing, then he shouted back, 'Yes!' He almost choked on the word, then managed to shout, 'Christ, Kilroy, it hurts! My fucking legs! Oh, my God! I can't move! Ah, Jesus!'

Kilroy glanced back over his shoulder to see that Alice and the three men were all standing up in the first Pink Panther, straining to see.

'Stay there!' he shouted at them. 'Don't get out of the jeep. Geordie ran into a minefield. The whole gorge is mined.'

After a lengthy, shocked silence, Captain Williams shouted back, 'OK, Sarge! We're waiting right here.'

When Geordie screamed again, sounding almost inhuman, Kilroy turned back to the front and saw him beating his clenched fist on the ground as his smouldering, mangled legs twitched repeatedly, this now being the limit of their mobility.

'Geordie!' Kilroy bawled.

'Yes, Kilroy! Yes!'

'Can you move at all?'

'No! Oh, God, no! Jesus, Kilroy, it hurts! I think my legs are . . .' He hesitated, unable to state the awful truth, then shouted, 'It's bad, Kilroy. Real bad.'

Kilroy was silent for a moment, wondering what he could do, then he bawled, 'Try to hold on, Geordie. I'm coming to get you.'

'No!' Geordie shouted back. Then he screamed and started sobbing. He managed to control himself and shouted, 'No! The whole place is mined. There's more mines between me and you! Oh, God, Kilroy, I'm fucked!'

'You're not fucked. We'll think of something, Geordie. Just try to hold on there.'

'I'm fucked. You can't come in here, Kilroy. You have to explode the mines first. There's no other way. You have to blow the whole mine field up. Call in an air strike.'

'We can't call in an air strike while you're there.'

'Yes, you can. You've got to.' Geordie screamed in pain again, a terrible, lacerating sound, then he managed to control himself once more, repeating, 'You've got to. You can't get me out, Kilroy. I'm fucked and there's nothing you can do except clear the minefield. Never mind me. I'm fucked. I'm finished. I can't stand it. I'll end it. Call the aircraft in, Kilroy.'

Then he screamed again.

Kilroy turned away, crawled a short distance on hands and knees, then clambered to his feet and returned to the first Pink Panther, where Captain Williams, Wild Bill, Paddy and Alice were all standing upright in the vehicle, staring down with distraught eyes.

'He's in a bad way?' Captain Williams asked.

'Pretty bad,' Kilroy told him. 'I'd say it's just a matter of time, though it could be a long time.'

'We can't drag him out?'

'We can't get through the minefield. We have to blow up the mines to get through the gorge and he can't be moved first.'

'Dear God,' Williams whispered.

'Jesus Christ,' Wild Bill said.

'If we call in the aircraft, he's dead,' Paddy said. 'That's for sure.'

'He knows that,' Kilroy said.

'That doesn't mean we can do it,' Alice said.

'He said we should do it,' Kilroy told her. 'He knows what's at stake here.'

'You can't do that!' Alice insisted.

'What's our option?' Kilroy asked her.

'There must be a way to get him out,' Alice said.

'What way?' Kilroy asked her.

He saw the shock in her eyes, mixed in with outrage, and, although he knew damned well that it was hopeless, he felt he had to try something. Turning from Alice to Williams, he said, 'There *is* a possibility that I could use two of the steel sand channels, pushing one ahead to ignite any mines between me and Geordie and holding the other one up to deflect the blast of them that go up. If I get to him that way, I can pull him out on the first sand channel. It might just work, boss.'

Williams thought about this for a moment. The steel sand channels were five-foot-long strips of metal, shaped like guttering but much wider, which could be slid under the wheels of vehicles trapped in soft sand to give firm support for the rotating tyres and make it easier to push them out. Having thought about it, Williams said, 'If a mine blows up beneath you, I don't think that a steel channel held up in front of you is going to protect you from it. You'll be too close for that.'

Another dreadful scream from Geordie made both men glance in his direction to see him writhing in agony again and hammering the ground with his clenched fist. The other hand, they now noticed, was as mangled and bloody as his legs. If rescued, he would certainly not survive, but that was hardly the point.

'That's a chance I'm willing to take, boss,' Kilroy said, turning back to Captain Williams. 'We can't leave him out there. And we can't get through unless we remove him and have the gorge cleared with an air attack. It's sticks and stones, boss.'

Williams sighed. 'OK, Sarge, let's try it.'

'That's goddamned suicidal,' Wild Bill said to Kilroy. 'Even *I* couldn't hold one of those sand channels upright against the blast of a landmine planted as close as you're going to be – and I'm as strong as a mule. That steel channel will be scorched and buckled and blown back into your face, probably killing you before the actual blast does. It's suicidal, believe me.'

When Geordie screamed again in his terrible agony, Paddy, looking distraught, said, 'If Sergeant Kilroy doesn't try it, I will. We can't leave Geordie out there.'

'So let me try it,' Kilroy said.

Without waiting to be contradicted, he proceeded to untie the steel channels from the side of the Pink Panther. Once they were loosened, he humped them up onto his shoulder and walked back to what he believed was the front edge of the minefield, approximately two hundred yards away. There, he went onto his knees, removed the two steel channels from his shoulder, and laid one flat on the ground with the channel pointing directly at the groaning, sobbing Geordie. He then lay on his belly and, using his right hand, raised the second steel channel horizontally in front of him, forming what he hoped would be a blast-break. Instantly, he felt the strain in his arms, the pains darting between his shoulder blades, and understood that what he was attempting might be next to impossible.

Nevertheless, when Geordie screamed out again, Kilroy knew that he had to at least try it.

'Geordie!' he bawled. 'It's me! Kilroy! I'm coming out to get you. Hang on there, Geordie!'

Lying flat on his back, Geordie managed to raise his head high enough to see Kilroy stretched out on the ground behind the horizontally raised length of steel channelling. Exhausted by even that small effort, Geordie dropped his head again. That effort alone was enough to make him scream out in agony. Then he caught his breath and shouted, 'No, Kilroy! Don't try it! You won't make it! The mines are too close together for that! We'll both cop it, Kilroy!'

Sweating profusely, with his arms already aching and pains darting between his shoulder blades, Kilroy held the horizontal channel in his right hand and tentatively pushed the other one forward, inch by inch, until he had moved it about twelve inches. Hitting no landmine, he lowered the steel channel raised in front of him and tried to relax his arm before repeating the process.

'No, Kilroy!' Geordie shouted. 'No farther! Go back, please go back! I'm finished anyway! It's over!'

'We have to clear the minefield,' Kilroy shouted at him. 'We have to call in an air strike. It's not just for you, Geordie, it's for all of us, so I'm coming to get you. Hang in there, mate.'

'Then call in the air strike!' Geordie shouted. 'It makes no difference to me! I'm finished, Kilroy. I'm fucked. Jesus, Kilroy, don't try it.'

'I'm coming to get you,' Kilroy shouted back, then reached down with his right hand to raise the steel channel in front of his face again.

'Oh, God, what's he doing?' Alice cried out behind him, from where she was standing upright in the Pink Panther, suddenly staring even more intently at where Geordie was lying.

When Kilroy lowered the steel channel to look ahead again, he saw Geordie wriggling frantically on the ground, trying to draw his Browning handgun from its dusty leather holster.

'Ack, Jesus!' Paddy exclaimed. 'Sure he's gonna take the fuckin' Exit Club. Don't, Geordie! *Don't*!'

But even as Paddy bawled that entreaty, Kilroy saw Geordie withdrawing the Nine-Milly from his holster. Then he cocked it and held it to his temple.

'Ah, God!' he sobbed.

He squeezed the trigger and blew his own brains out. His head rocked once and then was still; the pistol fell from his hand.

'Oh, Christ!' Kilroy said softly.

He dropped the steel channel and laid his forehead upon it, gazing into the darkness behind his closed eyes and taking deep breaths to still his racing heart. Finally, after what seemed like an eternity, he raised his head again and looked along the ground to where Geordie was lying. There was no movement there. Geordie's head was a mess. The Browning lay beside his outstretched hand. Kilroy stared at him, trying to accept what had happened. At last accepting it, he placed the two steel channels together, one on top of the other, then stood up and made his careful way back to the jeep.

Alice had turned away and was dabbing at her eyes with her tear-soaked *shemagh*. Wild Bill and Paddy were both looking shocked. Williams was staring down at him, trying to control his emotions.

'He knew we couldn't get through without clearing the minefield,' Williams said. 'He also knew that we couldn't do that while he was still alive. That's why he took the Exit Club, Sarge. It wasn't your fault. Now let's call in that air strike.'

While Kilroy strapped the steel channels back onto the side of the Pink Panther, glancing up occasionally to see Alice drying her tears, Williams had Paddy contact HQ Riyadh on the SATCOM system, using short-burst transmissions, then he called up an air strike by AWACS command aircraft.

Thirty minutes later, two US Strike Eagles arrived. Guided precisely to the target by the Military Grid coordinates given on Williams's Magellan GPS 1000M receiver, they dived out of the dawn sky to rake the gorge with AIM-9L Sidewinder rockets and M61A1 20mm rotary cannons, turning it into a nightmare of exploding sand and soil, sheets of vivid white-and-yellow flame, and boiling black smoke. Instantly, the explosions from the Strike Eagles' rockets and cannons ignited the many landmines planted along the gorge and they, too, exploded, adding to the fiery, noisy spectacle. Within minutes, the whole gorge had been obscured in spiralling sand, soil and smoke, with explosions continuing farther along and great chunks being torn from the rocky walls to crash down onto the desert floor, creating more clouds of dust.

The Strike Eagles made three attacks, sweeping down and across the desert with awesome precision, one close behind the other, and then rolling in salute to the men below before flying away for good. Eventually, when the planes had gone and the silence had returned, the spiralling sand, soil and smoke subsided to let the gorge reappear.

The ground where Geordie had been lying – and the floor of the gorge beyond it – was now no more than a series of blackened shell holes surrounded by widely strewn, smouldering rubble. There was no trace of Geordie.

'Let's move out,' Williams said.

No other word was spoken as the two Pink Panthers advanced carefully into the gorge, passed slowly through it, and emerged eventually in one piece from the other side. There they were dazzled by the sunlight on the plains, which were vast, sunscorched and seemingly empty. The Pink Panthers moved on.

CHAPTER TWENTY

After the biting cold of night, the heat seemed doubly fierce and soon Alice was sweating profusely, as were all of the others. The Pink Panther was making good speed across the vast, flat plain, heading towards a dark line of mountain ridges on the horizon, and the wind rushed across it, making the many communications antennae quiver like bowstrings, giving off whistling sounds, and whipping sand into Alice's face. Luckily, she had the *shemagh* back up over her face, protecting her nose and mouth, but she felt grains of sand attacking the skin around her eyes, which were covered with Litton night-vision goggles under the wide-brimmed desert hat. The four men in the jeep were wearing the same, though with berets instead of hats, and it made them look like strange, inhuman creatures in the howling dust and blazing heat of an alien planet.

They were unusually subdued. The death of Geordie had obviously shocked them, as indeed it had shocked Alice, and now they were content to be silent and concentrate on the vast, desolate desert.

Though the plain was flat and seemingly featureless, it was

not as easy to travel on as it looked, being a treacherous combination of soft sand, loose gravel, smooth lava rock, sharp stones and wadis, all of which could occasionally trap even the highly sophisticated Pink Panthers. Though specially modified to enable them to roam virtually at will anywhere in the desert, the Pink Panthers could still become bogged down in soft sand and then had to be pulled out with the help of the steel channels first used by Major Bagnold in Africa in the 1930s. In order to do this, they had to unload the vehicle to make it lighter, then laboriously dig and scrape the sand away from the trapped wheels. When the wheels were freed, the steel channels were slipped between them and the soft sand; then the vehicle, with its engine running in low gear, could be pushed forward over the steel channels until it was free. It then had to be reloaded with all the kit before the team could move off again.

The releasing of trapped vehicles was a backbreaking, time-consuming task that was done in the fierce heat and constantly blowing sand of the open plain. As each of the two teams was responsible for its own Pink Panther, the other team kept watch for enemy patrols while the men with the trapped vehicle sweated and struggled in the blazing sun to set it free.

Alice had already taken part in just such a rescue operation, sliding the steel channels under the wheels of Captain Williams's Pink Panther while Wild Bill, Kilroy and Paddy Magee pushed the vehicle out; now it was her team's turn to keep watch while the men of the other team engaged in the same arduous task, all of them pouring sweat as they pushed and pulled in the suffocating furnace of high noon.

Sitting beside Wild Bill in the Pink Panther, scanning the desert through binoculars, Alice was surprised at how empty it all seemed when it was, as she knew, being crisscrossed with enemy troop trucks. Finally deciding to rest her eyes, which had started watering from the sheer brightness the minute she had removed her night-vision goggles, she placed the binoculars on her raised knees, pointed towards the distant mountain ridges and asked, 'Is that Scud Boulevard over there?'

'More or less,' Wild Bill replied. 'Combined, we call our Scud Boulevard and the Brits' Scud Alley the "Scud box" because that area's crawling with Iraqi mobile Scud launchers. It's spread out over approximately two hundred forty square miles beyond those mountains, which are part of the Jordanian lava plateau.'

'We're going to have to cross them?' Alice asked.

'Yep.'

'What are they like?'

'High and hilly. Crisscrossed with deep wadis that often get flash-flooded after storms. Loose rock instead of sand, though dense sandstorms are blown in from other areas. Lots of rain and fog instead of burning sun. Freezing cold at nights. Sleet, snow, hail and frost. Nothing like you'd imagine the desert to be. It's a whole different ball game.'

'It sounds like hell,' Alice said.

'It's not heaven,' Wild Bill said.

'You think we'll make it?'

Wild Bill sighed. 'We might.' He nodded at Kilroy, sitting behind the front-mounted GPMG and grimly scanning the desert, then at the men digging out the trapped Pink Panther. 'These SAS guys are pretty damned exceptional. They know what they're doing and they're not easily stopped. If anyone can get us out, they can. As for me, my brief's to return you safe and sound and I'm determined to do it.'

'That's good to know,' Alice said.

'You didn't smile when you said that, Lieutenant, so I guess you resent me being here and placed in charge of you. More so because you outrank me.'

'I don't resent you and I'm not worried that a Delta Force NCO's been put in charge of my safety. I just don't smile easily. Given what I've been through since joining the Air Force, smiling doesn't come naturally.'

'Yeah, it couldn't have been easy,' Wild Bill said, obviously thinking she meant only her capture and imprisonment by the Iraqis. 'You've had a pretty rough ride. Don't know that I could have taken it so well myself. You did well, Lieutenant.'

Alice glanced up at Sergeant Kilroy. She wondered if he could hear the conversation and she wanted him to.

I want him to think well of me, she thought, startled to realise what she was thinking. I must be still wet behind the ears. Why him of all people?

'You think these guys are as good as the Delta Force?' Alice asked.

Wild Bill grinned and shook his head ruefully. 'There's no way I can answer that, Lieutenant, without cutting my own throat. They're damned good – but so are we. We cross-train with each other and sling shit at each other when we do so, but secretly we respect each other and are mutually supportive. Who's best? I wouldn't even attempt to answer that question. But this bunch? Yeah, they're good.'

'They're tough, but not rough,' Alice said. 'I mean, given what they're called upon to do, they seem pretty well mannered.'

'You mean to you?' Wild Bill asked bluntly.

'Yeah, Sarge, I guess so.' She blushed a little when she confessed that. 'I mean, I thought they'd resent me more than they do, but most of them seem to treat me as an equal. That kinda surprised me.'

'Why? You're an officer and a pilot with combat experience. You've already earned their respect.'

'I still didn't expect it. It's not what I got at . . .' She hesitated, still pained by the memory. 'At the Air Force Academy. Since then I've always been wary.'

'They gave you a rough time?'

'More than that.'

'What does that mean, Lieutenant?'

'I don't want to talk about it,' Alice said. 'But it sure coloured my thinking. That's why I'm so surprised that most of these men treat me with respect. I wasn't expecting that.'

They were silent for a moment, watching the men struggling with the trapped Pink Panther about a hundred metres away, Major Phillips revving the engine while it was in second gear, the others stretched out at an angle behind it, their feet braced against the ground as they pushed it along the steel channels to get it out of the sand. They were so soaked in sweat, they all looked as if they had just been drenched in a rainstorm.

Snorting with impatience, Kilroy clambered down from his GPMG and marched off to help the other men. Alice watched him departing.

'You said *most* of them, Lieutenant,' Wild Bill said. 'Who's the odd man out?'

'Him,' Alice said, pointing at Kilroy as he approached the trapped jeep and the men struggling behind it.

'Kilroy?'

'Yep.'

'I don't think he's the kind to treat a woman with disrespect,' Wild Bill said. 'A bit distant, maybe, a bit cold, but he's not disrespectful.'

'He doesn't like women.'

'He doesn't think women should be in a war and that's an entirely different matter. I don't agree, but that's just the way he thinks.'

'No,' Alice said. 'It's more than that. Something about me makes him uncomfortable. I can tell by the way he looks at me. He sure as hell makes *me* uncomfortable.'

'He's a strange one,' Wild Bill said. 'That's for sure. But a damned fine soldier.'

'What makes him so different from the others?'

'He has the killer instinct.'

'You mean he's violent?'

'He'd certainly have a strain of that in him, but a man with an overtly violent nature won't make a good soldier. Self-control is what makes a good soldier and Kilroy certainly has that.'

'I think he's violent,' Alice said. 'It may be controlled, but it's always there, ready to explode.'

'Maybe that's why he's so distant,' Wild Bill said. 'Why he's cooler than most. Some men become soldiers to contain the violence they feel inside themselves: to give it an outlet. Some men become soldiers for the discipline. Some men need both. I think Kilroy's that kind.'

'Yeah,' Alice said. 'I think he's shown that violence in the past and now he's keeping the hatch battened down.'

'Maybe,' Wild Bill said. 'That's certainly why a lot of men become soldiers.'

'What about you?' Alice asked, trying to get off the subject of Kilroy and onto more neutral ground. 'Is that why you joined the Army and ended up in the Delta Force?'

'I don't know that I was ever violent,' Wild Bill said, 'but I sure needed excitement. Still do, I guess.'

'Yet you're married and have kids.'

'*Happily* married,' Wild Bill emphasised, 'with very happy kids. The need for excitement, for danger, doesn't mean you can't be a decent husband and father. It just means, in my case, that I'm away from home a lot more than my wife likes; but she's learned to accept that. I mean, men working in factories often work more and are home a lot less. Everything evens out.'

'Why do you need excitement and danger?' Alice asked.

'Because I'm easily bored.'

'Men are such sad sacks,' Alice said.

'We have our good side,' Wild Bill replied.

Phillips's Pink Panther had finally been pushed out of the sand and Alice saw the dark, intense Trooper Roy Collinson tying the metal channels back on as Kilroy returned to his own vehicle. He glanced at her as he clambered back up into the jeep and took his seat behind the front-mounted GPMG, just behind the head and shoulders of Captain Williams who had been using the break to study the map opened up on his lap. Oddly disturbed by that brief glance, feeling as if she had been violated, Alice felt her cheeks burning and busied herself with checking the SLR she had been given by Williams.

'Are they set to go over there?' Williams asked, folding up his map and tucking it away.

'Yes, boss,' Kilroy replied.

'Good,' Williams said. He turned on the ignition of his vehicle, let it tick over, raised and lowered his right hand, indicating that he was about to advance, then moved off again.

Within seconds, with the increasing speed of the Pink Panther, Alice was forced to lower the goggles over her eyes and raise the *shemagh* to protect her mouth and nose from the beating sand. The afternoon heat was truly appalling and the desert seemed to stretch on for ever. For the first few hours, they made no contact with enemy transports or tanks, though they did see the odd Bedouin caravan, the Arabs in fluttering robes, astride camels burdened with carpets and woven bags filled with a wide variety of wares which they were taking to market regardless of the war being waged all around them.

Eventually, however, as the two SAS Pink Panthers drew closer to the mountains, the north–south border of the Scud box, Alice saw distant columns of dust, indicating the movement of enemy troop trucks or convoys. Assuming that these were the vehicles of the Iraqis reported by Geordie as spreading out all over the area in a determined bid to find the SAS rescue teams, Williams kept changing direction to avoid them. This tactic gradually forced them north, parallel to Scud Alley, patrolled by SAS units, but each time they tried heading in that direction, they were blocked by the distant clouds of boiling sand being churned up by the Iraqi patrols.

Finally, as they crossed a main supply route, the two Pink Panthers were so close to the Scud box that the enemy trucks were clearly visible in the distance. To avoid them, Williams signalled for the second Pink Panther to follow him, then he drove down a dangerously steep slope of loose gravel, shifting sand and smooth lava rock, into a dusty culvert under the road. There they waited, still sitting in their vehicles, until the enemy convoy had passed, rumbling practically overhead. When the sound of the last truck had faded away, Williams clambered up the side of the culvert, followed by the other members of his team, and scanned the north-westerly border of the Scud box through his binoculars.

'Damn!' he exclaimed softly, lowering the binoculars and wiping sand and sweat from his high forehead. 'We're so damned close to the Scud box, which our own men are patrolling, but the whole area between here and there is crawling with heavily armed Iraqi troops, all looking for us. We're only about ten miles from the Scud box and if we could get into it, we'd be home and dry. If we can't get into it, we'll have to head for Syria, which is a hell of a lot farther away, along an enemy-held route.'

'That doesn't sound like a good choice,' Wild Bill said.

'No, it's not,' Williams said.

They all studied the terrain ahead in silence, watching the shifting clouds of dust, then Kilroy said, 'If we head for Syria, we have to accept that we're going to be travelling for two or three days, through enemy territory, with our food and water supplies getting lower all the time. On the other hand, if we break through to the Scud box, we'll be in SAS territory in less than an hour. The question is: can we break through and is the chance worth the taking?'

'It's a long chance,' Wild Bill said, 'and if it fails, we'll either be caught or wiped out. On the other hand, if we head for Syria and get as far as Al Qaim, we could turn south there and make our way into Scud Boulevard, patrolled by my Delta Force buddies.'

'What are the odds on reaching Al Qaim?' Alice asked.

'Higher than those for breaking through to the Scud box,' Kilroy flatly informed her, 'though it's still bloody dangerous.'

'The thought of being inside the Scud box within the hour is very tempting,' Williams said. 'We also have to consider our rapidly diminishing food and water if we make the longer journey to Al Qaim.'

'We have enough water and food for another twenty-four hours,' Kilroy said. 'After that, we'll have to forage for both.'

'How do we do that?' Alice asked him.

'Either we take fossil water from prehistoric aquifers beneath the desert floor or we negotiate with local landowners to take water from their artesian wells. We also negotiate with the locals for food – either that or we steal it.'

'That's dodgy enough,' Wild Bill said. 'If we have to negotiate with locals, we won't know who's gonna help or who'll turn us in. Each time we have to do that, we'll be taking a long chance.'

'And over there,' Paddy said, 'ten miles away, our own mates are patrolling. I say let's take that chance.'

A thoughtful silence ensued. Alice knew that she had just taken part in the informal exchange known in SAS parlance as a 'Chinese parliament' and that all views were welcomed, regardless of the rank of the individual. It was, she thought, an admirable system that minimised the chance of unspoken resentment if things went wrong later. No wonder she was beginning to respect these men: they were actually civilised.

Finally, when the silence had stretched out long enough, Captain Williams said, 'Right. I think we're all agreed that we should try to break through to the Scud box. Stay here and keep watch while I propose it to Major Phillips and his men. I'll be back in a short while.'

He clambered to his feet and made his way back down into the dusty, rubbish-strewn culvert, where he spoke at length to Phillips and his men. While waiting for him to return, Alice and the other three continued lying on their bellies on the sloping rim of the culvert, watching out for advancing Iraqi patrols. Occasionally, Alice would glance sideways at Kilroy, who was just a few feet from her, but his gaze was focused steadily on the flat plain that stretched out before him. Returning her gaze to the front, feeling vaguely disappointed, Alice counted the separate columns of dust that were spiralling over the flat plain in the distance and guessed from what she saw that nearly a dozen Iraqi patrols were covering the area, all within eyeball contact of one another, forming an almost solid block across the north–south length of Scud Alley, between RT 10 and the location of the old SAS Road Watch North, which would be their escape route to Syria if things went wrong.

'There's a lot of them out there,' she said finally.

'Too many,' Kilroy replied flatly.

At that moment, Williams returned to say, 'Major Phillips and the others agree, so we're moving out immediately. Take up your positions in the jeep and prepare your weapons for firing. We're going to try to break through using the speed of our vehicles and the element of surprise; and if either of the two jeeps break through to Scud Alley, it's to keep going despite what happens to the other. OK, let's hop to it.'

Knowing the odds against them, Alice felt a twinge of fear lancing through her, but it subsided as soon as she was back in the Pink Panther, hemmed in by boxes of supplies and ammunition, with Kilroy only a few feet away, seated behind his front-mounted GPMG, Wild Bill right beside her, his Heckler & Koch MP5 across his heavy thighs, his Stinger SAM system propped up between him and the boxes of hand grenades, and Paddy Magee back on the rear-mounted 0.5-inch Browning heavy machine gun.

When they were all in position, Williams started up the Pink Panther and moved off, the engine screeching in first gear as the vehicle inched laboriously up the steep gradient, its tyres spinning in loose gravel and sand. Eventually, after sliding back a few times, it bounced back onto level ground and accelerated across the flat, sunscorched plain.

Instead of fear, Alice experienced a keen, almost unnatural exhilaration as the Pink Panther raced towards those distant columns of dust and sand, its wheels making a rhythmic drumming sound of the ground's combination of hard-packed sand, loose gravel and smooth lava rock, the wind making the communications antennae whistle, beating noisily against the sides of the vehicle, and slapping at her face, making the *shemagh* flutter wildly over her nose and lips. Glancing east, she saw the other Pink Panther also racing across the plain, about a hundred metres away, pacing the vehicle she was in, with Corporal Townsend on the front-mounted GPMG, Roy Collinson on the rear-mounted heavy machine-gun, and Staff Sergeant Morrissey and Sergeant Spooner huddled between them, taking care of the LAW 80 anti-tank weapon, PRC 319 radio system, personal weapons and crates of explosives. Alice held her SLR firmly across her lap and prepared to use it.

In less than ten minutes they had crossed six miles of ground and the columns of dust in the distance were clearly taking shape as Iraqi troop convoys on the move. Heading away from the convoys, towards an area free of boiling dust, the Pink Panthers were soon racing directly towards a laager of parked Iraqi troop trucks. As they approached the laager, trying to circle around it while staying out of firing range of the Iraqi guns, the trucks of the convoys in the distance broke apart to spread out across the plain and head in their direction. At the same time, as the Pink Panthers crossed west of the Iraqi laager, the troops inside the laager hurried away from their campfire to take up protected positions behind the parked trucks and open fire with a combination of machine guns, semi-automatic assault rifles and, finally, mortars.

Explosions from the Iraqi mortars tore up the ground between the two racing Pink Panthers as bullets from the machine guns and rifles ricocheted noisily off them. Instantly,

Kilroy and Paddy returned the fire with their mounted machine guns, creating a deafening din, and kept firing, trying to keep the Iraqis pinned down, as their Pink Panther raced past the laager. More bullets ricocheted off the Pink Panther, snapping off one of the whipping antennae, which flew away in the wind, glittering like a spinning dagger, as three troop trucks from one of the convoys spread out in a long line that forced Williams to turn away and circle around the laager, trapped within firing range of the enemy guns. When more mortar explosions tore up the ground between the two Pink Panthers, both drivers started frantically weaving to avoid them.

As Williams's Pink Panther circled around the laager, trying to find a clear way west, towards Scud Alley, Alice saw Kilroy swinging his mounted machine gun from left to right, both of his legs braced, to rake the parked trucks and those firing from behind them. The canvas coverings of the troop trucks were torn to shreds and sand exploded inside the laager as Kilroy's fusillade of bullets, augmented by Paddy's, caused devastation and sent men bowling dead or wounded to the ground.

The mortar explosions forced the Pink Panthers away from the laager just as one of the Iraqi trucks, obviously containing ammunition, exploded with a shocking roar and turned into a searing ball of yellow flame that licked out to engulf some of the Iraqi soldiers. Turning into human torches, they screamed and ran this way and that until, still burning and smoking, they either collapsed or were cut down by more bullets from the SAS machine guns.

The two Pink Panthers were now heading directly towards Scud Alley, but three Iraqi open-topped trucks were fanning out to box them in. The Pink Panthers were still advancing parallel to each other, though spaced well apart, and now they began zigzagging across the plain to confuse the Iraqi drivers and make themselves more difficult to hit. Nevertheless, the Iraqi troop trucks managed to fan out far enough to give the machine-gun crews in the rear a clear line of fire. As those machine guns opened fire, and as Kilroy and Paddy returned the fire with their own weapons, Wild Bill grabbed his Stinger SAM system, loaded it, braced himself, took aim and then fired. The Stinger belched fire and smoke and its HEAT missile hurtled across the plain to explode inside one of the advancing Iraqi trucks, blowing pieces off it and turning it into a ball of fire that came to a shuddering halt in boiling clouds of sand. The Pink Panthers then raced past the other two trucks, forcing them to turn around and circle back on screeching tyres, with one of them toppling over and crashing onto its side, spilling out its screaming men and obscuring them in clouds of raging sand.

As the Pink Panthers raced away from the open-ended trucks trying to catch up with them, a great number of Iraqi troops were jumping out of other trucks that had parked in line over a mile-long front and were running to spread out and form a solid wall of defence. As they were doing so, other Iraqi troops were setting up mortars spaced out in a similar line behind them.

More bullets ricocheted off the sides of the Pink Panther as Alice leant forward, adopted a firing position, and prepared to open fire on the troops kneeling between the Iraqi trucks and blocking off the way to Scud Alley. She heard the distant *crump-crump* of the Iraqi mortars, then the shells exploded in front of, and between, the two racing Pink Panthers, tearing up the earth in roaring, spiralling columns of dust, sand, gravel and smoke. A couple of the shells exploded directly in front of Williams's Pink Panther and Alice felt the blast, a wave of searing heat, as the vehicle rocked wildly and then plunged through the murk to emerge to the dazzling light at the other side. Swept by streaming sand, Alice caught a glimpse of the Iraqi troops kneeling to the front, saw the flashing of their rifles, then a hail of bullets ricocheted off the Pink Panther and it started zigzagging.

Two more mortar shells exploding out front forced Williams

to go into a sharp turn that brought him to a shuddering halt facing sideways to the firing Iraqis. He and the others ducked as low as possible when a hail of bullets whistled and whined around the Pink Panther and ricocheted off the side exposed to the enemy. In the split second between that hail of gunfire and the next, Kilroy and Paddy straightened up to pour a hail of fire into the Iraqis and enable Williams to frantically gun the engine and get the Pink Panther moving again.

Racing parallel to the line of kneeling Iraqi soldiers, backed up by the constantly firing mortars, which were laying down a line of explosions through which he could not drive, Williams was forced to turn back and head towards the two open-ended Iraqi troop trucks that were still pursuing him. As he turned towards them, Alice opened fire with her SLR, aiming at the kneeling soldiers, and saw some of them flinging their arms up and being punched back by a hail of bullets. Not knowing if she had hit them, or if Kilroy and Paddy had hit them, not caring either way, she kept firing until the Pink Panther was turning away from them and racing back the way it had come, straight towards the advancing Iraqi machine-gun trucks.

At that moment, Wild Bill, aiming out of the back of the Pink Panther, fired his Stinger SAM system at the kneeling men, blowing a whole bunch of them apart in a fiery explosion and creating a temporary breach in the line. Phillips's Pink Panther was racing towards that breach with its machine-gunners, Townsend and Collinson, firing on the move. As the Pink Panther approached, the Iraqis nearest to it fired a vicious fusillade and a mortar shell exploded in front of it, nearly under it, with the erupting earth lifting its front off the ground and nearly turning it over. Instead of crashing, however, it bounced back to earth and plunged into the seething smoke just as Roy Collinson was struck by the hail of bullets and punched out of his seat.

Collinson was still falling off his seat, his machine-gun barrel swinging wildly, as the Pink Panther disappeared in the dense smoke – but when it emerged at the other side, he was nowhere to be seen.

The Pink Panther raced on through the breach in the line, both machine-gunners firing at the Iraqis kneeling on either side, when Collinson emerged from the angry smoke, his clothing in shreds and soaked in blood. Dazed, riddled with bullet holes, trying to walk on wounded legs, he staggered forward a few feet, clawing automatically at the Browning 9mm High Power handgun in his holster, though he lacked the strength to withdraw it fully.

'Pick him up!' Kilroy bawled.

Phillips's Pink Panther was already through the breach in the Iraqi lines and racing towards the safety of Scud Alley when Williams turned the steering wheel sharply on his own vehicle, putting it into a screeching turn that took it away from the advancing Iraqi trucks, but made it run dangerously parallel to the kneeling enemy marksmen, straight towards Roy Collinson. Roy was still standing in subsiding clouds of sand, groping dazedly, uselessly, at his holstered Nine-Milly, and Kilroy was already leaning sideways out of the Pink Panther to grab him, when a fusillade from the Iraqi marksmen tore up the ground around him, peppering him with bullets that punched him this way and that in a convulsion of spitting sand before finally throwing him violently to the ground, his shivering body spurting blood from the many bullet holes.

'Keep going!' Kilroy bawled and jerked back into the jeep, behind his mounted GPMG, as Williams accelerated, swerving around Collinson's lifeless body and turning away from the Iraqi troops as they raced in at the crouch, firing on the move, to close the breach in their defensive line. Phillips's Pink Panther raced away in the distance, heading for Scud Alley, and soon disappeared in a cloud of boiling sand, well out of range of the Iraqi guns.

'They made it!' Alice shouted in automatic exhilaration.

'We didn't,' Kilroy said grimly. 'Neither did Collinson.'

Alice flushed with embarrassment, shame and a touch of anger, but was mercifully distracted when a mortar exploded right beside the Pink Panther, showering her in hissing sand and making her choke temporarily in the smoke.

As Williams now headed in the only direction open to him – straight between the two Iraqi machine-gun trucks – more trucks came racing in from all directions, hoping to encircle him. Kilroy and Paddy opened fire with their mounted machine guns, Kilroy aiming at one truck, Paddy at the other, and poured a hail of bullets into them as the Pink Panther raced between them before they could close the gap. Some of the machine-gun crews were hit and toppled backwards off the trucks, their bodies thudding into the ground and kicking up clouds of sand. Then the fuel tank of one truck was hit and exploded, blowing pieces off the engine, setting it on fire, and making the truck grind to a halt in a greater cloud of frenzied sand.

As Williams's Pink Panther raced past the other oncoming trucks, Alice supported Kilroy and Paddy with bursts of semi-automatic fire from her SLR. Wild Bill, meanwhile, had braced his thick legs against the crates of hand grenades and he fired his Sting SAM system as they drew abreast of the enemy truck. The HEAT anti-tank rocket shot across on a trail of white smoke and smashed into the side of the truck, its explosion blowing off the rear wheels and making the tailboard slam into the ground, where it made a dreadful grinding sound as the machine-gun crew slid off the back and plunged bawling and screaming into the boiling sand, followed by their weapon and its mangled tripod. The truck then shuddered to a halt and was racked with a series of internal explosions as Williams's Pink Panther raced on.

'They're closing in on us!' Kilroy bawled, meaning the other trucks now moving in on them from the east, west and south.

'Not for long!' Williams shouted back as he wrenched at

the steering wheel, turning the Pink Panther into a screeching, shuddering turn, then headed north, away from the Iraqi trucks.

Those trucks tried following, but they couldn't keep up with the more sophisticated, powerful Pink Panther being driven by Williams and soon it was well ahead, still gaining speed, and increasing the distance between itself and those trying to catch up with it. Williams kept driving until the trucks trying to follow him had disappeared over the horizon. Then he slowed down and drove more carefully until he reached the main supply route at the approximate location of the old SAS Road Watch North. He drove across the MSR, cut across the flat plain, and finally made his way down into a shallow wadi and braked to a halt. From there they could all look out over the desert that ran the whole way to Syria.

'We've no choice now,' he said. 'The others made it, but unfortunately we didn't, so now we're heading for the Syrian border or, hopefully, Scud Boulevard.'

'At least that other jeep held all of the former SAS prisoners,' Paddy Magee said. 'The Iraqis won't get *them* back.'

'Right,' Wild Bill said. 'Now we've only one former prisoner to deliver.'

'Yeah,' Alice said. 'Me.'

'I'll wear that,' Kilroy said.

CHAPTER TWENTY-ONE

Hardly able to believe what Kilroy had just said, not too sure if it was a compliment or not, Alice glanced at him but saw only his impassive face, those handsome features slightly brutalised by that two-inch scar running down his right cheek, his glacial, unfathomable gaze taking in the mountains in the north, beyond the flat, open desert.

'If we're going, we should go now,' he said, 'before those Iraqis catch up with us. That won't take them too long.'

'I agree,' Williams said. 'They'll be even more determined to catch us now that the other Pink Panther's made its escape. Saddam's going to be bloody furious with them, so they'll be even more desperate to catch us. They certainly won't give up now.'

'Well, at least the others made it,' Wild Bill said. 'Every damned one of the SAS prisoners, so already you've gained your propaganda victory.'

'Which is why the Iraqis will be even more keen to catch us,' Kilroy said.

Williams glanced at his wristwatch. 'Two hours to last light,' he said, looking up again. 'That gives us time to put a great deal of space between us and those following us. I suggest you all have a quick drink of water – a very *short* drink of water – and then we'll move on again.'

'Sure I thought you'd never mention it,' Paddy Magee said, enthusiastically unscrewing the top of his water bottle. 'An' me dyin' of thirst, like.'

'Go easy on it, Paddy,' Kilroy told him. 'The spare water's in short supply.'

'Sure I'll make another desert still,' Paddy replied, having had a quick drink and now wiping his lips with the back of his hand. 'No problem at all.'

'The problem,' Williams said, 'is that we'll be travelling through the night, so you won't have the sunshine you need for condensation. That rules out a desert still based on your holy Irish urine.'

'Oh,' Paddy said, disappointed, then he shrugged and grinned at Alice as she, too, had a drink from her water bottle, swirled it around in her dry mouth, hardly able to bear losing it, then swallowed it just before it turned warm. 'God, I needed that,' she said, almost gasping, as she screwed the lid back on and clipped the bottle to her webbed belt. 'It tasted just like champagne.'

'You drink champagne a lot?' Kilroy asked her without the trace of a smile.

'No. But I've had the odd glass. Special occasions and so on.'

Kilroy nodded solemnly. 'I'm not one for the bubbly stuff myself. Beer's more in my line.'

'Sure yer just common muck,' Paddy told him, 'with the tastes of the lowest.'

'You and me, both,' Kilroy replied.

'May I suggest,' Williams said, 'that we take this opportunity to quickly check our vehicle and fill up the fuel tanks? With that done, we can run as quickly as possible for as long as the petrol lasts.'

'Good thinking, boss,' Kilroy said, then he turned to Paddy Magee and indicated the sloping wall of the wadi with a nod of his head. 'Get yourself up there, Paddy, and keep watch while I check the Pink Panther. Take Lieutenant Davis with you. She seems to be a dab hand with the SLR, so she could come in handy.'

It was an off-handed compliment but it seemed sincere enough and Alice was very surprised by how much it pleased her. Rather than showing that pleasure, however, since it might backfire on her, she simply nodded, removed her SLR from where it was lying in the Pink Panther and then followed Paddy up the slope.

'Anything I can do to help?' Wild Bill asked as Alice started up the slope.

'Yes,' Kilroy replied. 'You can help me check the Land Rover.'

'I'm your man,' Wild Bill said.

Reaching the top of the slope, Alice followed Paddy's example and lay belly down on the ground, which gave her a panoramic view of the vast plain below, divided by the straight line of the MSR. Glancing back over her shoulder, she saw Kilroy and Wild Bill leaning over the raised hood of the Pink Panther. They would, she knew, check and clean the carburettor, special filters, fans, radiators, condensers, water and fuel tanks, any movable parts that could become jammed up with sand, including the sextants and compasses and, finally, the pressure and general condition of the unusually wide, reinforced sand tyres. Captain Williams, on the other hand, was sitting in the front seat with a map spread out on the steering wheel and a cigarette smouldering between his fingers.

Turning back to the front, Alice surveyed the vast expanse of the desert, looking for signs of advancing enemy trucks but seeing only the usual clouds of dust and sand drifting lazily across it. Eventually, however, after a lengthy silence, she asked Paddy about something that had been troubling her.

'Excuse me if I'm speaking out of line, Paddy,' she said, now using the informal mode of address favoured by the SAS, 'but I wanted to ask you about something I noticed back there.'

'Back *where*, Lieutenant?' Paddy replied.

'Just down the hill there, when we were talking.'

'Yeah?' Paddy asked. 'What about it?'

'I noticed that no one mentioned the fact that Roy Collinson had been killed. No one showed any emotion about it. The subject wasn't even raised. Now I know you guys are fond of each other and that you and Roy, in particular, were good buddies, so I know you cared for him. I just thought it was odd.'

'Sure there's nothing odd about it at all,' Paddy replied in his rough Ulster accent. 'We never discuss those who fail to beat the clock. It's kind of a regimental tradition – maybe a superstition. We just don't do it, that's all, like.'

'Fail to beat the clock?' Alice asked.

'Aye. Beating the clock is staying alive,' Paddy informed her. 'To fail to beat the clock is to be killed in action. We never discuss those who fail to beat the clock, but their names are inscribed on plaques originally fixed to the base of the clock at our regimental base, Stirling Lines, in Hereford – so that's why we use that particular expression. Of course, when the new spider was completed—'

'Pardon?' Alice interjected, puzzled.

'Spider – barracks. Sure when the new barracks was completed, the tower was left in place but the plaques were resited outside the regimental chapel. So we still talk about beating the clock, but we never discuss the dead.'

They both were silent for a moment, surveying the empty desert, then Alice said, with a sigh, 'You guys sure have a language all your own.'

'Ackay, we do that.'

'Teach me the language, Paddy.'

Paddy grinned. 'You want an A-B-C, like?'

'More or less,' Alice said.

'Let me think.' Paddy wrinkled his forehead in thought. 'Well, now, let's start with a basha. That's a waterproof shelter made with a poncho or from local materials – foliage and sand or whatever. On the other hand, basha's also used to describe a small canvas tent, a barracks, a house or a bed; and to basha down is simply to have a kip, meaning a sleep. We've already discussed beating the clock, but a beat-up march is the series of progressively harder marches over the Brecon Beacons, in Wales, used to weed out good candidates from bad, like. Those who fail their beat-up march are RTU'd, which means being returned to yer original unit with yer tail between yer legs. Still on the Bs, there's the Belfast Cradle, which isn't what I was reared in. It's actually a way of holding yer weapon crooked in yer forearm for a quick response during surprise encounters with the enemy.'

'Bergen?' Alice asked.

'Bergen's a town in Norway that became the operational base for SAS Brigade HQ in 1945, but a bergen, on the other hand, is the standard-issue British Army backpack used by the SAS. To bin is to reject a plan or unpopular bloke, a bingo book is a journal containing the details of wanted terrorists and a bivi-bag is a waterproof sheet used when yer raisin' a temporary basha.'

'Goddammit, Paddy,' Alice exclaimed, 'you're still with the Bs!'

'Aye,' Paddy replied, amused. 'There's a lot of Bs, including bullshit, which you can guess, though it doesn't relate to cowshit. Then there's bumped, which is what happens when a friendly patrol is observed or attacked by the enemy.'

'Get off the Bs,' Alice implored him.

'Right,' Paddy said agreeably. 'A CasEvac is a casualty evacuation, usually by helicopter; a Chairman Mao suit is a standard-issue British Army padded suit designed for extremely cold conditions; a crap-hat is a failure or a member of the regular army; and a Chinese Parliament is—'

'I know that one already,' Alice told him. 'Move on in the alphabet.'

Paddy sighed. 'My wee brain's already frazzled with all this. You're pretty demanding, Lieutenant.'

'Most women are,' Alice said.

Paddy nodded. 'OK.' He was still scanning the sun-hazed horizon. 'A double tap is two-to-thirteen rounds fired in quick succession from the Browning Nine-Millimetre High Power handgun, or Nine-Milly; a fan-dance, also known as the Long Drag, is a sixty-kilometre, solo, timed navigation march over the Pen-y-Fan, the highest peak in the Brecon Beacons; a flash-bang is a stun grenade; a gimpy is a GPMG or general-purpose machine gun; a golok is a fighting knife; the green slime is the Intelligence Corps who wear green berets instead of our maroon; a Head Shed is a senior officer; hot bedding is—'

'Don't tell me,' Alice interjected.

Paddy grinned again. 'Hot bedding's the sharing of one or two sleeping bags between the members of a four-man patrol.'

'I'm relieved,' Alice joked without smiling.

'And to skip a few,' Paddy said, obviously feeling brain-drained, 'the Kremlin is the nickname for the intelligence section of regimental HQ, Stirling lines; a Lurp is an LRRP, or long-range reconnaissance patrol; and LUP is a laying-up position; the maroon machine is the name we give to the Parachute Regiment; a mixed-fruit puddin' is two high-explosive shells to one white phosphorous, fired by mortar; a percentage player is someone who steals credit from others or takes big chances; a Rupert is an officer, particularly one not respected by the men; a sit rep is a situation report; scran is food; a Startrek is an airstrike; tab is a forced march carrying a heavy load; a vet rep is vertical replenishment by helicopter; a wad is a sandwich; a washup is a debriefing; a wet jump is a parachute drop into water; and a wet rep is a weather report. Sure that's my lot, Lieutenant.'

'It's enough,' Alice replied. 'It's well known that the Irish have a gift for language and you've sure proved the point.'

'Not *my* language,' Paddy reminded her. 'SAS language. I just picked it up, like.'

'I'll try to remember it,' Alice told him. 'It might save some confusion.'

'It'll help,' Paddy said. He stopped grinning and stretched out farther, like a hunting dog sniffing, and Alice followed the direction of his gaze and saw, coming up over the distant horizon, two black dots that were flying so low in the sky, they were sucking up spiralling clouds of sand.

'Choppers,' Alice said.

'That's right, sure enough. They musta bin called up by those troops and now they're comin' to find us. I'll stay here and keep my eye on 'em; you go tell the others.'

'Right,' Alice said. Glancing once more at the horizon, she saw that the dots had already taken shape as helicopter gunships and were approaching the ridge at good speed. Without further ado, she slithered back down the slope of loose gravel and stood upright beside the Pink Panther when she reached the bottom. Kilroy and Wild Bill had just completed their maintenance job on the vehicle and were wiping their oily hands with rags. They both looked up as she approached, as did the schoolboyish Captain Williams, who had completed the reading of his map and was smoking another cigarette.

'Yes, Lieutenant?' he said.

Alice jabbed her finger back up the hill, indicating the sky. 'Two helicopter gunships are on their way toward us and will be here within minutes. I think we'd better move out.'

'I think not,' Kilroy said. 'I think we should stay put. Once we're out in the open we'll be fully exposed to those choppers.

If we stay here and camouflage the Pink Panther, there's a chance that they'll miss us.'

'My very thought,' Williams said, 'so let's cover up quickly.'

'I don't think we have that kind of time,' Alice said. 'Those choppers will be here any minute now. They're practically on top of us.'

'The Pink Panther already blends in with the desert,' Wild Bill said, 'so why not just get the hell out of sight and pray that the chopper pilots don't see us?'

'Let's try that,' Williams said.

'Here they come!' Paddy shouted from the rim of the wadi, then he slid down backwards on his belly, leaving a trail of spiralling dust behind him, as the others scattered to hide under sand-covered rock outcroppings. When Paddy reached the dried-out bed of the wadi, he too ran at the crouch to take shelter in the shadow of some rocks, mere feet from where Alice was already crouching. 'Christ, I'm hot!' he exclaimed.

The remark was enough to remind Alice that she, too, was burning up from the sun and so soaked in sweat that she was practically dripping. Wiping the sweat from her forehead with her *shemagh*, she heard the approaching roar of the two Iraqi choppers and automatically held her SLR at the ready. Kilroy was pressed against a large rock about eight feet away, almost directly opposite, and she caught his glance, which dropped from her face to her weapon, then flicked away.

He's starting to admire me, she thought. Jesus, what am I *thinking*?

The roaring of the choppers grew louder and then suddenly they were directly above, fairly high up, though low enough to whip up the sand and make it swirl violently over the rocks and the Pink Panther between them. Looking up, Alice caught a glimpse of the two machines, their rotors spinning so fast they were a blur, their rocket ports like black eyes, machine-gunners sitting at open bays and scanning the plain below. They passed on without hovering or dropping any lower, and Kilroy, with his gaze still fixed on the sky, tentatively raised his right thumb.

His optimism was short-lived. The choppers had barely passed over and away when they moved off in opposite directions, then circled back to fly towards the Pink Panther, one after the other. Paddy raised his SLR to fire at the first one, but Kilroy slapped his gun barrel down and shook his head vigorously, indicating, 'No.' The first chopper came lower, hovered just above the ridge, then it descended directly over the Pink Panther and the machine-gunner in its open bay suddenly opened fire.

The harsh chatter of the machine gun cut through the roaring of the chopper and a hail of bullets tore up the ground around the Pink Panther, ricocheted off its sides and then moved forward to locate those hidden in the shadow of the rocks.

Kilroy and Paddy opened fire with their SLRs, trying to hit the helicopter, and Wild Bill, Williams and Alice all followed suit.

When the helicopter rapidly ascended out of firing range, Williams bawled, 'Bug out!'

Taking advantage of the chopper's ascent, they all raced for the Pink Panther and clambered up into their usual positions. Even as Williams was turning on the ignition, the second chopper was descending with its rocket ports belching smoke and flame. The Pink Panther lurched forward and away just as the two rockets swooshed down into the wadi and exploded with a dreadful bellowing right behind them. Alice was smacked by the blast, felt a wave of heat sweeping over her, then was deluged in a shower of gravel and sand and nearly choked by swirling smoke.

The Pink Panther kept going, bumping up out of the wadi, its tyres screaming as they spun on loose gravel before taking a firm hold. Kilroy leant back in his seat, bracing his legs, practically hanging backward from the handles of his GPMG, then he opened fire on the helicopter, as did Paddy behind him. Their hail of bullets struck the helicopter, ricocheting noisily off its fuselage, making it ascend out of range as the Pink Panther bounced back onto level ground and raced across the flat plain.

'They're coming back!' Wild Bill bellowed.

The first chopper was indeed returning, dropping vertically and then flying at low level over the ground to give its machine-gunners a clear line of fire. It fired two rockets at the Pink Panther, but they both exploded ahead of it, making the ground erupt in great columns of spinning soil as Captain Williams wrenched the steering wheel to put the Pink Panther into a zigzagging forward course. He drove through the geysering earth, the swirling clouds of black smoke, and emerged to clear air as the man in the open bay of the same chopper opened fire with his machine gun. A line of spitting sand raced towards the Pink Panther, almost hit it, missed and passed on, as Kilroy and Paddy swivelled their machine guns and again opened fire. Their combined fusillade went into the chopper, right into the open bay, and the gunner jerked like a puppet on strings back into the chopper, then fell out as the chopper tilted wildly. He plunged screaming, limbs akimbo, to the ground, thudding into the sand, his broken body raising a cloud of dust that looked like a small explosion.

The chopper, now pouring smoke, turned away and headed back where it had come from as the second one came in low to fire two more rockets.

Again, the rockets exploded just in front of the Pink Panther, but this time close enough to blow off the spare wheel fixed above the front bumper and send it flying, in flames, spinning rapidly, through the air to bounce a few times off the ground, its motion marked by trails of smoke, before finally coming to rest on its side where it continued to burn. The Pink Panther kept going, but its front bumper had come loose with its loose end dragging on the sand and lava rock, making a hideous shrieking noise and slowing down the vehicle.

When Williams cursed and tried in vain to accelerate, Wild Bill shouted, 'Keep me covered!' then clambered over the front seats and onto the pink-painted, dust-covered bonnet. Whipped by wind and flying sand, exposed to the machine-gun fire of the incoming helicopter, he nevertheless kept crawling forward on his belly until he had reached the front of the vehicle, where he gripped the sextant to keep himself from falling off. Kilroy and Paddy opened fire with their machine guns, and were aided by Alice's SLR, trying to keep the chopper gunner pinned down, as Wild Bill clung to the sextant with one hand, removed his .45-inch calibre Colt handgun from its holster, then aimed downwards and fired repeatedly at the fixed end of the damaged bumper until it broke free and disappeared from sight under the racing vehicle.

Instantly, the Pink Panther picked up speed and Wild Bill began crawling backwards along the hood, his right foot nearly kicking Williams in the face. Leaning his head to the side, still driving wildly with one hand, doing fifty miles an hour, Williams grabbed Wild Bill's ankle, tugged the booted foot away from his face, then helped him by tugging him back into the vehicle. Wild Bill had just managed to get his feet over the back of the front seat and was dropping on both hands onto the seat itself, his head down and out of sight, his backside thrusting up to the sky, when the descending helicopter's machine gun roared and bullets again ricocheted off the Pink Panther, blowing the sextant to pieces and peppering the pink hood with holes.

'We've been hit!' Williams bawled.

Nevertheless, he kept driving, feeling no sudden drop in acceleration, as Kilroy and Paddy between them poured a fusillade of machine-gun fire into the helicopter, forcing it to ascend once more out of range of the guns.

'He's going to come back!' Wild Bill shouted. 'To hell with it! Let's *get* him!'

As the Pink Panther crashed and banged over the stones and potholes of the deceptively flat plain, Wild Bill struggled to load the Stinger SAM system with a HEAT rocket, balance it on his shoulder and aim it at the incoming helicopter. As he was doing so, Kilroy and Paddy, supported by Alice on her SLR, continued firing up at the same machine, hoping either to damage it or to knock out the pilot. This time, however, the helicopter was keeping out of their firing range and angling itself to release its rockets. Just before it managed to do so, Wild Bill caught it in his sights and fired his HEAT rocket, which soared up on a column of white smoke that showed its trajectory and slammed into the fuselage just above the firing bay for the machine gun. When the rocket exploded, pieces were torn off the side of the helicopter and the machine-gunner and his weapon, both in pieces, were thrown wide and went sailing down to earth with the smoking debris. Even before they had hit the earth, the helicopter exploded into flames, suffered a further series of internal explosions, and then turned into an immense ball of flame that plunged to earth and exploded for the final time.

Wild Bill and Paddy cheered, but their joy was short-lived when the first helicopter, which they had thought was returning to Baghdad, appeared over the now distant wadi and, no longer trailing smoke, glided towards them.

'Goddammit!' Wild Bill exclaimed. 'It must have just been a small fire inside the cabin – but those bastards are gutsy.'

'*Rockets!*' Kilroy bawled.

Racing towards the distant mountain range that would be their escape route to Syria, Williams went into another sharp zigzagging pattern as two rockets fired from the helicopter flew towards the Pink Panther. This time they exploded on both sides of the vehicle, one so close that it blew off the steel sand channels, which flew spinning and shrieking through the air, as well as one of the spare cans of water, which exploded and bounced away in the Land Rover's wake. Showered in spewing sand and gravel, Williams nearly lost control of the vehicle, managed to straighten it out, then found himself bouncing and banging down into another dried-out wadi bed with pieces of equipment either being torn off or flying out of the vehicle. When the Pink Panther hit the bottom, it practically bounced off the stone bed, then started rolling over.

'*Jump!*' Williams bawled.

Alice jumped with all the others, not knowing where she would land, and crashed into the ground and rolled over in a shower of stones and dense dust, still holding her SLR. Righting herself, she saw the side of the Pink Panther crashing down where she had been, then, as a hail of bullets from the helicopter's second machine gun turned the ground around the Pink Panther into a convulsion of spitting sand and ricocheting, whining bullets and debris, she jumped up and followed Kilroy and Williams farther along the bed of the wadi. When they stopped and turned around, she did the same and saw Wild Bill and Paddy standing upright, legs spread, spines curved, firing their weapons almost vertically. The second machine-gunner fell out of the helicopter in a tangle of arms and legs, his scream filled with terror, and dropped a hundred feet through the air to smash to the ground in a cloud of dust and billowing sand.

The helicopter ascended again, heading back for Baghdad – but its fading roar was swiftly replaced by the growling of trucks.

Scrambling back up the sloping side of the wadi with the others, Alice was shocked to see a horde of Iraqi soldiers, obviously guided in by the choppers, pouring out of troop trucks and advancing on the wadi. They were at least half a mile away and not yet firing their rifles.

'Jesus H. Christ!' Wild Bill exclaimed. 'They're swarming like ants out there.'

Williams looked to the west, at the nearby mountains, then glanced at his wristwatch. 'The sun's going down,' he said. 'At last light, we can hike it to those mountains and lose ourselves there. The sun should sink in ten minutes.'

'Those sonsofbitches will be swarming all over us in five minutes,' Wild Bill said. 'We don't *have* ten minutes.'

'We have to take everything we can carry from the Pink Panther,' Kilroy said, 'so I suggest that we get back to it, unload it and then bug out to the mountains.'

'We'll be shot to pieces,' Wild Bill said.

'No, we won't,' Kilroy said. 'The engine of the Pink Panther was still running – wasn't it, Captain?'

'Yes,' Williams confirmed. 'I turned off the ignition just before we tipped over.'

'Then we switch on the smoke dischargers,' Kilroy said, 'and create a wall of smoke between us and those troops. The smoke'll blind them for a bit, and choke them – maybe long enough for us to make our way to the base of the mountains, by which time it'll be dark. I say we move now.'

'Let's go,' Williams said.

Together, they slid back down through the loose gravel and dust of the slope and then ran at the half-crouch along the bed of the wadi. Reaching the overturned Pink Panther, they found that it had spilt a lot of their kit onto the wadi bed, including the smashed pieces of the two mounted machine guns. While Williams, Wild Bill and Alice removed what they could from the badly damaged Pink Panther, including the Stinger SAM system, a portable GPMG and the last of their spare water bottles, Kilroy and Paddy, on Williams's instructions, clambered back up the slope to hold off the advancing Iraqis with sustained bursts of fire from their SLRs.

Hearing the return fire of the Iraqis, Alice realised they must be close and found herself labouring with unexpected energy to help sort out the kit into five manageable piles. She was clipping as many hand grenades as she could to her webbed belt when Kilroy bawled from the top of the wadi, 'Move out! They're practically on top of us! *Move out now!*'

Glancing sideways, Alice saw that Wild Bill had strapped the main components of the GPMG to his broad back and was picking up the Stinger SAM system and preparing to run. Williams was carrying the rest of the GPMG and was otherwise heavily burdened with as much kit as he could carry. Two piles remained to be picked up by Kilroy and Paddy when they made it back down the slope.

'Bug out!' Williams shouted, then he led Wild Bill and Alice up the other side of the wadi and onto the flat plain that fell away to the base of the mountains. As Alice was clambering over the rim of the slope, she glanced back over her shoulder and saw Kilroy and Paddy sliding down in clouds of dust to the overturned Pink Panther.

Once on the rim of the wadi, Williams bawled, 'Give them covering fire!' and opened fire with his SLR. Dropping to one knee and aiming along the sights of her SLR, Alice saw hordes of Iraqi troops advancing on the wadi from the other side, firing on the move. Bullets stitched the earth around her, but she ignored them and opened fire, swinging the barrel of her weapon from side to side, to cover as broad an arc of fire as possible as Wild Bill did the same with his MP5.

'Oh, God!' Alice heard herself whisper as the first of the Iraqis reached the far rim of the wadi and started lowering the barrels of their rifles to fire down into it.

Paddy had now gathered up his personal kit and was clambering up the nearside of the wadi towards Alice. The Iraqis fired down into the wadi and bullets ricocheted off the Pink Panther as Kilroy, hiding behind it, reached in to turn on first the ignition, then the smoke dischargers. The back of the overturned Pink Panther was facing the far side of the wadi and two streams of dense smoke shot out like water from hosepipes, then were blown along the slope by the wind, obscuring the Iraqi troops on the rim.

Kilroy jumped up and threw two hand grenades, one after the other, as the Iraqi troops were engulfed in the smoke. The grenades exploded in the midst of the Iraqi troops, blowing some of them apart and creating a further screen of smoke and swirling sand, as Kilroy grabbed his kit and started clambering up the nearside of the wadi.

Reaching the rim of the wadi, about six feet from Alice, Paddy turned back to add short bursts from his SLR to the covering fire already being laid down by the others. By now, Iraqi bullets were stitching the ground all around Kilroy, but the firing diminished as the smoke from the Pink Panther's dischargers thickened and covered the whole of the far side of the wadi, blinding and choking the troops trying to advance down into it. Given this temporary protection, Kilroy managed to make it up to the others. Williams, without a word, turned and ran at the half-crouch towards the base of the nearby mountains, signalling that the others should follow suit.

Alice heard the distant *crump-crump* of an Iraqi mortar being fired as she turned to follow Wild Bill across the flat plain. Suddenly, she heard a dreadful roaring, was deafened and crushed, felt herself being sucked up into a maelstrom of heat and beating sand. Stars exploded in her head and she felt herself choking. Then something tugged at her, pulled her upright, and threw her forward again. She saw Kilroy's bright eyes, the grim line of his lips, and realised, as sand swirled and hissed around her, that she had been bowled over by a mortar explosion and then picked up and pushed forward by him. Dazed and confused, fighting the urge to throw up, she followed Kilroy across the flat plain, weaving left and right to avoid more mortar explosions, and finally caught up with the others as they reached the lower slopes of the mountains and made their way into a honeycomb of high, protective rocks.

They did not stop when they reached the rocks, but continued to climb up the lower slopes, darting from one rock to another, until the sporadic gunfire that had been dogging them gradually tailed off and the sun sank beyond the western horizon, plunging the desert into moonlit darkness.

Stopping for a short break, they all gazed back down the rocky slopes to the flat plain below. Alice saw striations of moonlight streaking the dark plain, the darker wall of the smoke that had drifted along the wadi, the Iraqi soldiers stopping on the flat ground of the nearside rim, looking left and right, trying to find their quarry and failing to do so. Realising that she had escaped once again, she heaved a sigh of relief.

'Don't think of resting on your laurels,' Kilroy said as if reading her mind. 'We have a long way to go yet.'

'I'll go as far as you can take me,' Alice replied.

'I don't doubt it,' Kilroy said.

CHAPTER TWENTY-TWO

The cold was shocking. Kilroy felt it as soon as the sun went down and felt it even more when they laid up in the shelter of the rocks a good way up the hill. It would, he knew, get worse and he was even more convinced of this when he glanced at the night sky and saw thunderous clouds shifting across the moon, blotting out the light. Moving his gaze, he was surprised to see, even from this great distance, the web of purple tracers, jagged, silvery explosions and crimson flames that indicated that the nightly Coalition air raid on Baghdad had commenced again. Lowering his gaze, looking down the rocky slope, he saw the Iraqi soldiers spreading out east and west along the rim of the wadi, searching in vain for their quarry. They had not yet advanced to the foot of the mountain and would probably not attempt to do so until first light. Kilroy sighed with relief.

Gazing around him, he saw Wild Bill, Paddy and Alice sitting on the ground with their backs against the rocks, eating the last of their cold, high-calorie rations because they did not dare light their portable hexamine stoves lest the Iraqis see the faint glow of the flames. Captain Williams, sitting nearby, was biting on a bar of chocolate, taking sips from his water bottle and glancing constantly, restlessly, around him, obviously still working out what they should do next. He looked like a schoolboy, but he knew what he was doing. A damned good officer, Kilroy thought.

Kilroy didn't like chocolate, no matter how much energy it gave him, so he unwrapped the last of his wads and bit into mouldy bread and some kind of processed meat paste. It tasted vile, but he swallowed it, washing it down with cold water, wary of drinking too much as his supply was running out.

His gaze came to rest on Alice. She had removed her desert hat and her short-cropped blonde hair was framing a face smeared with sweat, sand and dirt, yet she still looked beautiful. That she also resembled his wife was a fact that Kilroy could not ignore. Nor could he ignore the pain that seared through his heart each time he thought of that other woman, back home in Hereford. The horror of what had happened there would haunt him for ever, remain his dark secret, remind him of the violence that he had to contain. But he still couldn't help studying the face of Alice Davis and feeling the need to reach out to her.

She didn't like him – he sensed that much. At least, she was uneasy with him. She was defensive and quick to take offence and he wondered why that was so. He thought she might be one of those awful politically correct American women, despising men and yet forced to coexist with them in what she viewed as their world. Kilroy couldn't stand that crap. She must have known what she was joining when she enlisted in the Air Force. Yet the decency in her features, the courage she had displayed, made him feel that it had to be something else, something deeper, more hurtful.

She would have suffered under the Iraqis. Maybe that was the cause of it. Yet even that was unlikely to account for what he sensed was her fear of men. Certainly, she feared him. He could tell that from her eyes. She probably thought he was a violent brute with few feelings and she had good cause to think so.

Geordie Welsh and Roy Collinson.

Kilroy's mates. His friends. When he thought of how Geordie had died, taking the Exit Club, and of Roy being chopped to shreds by Iraqi bullets, he filled up with a grief he could not show. Maybe that was why Alice despised him, thinking him unfeeling. She didn't know that you never discussed those who failed to beat the clock, never mentioned the dead or displayed your grief. It wasn't only him – it was the SAS way – but all Alice had seen was a singular lack of sympathy for Geordie and Roy. She must have been shocked by that.

Kilroy finished his wad, washing the last of it down with a tiny sip of water, then screwed the cap back on his water bottle, clipped it to his webbed belt, and picked up his SLR to check it for sand ingestion and then oil it and clean it. As he was doing this, he glanced frequently, slyly, at Alice and was torn by what he saw: a woman he respected, was drawn to, but who also reminded him of his wife and what had gone down at home.

What had happened was his fault.

The pain was there again, churning around his heart, and he glanced at Alice and felt a stab of guilt that could never be deadened. Gazing at Alice, he saw the face of his wife, her equally beautiful but frozen features, her wide green eyes accusing, and he knew that his need to reach Alice was a need to atone. He wanted to confess his sins, to unburden himself, but he sensed that if the American woman knew what he had done she would fear and loathe him even more. She was frightened by what she sensed was in him as only a woman could. If she knew about his past, about his wife, her fear would turn to revulsion.

I'd deserve that, he thought.

Trying to distract himself from his dark thoughts, from his yearning for Alice Davis, he cleaned and oiled his SLR, checked the firing mechanism, then carefully reloaded it. The clouds around the moon had now thickened and the wind was blowing harder, much colder, making him and the others shiver as they worked at their separate tasks. When everyone was ready to move out, Captain Williams, looking too young for the job but doing it well, gathered them around him for a Chinese parliament.

'From this perspective,' he said, waving his right hand to indicate their location and the surrounding terrain, 'it's clear that we're not on a mountain but merely high and hilly terrain. It's crisscrossed with deep wadis which, in this area, are prone to being flash-flooded after storms. Judging from the climb we've just made, the hiking route is composed mostly of loose rock instead of sand, though we can expect sandstorms to be blown in from other areas. We can also expect rain and fog instead of burning sun, and then sleet, snow, hail and frost as we move farther north-east, heading for Al Qaim.'

'Sounds like heaven,' Wild Bill said laconically.

'At least it's passable,' Williams responded, 'and, given that we no longer have transport, that's a small blessing.'

'Amen to that,' Paddy said.

'We'll be hiking in file formation,' Williams continued, 'with Sergeant Kilroy taking the first point duty, myself second in line as PC, Lieutenant Davis in the middle, followed by Master Sergeant Kowalski, who remains responsible for Lieutenant Davis, and Trooper Magee bringing up the rear as Tail-end Charlie.'

'I'm always last in line,' Paddy said. 'It's the fate of the Irish.'

Williams grinned. 'Our main priority throughout the hike back,' he said, 'remains the safe return of the last of the hostages – namely Lieutenant Davis.' He nodded in Alice's direction and Kilroy saw her glancing left and right, down at her feet, up again, as if embarrassed to be the focus of their attention. 'As Lieutenant Davis is the last of the hostages,'

Williams continued, aware of Alice's discomfort but unable to avoid the issue, 'her safe return is of particular importance in terms of propaganda and it must be attained at all costs. I repeat: at *all* costs.'

'Captain—' Alice started protesting.

'No, Lieutenant,' Captain Williams interjected, waving his hand to silence her. 'You have no say in this matter. Your safe return has to be our prime concern and that's all there is to it. I know this makes you uncomfortable, but getting you back safe and sound will be an invaluable contribution to the war effort. If you're embarrassed, consider yourself an unwilling pawn in the propaganda war. That's your part – your unavoidable part – in this whole operation. The rest of it, our own safe return, is relatively unimportant in relation to that goal.'

'OK,' Alice said, though she still looked uncomfortable.

Williams glanced at everyone in turn. 'Any questions?' he asked.

'Yeah,' Wild Bill responded. 'Are we heading for the border of Syria or for Scud Boulevard?'

'That depends on obstructions,' Williams replied. 'My first objective is Scud Boulevard and your US Delta Force, but we may be forced to turn away from that and try crossing the border. We'll have to play it by ear.'

'Fine,' Wild Bill said.

'Any *more* questions?' Williams asked. When a general shaking of heads indicated that there were no more queries, he stood up and said, 'Fine. Let's move out.'

As Williams had instructed, they fell automatically into file formation, with Kilroy well out front, taking the 'point' as lead and constantly checking what lay ahead through the infrared night-sight of his SLR. The others were strung out behind him, a good distance apart, maintaining irregular spaces between them to avoid unnecessary, or too many, casualties if attacked. Marching behind Kilroy, Williams, as PC, was second in line with Wild Bill behind them, Alice behind Wild Bill, and Paddy in the signaller's position, though the PRC 319 radio set had been destroyed when the Pink Panther overturned and he now had only a hand-held SATNAT GPS, as did Williams. Burdened not only with their heavy bergens, but also with personal kit belts laden with basic survival gear and SARBE surface-to-air rescue beacons, as well as hand grenades and spare ammunition, they were like beasts of burden and soon began sweating profusely even in the night's freezing cold.

Marching out ahead on point, Kilroy had the worst job of all, not only being heavily burdened like the others, but compelled to be attentive every second, constantly attuned to the slightest sound up ahead, scanning the moonlit darkness for the slightest movement and the ground before his feet for any sign of landmines. That landmines would be highly unlikely in this high and hilly terrain did not lessen his need for vigilance, since a previous action may have caused the Iraqis to plant them in a fit of pique. Also, the wind, at once chilling and eerie, constantly blew sand and dust across the hills, covering up small rocks that could trip him and wadis into which he could fall.

Worst of all, however, was the constant straining to see and hear any signs of enemy movements up front. This placed an almost intolerable burden upon him, but he survived it by recalling other tests of his endurance: trapped on the summit of the Fortuna Glacier in South Georgia in the middle of a freezing, blinding white-out; eating, sleeping, shitting and pissing in a covert OP in the loft of a terraced house in Belfast during surveillance of suspected IRA terrorists; escaping from a crashed Sea King helicopter into the Atlantic off the Falkland Islands and spending hours in his lifebelt in the stormy, freezing sea, waiting for the rescue choppers to arrive; marching all the way from Goose Green to Port Stanley, with nights spent in rainswept, freezing LUPs.

It was a terrible truth that operations such as the embassy siege in Princes Gates, London, and even the stalking and 'neutralising' of three IRA terrorists in Gibraltar made the adrenalin rush with excitement, whereas the real torment in his business was to be found in more mundane activities involving lengthy hikes, uncomfortable surveillance operations, and the vagaries of antagonistic weather, such as he and the others were experiencing right now.

Indeed, as the hike continued and the weather grew worse, with frost glinting on the rocks and sleet sweeping across the windblown hills, making Kilroy's point duty even more difficult, he was reminded of what real soldiering was all about and took his strength from the pride he had in doing it.

They marched throughout the night, stopping every couple of hours to rest up and shit or piss with as much privacy as was possible in the circumstances, usually by taking themselves behind rock outcroppings and exposing their backsides to the raging elements. This, Kilroy sensed, was embarrassing for Alice, but she put a brave face on it and the men were careful not to joke about it or otherwise pass comment. When they had rested, they moved out again, still in file formation.

Four hours before first light, they found themselves in another hilly, rocky area, splashed here and there with white patches of snow, ice and frost, with dense fog making the prevailing darkness even more difficult to penetrate. The wind blew constantly and the temperature barely rose above freezing point. Realising that it would be dangerous to attempt going farther in such conditions, Williams called a halt and ordered the construction of a rectangular OP that would accommodate the five of them at the bottom of a water-logged wadi, which was the only half decent place they could find.

The OP was constructed with a camouflaged roof of netting, waterproof canvas, hessian and sand, as well as plastic sheeting to cover the bottom of the wadi. The wadi itself was long, narrow, cold and damp, with the wind howling eerily through it, but the OP gave them some measure of protection and enabled them to catch up on badly needed sleep in two-hour shifts.

'It ain't a Hilton hotel,' Wild Bill said, 'but it has its own little comforts. I've slept in worse in my time.'

'Sure the only thing worse than this would be yer grave,' Paddy informed him. 'An' then you wouldn't know better.'

Having been given the worst duty, being out on point, Kilroy was allowed to sleep first, along with Paddy, who'd had the second worst duty, being Tailend-end Charlie, and Alice, who was being given the first privilege of a lady. As he was settling in to sleep, stretched out in his zipped-up sleeping bag, Kilroy wondered if she resented even this gentlemanly gesture, but he guessed that Captain Williams's pep talk about propaganda might have soothed her womanly pride.

Almost smiling at the thought of her, he closed his eyes and drifted into a sleep in which he dreamt that he was in the Pink Panther that had made its escape. He awakened briefly, still caught up in that dream, thrilled by the knowledge that the others had got away, but then he drifted off again and saw Alice glaring accusingly at him from the chair his wife normally used in their house back in Hereford. Retreating from that nightmarish image, he felt himself being aroused to unnatural heights by the gently massaging fingers of a feminine hand, then saw a thin wrist, a pale, smooth-skinned arm, a bare marble shoulder, a delicate, swanlike neck and, finally, the face of Alice again. This time she was smiling at him, her fine-boned features framed by that blonde hair, and he reached out to cup her chin in his hand and tug her towards him.

'Waken up, Sarge! It's your turn on watch.'

Awakened by the forceful shaking of Wild Bill, Kilroy shook his head to clear it, then unzipped his sleeping bag, wriggled out of it, and crawled away to the watch position while Wild Bill replaced him in the sleeping bay. Kilroy's watch position was slightly down the sloping side of the wadi, in front of the

OP, and to get to it he had to crawl past Alice, who had also been awakened and was replacing Captain Williams as the sentry at the viewing hole. He caught her glance as he passed, but she merely nodded sombrely at him, and he nodded back, then slithered down the slope to take up his watch position. He felt oddly disturbed.

She's getting to me, he thought.

It was a miserable watch period. The wind howled relentlessly and swept rain across him, drenching him and making the bitter cold worse. Eventually, however, the wind settled down, the rain ceased to fall, and dawn came with pale fingers of light poking through foggy darkness. The darkness faded gradually, but the fog remained longer and, even before it thinned out, he heard dogs barking nearby.

Instantly alerted, he strained to see through the fog and gradually discerned, as it thinned out, an Arab hamlet at the bottom of the slope. It was no more than a random collection of rectangular mud huts with a small patch of cultivated earth on its eastern side, dogs and chickens roaming freely between the buildings, and goats feeding on the sparse vegetation of the lower slope.

Now even more alert, Kilroy left his watch position and hurriedly made his way back up to the OP, clambered past Alice, who again nodded sombrely at him, and then crawled along the trench to shake Captain Williams awake.

'There's people down there,' Kilroy said.

Without a word, Williams unzipped his sleeping bag, wriggled out of it and made his way to the viewing hole of the OP to survey the scene below. Behind him, Wild Bill and Paddy Magee did the same, until eventually all of them were at the viewing hole, bunched up beside Alice. Williams indicated with a wave of his hand that no one was to speak.

No one said a word.

CHAPTER TWENTY-THREE

As the fog disappeared, letting the light of day break through, three Arab goatherds, wearing the customary headcloth, the *keffiyeh*, draped over their head and shoulders, and the *dishdisha*, the plain one-piece shirt that Alice had been wearing when rescued, emerged from the huts and started making their way up the slope towards the goats. Less than a minute later, as the goatherds were still ascending the slope, an Iraqi Army jeep came driving down the western hill and braked to a halt in the clearing between the mud huts. Glancing up that slope, to where the jeep had come from, Kilroy saw an S60 anti-aircraft gun emplacement, surrounded by sandbags and manned by Iraqi soldiers. When he looked at the eastern hill, he saw a similar gun emplacement, this one containing Triple A anti-aircraft guns and manned by even more troops.

'We couldn't have picked a worse place if we'd tried,' Williams whispered, finally breaking the silence.

'Why are you whispering?' Wild Bill said. 'They can't hear us from here.'

'But they'll see us if we make a move,' Kilroy said, 'which means we're trapped here till nightfall.'

'If those goatherds don't find us first,' Williams said. 'So let's pray that they don't.'

The bottom of the OP was covered with water and all of them were soaked and shivering. Glancing sideways, Kilroy saw that Alice was pale and drawn from exhaustion, though she was holding her own. Looking back down the hill, he saw that an Iraqi Army officer had climbed down from the jeep and was gesticulating angrily at an elderly Arab who had emerged from one of the mud huts and was standing in front of some clearly frightened women and children. As the officer shouted, his men climbed down from the jeep and began running around the clearing, scooping up what chickens they could catch and laughing as they did so. The elderly Arab must have been protesting, because the officer slapped his face and then pushed him contemptuously back into the arms of the women. When his men had gathered up as many chickens as they could handle, they clambered back into the jeep and the officer followed suit and was then driven off. The elderly Arab stepped forward again and looked forlornly at his few remaining chickens, then, shrugging fatalistically, he followed the women and children back into the mud hut.

'Sure those bastards are havin' chicken for breakfast,' Paddy said indignantly, 'while those poor peasants starve.'

'Which means the peasants might be on our side,' Williams said pragmatically. 'We might have to depend on that.' He glanced east and west, at the S60 and Triple A gun emplacements on the facing hills, above which the sky was dark with dense clouds. 'More rain coming,' he said.

'Ackay,' Paddy said. 'An' we're ankle deep in this water already. We're gonna die of pneumonia.'

'There are worse ways to go,' Will Bill said, 'so I'd count my blessings if I were you.'

'If I were Catholic I'd cross m'self,' Paddy rejoindered, 'but I've got nothin' to lean on.'

'The Irish Prods are a miserable race,' Wild Bill told him. 'They lack faith and always take the gloomiest viewpoint.'

'Sure I'm gloomy because I'm soaked and freezin' cold. That's reason enough for me.'

'Me, too,' Alice said.

Kilroy glanced at her and saw her solemn face, realising that he had not yet seen her smiling and wondering why that was so.

I rarely smile myself these days, he thought. Who am I to complain?

'So what do we do?' he asked.

Williams sighed. 'We sit tight,' he said. 'We can't advance past that hamlet until it's dark, so we don't have a choice. Let's just pray that the Iraqis up on those hills don't go out on patrol. Let's hope they don't come up this far.'

'The goatherds might,' Wild Bill said.

'If they do, we might be able to bribe them,' Williams said. 'We can give them compensation for their chickens and maybe get them on our side.'

'Hearts and minds,' Kilroy said, referring to the old SAS campaigns in the Far East.

'That's right,' Williams said. He glanced again at the two gun emplacements on the facing hills, nodding silently, as if speaking to himself. 'So,' he said finally, 'we might as well dig our heels in and see what transpires. Relax. Have breakfast. If nothing happens between now and last light, we'll move out then, under cover of darkness.'

'Who's on watch?' Wild Bill asked.

'I'll take the first watch,' Williams replied, 'while the rest of you snatch a bite of eat. No brew-ups, however. We don't want them to see the smoke. So let's get to it.'

While Williams positioned himself at the viewing window of the OP, the others seated themselves around it and tucked into the last of their cold, high-calorie rations. Alice was sitting well away from Kilroy, but he caught her glance often.

'Christ,' Wild Bill said when they were in the middle of eating their canned food, 'this is Godawful swill!'

'Good British tucker,' Paddy replied. 'We're not spoilt like you Yanks.'

'We're not really spoilt, Paddy. We just happen to be better at most things than you fucking Brits.'

'Oh, yeah? Such as?'

'Instant food, for instance. Our instant food's better than your average Brit's so-called roast dinner. Just because we don't chop the legs off frogs doesn't mean we don't eat well.'

'Sure most Americans are too fat,' Paddy retorted. 'They've got bellies like Michelin tyres, like, 'cause they live on hamburgers, chips – that's French fries to you – and Coca-Cola. From what I hear, they go down like flies from heart attacks when they're scarcely out of their nappies.'

'Bullshit!' Wild Bill retorted, obviously enjoying himself. 'We're healthier than your bunch and we don't have bad teeth and blackheads sprouting like turnips on our kissers. Look at me: I'm the picture of perfect health. A shining example of fine American manhood. You don't match up, Trooper.'

'Paddy's been trimmed down by hard duty in the SAS,' Kilroy said. 'You'd look like him if you'd been through what he's been through and lived to tell the tale.'

'Don't shit me,' Wild Bill retorted. 'I do OK for an old man. I had two tours of Vietnam, picked up a Purple Heart and Bronze Star, and now I've got three years of covert activity with the Delta Force behind me, including service in Grenada, in Panama, and now here in the Gulf. I may be big, but I'm still as fit as a fiddle and can match you pair any day.'

Kilroy couldn't help grinning.

'Shit, the guy smiles!' Wild Bill exclaimed. 'I never thought I'd live to see the day. That's one up for me.'

Kilroy saw Alice glancing at him, but she still wasn't smiling. Having finished his rations, he cleaned up his patch, then turned away from the others. 'Back to work,' he said.

Sliding up beside Williams, who was still at the viewing hole, he gazed down the hill. Smoke was coming out of the chimneys of the mud huts, children were playing with the goats and chickens in the clearing, and the three Arab goatherds were tending to the goats on the lower slopes, one of them gradually advancing up the hill to round up the strays. Some of those strays were just below the OP, chewing on the sparse grass.

'Shit!' Kilroy said. 'If that bastard comes any higher, he's going to see the OP.'

'My thought exactly,' Williams replied.

The others had now made their way up to the viewing hole to see what was going on below. All of them watched in an increasingly tense silence as the leading goatherd continued advancing up the hill, calling out in Arabic to his goats and frequently slapping them into line with a gnarled stick. As he tried to get the animals to bunch together, some of them retreated from him, even farther up the hill, until they were practically in front of the OP.

'He's coming up,' Kilroy whispered.

'If he sees us and doesn't instantly scream a warning, I'll try talking to him,' Williams said. 'No point in shooting him – that would just draw the attention of the Iraqi gunners on those hills. Oh, oh, here he comes!'

One of the goats was practically standing on the lip of the OP, blocking part of the view, and the goatherd, still bawling in Arabic, made his way up to bring the animal down. It was clear even before he reached the OP that he could not possibly miss it, and sure enough, when he reached the goat and was about to whip it back, he glanced down and saw Williams and Kilroy staring up at him. He froze immediately, his brown eyes widening under his *keffiyeh*.

Before the Arab could say anything or shout a warning to the Iraqi troops, Williams waved his hand from left to right and then put his index finger to his own lips. The Arab stared steadily at him, more startled than frightened, and Williams waved his right hand, signalling that the Arab should come in closer and kneel down to speak with him. After glancing back over his shoulder, instinctively checking that he wasn't being observed by the Iraqi soldiers on the distant hills, he lowered himself to one knee and peered into the OP. He had a face so brown and wrinkled by the sun that his age was impossible to gauge. His smile revealed missing front teeth.

'You speak English?' Williams asked in Arabic.

The Arab shook his head from side to side.

'We are British soldiers,' Williams said. 'We are not here to fight. We want to get back to our own lines without being seen. Do you understand that?'

The Arab nodded.

'We wish to remain here until nightfall,' Williams said, still speaking in crude Arabic, 'and then move on under cover of darkness. Do you understand that?'

The Arab nodded again.

Williams pointed to the facing hills behind the Arab and said, 'Those Iraqi soldiers are treating you badly. Yes?' The Arab stared thoughtfully at him, then nodded. 'They steal your food and livestock?' The Arab nodded.

Williams groped about in a pouch on his webbed belt and withdrew one of the small gold bars that each SAS man had been given to help buy favours from the Arabs in circumstances like these. When he handed the gold bar over, the Arab's brown eyes lit up.

'That gold is worth a lot of money,' Williams said. 'It is enough to buy you more chickens and goats than you had before. It will also buy you many other things. I give you this gold in return for your silence until we move out of here tonight. Is that agreed?'

The Arab was staring disbelievingly at the gold bar.

'Is that agreed?' Williams asked.

Shoving the gold bar into a pocket in his ankle-length *dish-disha*, the Arab nodded vigorously.

'You will not mention our presence to the Iraqi soldiers?'

The Arab shook his head from side to side.

'Good,' Williams said. 'Now please take your animals back down the hill, well away from this place, and do not return until tomorrow morning.'

The Arab nodded, indicating that he understood, then he clambered back to his feet, turned away from the OP and started whipping the goats back down the rocky, windswept hill.

'What do you think?' Wild Bill asked.

'I think we might be lucky,' Williams said, 'but I don't guarantee it. It's pretty clear from what we've seen that those Arabs have no love for the Iraqi soldiers. On the other hand, they're bound to be frightened of them, so God knows how they'll turn.'

'He looked greedy,' Wild Bill said, 'and that gold made his day.'

'And being greedy,' Kilroy said, 'he might try to get similar from the soldiers by telling them we're here. We should get ready to bug out.'

'Damned right,' Williams said.

They watched the Arab as he herded his stray goats down the hill until they had joined up with the others. He did not, as Kilroy noticed, talk to the other two goatherds, but instead continued bawling at the animals, urging them down the hill. When the goats were all back on the lower slope, they were left in the care of the other two goatherds and the one Williams had spoken to, clearly the eldest, made his way back to the hamlet, where he disappeared inside one of the mud huts.

'Lunchtime,' Williams said, checking his wristwatch.

'Not for us,' Paddy murmured.

The sun was now high in the sky and the freezing cold of night had been replaced with fierce heat. Though drenched throughout the night, the clothes of those in the OP were giving off steam while they dried. Glancing sideways, Kilroy saw Alice wiping sweat from her brow and adjusting the wide-brimmed desert hat on her head. She caught his glance and hurriedly looked away, as if slightly embarrassed. Licking off the sweat that had trickled onto his upper lip, Kilroy glanced back down the hill and saw the Arab emerging from his mud hut to sit on a bench outside it, where he proceeded to smoke a cigarette.

'He seems contented enough,' Wild Bill said.

'Let's hope so,' Kilroy replied.

But he felt uneasy. He didn't trust that Arab. When greed and stupidity came together they could lead to problems. It was obvious that the Arab didn't like the Iraqi soldiers – they were stealing his livestock, after all – but if he thought they would reward him as Captain Williams had done, he might try to play a double game and tell them about the OP. Kilroy kept his eyes on him.

A jeep came down from the western hill and the same Iraqi officer got out and approached the Arab. The Arab stood up. The Iraqi officer shouted and gesticulated. The Arab nodded obediently and the officer slapped his face and then returned to his jeep, which then turned around and headed back up the hill, to the S60 gun emplacement. The Arab then sat back on his stool and lit another cigarette. Kilroy sighed with relief.

Thirty minutes passed. Heatwaves shimmered up off the ground. Kilroy felt himself tensing when a cloud of dust beyond the hamlet announced the arrival of some kind of transport. It materialised in the clearing in the middle of the hamlet as a self-sustaining Iraqi Army unit with command vehicle and tracked carriers. An officer jumped out and shouted at the Arab. The Arab pointed up the hill, indicating the exact location of the OP. The officer turned away and shouted at the men in the tracked carrier behind him. Instantly, the canvas covers were whipped off the trucks and a battery of low-level anti-aircraft guns were revealed.

'Shit!' Wild Bill exclaimed. 'That sonofabitch has turned us in. He told that bastard from the gun emplacement that we were here and they must have phoned through to bring up that mobile unit. It's fried-chicken time, folks.'

'Damn!' Williams exclaimed softly.

The roar of the Iraqi low-level AA guns split the afternoon silence and purple tracers streaked up the hill towards the OP to make the soil explode along the front of it. At the same time, machine guns from the gun emplacements on both hills opened up, creating a dreadful din and also peppering the rim of the wadi with bullets. Just before he ducked low with the others, Kilroy caught a glimpse of Iraqi soldiers leaping out of the tracked carriers and advancing to the foot of the hill.

'They're coming up!' he shouted.

'Bug out!' Williams bawled. 'Head east along the wadi. We'll try circling around that eastern hill out of sight of the gunners. Leave the heavy weapons behind. Go now! *Go!*'

Without a word, Paddy turned away and ran at the half-crouch along the waterlogged bottom of the wadi, carrying his SLR at the ready. Alice hesitated, glancing at Kilroy, but Wild Bill tugged her upright and pushed her ahead of him as he followed Paddy along the wadi, wading through the deep water. Iraqi bullets were tearing the waterproof canvas of the OP to shreds and thudding into the rim of the wadi so relentlessly that they made a constant drumming sound. Determined to give Alice and the others cover, Kilroy stuck his head up long enough to see the Iraqis advancing up the hillside and get off a couple of short bursts at them. Two flung their arms out and spun away in a dance of death as Kilroy dropped low again and saw Williams doing the same, firing his SLR in short bursts.

'Got some,' he said, crouching beside Kilroy, beneath the viewing hole.

'They're still advancing,' Kilroy said, then he crouched even lower as more bullets tore the canvas roof of the OP to shreds, with pieces of canvas and netting raining down upon him and Captain Williams. The Captain jumped up, fired another short burst from his SLR, then dropped down again as the ground around the front and sides of the OP was turned into a veritable convulsion of exploding soil and spitting sand by the combined fire power of the S60 and Triple A anti-aircraft guns on both hills, as well as the small-arms fire of the troops advancing up the hill and the low-level AA guns in the tracked carriers below them.

'Damn!' Williams exclaimed, spitting dirt from his mouth and clearing it from his eyes. 'We'll be torn to bloody shreds if we stay here. We have to leave now.'

Glancing east along the wadi, Kilroy saw the retreating backs of Wild Bill and Alice, with Paddy out ahead, all making slow progress through the ankle-deep water. He then glanced about him and saw the heavy weapons – the GPMG and American Stinger SAM system amongst them – piled up in the well of the OP.

'Those Iraqis are going to reach this OP,' he said, 'before we can get out of the wadi. If they do, they'll have a clear line of fire to us and we'll end up as chopped liver. They'll also capture our heavy weapons. We can't hold them back, so I suggest we give them a hot reception. Keep them pinned down for a couple of minutes, boss, and I'll lay down a welcome mat.'

'Right,' Williams said.

Williams kept the advancing Iraqis at bay as best he could by firing short, blind SLR bursts down the hill. Kilroy opened the shoulder bag he had been given by the escaped demolitions expert, Sergeant Spooner, and withdrew some C3/C4 plastic high explosive, blasting caps and an initiator. While Williams continued firing, Kilroy connected a time fuze to the non-electric blasting cap – a thin aluminium tube 250mm long – and embedded the blasting cap in the explosive charge.

He then attached a safety fuze, in the shape of a length of flexible detonating, or 'det', cord, to the blasting cap and then moved backwards out of the OP, along the floor of the wadi, uncoiling the det cord as he went. The det cord was reinforced primacord consisting of a small high-explosive core protected by six layers of material and connected to the non-electric blasting cap. When the cord had stretched out as far as it would go, about fifteen metres from the outer edge of the OP, Kilroy attached it to a remote-control firing device – a 'button job' – and then signalled for Williams to come and join him. Williams immediately scrambled out of the side of the OP, which was still being torn to shreds by a fusillade of Iraqi bullets, and crawled along the bed of the wadi, splashing through the water, until he reached Kilroy.

'They're only yards away from the OP,' he told Kilroy. 'I think we better go now.'

'I'll wait until they enter the OP,' Kilroy said. 'Then I'll blow them to hell and run. You better go now, boss.'

'No,' Williams said. 'I'll keep you covered until you use the button job.'

'That's cutting it close, boss.'

'For both of us,' Williams said.

The ferocious fusillade of bullets on the OP was causing total devastation, with lumps of waterproof sheeting, hessian and netting flying off in all directions through clouds of boiling dust, spitting sand and exploding soil. It eased off, however, when the Iraqi troops approached to just below the OP, and stopped entirely to allow them to reach it. When they did so, they approached it carefully, then stood over it to rake it with bullets from their semi-automatic assault rifles. Receiving no response, they swarmed all over it, with some crawling into the OP via its side entrance and the others bunching up in the wadi and then glancing along it.

More Iraqi troops were pouring over the rim of the hill and jumping down into the wadi when Williams opened fire with his SLR, cutting them down, the bullets punching some back in a tangle of arms and legs into the side of the OP, which collapsed upon the men already inside. Just as the others were raising their assault rifles to fire on Williams and Kilroy, Kilroy pressed the button job, detonating the plastic HE. The explosion was catastrophic, blowing the OP apart, bowling over the men nearest to it and setting others on fire.

As they screamed and ran this way and that before collapsing, and as the remainder were bowled over by the blast or deliberately flung themselves to the ground, Kilroy turned away and hurried along the wadi, followed by Williams. He had gone only a few metres when some Iraqi soldiers materialised on the rim of the hill, raising their weapons to fire. Kilroy fired first, while still on the move, and the Iraqis screamed and shuddered and collapsed, some falling backwards out of sight, probably rolling back down the hill, and others plunging into the water. Still moving at the half-crouch, Kilroy stepped over the bodies and continued along the wadi until he saw Wild Bill, Alice and Paddy up ahead. They had stopped to rake the rim of the wadi with gunfire, where more Iraqi troops had appeared. More bodies plunged into the water of the wadi as Kilroy continued advancing.

Suddenly, Kilroy felt himself picked up in a maelstrom of heat and light, then he was flung face down into the water. Instantly rolling over, shaking his head to clear it, he heard a high, daggering scream and sat up to see Williams lying on his back in the water, screaming in agony, his left leg shuddering spasmodically, his right leg dismembered from the hip, with blood pouring out of the stump and turning the water red.

Even as Kilroy was clambering back to his feet, he saw Iraqi troops advancing along the wadi, one of them swinging his arm to throw another hand grenade. Instinctively, Kilroy dived farther along the wadi, in the direction of Wild Bill and the others, and was splashing belly down into the water again when the second hand grenade exploded behind him, close to

Captain Williams. Kilroy felt the blast, a wave of heat passing over him, then he clambered to his feet as the Williams's body bounced off the wall of the wadi and splashed face down in the water, his shredded left arm floating out to the side.

Filled with grief and savage fury, Kilroy raised his SLR and fired a sustained burst that decimated the Iraqis coming towards him. He was still firing when Wild Bill, leaving Alice and Paddy together, came back along the wadi and tugged him around, bawling, 'He's dead! Let's get the hell out of here!'

Kilroy tried to jerk free, turning back to face the Iraqis. 'Fuck this!' he snarled.

'Fuck *you*!' Wild Bill retorted. 'Our brief's to get that woman back safe and sound and that's what we're doing. Come on, Kilroy, let's go.'

Seeing that the Iraqis, though badly depleted in numbers, were still advancing along the wadi, Wild Bill unclipped a hand grenade from his belt, pulled the pin and hurled it, then grabbed Kilroy and dragged him away as the grenade exploded, blowing more of the Iraqi soldiers apart. Now getting his senses back, Kilroy did as he was told and followed the bulky American along the bed of the wadi until he had rounded a bend in it, out of sight of the Iraqis, where he found Alice and Paddy waiting for him.

He saw Alice's wide green eyes, the concern in her gaze, then he followed her and the others along the wadi, letting Paddy take the lead on point, himself the last as Tail-end Charlie, and with Wild Bill and Alice in the middle, which was the safest position. They moved as fast as they could, wading through the muddy water, and soon found themselves climbing upwards, out of the water, and back to dry ground. The wadi curved to the north, circling around and behind the Iraqi gun emplacements. The sounds of gunfire tapered off behind them and eventually stopped completely. The Iraqis had lost them.

Shocked by the death of Captain Williams, depressed by

the fact that they no longer had their heavy weapons, they nevertheless kept moving until they reached the end of the wadi, where they were forced back to high ground. They emerged to a sunscorched, hilly terrain that stretched as far as the eye could see. A great silence hung over it.

'Now we leg it,' Wild Bill said.

CHAPTER TWENTY-FOUR

'No,' Kilroy said. 'Not yet. We'd be burnt to a frazzle out there. That's hilly territory too. Little protection other than wadi beds. So I say we leg it when the sun's gone down.'

'No argument,' Wild Bill replied. 'That sounds sensible enough to me. I guess we could all do with a break, particularly after—'

Clearly he was going to mention the death of Captain Williams, but Kilroy cut him short with, 'Anyone got any water left?' They all shook their heads, indicating either that they had no water at all or that they had little left. Kilroy turned to Paddy. 'What about a desert still?' he asked. 'You think there's still time for that?'

Paddy squinted up at the sun, then checked his wristwatch. 'Maybe,' he said. 'It's still a long time before the sun goes down. Sure that might be just long enough to get enough condensation to make water. Not much, but a little. You want me to try?'

'Yes.' Kilroy turned to Wild Bill and Alice. 'We'll lay up here,' he said. 'Shallow scrapes for LUPs. We'll move out shortly after last light. Now go pass water, Paddy.'

Paddy didn't respond with his usual grin – obviously he was, like the rest of them, shaken up by the death of Captain Williams – but he dropped his bergen on the ground and loped off out into the plain, carrying only what he needed for the still and his SLR.

'Right,' Kilroy said to Wild Bill and Alice. 'We might as well relax.'

Noting that the surrounding terrain was composed of smooth lava rock and irregular patches of sand, Alice picked a spot in low, sandy ground shadowed by rock outcroppings and, like the other two, scooped out the sand with her small spade until she had a slight depression long enough to hold her body. As there were no sticks in the area, she couldn't make a lean-to with her poncho, so she just rolled her sleeping bag out in the shallow, deciding that she would stretch out on top of it, rather than in it. Before that, however, she needed to go to the toilet and she was surprised at how self-conscious she still was about it when she made her way behind some other rocks, carrying a roll of tissue paper in her hand.

'Don't use any of your water to clean your hands,' Kilroy called out to her. 'It's too precious for that. Clean your hands by wiping them with hot sand and dry paper. You'll survive the experience.'

'Thanks a lot for the tip,' Alice replied. 'Why not come and hold my hand?'

'Sorry,' Kilroy said.

Slipping behind the rocks, she could feel her cheeks burning with a combination of embarrassment and resentment that Kilroy should have even raised the subject. On the other hand, he was right and her water bottle was practically empty. She knew that, but she still resented him as she squatted on the ground, feeling undignified. When she urinated in the silence, she thought the sound would travel for miles and felt even more embarrassed.

You're a grown woman, she thought. Not a child. Stop acting this way.

But she couldn't help herself. When she had finished and wiped herself clean, she buried the tissues in the sand, then scooped sand up and rubbed it vigorously between her fingers and hands, rubbed until it hurt, then wiped her hands with a dry tissue and buried that as well. As she was doing so, she heard Kilroy and Wild Bill urinating behind some other rocks. That embarrassed her as well, reminding her that they must have heard her when she was doing the same thing.

We're down to basics now, she thought ruefully. I'm going to have to get used to this.

She waited until the sounds of the two men urinating had ceased and only then emerged from behind her rocks. Kilroy and Wild Bill were doing the same, the American still zipping up his pants. He grinned sheepishly at her.

'Well, that's a relief,' he said.

Kilroy stared sombrely at her. 'You better try to catch some sleep,' he told her.

'I don't think I can sleep.'

'Then just lie down and close your eyes. It may not be sleeping, but it helps. At least your eyes won't be so tired.'

'I'll buy that,' Alice said.

She glanced across the hilly plain and saw Paddy digging a three-foot hole for his desert still. Not wanting to see him urinate into it, not wanting to be reminded of what she would soon be drinking, she stretched out on top of her sleeping bag and closed her tired eyes. Kilroy was right: she had needed to close her eyes. Nevertheless, she opened them again and glanced to the side. She saw Kilroy and Wild Bill in their separate shallow scrapes, though neither had lain down. Wild Bill was stretched out, but lying on his side, wearing spectacles, which made him look remarkably less a man's man, and reading a letter. Kilroy was still sitting upright, his SLR resting across his lap, his steady, still slightly unnerving gaze fixed on the horizon. Alice sat up again.

'What's that you're reading?' she asked of Wild Bill.

His massive bulk shifted slightly as he turned to gaze at her, his bright blue eyes staring over the rim of his spectacles.

'Letter from home,' he said.

'From your wife?'

'Yeah,' he said.

'How long have you had it?' Alice asked him.

'Eight days,' he told her.

'How often have you read it?' she asked him.

He shrugged. 'Lotsa times.'

'You happily married?'

'It's had its ups and downs.'

'But you've read that letter lots of times.'

'I reckon,' Wild Bill said.

'That says something,' Alice said.

'I reckon,' Wild Bill said again.

Alice lay down again. She felt a deep, indescribable yearning. She closed her eyes and felt a great peace, then opened her eyes again. She looked at Kilroy, sitting cross-legged in his shallow scrape, and although he was English, as unreadable as the moon, he reminded her of some wild Indian chieftain, surveying his domain.

God, she thought, I must be going crazy. I'm losing my mind out here.

The sound of booted feet on the sand announced Paddy's return and Alice turned her head and looked up again. Paddy walked past her, stopped between the three of them, looked around him and said, 'All nice and cosy here. I'm the only one who's been workin'.'

'You made the still?' Kilroy asked him.

'I relieved my bladder,' Paddy said. 'Sure I don't guarantee that it'll work, given the time an' all, though I certainly soaked it.'

'We live or die by his piss,' Wild Bill said. 'I never thought I could sink to this.'

'Rather my piss than yours,' Paddy retorted. 'At least I don't eat hamburgers.'

'You're fucking Irish,' Wild Bill said, 'but you don't even have an Irish accent, so don't shit on my shoeshine.'

'I don't sound Irish?' Paddy asked.

'Not any Irish I'd recognise.'

'Sure the only Irish you'd recognise is that shite they all talk in Hollywood. Victor McLaughlin, like. *The Quiet Man* an' all that. I speak Ulster Irish. Prod Irish. What the fuck would you know?'

'I know your piss makes a decent drop of water when a man has the thirst.'

Paddy laughed. 'Now is that a fact?'

He removed his small spade from his webbed belt and made a shallow scrape, then laid his sleeping bag down in it and stretched himself out.

'Are you on watch?' he asked Kilroy.

'Right,' Kilroy said.

'The world's greatest conversationalist,' Paddy said and then closed his eyes.

Alice closed her eyes as well. She felt a great contentment. She was filthy and exhausted and hungry, but peace descended upon her.

They're OK, she thought. They're better than those I knew. They might be better than most men I've met, though I'm not sure what that means.

She was thinking of the Academy. Her thoughts always went back to that. It was a nightmare more vivid that her interrogations by the Iraqis and it burned like a tormenting flame inside her, scourging her innards. She wanted to release the flame, to dim the light on her recollections, but the memory of what her own kind had done to her would not leave her alone. They had abused and degraded her, filled her with shame and fear, and she had thought, when they were finished, that she would never look a man in the face again without wanting to spit at him. Then she had met Dave Bamberg, Captain, USAF, and in a few brief, heady days, in war and in peace, braving Iraqi guns while flying in the Black Hawk or sitting in the mess hall, sharing beers, talking a torrent, he had given her back her self-respect and made her fall in love with him. Then Dave Bamberg had died. She had watched him burning up. Thank God, he had died in the crash and his burning was painless. For him, but not for her. She had seen him blister and burn. She had smelt his roasting flesh and heard her own demented screaming as she clambered instinctively from the cockpit and fell to the earth. She had wanted to die with him.

She didn't die.

Dave Bamberg did.

Alice wanted to cry but the tears refused to come and she felt as though the very earth beneath her was opening up to swallow her. A few days ago, she would have welcomed that, but now she wanted to live.

Yes, I do, she thought. Definitely.

She lay there as the others did – all waiting for the sun to sink – and she thought about the Academy and her Iraqi interrogators, about male brutality and the fear it had engendered in her before the healing began.

My father, she realised. I thought about him a lot. He loved the Air Force so much, and I loved him so much, that I couldn't even tell him what they'd done to me in case it would break his heart. I loved my dad and still do. God, I did. God, I do. And I loved Captain Dave Bamberg.

So not all men were brutes. She had thought about that in the prison. She had survived the terrors of the Academy, the interrogations of the Iraqis, the brutality of men who had a woman at their mercy, ironically because of her love of the men who loved her.

My father, she thought. Dave Bamberg. And now . . . No, this can't be.

'Up you get, Lieutenant,' Kilroy said. 'The sun's down. Time to move out.'

Alice opened her eyes. She saw Kilroy standing above her. He was looking down upon her, his face revealing nothing, the two-inch scar on the side of his cheek making him look like a brute. Alice wanted him to smile, to show her something, but his face was carved out of granite. She thought of Captain Williams lying back there in the wadi, torn to shreds by the hand grenades, and she knew that Kilroy must have thought about him as well, though he was showing her nothing. None of them, not one of these men, would show their feelings about that death. Especially not Kilroy.

'You were sleeping,' he said.

'No, I wasn't,' Alice replied.

'Right,' he said. 'I'll take your word for it. But we're moving out now.'

'Fuck you,' Alice said.

He didn't actually grin, but his lips moved a little and he turned away before she could see more.

I'm going crazy, she thought.

Rolling out of the shallow scrape, she folded up her sleeping bag and packed it back into her bergen, then picked up her SLR. Though convinced that she hadn't slept, she felt extremely drowsy and glanced about her to get her senses back. The sun had indeed gone down. Dark clouds blacked out the stars. The heat had already been replaced with freezing cold and the wind was as cold as ice. Alice shivered and rubbed her eyes and looked around her again.

'Jesus,' she whispered.

Paddy Magee was standing between Kilroy and Wild Bill, pouring water from a can into their water bottles, saying, 'A Catholic would give it as a blessin', but bein' a Prod I can't do that.'

'Your piss, my blessing,' Wild Bill replied.

'Sure that's a fine thing to say.' Paddy turned towards Alice, holding the can up invitingly. 'Even my piss can't produce champagne,' he said, 'but it's better than nothin'.'

'It sure is,' Alice said.

She held out her water bottle and let Paddy pour water in. When he had filled about a quarter of the bottle, he said, 'That's yer lot. Sure I've barely got enough to go around, but it's enough for emergencies.'

'I'm dying of thirst already,' Alice said.

'Don't drink until you feel worse.'

'Let's move out,' Kilroy said.

'I'm starving,' Alice said.

'Do you have food?'

'No,' Alice said.

'Then starve,' Kilroy said. 'OK, let's move out.'

They marched into the freezing night, in single file again, with Kilroy out front, Paddy bringing up the rear and Wild Bill and Alice in the middle. Alice felt protected there and no longer resented it; she realised that these men had a job to do and that she was the job. They would do their job or die in the attempt and she had to respect them for that, though now she felt love as well. It was a familiar kind of love – the kind she felt for her family – and she understood at last what it was that these men found in war. She felt that as well now – solidarity, comradeship – but she also felt something much deeper and she felt it for Kilroy. She just didn't know why.

You damned fool, she thought.

The night was bitterly cold and growing colder by the minute. Two hours later, when they had settled down for a rest, the wind swept rain and sleet across. Alice couldn't believe it. She was frozen to her very bones. She wrapped herself up in her poncho and shivered uncontrollably and could hardly believe that this frozen wasteland was a desert, scorching hot in the daytime.

'We better keep moving,' Kilroy said when they had been resting for only five minutes. 'If we don't, we're liable to get hypothermia. We have to keep on the march, keep the blood circulating, and if we sit here too long we won't get up, so I say let's go now.'

'I'm with you, pal,' Wild Bill said.

As the march continued, the sleet was followed by snow and Alice started turning numb with cold and felt dazed by exhaustion. The only sounds she heard were the howling of the wind, the jangling of the kit of those in front and behind, and the frequent droning of aircraft overhead, reminding her that the war was continuing elsewhere. Kilroy marched them without break – it was the only way to beat the cold – and called a brief halt only when they had to lie down until enemy search and reconnaissance helicopters had passed overhead, beaming searchlights down on the ground, trying to find the escapees.

Reminded thus that she was not out of danger, that she could yet be recaptured, Alice, shaking with cold and growing ever more exhausted, felt a dreadful tension building up inside her and had to fight to contain it.

'Where are we?' she asked when they had stopped to let Kilroy check their route with the aid of a button compass and a small-scale map taken from his escape belt. 'Are we even close yet?'

Kilroy looked up from the map and studied her with eyes still slightly veiled, but showing hints of concern. 'Your teeth are chattering,' he said. 'How do you feel?'

'Never mind how I feel,' she replied. 'Just tell where we are, Kilroy.'

'About twenty kilometres from Al Qaim. We should get there before noon.'

'We'll never make it,' Alice said.

'Yes, we will,' he insisted.

'We'll all freeze to death first,' Alice said.

'We'll be OK in daylight.'

'We're gonna march in daylight?'

'We don't have a choice. We'll hike and lay low when required until we reach a safe area.'

'Across the border?'

'Maybe into Scud Boulevard. It depends on what we meet up with.'

'Great,' Alice said.

'Your teeth are chattering,' he repeated. 'That means you're a lot colder than you think. Let me give you my jacket.'

'No, thanks,' Alice said.

'It isn't a favour,' Kilroy told her. 'It's important that we get you back alive and you've got to help us do it.'

'Here,' Wild Bill said, removing his fur-lined desert jacket. 'Take mine. Being a Yank who eats hamburgers, I've a lot more fat on me than Kilroy. I can stand the cold better. Come on, Lieutenant, please take it.' Alice hesitated, but Wild Bill shoved the jacket at her. 'I'm personally responsible for you,' he said, 'and I don't want to lose you. Take the jacket, Lieutenant.'

Alice took the jacket from him and put it on.

'Let's move on,' Kilroy said.

The hike continued and the weather grew worse, with more snow and ice gleaming on the rocks between great swathes of sand. Alice felt marginally warmer in Wild Bill's fur-lined jacket, but even with the *shemagh* covering her eyes and lips, even with gloves on her hands, her face and fingers felt numb and her body was aching. She could hardly breathe. Her thoughts were in disarray. An hour later, pains were darting through her feet and it hurt worse each time she placed one on the ground, making her wince. She realised that her feet were frozen, but that they also had blisters, and although the pain became excruciating she kept her mouth shut.

What they do, *I* can do, she thought.

She kept marching, seeing Wild Bill's broad back just in

front of her, hearing Paddy's equipment jangling softly behind her, aware that Kilroy was still out ahead on point, scanning the dark terrain through the night-vision sight of his SLR for signs of enemy movement. It was a demanding job, she knew, made no easier by this weather, and she felt her heart go out to him despite her own suffering.

God, this is hell, she thought as the howling wind whipped snow into her face and she realised that she was turning weak from hunger, with thirst, with the pains that were darting through her feet and with the aches in her bones. I don't think I can make it.

Dawn finally came, bleeding through the dense fog, and the wind gradually faded away and let the snow settle down. They were now heading north, towards the Syrian border and Scud Boulevard, and the farther they marched, the more densely populated the area became. This forced them to stop frequently and lie low until the Arabs had passed.

Here there were many roads, used since ancient days for trading between the locals and those across the frontier. Ignoring the war going on around them, the Arabs, all dressed in the traditional *keffiyeh* and *dish-disha*, carried their wares on makeshift rucksacks on their backs, on old, creaking carts hauled by donkeys, or on camels, often with vicious dogs snapping at their heels. The war, however, was certainly still engaged, as the many dead civilians on the roads and in the fields testified, their corpses torn to pieces by the wildlife and covered with black, buzzing flies.

'The Iraqi soldiers are touchy here,' Wild Bill explained to Alice as they lay together in a wadi, hiding out from a passing Arab camel train, both wet from their night of falling snow, both shivering with cold. 'They know my pals of the Delta Force are working inside Scud Boulevard, which runs along the border with Syria, and they're scared shitless that they'll be attacked either from the Scud box or from across the border. That gives them itchy trigger fingers. They're inclined to open fire on anyone not instantly recognisable as a local trader. The innocents always cop it in a war like this and the body count is high here.'

'The Arabs have gone,' Kilroy said. 'Let's get on the move again.'

'I can't get up,' Alice said.

'Neither can I,' Paddy said. 'Sure m' hands are startin' to turn black with cold an' I can't feel m' feet.'

'Get up, both of you,' Kilroy said. His face was again like granite. 'If you stay here, you'll *never* get up and then you'll both freeze to death.'

Alice stared at him with hatred. She thought the bastard was inhuman. He stared back, then reached down and grabbed her wrist and hauled her to her feet.

'You're going back whether you like it or not. Now pick up your weapon.'

Alice tried to stare him down, letting the hatred give her strength, but she was still too weak and dazed to resist, so she picked up the SLR.

'I'm ready when you are,' she said.

'Good. You, too, Paddy.'

'Yes, boss,' Paddy said. He stood up very slowly, swayed a little from side to side, then rubbed his bloodshot eyes with his blackening hand and whispered, 'Let's get to it.' He looked pretty damned awful.

'Let's go,' Kilroy said.

They marched in single file over the low, snow-covered hills as the wind started blowing again and snow swirled about them. Alice thought she was going mad. She felt weak and half deranged. She was convinced even more of this when they had marched for another hour and the wind settled down, the snow ceased to fall, and brilliant sunlight poured over a view she could scarcely believe. She saw a flat plain far below, a winding ribbon of muddy water, palm trees and mud houses scattered along its banks, small villages in irrigated fields, surrounded by more palms. The river, when she focused properly upon it, coiled back to the horizon.

'The Euphrates,' Wild Bill explained. 'We must be nearing Al Qaim.'

It took them another hour to make their way down the hills, past more dead, rotting civilians, and when they reached the flat plain below they saw the river more clearly, partially obscured by lines of palm trees and mud-and-thatch huts. Smoke was rising from the chimneys of the huts and dogs barked in the distance.

'We can't cross the river,' Kilroy said, 'so we'll make our way north along the bank and hope it brings us to Al Qaim. We should find friendly forces there.'

'Why can't we cross the river?' Wild Bill asked.

'It's four hundred feet wide.'

'You win,' Wild Bill said.

To get to the river bank, they had to make their way across the flat, irrigated fields, which would leave them exposed, and then head for the shelter of the palm trees. Falling into diamond formation, which afforded them better protection in exposed areas, they left the shelter of the rocks on the lower slopes of the hills and advanced with great caution across the first irrigated field they came to. It was a broad, flat field of maize, soaked with rain and snow, and their feet sank into the slimy mud, which made walking difficult.

Alice thought she might not make it, finding it hard to lift her feet, feeling that the mud was dragging her down and growing weaker each second. Nevertheless, she kept going, determined not to give in, and was encouraged by the sight of the palm trees a few hundred yards away. The river was beyond the trees. She could see its muddy surface. She knew she would feel better once she reached the river bank and she sensed that if she could only make it that far, she might get her strength back.

Then the gunshots rang out.

CHAPTER TWENTY-FIVE

Shocked by the gunfire, Alice glanced to the left and saw two Iraqi Army troop trucks disgorging soldiers, some of whom were already advancing and firing on the move. Bullets stitched the field about her, causing water to spit upwards, and Kilroy dropped onto his belly, splashing into the muddy water, and bawled to the others, '*Get moving!*' and opened fire with his SLR.

'Come on!' Wild Bill bawled and grabbed Alice by the shoulders to drag her on towards the line of palm trees. 'Let's get the hell out of here!'

Alice ran automatically, having no time to think, and was rushing past Kilroy as water spat up all around him and bullets whined past her.

'Get her out of here!' Kilroy bawled.

Wild Bill kept hold of her, making sure she came with him, but this time she followed him willingly as they hurried towards the trees, their feet sinking and slipping in the mud and kicking up water. Alice felt her heart racing, the burning of her lungs, but she didn't look back, didn't hesitate, until she was in the shelter of the trees with Wild Bill just ahead of her. Wild Bill turned around immediately, pressing himself to a tree trunk, and bawled, 'Give them covering fire!' as he raised his MP5. Alice did as she was told, though feeling breathless and dazed, and opened fire on the Iraqi troops a few seconds after Wild Bill had done the same. The sound of their rifles was deafening, a nerve-racking crescendo, as they both raked the advancing Iraqis, trying to keep them pinned down. Some Iraqis were hit and fell, others threw themselves to the ground, and the rest of them rushed back behind their trucks to continue the fight from there.

'Run!' Wild Bill bawled.

Glancing to the side, Alice saw Kilroy clambering to his feet, firing his SLR from the hip, and then running towards the palm trees, firing on the move. Paddy had also lain on the ground to give Alice and Wild Bill covering fire and now he jumped up and followed Kilroy, also firing on the move. Both men zigzagged at the half-crouch, trying to dodge the hail of bullets, and Kilroy managed to get to the trees, throwing himself the last few feet and rolling through the undergrowth. Paddy had farther to run, being the last in the line, and before he could make it to the trees a round of bullets stitched the watery ground around him and finally found him. He screamed and jerked convulsively, dropping his weapon, then spun sideways and fell into the water and started crawling towards the trees. His blood was reddening the water around him and he moved like a snail.

'I can't make it!' he bawled.

'God, not Paddy!' Alice exclaimed.

'Keep firing!' Kilroy bawled. 'Keep those bastards over there pinned down until I bring Paddy in.'

'No!' Alice screamed, hardly aware that she was doing so, then she opened fire again with her SLR as Wild Bill threw a hand grenade. The grenade arched through the air, as if in slow motion, and exploded right in the middle of the Iraqi troops firing from the ground. Kilroy ran when it exploded, crouched low, zigzagging, and managed to reach the still-crawling, wriggling Irishman before the other troops could open fire again. He grabbed Paddy by his shirt collar, dragged him backwards through the mud, as Alice and Wild Bill poured a hail of gunfire into the Iraqi troops. They were covering as broad an arc as possible, keeping most of the troops pinned down, but the ones behind the trucks were still firing and bullets made mud and water spit upward about Kilroy and Paddy.

Wild Bill threw another flash-bang, an incendiary grenade, and it exploded against the side of a truck, blowing chunks off it and setting its canvas top on fire. The smoke swirled across the field, obscuring Kilroy and Paddy, who was screaming with pain as he was dragged through the mud, and eventually they reached the shelter of the trees, where Kilroy almost collapsed.

'Shit!' he gasped. 'Jesus!'

'Leave me!' Paddy bawled. 'Go!'

'We can't leave him to those bastards,' Wild Bill said. 'But where can we take him?'

'To the river,' Kilroy said. 'We'll try to escape along the river bank, but he'll have to be carried.'

'No!' Paddy bawled. Alice looked down in horror. Paddy's shattered hip bone was visible through his shredded trousers and blood was still pouring out of it. He was shivering helplessly and his hazel eyes gleamed too brightly from the mud on his face. 'You'll never make it if you try to take me. Prop me up against a tree and give me an SLR. I'll hold them off while you—'

'Shut up,' Kilroy snapped. He glanced back over his shoulder and saw the Iraqi soldiers advancing across the field, firing on the move. 'You're not staying here, Paddy.'

He bent down to pick Paddy up, but Wild Bill brushed him aside and spread his legs beside Paddy. 'I'm bigger than you,' he said, 'and I've got to get Lieutenant Davis out of here. I'll carry him while you hold them off.'

'Right,' Kilroy said. 'Do it.'

'I'll hold them off as well,' Alice said.

'No, you won't,' Wild Bill said. 'You're coming with me. You're why we're all here.'

'Jesus!' Alice exclaimed.

'Run!' Wild Bill bawled, and bent down to pick Paddy up as Alice started running and Kilroy opened fire with his SLR, firing short, precise bursts.

Alice heard Paddy screaming behind her as Wild Bill picked him up and that made her run faster. She smashed her way through the undergrowth, tripped and fell, jumped up and ran, and she felt the tears pouring down her cheeks as branches lashed at her face. She burst through to the muddy bank, saw that vast expanse of water, and looked back to see Wild Bill coming after her, his MP5 in one great fist, his huge body bent over with Paddy slung roughly across over his back and still screaming in pain. Kilroy's SLR kept chattering. Wild Bill smashed through the undergrowth. He reached Alice and stopped, gasping, while Paddy still screamed in pain, and then he looked left and right along the bank and said to Alice, 'Let's go.'

'What about Kilroy?'

'What about him? He'll do what he has to do. Come on, let's get moving.'

He headed right, going north, along the river bank, and Paddy writhed and screamed, 'Jesus Christ! Put me down! You're killing me! Please God, put me down!' Wild Bill ignored him and Alice followed Wild Bill, holding her SLR at the ready and filling up with pain and fear. It wasn't fear for herself. It was fear for Kilroy. It increased when his SLR stopped firing and the Iraqi guns tailed off.

'They've killed him!' she screamed.

'Keep moving!' Wild Bill bawled.

Alice kept moving, not knowing what else to do, and was blinded by the tears in her eyes and the fear that had stripped her mind. Then the undergrowth moved ahead, making a noisy thrashing sound, and Kilroy burst out from the trees and waved his hand to stop them.

'We can't go this way,' he said. 'They're circling around to cut us off. We have to go in the opposite direction. There's no other way.'

'We can't go in the other direction,' Wild Bill replied. 'It leads us away from where we need to go.'

'They're coming *right now!*' Kilroy bawled. 'Now get the fuck out of here! Turn back and keep going.'

Alice fired her SLR. She had seen the undergrowth moving. Someone screamed and an Iraqi soldier fell out from the trees, just behind Kilroy. He spun around and fell to one knee, fired his own SLR, and his bullets sent leaves and branching flying and more screams were heard.

Wild Bill turned back the other way. 'You're fucking good,' he said to Alice. She turned away and ran back along the bank with Wild Bill behind her. Paddy was still screaming. His pain had to be horrendous. Kilroy's SLR was firing behind them and more screams were heard. Alice kept running, impelled by Paddy's screaming, and then she rounded a bend in the river bank and saw more Iraqi soldiers ahead, bursting out of the trees. That made her stop running.

'Oh, my God!' she said softly.

Wild Bill stopped beside her.

'Put me down!' Paddy screamed. 'I'm fuckin' dyin' here! I'm being torn apart by all this movement. Put me down! Let me hold them off!'

'Shut up,' Wild Bill said.

Kilroy rushed up beside them, saw the Iraqis farther along, then glanced right, across that broad expanse of water, and said, 'There's only one way left.'

The river was rushing like a torrent and they knew it was icy cold.

'Shit, no!' Paddy screamed.

'Shit, yes,' Wild Bill said. 'We go now or we don't go at all and I say we go now. I can drag Paddy with me.'

'*No!*' Paddy screamed.

'Let's go,' Kilroy said. 'You first, Alice. Get in there. Leave your weapon behind you.'

He used my first name, Alice thought. She was dazed and felt half crazed. She turned away from him and slipped down the muddy bank and then sank up to her waist in the water and was shocked by the cold. She released the SLR, let it sink into the water, then kicked herself off and started swimming, wondering how she could do this. The cold was appalling. The current was strong. The farther out she swam, the stronger the current became and she thought that she would either be frozen to death or be swept away by that current. Soon exhausted, she stopped, rolled over, did a backstroke, and saw Wild Bill swimming with one hand and dragging Paddy behind him. Paddy wasn't screaming now. He was trying to help Wild Bill. He was kicking his good leg, which must have caused him horrendous pain, and his pale face was turned up to the sky as he gasped desperately for breath. Alice couldn't believe it. His courage shamed her and gave her strength. She saw Kilroy on the bank, facing the Iraqis, down on one knee and firing his SLR in short, precise bursts. His control was absolute. He was a killing machine. He fired a final burst, then slithered down the muddy bank and let his SLR drop into the water and then started swimming.

If I make it, he will, Alice thought.

Rolling over again, she started swimming with all her might, realising that the current was getting stronger and making her fight it. She fought it and started losing, fought again and started winning, then bullets stitched the water around her and she fought even harder. She crossed the halfway mark, fought for breath, almost vomited, then breathed deeply and started swimming again, lured on by the approaching bank. The Iraqi gunfire tapered off and her heart soared like a bird.

She knew, by the tapering off of the gunfire, that they were now out of range. She fought the current and kept swimming, was swept sideways and kicked free, then realised that the freezing cold had made her numb and that she couldn't feel anything. That made her lose control. She couldn't feel her arms or legs. She didn't know if she was swimming correctly and again she was swept away.

If I make it, he will, she thought again, and that somehow sustained her. She fought the raging current, choked and coughed, sank and surfaced, then reached out and grasped the reeds by the river bank and pulled herself out. She fell in the mud and vomited and rolled over and then sat up and looked back.

'Please, God, no!' she murmured.

Wild Bill was struggling in the current, with Paddy kicking one leg behind him, but the current was too strong for even Wild Bill because he had Paddy with him. Paddy screamed and then went under, leaving Wild Bill alone, and as Wild Bill rolled over, obviously looking for Paddy, the trooper drifted back to the surface and was then swept away.

'*No!*' Alice screamed.

Paddy was swept out of view, no longer screaming, just drifting, and Wild Bill rolled onto his belly again and swam for the shore. He clambered out onto the mud and Alice rushed to help him up, helping him to get back to his feet as Kilroy swam up behind him. Kilroy climbed out as well, smeared with mud like Wild Bill, and they both turned and looked along the river like men in a trance.

'Fuck you!' Alice screamed. 'We've got to find him!'

'Let's go,' Kilroy said.

They ran along the river bank, stumbling through the undergrowth, out of range of the Iraqi guns but being cut and whipped by the gnarled branches, their skin breaking and bleeding. They ran for a long time, forgetting their own exhaustion, and eventually found Paddy washed up on the bank, covered in mud and bark, the blood washed from his shattered hip bone, arms outflung, his eyes staring at the sky, though as dead as the moon.

Alice fell to her knees beside him and reached down to put her hand on his forehead. Paddy didn't respond.

'He's dead,' Wild Bill said.

'You did your best,' Kilroy told him.

'My best wasn't fucking good enough. That poor bastard. Those shits.'

'We've lost Al Qaim,' Kilroy said.

'Scud Boulevard,' Wild Bill said. 'It's just across that hill, across the desert, about ten miles from here. If we get there, we're safe.'

'Let's go,' Kilroy said.

Alice turned away from Paddy, filling up with grief and rage, and heard someone – it certainly didn't sound like herself – saying, 'What about Paddy?'

'What about him?' Kilroy asked.

'We have to bury him,' Alice said.

'We didn't bury any of the others,' Kilroy said, 'and we're not burying him.'

'*What?*'

'We haven't time. Those Iraqis won't give up now. They won't give up until we're in Scud Boulevard, so we have to move now.'

'You bastard,' Alice said. It didn't sound like herself at all. 'You're going to leave him to lie here and rot or be chopped up by them?'

'He won't feel a thing,' Kilroy said. 'Now get up and let's go.'

Alice exploded, went wild on the instant, rising up and grabbing Kilroy by his tunic and shaking him viciously. 'You brutal bastard!' she screamed. 'You mindless, vicious thug! All you bastards, you big men in uniforms, you don't feel a fucking thing! I hate you all – you understand that? I can't stand the sight or smell of you. You think you're fucking heroes, the élite of the forces, but you're just another bunch of fucking animals who glory in war. Do you know what you did to me? Have you any idea? Do you know what it is to be a woman in a world of you men? Where the fuck do you get off? What the hell makes you tick? Do you have any kind of decent feelings that a woman could recognise? *Fuck* you, you bastard! I don't want to be saved by you! I don't need your male protection, your fucking hardness, your masculinity, your fucking ego and the destruction you bring and the pride you take in it. You *bastard*! You and your kind destroyed me! Now go bury your friend! Make amends! Don't destroy me. *I want Paddy buried!*'

She shook Kilroy once more, slapped his face, turned away, burst into tears and ran into the undergrowth and threw herself on the ground.

'Jesus Christ!' she heard Wild Bill say. 'What the hell do we do with this?'

She knew he was concerned. That made her sob all the more. She shed her tears into the earth, felt the wet leaves, the mud, and wanted to bury herself in it and never rise to the light again. Her heart was breaking. She felt love and rage at once. She wanted Kilroy to atone for the sins of the men who had shamed her. She wanted Kilroy's respect.

He came through the undergrowth, knelt beside her, stared at her. She sat up and dried the tears from her eyes and refused to look at him. She felt like a child.

'What the fuck is it?' he said. 'What the hell's going down here? You better spit it out, Alice. What did they do to you?'

'The Iraqis?'

'Was it them?'

'No, it wasn't.'

'The Academy.'

'Yes.'

'I might have known,' Kilroy said.

She knew then that she could tell him. She knew that he

understood. She knew that he knew more than he let on, but that he kept it all hidden. He had his secrets as well. That made it easier for her.

'I was so proud,' she said. 'I'd always wanted to enlist. My father'd been in the Air Force all his life and I surely loved him – so, you know, that was *my* life.'

'Yes,' Kilroy said.

'I enlisted,' she told him. 'I was so goddamned proud. I went in like a kid biting cookies and then they shat on me.'

'I'll bet,' Kilroy said.

'They didn't want girl recruits. They accepted them, but they hated them. I arrived at the Academy and they treated me real nice, then the training started and they went to work on me and I knew what the score was.'

'Not good,' Kilroy said.

'No,' Alice said. 'Not good.'

She shut up for a moment, trying to gather her thoughts, trying to find the courage to talk to this strange man and release what had tormented her. She finally gave him her trust.

'They came for me at nights,' she said. 'The other cadets. I think some of them were as scared as I was, but they did what they were told. They dragged me out of bed. They didn't let me get dressed. I was only wearing my fucking nightdress and that's just what they wanted. They walked me out of the dorm, across the goddamned quadrangle, in full view of the other cadets, and then into another building, the male dorm, and finally into a bare room. Real bare. Just a light bulb. A wooden chair in the middle. They sat me down and started shouting abuse at me and most of it was sexual. I was a cock-teasing cunt. I was a bitch and a whore. I'd only enlisted, they said, for some good fucking and they would give me just that. They didn't, of course. They just played their games with me. They unzipped their fucking pants and said suck on this, baby, and then laid me on the floor and spread my legs and threatened to rape me – a gang bang, the whole works – they had me really convinced. And you know what, Kilroy? I really thought they were gonna do it. It was all a game at first, but they were sweating and then they were breathing hard. God, it was terrifying. I really thought they were gonna do it. One of them held my shoulders down and another spread my legs and I felt a hand sliding up my thighs and I thought I would die. I nearly died. I *was* dying. I was breathless with fear. Then they laughed and picked me up and walked me back out, back across the quadrangle with the other cadets laughing, then slammed me back down on my bed and promised the same for the next night. That promise was kept.'

She recalled it so vividly. It came back like flame to scorch her. She felt the air being sucked from her lungs as it had been at the time. The returning fear shook her.

'They did it night after night,' she said. 'Each time worse than the last. They did it so often that I thought they must do it truly, eventually, that the game would become real. When I thought they were really gonna do it, I gave up and reported them.'

'Then the real flak came,' Kilroy said.

'Yeah,' Alice said. 'Right. Then I knew what betrayal was.'

She stopped to gather her thoughts. It wasn't easy, but she did it. Soaked from the river, shivering with cold, exhausted beyond any known measure, she was not quite herself, but she had to tell Kilroy. He was hard. He was the rock in her storm. He was strong in the right way.

'I went to my commanding officer. I told him what was going on. He told me that he knew what was happening and that he fully condoned it. It was for my own good, he said. I was a woman, he said. War was no place for women, the bastard said, and so I was a special case. I needed special conditioning, to be prepared for rape, to learn to withstand all the vileness that men could inflict on me. And after all, they hadn't actually raped me – they'd only pretended. That's what that bastard said. He was smiling as he said it. He said that if I couldn't stand the heat I should get out of the kitchen. I said I didn't want that, that I wanted to stay in, that I wanted to register a formal complaint and put an end to my torment. He said that if I did that, if I caused him any problems, he would find a way to have me thrown out and that I'd never get back in. I knew I couldn't stand that.'

'Why?' Kilroy asked. 'Did you want in that much?'

'Yes,' Alice said. 'It was in the blood, Kilroy. Why the hell do I always call you Kilroy? It isn't even your Christian name.'

'They all call me that,' Kilroy said.

Alice sighed. She felt a weight lifting off her. 'It was my father, Kilroy. I loved my father with all my might. He was the kind of father most girls only dream of and I couldn't hurt him. Not by leaving the Air Force. It wasn't that at all. It was the fact that he loved the Air Force, believed in it, was proud of it, and if he'd known what those bastards had done to me, it would have broken his heart. I loved my father so much, I stayed in and I'm proud that I did it. That's my one ray of hope in this.'

'Not all,' Kilroy said.

'No,' Alice confessed. 'Not all, Kilroy. What they did to me made me fear men, but you guys taught me better. I've hated you sometimes – I've feared you – but now I know you're not all the same. You guys hurt, but you know you can't show it because the showing would break you. It almost broke me with Paddy. I'm sorry, Kilroy. I owe you one.'

'You owe nothing to anyone,' Kilroy said. 'You just have to get back. That's part of your job.'

'Thanks, Kilroy. Dear Jesus.'

Alice started to cry again. Kilroy reached out and slid his hand behind her head and then pulled her face into his body and said not a word.

Alice wept into his hard shoulder, letting trust mend her wounded heart.

CHAPTER TWENTY-SIX

In deference to Alice, they buried Paddy by the bank of the river, scooping out the grave with their short spades as they would a shallow scrape to sleep in. They put Paddy into it and covered him up and no one said a word. There was nothing to say. Then they moved on again.

This final hike took them over frost-covered hills, through more rain and sleet, and then they made their way back down to a flat plain that burned like God's anvil. Alice couldn't believe it. She moved from one world to another. From the hellish damp and cold of the hills back to the heat of the desert. The sun burned down like pure flame, scorched her skin, made her dizzy, and she felt like she was floating on air, divorced from herself. It was hunger, she realised. They hadn't eaten for two days. She knew that Kilroy and Wild Bill felt the same, but they weren't going to show it. They were dying of thirst as well. Her own thirst told her that. She felt the screaming of a child well up inside her, demanding its sustenance. I want the nipple, she thought. I need the comfort of the breast. It was a need that could not be denied, but she refused to give in to it.

She marched on in the single file, Kilroy out front, Wild Bill behind, and she knew that they would not break that formation, that for now she was in the womb. The sun blazed down upon her. The wind blew the sand across her. She saw heatwaves rising from the plain and distorting the landscape. Kilroy loves me, she thought. He doesn't know it, but he does. I don't love him, or I refuse to believe I do, because I once loved Dave Bamberg. God, yes, there was the pain. It came back to torment her. Though fearing men, she had fallen in love with Dave Bamberg and then watched him die.

God's punishment, Alice.

And now she had Kilroy. She didn't know about this man. He was as dark and as deep as a great lake, and as with a lake she could drown in him. What was it with Kilroy? What had drawn her towards him? What was it that had made her confide in him and in so doing free herself?

I could love Kilroy, she thought. For that, if nothing else. And the truth be told, nothing else really matters. It all begins and ends there.

She was coming unglued, she thought. The heat and thirst were getting to her. She licked her lips and felt the pangs of a hunger that could drive her demented. It was the heat. It was the light. That great silvery sun dissolved her. She vaporised, she melted into herself, then felt the earth shift beneath her.

I want my mom and dad, she thought. I want my brother and sister. I want the comfort of the familiar, the security of hearth and home, and I mustn't despise this in myself because it's what gives me strength. I also love my dad. I love Dave Bamberg. And despite all my fears that I feared men, I love men who respect me. I might even love Kilroy. Kilroy's shoulder – his hard, muscular shoulder – was finally home to me. I must be losing my mind.

She felt pain in her head, in her bones, in her feet, and the pain in her feet became worse and finally made her give in.

'I can't walk,' she said. 'Sorry. My damned feet are killing me.'

'Blisters,' Kilroy said.

'*What*?'

'Blisters,' Kilroy repeated. 'Take your boots off.'

Alice took her boots off. Her feet were badly blistered and the blisters were suppurating.

'Try wrapping them in bandages,' Wild Bill said. 'It might hurt, but it sometimes works.'

Alice wrapped her feet in bandages withdrawn from her kit belt, but her feet were so swollen that she couldn't get them back into her desert boots with the bandages on.

'This is hopeless,' she said.

'Never give up,' Kilroy said. 'Just sit back and grit your teeth.'

As Alice sat back and gritted her teeth, Kilroy withdrew a small knife and matches from his escape belt. He sterilised the knife by holding it in the flame of a match, then, while Alice gritted her teeth even harder, he lanced the blisters one by one. It took a long time and hurt like all hell, but it hurt even more when Kilroy swabbed the raw wounds with TCP, then smeared two separate short strips of bandage with antiseptic cream and placed them once around Alice's feet.

'How does that feel?' he asked her.

'Lighter than the bandages,' she replied.

'And thinner,' he said. 'You can put your boots on now.'

He was still holding her foot and it felt very intimate. Alice blushed and looked up to see that Wild Bill was scanning the desert, looking out for the enemy.

He knows what's going on here, she thought, and he's politely ignoring it. That big brute's a real gentleman.

'Thanks,' she said to Kilroy, putting her desert boots back on. 'They feel better already.'

'My pleasure,' Kilroy said.

They moved on again. Kilroy had lost his button compass

in the desert, so he improvised a compass by stropping a razor blade against the palm of his hand, then dangling it from a piece of thread taken from his survival kit.

'Scud Boulevard's over that way,' he said, indicating south-west.

'And if my memory serves me correctly,' Wild Bill responded, 'we're practically entering it.'

'How far?' Kilroy asked.

'A couple of miles,' Wild Bill said. 'Maybe more. Maybe less. Not much in it either way. We're home and dry, pal.'

'Don't count on it,' Kilroy said.

They moved on, walking slowly, their steps faltering as they weakened, dehydrating and suffering from hunger pangs that filled their bellies with pain. Alice knew what they were suffering. She was suffering the same. She thought she might die, that the earth might devour her, but somewhere, sometime, in that hallucinatory march, Wild Bill wandered out on his own and found them some water. He knew this territory, had explored it with the Delta Force, and he located an aquifer beneath the desert floor and managed, with some digging and much cursing, to extract a little fossil water from it.

'Mother's milk!' he exclaimed.

They drank with animal greed, slaked their thirst, felt revived, then moved on into the furnace of the desert, towards the hills that Wild Bill knew. He was out in front now, leading them through familiar terrain, and Alice felt a great weight lifting off her, sensed the sweet smell of freedom. The sun was a silvery orb. The hills shimmered beyond heatwaves. They marched under a great umbrella of silence and felt divorced from the real world. Alice thought that she might survive. They were together now, as one. They were two men and one woman pitted against a hostile world, but the conflicts that might once have divided them had been reconciled. They would beat this together.

'I'm dizzy,' she told Wild Bill.

'Most people are,' he replied.

'I don't don't think I can go much further,' she confessed.

'You'll go further. We all do.'

'You love your wife and kids, don't you?'

'I reckon,' Wild Bill said. 'It's not something I think about too much, but I don't think there's much else.'

'I bet you're a good father.'

'I like to think that my kids think so.'

'I think my dad's terrific,' Alice said. 'I count that as a blessing.'

'It surely is,' Wild Bill said.

'Are you as happy?' she asked Kilroy.

'You talk too much,' he said.

'If I don't talk to you guys,' Alice said, 'I'll probably talk to myself.'

'You're wasting energy,' Kilroy said.

'I've none to waste,' Alice answered. 'So tell me, Kilroy, are you happy? Just answer the question.'

'Go fuck yourself,' Kilroy said.

Alice didn't feel offended. She heard Wild Bill chuckling. She wanted to chuckle the same way, but when she tried, she just choked.

'Throat's dry as a bone,' she said.

'Same here,' Wild Bill said.

'Practise swallowing instead of talking,' Kilroy said, 'and your throats won't be so dry.'

Wild Bill chuckled again. 'We live or die by Kilroy's wit.'

'The day Kilroy makes a witty remark,' Alice said, 'I'll kneel on a fucking bed of nails and thank God for the miracle.'

'There's something out there,' Kilroy said.

They all froze on the instant. The silence overwhelmed them. Kilroy stepped out ahead, moving gracefully, like an animal, and raised his binoculars to his eyes and seemed to take an eternity. When he lowered the binoculars to his chest, his eyes shifted left and right.

'What's up?' Wild Bill asked.

'An Iraqi jeep,' Kilroy said. 'It has a machine gun in the rear and it's coming straight towards us.'

'Fuck,' Wild Bill said. 'We're practically in Scud Boulevard. Those bastards must be patrolling the perimeter. Those motherfuckers are always there.'

'Now he tells us,' Kilroy said.

'It's the luck of the draw, pal.'

Kilroy looked left and right, an eagle searching for its prey, and then said, 'There's a wadi over there. Let's get the hell into it.'

'Fucking A,' Wild Bill said.

Alice felt destroyed by fear. It just swooped down to crush her. She had sensed the sweet smell of freedom and now it was threatened.

'No!' she hissed with a venom that startled her. 'I won't be stopped now. *I won't let them take me back!*'

'They won't take you back,' Kilroy said.

He took her by the hand and ran her to the wadi, then practically threw her down the slope and into the dried-out bed. Wild Bill followed, sliding down in a shower of dust, and soon landed heavily beside them, wiping sand from his face.

'We've no fucking weapons,' he said. 'If they find us, we're finished.'

'Think positive,' Kilroy said.

He slithered back up the slope and squinted into the blazing sunlight. Alice and Wild Bill did the same and saw the jeep coming towards them. It was churning up the sand, leaving a billowing trail behind it, and it kept coming until it approached the wadi, where it gradually slowed down. There were two Iraqi soldiers in it, the driver and the gunner, who was leaning out to the side to check the sand for footprints. When he saw the prints leading to the wadi, he called out a warning.

'Shit!' Wild Bill exclaimed softly.

The driver braked to a halt and dropped low in his seat.

The gunner did the same, but then sat upright and looked down at the sand again. His gaze followed the footprints. They led straight to the wadi. He said something in Arabic to the driver, then swivelled the machine gun on its mount until it was aimed at the wadi.

'Let's go,' Kilroy said.

'Where?' Wild Bill asked.

'Along the damned wadi,' Kilroy said. 'Where *else* can we go?'

'We can't go fast enough,' Wild Bill told him. 'This wadi's straight as a fucking slide rule. No matter how fast we go along the wadi, those bastards will see us and they'll shoot us to shreds.'

'We've no weapons,' Kilroy said.

'We've hand grenades,' Wild Bill reminded him. 'So one of us goes up there and lobs a few flash-bangs while the other takes Lieutenant Davis out of here and heads for Scud Boulevard. What else *is* there, amigo?'

Kilroy stared at him, then reached down to touch his webbed belt, his fingers curving around the incendiary grenades as if touching diamonds. Then he looked up again.

'You know, I can't believe I forgot those,' he said. 'You've got one up on me, Wild Bill.'

'Get going,' Wild Bill said.

'She's your responsibility, Wild Bill.'

'Fuck you both,' Alice said. 'I'm staying here to take those bastards out.'

'No, you're not,' Wild Bill said. 'You're going back safe and sound.'

'And she's your responsibility,' Kilroy repeated, 'so you better get up and go.'

'You take her,' Wild Bill said. 'You two have a rapport.'

'I'm not something for trade, you chauvinist pigs, and I'm staying right here.'

They both stared at her, surprised.

'You've got to go,' Kilroy said. 'No matter which one of us takes you, you're the one who lights out of here.'

'I'm not going,' Alice said.

'Yes, you are,' Kilroy said. 'A lot of good men died for you, Lieutenant, so you can't let them down.'

'You bastard,' Alice said.

'That's not the point,' Kilroy said. 'If you don't get back, this operation's been wasted and good men have died in vain.'

'Fuck you, Kilroy,' Alice said. There were tears in her eyes. 'You don't know what you're doing when you say that. You just don't fucking know.'

'Yes, I do,' Kilroy said.

'And he's right,' Wild Bill said. 'Either Kilroy or me takes you out, but you've got to go, kid.'

'I'm not a kid – I'm a lieutenant.'

'Then get the hell out, Lieutenant.'

'OK, I'll get out,' Alice said. 'Now why not toss a coin?'

'She's your responsibility,' Kilroy said to Wild Bill, 'and your friends are just across that strip of land. You know that land. Now get out of here.'

'Let's go,' Wild Bill said.

He grabbed Alice by the wrist and tugged her to her feet, then raced her along the bed of the wadi, both at the half-crouch. Alice was sobbing. She felt like a child. She was letting herself be ruled by these men and they had her hands down. For that reason, she kept running. She didn't know what else to do. She kept thinking of Kilroy and the two Iraqis and she filled up with pain. When that happened, she stopped running. She tried to turn back. She caught a glimpse of Kilroy, clambering up out of the wadi, and then Wild Bill grabbed her by the wrist again and pulled her behind him. She stumbled after him, sobbing. She heard the hand grenade exploding. It was followed by the roaring of the machine gun and that made her look back again. When she saw Kilroy falling backwards into the wadi, she put her hands up and screamed.

'Jesus Christ!' Wild Bill said.

He stopped running and looked as well, saw Kilroy lying on his back, clearly wounded and writhing in the dust that was subsiding around him. An Iraqi solder materialised on the rim of the wadi, holding a sub-machine gun in his hands and looking down warily. He saw Kilroy lying there, still writhing in the dust, and he raised the sub-machine gun to his shoulder and carefully took aim.

'*No!*' Alice screamed.

That scream startled the soldier, made him hesitate and look around, his gaze taking in the length of the wadi and then Wild Bill and Alice. He turned to take aim again and took his time when doing so.

'Fuck it!' Wild Bill bawled. 'Run, Lieutenant! Get the hell out of here!'

Alice ran along the wadi, not thinking, doing her duty, but when she heard the savage roar of the sub-machine gun, she stopped and looked back. The ground was spitting around Wild Bill. The bullets chopped a line across him. Alice saw his legs breaking – they just buckled and bent – and he screamed in the helplessness of anguish and keeled over and hit the dirt. Alice looked on, horrified. The Iraqi headed towards Wild Bill. He was heading along the rim of the wadi, determined to finish him. Wild Bill writhed in the dirt, clawing at it, his legs useless. Then he wrenched a hand grenade from his webbed belt and somehow managed to throw it. The Iraqi fired at the same time, cutting Wild Bill to shreds. Then the hand grenade exploded and the Iraqi was thrown back and disappeared in white phosphorous and streaming smoke. He appeared again, falling out of the smoke, and rolled down into the wadi, coming to rest beside Wild Bill.

Alice looked on, paralysed by dread and horror, and then she saw Kilroy. He was still lying on his back on the wadi, still alive, and she ran to him.

She didn't get far.

The second Iraqi appeared on the rim of the wadi, also carrying a sub-machine gun and looking down on Kilroy.

Alice slid to a halt.

Her foot touched something soft. She looked down and almost retched. The toe of her boot had pressed into the bloody hole that had been Wild Bill's ribcage. She gasped and stepped back, looked up again, saw the Iraqi. She saw him gazing down upon Kilroy and then turning his head.

'No, you don't,' she said. 'Not now!'

Moving before the Iraqi saw her, she clambered up the side of the wadi, hidden from the Iraqi's view by a shelf of high rocks. She remembered the knife then – the knife Kilroy had given her – and she tugged it from its sheath without thinking as she reached level ground. She lay flat on her belly. The rocks were still protecting her. Glancing sideways, she saw the Iraqi soldier staring into the wadi. He must have seen his dead friend, for he let out a curse, then he turned his head to look back down at Kilroy and he decided to finish him.

He started down into the wadi. Alice jumped up and ran towards him. She was running along the rim of the wadi and coming up behind him. He slipped and slid into the wadi, his weapon at the ready. Alice reached the starting point of his descent as he stepped up to Kilroy. He looked down at Kilroy, still alive, still on his back. Kilroy returned his gaze with that steady stare which Alice knew so well.

She inched down the wadi slope. She tried not to make a sound. The Iraqi was raising his sub-machine gun when she came up behind him. She hardly knew what she was doing. She only knew she had to do it. Coming quietly up behind him, she slapped her hand across his mouth, jerked his head back, then slashed his throat with the sharp knife and hurriedly stepped back. The Iraqi made a dreadful gurgling sound as his blood spurted forth. Alice, realising what she had done, dropped the knife and stepped back. The Iraqi shivered and fell.

'Good girl,' Kilroy said.

Those words held her together. She breathed deeply and calmed down. The sun was sinking over the western horizon and the shadows fell over her.

'You'll have to help me up,' Kilroy said. 'I don't think I can walk.'

'We've got transport,' she told him.

She helped Kilroy up. He wasn't wounded too badly. His left leg was a pretty bad mess, but otherwise he was fine. Alice supported him, putting her arm around his waist, then she helped him up out of the wadi, inch by painful inch, and then half walked, half dragged him across the flat plain to the Iraqi jeep. She pushed him up into the front seat, beside the driver's seat, then she went back down into the wadi for the body of Wild Bill.

He was a very big man, much heavier dead than alive, but she overcame her natural revulsion to drag him up the steep slope. It was a hell of a job and took a very long time, but when she had him on the rim of the wadi she went back to the jeep. She drove it up to the wadi. Kilroy didn't say a word. She got out and dragged Wild Bill to the jeep and then, with a great deal of difficulty, managed to hump him up into it, laying him across the back seat, just behind the machine gun.

'He was determined to get back with me,' she said, 'and that's just what he's going to do.'

'Damned right,' Kilroy said.

Alice drove them both back. Kilroy slept most of the way. Alice didn't know where she was going and she didn't give a damn, but when she saw American soldiers, Wild Bill's pals of the Delta Force, as well as the others who'd made it back – Major Phillips, Sergeant Spooner, Staff Sergeant Morrissey and Corporal Townsend – she skidded to a halt and stood upright in the jeep and then exultantly raised her hands to the heavens. All those guys – they just cheered her.

Alice sobbed and collapsed.

CHAPTER TWENTY-SEVEN

Alice visited Kilroy in a hospital in Kuwait when the pall of smoke that covered the city had turned the sky into an almost total, nightmarish blackness. This was rendered even more frightening by the dark smoke pouring in from the six hundred oil wells set on fire by the Iraqis and still blazing furiously. The war had almost ended, but odd gunshots still rang out and aircraft still flew through the murk. All around the city, under that fearsome black sky, the burning oil wells had created a great wall of vivid yellow fire that must have appeared to some to be the end of the world.

The end of something, Alice thought as she tentatively entered Kilroy's ward. The beginning of something new.

It was one of the better wards, containing those not badly wounded, and she found Kilroy standing out on the porch, leaning on crutches, gazing across green gardens and the desert beyond at that great wall of searing flames and its vast umbrella of black smoke. Kilroy was wearing a blue dressing gown over pyjamas and his left leg was encased in thick bandages, but otherwise he looked fine.

'Hi, Kilroy,' Alice said.

He turned his head to stare at her, then awkwardly turned his body towards her, using his crutches with some discomfort, then leant back against the low steel railing to stare thoughtfully at her. He was taking her in, she knew, studying her washed face and hair, the curves of her body in a clean and newly pressed uniform. He liked what he saw.

'Hi, Lieutenant,' he said. 'Good to see you. You look pretty good.'

'Thanks,' Alice said. 'You don't look bad yourself.' She nodded, indicating his wounded leg. 'So how's it going?'

'It'll mend,' Kilroy told her.

'I'm glad,' Alice said.

They were silent for a moment, neither knowing what to say, then Alice said, 'I'm going back tomorrow.'

'Good,' Kilroy said. 'You've done more than enough.'

'When are you going back?'

Kilroy shrugged. 'A week or two.'

'Back to your wife and kids.'

'That's right, Lieutenant.'

'You don't love your wife, do you?'

Kilroy blinked, then turned slowly away. 'No,' he said, 'I don't love my wife, but I have to go back to her.'

'Yes, Kilroy, I know you do.'

But the pain of loss was there. It was a vice around her heart. She knew that she wouldn't see him again and that the pain would be bad. She would have to get used to that.

'I had you all wrong, Kilroy.'

'What does that mean, Lieutenant?'

'I thought you were like the others – those bastards back at the Academy – and I feared you as I'd feared so many men and now I know that was wrong. You're not like them at all. You're not a brute and you're not violent. You're pretty reserved, you're practically hidden away, but you're a decent man, Kilroy. You even have your sweet side.'

'Thanks,' Kilroy said.

He had turned his back to her and was staring at the flames, locked up in himself as he always was and maybe always would be. He didn't speak for a long time.

'You're wrong,' he said finally. 'I'm a violent man, Lieutenant. That's why I joined the Army – to use it up – but it didn't always work for me. I had a pretty bad marriage. It wasn't a marriage we wanted. I got her pregnant the first time we made love and then I did the right thing, which is how I was brought up. It didn't work out, of course. We both knew it was all wrong. She hated me because I didn't love her and we fought like cat and dog. I started drinking and brawling. I was right off the wall. I enlisted to get away from home and to use up my violence. That didn't work out, either. It helped, but not enough. We had two kids and she treated them fine, but she hated me even more. You know what that's like, Lieutenant? It's a dark place to be in. Both sides see their lives slipping from them and they can't find a way home. I went home when I had to – during leaves and holidays – but each time I went back, it got worse and my drinking increased. She was drinking as well by then, night and day, in a stupor, and often, when she was on one of her binges, she would go for me physically, slapping and kicking, the whole works. I was pretty bad by then. I guess I needed a war to fight. She exploded one night and came at me and I slapped back, then punched her. She fell backwards down the stairs and I thought I might have killed her. I didn't, because she got up and ran and then jumped into our car. She was drunk and distracted, screaming abuse as she drove away, and five minutes later, not too far from where we lived, she turned out of the street into the main road and took a broadside from an oncoming truck that wiped the car off. She was lucky to survive – if survival you could call it. Now she's completely paralysed from the neck down and spends her days in a wheelchair. She's still back there, at home, looked after by her parents. Her eyes are all she can move now and I can't stand the sight of them. She has a steady, accusing gaze.'

Kilroy turned to face Alice, showing anguish for the first time, and Alice had to fight back her tears and keep control of herself.

'My wife looks like you, Lieutenant.' Kilroy kept his gaze upon her. 'You two could be sisters. My wife has green eyes and blonde hair and your nose and lips. She's a beautiful woman.'

Alice blushed. Her racing heart would not slow down. She turned away to hide her tears from Kilroy and said, 'Damn it, I could have loved you. You're the kind of man I could have lived with. I learnt to trust you and that's a kind of love, but there's someone else out there. He's dead, but he's out there and still inside me and I can't let him go yet.'

'I could have loved *you*,' Kilroy said, speaking quietly, 'but I have to go back to what I left behind and try to deal with it.'

'Yes,' Alice said. 'Naturally. So do I. That's something else we share, Kilroy.'

She took a deep breath, wiped the tears from her eyes, then finally got up the courage to turn and face him and look into his steady gaze.

'I can't believe what I did back there,' she said. 'I didn't know it was in me. I mean, cutting that man's throat.'

'It's in us all,' Kilroy said, 'when we need to do it ... and you did it for me.'

'Yes, I did,' Alice confessed. 'I did it for you. I didn't know I had it in me, but I have, and now I'll always know that as well.'

'You'll live with it, Lieutenant.'

They were silent for some time. Aircraft rumbled overhead. Gunshots could be heard in the distance, but the fighting would soon stop. Alice glanced at that wall of flame, at the pall of smoke above it, and realised that she thought it was beautiful in its own bizarre way. She lowered her gaze to Kilroy, who was staring steadily at her. Leaning forward, she kissed the scar on his cheek, then she stepped back again.

'I have to go,' she said.

'I'll go first,' he replied. 'I get tired if I stand up too long, so I'll hop back to my bed. You take care, Lieutenant.'

'You, too, Kilroy.'

He propped the crutches under his arms and hopped back into the ward. Alice had to wipe more tears from her eyes as she walked to the railing. She looked out at that wall of fire, at the black smoke above it, and saw in it a terrible beauty that she would never forget: the good and bad at the heart of the men she could never renounce. Then she felt someone coming up behind her and she knew it was Kilroy.

She didn't turn around to face him. There was no need to do so. She just stared at that fearsome, glorious sky, feeling no fear at all.

'Alice in Wonderland,' Kilroy whispered.

Alice finally smiled.

GLOSSARY

AWACS	airborne warning-and-control system
basha	waterproof shelter made with a poncho or available local materials; as verb, to 'basha down', i.e. to sleep
bug out	to make a hurried escape
Civaid	Civil Aid
crap-hat	1. failure; 2. SAS term for a member of the regular army
det cord	detonation cord (used as a fuse)
dibdibba	undulating gravel plain in the desert
dish-disha	a neck-to-ankle Arab shirtlike garment
ECM	electronic counter-measure
ECR	electronic surveillance measure
flash-bang	stun grenade
FOB	forward operating base
GMPG	general-purpose machine gun (often pronounced *gimpy*)
GPS	global positioning system (for navigation)
HARM	high-speed anti-radiation missile
HAS	hardened aircraft shelter

HE	high explosive
HEAT	high-explosive anti-tank (weapon)
keeni-meeni	Swahili term describing the movement in grass of a snake, used by soldiers to describe undercover work
laager	South African term for an encampment formed by a circle or semicircle of wagons; a circle or semicircle of military vehicles formed for defence
LAW	light anti-tank weapon
LRRP	long-range reconnaissance patrol
LSV	light strike vehicle
LUP	laying-up position
Lurp	way of saying LRRP (*q.v.*)
LZ	landing zone
MILAN	*missile d'infanterie léger antichar* (or 'light infantry anti-tank missile' – French-designed, but internationally marketed)
MSR	main supply route
OP	observation post
POST	Passive Optical Seeker Technology (said of a missile such as a SAM; *q.v.*)
Psyops	Psychological Operations
R and I	reconnaissance and intelligence (exercises)
REME	Royal Electrical and Mechanical Engineers
RTU	return to (original) unit – an SAS punishment for poor performance or insubordination
RV	rendezvous point
SAM	surface-to-air missile
SATCOM	satellite communications
SEAL	Amphibious Sea Air Land (units)
shemagh	veil worn by Arab people
SOV	special-operations vehicle
wad	sandwich
wadi	water course (usually dry except in the rainy season)